PRAISE FOR

The Reading Group

"A hot, soapy bubble bath of a novel. Go ahead and sink in."
—*Entertainment Weekly*

"This is funny, contemplative, and touching reading."
—*Publishers Weekly*

"Noble keeps engagement high as her characters connect and interconnect. . . . This entertaining read is very accessible."
—*Booklist*

"Goes down easily with brie and chardonnay."
—*Columbus Dispatch*

"[Elizabeth Noble is a] reading club goddess."
—*St. Paul Pioneer Press*

"A thoroughly accomplished debut novel which embraces a wide range of contemporary issues. Fresh and sharp. Funny and sad."
—Carole Matthews, author of *For Better, for Worse*

"Fast paced and funny, [it's] worth staying up past your bedtime."
—*Library Journal*

"This is a real female-bonding novel in the very best sense; it's witty, pacy, and immediately engaging, with a careful balance of poignant and feel-good moments."
—*Glamour* (UK)

David Galloway

About the Author

ELIZABETH NOBLE lives in Guildsford, Surrey, with her husband and two daughters. Her first novel, *The Reading Group*, was number one in *The Sunday Times* (London) bestseller list.

Also by Elizabeth Noble

The Reading Group

THE FRIENDSHIP TEST

Elizabeth Noble

Harper

An Imprint of HarperCollins*Publishers*

For his love, his patience, and his ability with Word,
my gorgeous husband David

First published under the title *The Tenko Club* in Great Britain in 2004
by Hodder and Stoughton, an imprint of Hodder Headline.

THE FRIENDSHIP TEST. Copyright © 2004 by Elizabeth Noble. All rights
reserved. Printed in the United States of America. No part of this book
may be used or reproduced in any manner whatsoever without written
permission except in the case of brief quotations embodied in critical
articles and reviews. For information address HarperCollins Publishers,
10 East 53rd Street, New York, NY 10022.

HarperCollins books may be purchased for educational, business, or
sales promotional use. For information please write: Special Markets
Department, HarperCollins Publishers, 10 East 53rd Street, New York,
NY 10022.

First U.S. edition published 2006.

Library of Congress Cataloging-in-Publication Data
Noble, Elizabeth (Elizabeth M.)
   [Tenko Club]
   The friendship test / Elizabeth Noble.—1st U.S. ed.
      p. cm.
Originally published as: The Tenko Club in Great Britain in 2004
by Hodder and Stoughton.
ISBN-10: 0-06-077774-5
ISBN-13: 978-0-06-077774-6
1. Friendship—Fiction.   2. Societies and clubs—Fiction.
3. Betrayal—Fiction.   I. Title.
PR6114.O25F75 2005
823'.92—dc22

                                                    2005050454

06 07 08 09 10   RRD   10 9 8 7 6 5 4 3 2 1

F
NOB

THE CHARACTERS

ENGLAND

Freddie	Founding member of the Tenko Club: frustrated, lonely, and unhappy. She just doesn't quite know why yet . . .
Reagan	Second founding member: spiky, difficult, and uncommunicative. If she stopped to think about it, she'd marvel that the others still bother with her, but thank God that they do.
Tamsin	Third founding member: nurturing, chaotic, and funny. To her, friends are family, and there is room in her heart and her home for all of them.
Sarah	Fourth founding member: beautiful, kind, and loyal. They would all agree—she was the best of all.
Adrian	Freddie's handsome, shallow, selfish husband. Golf addict, sex addict, and private school prat.
Neil	Tamsin's adoring, long-suffering medic husband.
Matthew	Sarah's husband. A handsome lawyer desperate for a family to love.
Antonia Melhuish	Ex-wife of Jonathan, and Adrian's mistress. High maintenance, low intellect.
Meghan	Tamsin's Australian au pair (aka total lifesaver)
Harry	Freddie and Adrian's precious only child. Being educated at boarding school, like his father before him, even though it breaks his mother's heart.
Homer, Willa, and Flannery	Tamsin's three beautiful children. Stuck with names of their mother's literary heroes and heroines, they avenge themselves by being noisy (always) and sticky (mostly). The fourth is in utero as the novel begins.

AMERICA

Thomas Jacob Valentine	Freddie's father: old-fashioned, critical, and stern. He can't show love, but can he feel it?
Rebecca	Freddie's mother, who did a disappearing act when Freddie was a small child, and hasn't been seen or heard from since.
Grace	Freddie's father's housekeeper, who raised Freddie after her mother left, and stayed with her father long after Freddie had fled.
Cosmo	Rebecca's gay housemate, dearest friend, and bestselling children's author. These two are more married than a lot of straight couples.
Eric	Reagan's all-American love interest—much deeper and nicer than she wants him to be.

Prologue

October 1985,
St Edmund Hall, Oxford

The rooms in the Kelly block were directly above the hall. One of the big plate-glass windows was slid all the way back. Freddie Valentine had one long leg in the room and the other over the sill, foot resting on the concrete balcony. She was smoking a Silk Cut, flicking the ash delicately into the night air. Tamsin wouldn't let her smoke in her room, but this one offered the best view of the top quad, where the rugby players were congregating before they went to the bop.

'Born in the USA' was blasting into the night air, Springsteen's every emphatic word crystal clear, even three floors up. God help anyone who was trying to work. Although if you were, three Friday nights into the Michaelmas term, it was the Devil's help you needed, not God's.

'Did you see him, last year, on tour?'

'Yeah. He was fantastic. Favourite Springsteen song?'

'Has to be "The River".' Freddie nodded approval. 'Yours?' Tamsin asked.

' "Drive All Night".' Tamsin didn't know it. 'It's on "The River". It has the best lyrics.'

'Right.' Tamsin made a mental note to get the album, although she couldn't possibly imagine someone thinking what Freddie was referring to. She'd never heard it. She was utterly in the thrall of her new friend Freddie.

They had met on the first day. After her mum and dad had gone, Tamsin had sat terrified on her narrow single bed three floors up among the dreaming spires, feeling bereft, and willed herself to go down for lunch. Everyone in the queue was chatting easily. Some people obviously knew each other already. Tamsin was the first kid from her sixth form ever to get into an Oxford college and she knew not one soul, unless you included that dopey-looking daughter of her mum's friend Muriel, and she wasn't at Oxford, she was at some secretarial college in the middle of the city. Although Tamsin had promised her mum and Muriel that they'd get together, she wasn't at all sure that they would. The girls in front were talking about hockey tryouts. Well, fat – pardon the pun – chance of making friends that way, unless there was a sumo team. Tamsin had always known she was overweight; and in the company of these slinky girls, all in their skinny-legged jeans, she felt positively elephantine. She hadn't cared before – at least, not enough to do anything about it – but now she was rather wishing she had.

She was just about to give up on lunch – start the diet now, then, shall I? – when she was trapped into the line by a new arrival. She was alone – that was good. But she was beautiful, and, if not exactly skinny, with a lovely shape, and Tamsin's heart sank again. But the girl was smiling at her. Then she held out her hand. When she spoke, it was with an American accent. 'Hi, I'm Freddie.'

'I'm Tamsin.' She couldn't think what else to say.

'Look,' Freddie was saying, 'I've been in there and had a look at what they're serving, and, frankly, I think we'd be better off at McDonald's. There is one here, I hope?'

'I think so – down the High Street, in the town centre.'

'Wanna come?'

And that had been it. She was called Freddie Valentine, she was five foot ten tall, and what Tamsin's mum would describe as statuesque – a proper woman. She had these big blonde curls and a widow's peak and these sort of aquamarine eyes, and Tamsin thought she was beautiful. Beautiful and funny and irreverent and wonderful. She lived in Emden, the block opposite – so they could beckon each other over, waving a kettle and miming biscuits – and she'd covered every wall and surface in her room with these amazing Indian scarves and throws she'd bought from some place in the Covered Markets, so that it didn't feel like you were in Emden but in Scheherezade's tent in the middle of the desert. She burned joss sticks, drank weird teas, and when Tamsin came back in the next life, she wanted to be her.

She didn't work out for a while that the feeling was

completely mutual. The Winnie-the-Pooh duvet cover she had started to loathe on day two, the hinged photo frame with her parents' pictures in it that she kept by her bed, the box of HobNob biscuits and sherbet fountains – Freddie loved it all. Tamsin's shyness had quickly given way to the warmth and capacity for fun that made her irresistible to Freddie and to others. Freddie's room had the exotic look, but Tamsin's was where everybody wanted to be, drinking tea, raiding the stores and being mothered.

They were there tonight, ready for the bop, but anxious not to go too early. Anyway, they were waiting for Sarah. She lived in the room two doors down from Freddie. They were separated by a geeky but kind third-year chemist, who had introduced them over an uncomfortable cup of tea in his room. They had bonded in a mutual protection society against further visits to Graeme's room, although they had felt bad when he went home the first weekend – for a Ramblers' Association 'get together' – and the other chemists had broken into his room to plant cress on his carpet. They had shared Freddie's room for a couple of nights while he slept in Sarah's and waited for the cress to be cleared up. Sarah had been at rowing tryouts all afternoon down at the river, but had promised to grab a shower and join them later.

Tamsin wasn't sure about the wisdom of entering any room with Sarah, who was so pretty that boys actually stopped talking mid-sentence when she passed them. Tamsin had thought women like her didn't exist

– but they clearly did, and they came from the Mumbles. She wasn't shopping, though, Sarah had told them, the first chance she'd got. She was well and truly attached, she had told them. Practically engaged, they were. Only he hadn't got her a ring and asked her straight out because he thought her parents might worry about them being so young. Wasn't that considerate of him? He was certainly handsome and, yes, they had to concede he looked a bit like Sting. They'd seen one or two pictures of him – all right, hundreds – in Sarah's room. If Freddie's room was a homage to Marrakesh, Sarah's was a shrine to Owen. He was coming down soon, Sarah promised, and they'd all have the chance to meet him.

'Can we bear the suspense?' Tamsin had joked to Freddie, mimicking Sarah's Welsh accent.

Of course, it hadn't bothered Tamsin so much since she'd met Neil. Well, collided with him. She'd liked the idea of bicycling around Oxford, but she wasn't much good at it, and had ploughed into him one afternoon in week one, outside the Radcliffe Camera. Luckily he was studying physiological sciences – pre-med – and dressed his own flesh wound in his room. He hadn't held it against her, if that massive snogging session at last week's Queen's College bop was anything to go by. Neither had he seemed put off by her rolls. She'd mentioned tonight to him, ever so casually, when she'd seen him in the coffee-house. Something told her he'd be there. She couldn't wait.

Freddie had finished her cigarette and closed the

window. She was wearing baggy denim dungarees – Tamsin knew they would make *her* look like a demented children's television presenter but on Freddie they just looked cool.

At least Reagan was here. She'd dragged her in from the corridor where she had allegedly been on the way to the law library, a poky room full of dusty books at the back of the general library, which was housed in an old church. Tamsin had never been there at night, partly from principle, but also because it was surrounded by a graveyard, which gave her the willies. Once she had established that Reagan was not going to the law library for some illicit tryst with a fellow lawyer, which Tamsin would have allowed on the grounds that it was romantic, but to actually engage with the tomes of tort, she forbade her rather dry and dreary neighbour to leave, and poured her a glass of cider. 'You're coming with us tonight. No arguments.'

Reagan was a bit strange, Tamsin thought. A tough nut to crack. She had one of those wipeable boards on her door, and it often said 'PLEASE DO NOT DISTURB! ESSAY CRISIS!' (obviously an attempt to sound cool, which failed miserably). One morning, after a particularly drunken evening, some wag had rubbed out 'ESSAY CRISIS', leaving the exclamation mark, and written 'I'M IN HERE WANKING'. Tamsin had rubbed it off as soon as she'd seen it, but she'd never discovered whether or not Reagan had already read it.

Now, Reagan was a skinny girl – and not in a good way. She had no chest, and not much bum. All her clothes were sort of brown – if those weren't the individual colours, that was certainly the overall effect – and droopy. She definitely needed work. Tamsin thought of herself in terms of the theme tune of the *Six Million Dollar Man*: 'Gentleman, we can rebuild this man. We can make him better than before.' Tamsin liked a challenge. Great name, though: Reagan had told them her mum's favourite Shakespeare play was *King Lear*, and that it could have been worse – one of Lear's other daughters was called Goneril. An exotic name was a good start, Tamsin thought. Think how much duller Reagan might have been with a different name. Reagan had just ruefully pointed out that her mum had made a hash of the only interesting thing she'd ever done – by spelling the damn name wrong.

She looked at her now, talking to Freddie. Reagan was smiling, and she was one of those people on whom a smile made a world of difference: it lifted the corners of her eyes, made her nose crinkle, and she became almost nice-looking.

Tamsin filled all their glasses and looked anxiously at her watch. What if Neil was already downstairs, trawling around for her, and she was up here? He didn't know which room she was in. Which didn't stop her heart banging against her ribs when there was a knock at the door. Maybe he'd found her. Maybe he'd been in the porter's lodge, looking at her pigeonhole and pressing the porter for information . . . and maybe a friend of hers had overheard him . . . and . . .

It was Sarah, still wearing her black Lycra rowing

shorts and a waterproof, her long dark hair in a pony-tail. She had clearly been crying for quite a while: her face was all blotchy.

Tamsin put her arms around her and pulled her off the threshold. 'What's the matter? Sarah?'

This show of sympathy unleashed a new peal of fresh sobs, and they had to wait for them to stop.

Reagan wished she were somewhere else. She was intruding, but no one else seemed to think so – they were all concentrating on Sarah.

Sarah was holding a letter, one side of small writing in black ink. She held it out as explanation, but no one wanted to take it: a letter was private. Sarah let it fall to the ground. 'Owen's dumped me.'

'Oh, you poor thing.' This was Tamsin.

'Bastard,' said Freddie.

'I'm sorry,' added Reagan quietly, as though she thought she ought to say something.

Sarah looked at her, and smiled weakly in acknowl-edgement. 'That's not the worst part. He's gone off, hasn't he? With my best friend. With Cerys.'

Cerys had stayed behind in the Mumbles. She was going to be a hairdresser, Sarah had told them. She had designs on a salon on the high street. And, apparently, on Owen.

'We were going to get married.' More sobbing. 'Now he says they're thinking of moving in together.'

'So much for his wanting to wait out of respect for your parents.' Freddie smiled, but Tamsin shot her a stern glance, and stroked Sarah's hair.

'I mean, it's only been three weeks – three weeks, for God's sake.'

They didn't know how to comfort her. None of them had come anywhere close to the kind of relationship where you thought you might actually get married. Tamsin's love-life until Neil had consisted of a few slow dances at the Young Farmers' dances at home, and one very disappointing encounter last New Year's Eve with a friend of her brother. She had thought she might let him go all the way, but frankly the first part of the journey had been such a let-down she'd changed her mind, straightened her skirt and gone back to the disco. Now that she'd met Neil she was glad she'd waited. She thought it might be more fun going all the way with him. That was, if they ever got to this bloody bop tonight.

Freddie had been all the way and back, as far as Tamsin could work out, with an impressive, or frightening, number of boys in America, but none seemed to have meant all that much to her. She certainly didn't talk about them.

Freddie was actually thinking that it was the best thing that could have happened. She really liked Sarah – she was good fun, and she'd probably enjoy the next three years way more without some gormless boyfriend pulling her back to Wales all the time. Freddie couldn't imagine getting married ever – but thinking about it when you were barely nineteen was crazy. There were so many boys. She'd just been casting her eye over a few on the top quad. It would be so much more fun trawling through them with Sarah.

Reagan felt something like envy, which confused her. Imagine feeling that strongly about someone. Of course, the heartbreak and the dumping bit were horrid, but to have had that feeling in the first place . . .

'Men are pigs!' Tamsin declared. She didn't mean it, but it seemed like the right thing to say.

'What about Cerys?' Reagan couldn't help blurting out. 'He's not doing this on his own, is he? Isn't this Cerys supposed to be your best friend?'

Sarah's face crumpled again.

'Reagan's right.' Freddie took up her theme. 'I mean, men, even the good ones, they're just simple creatures, aren't they? Ruled by their stomachs and their dicks, not necessarily in that order.'

Tamsin reflected that she probably wasn't qualified to comment, not having known many men – and certainly not 'known' any. Freddie seemed quite angry. Perhaps there had been more to those 'flings' than she had let on about.

'It's women you've got to watch,' Freddie was saying now. 'Women have so many more layers – we're so much more complicated. Look at this Cerys. Look what she's done to Sarah.'

'What? Behaved like a man, you mean? Thinking with her . . . well, you know.'

'I bet it's way more sinister than that. Sarah thinks it's only been going on for three weeks, but we all know women a bit better than that, don't we? Don't you think she's been planning this for ages – months, probably – maybe ever since she found out Sarah was going away to college?'

Tamsin wasn't convinced that Freddie's tack was particularly helpful, but Sarah was looking at her intently. Freddie had that kind of voice: maybe it was the accent, but when she spoke you wanted to listen to her.

'I mean, think back, Sarah,' Freddie went on. 'Think about how they were, those two, leading up to you coming away. Think about how Cerys was with you . . . with him.'

Sarah's gaze went middle-distance for a minute. Then her eyes narrowed and she nodded. 'I know what you mean . . . yes.'

'See? Women.'

Freddie sat back, satisfied.

Reagan was impressed. 'You should be reading law,' she said.

Freddie's eyes flashed. 'No way! I hate lawyers. My dad's a lawyer.' Reagan wished she'd stayed quiet.

'I don't think that's quite fair, Freddie,' Tamsin objected. 'We're women, aren't we? Are you saying none of us can ever trust each other? Because I'm not like that, and I don't think anyone here is either.'

A damp Sarah shook her head emphatically.

'Did any of you watch *Tenko*?' Reagan asked.

Sarah and Tamsin nodded.

Freddie shook her head. 'No.'

'It was this drama on TV about five years ago, I think. It was about this bunch of women who were taken prisoner by the Japanese in somewhere like Singapore, English women, mostly. They were in a POW camp, no men, just women. It was brilliant. I think you can look at a woman, or talk to her, or listen to her, any woman, for five minutes and you'd know how she'd behave in that situation, in one of those camps, and once you've figured that out, you know pretty much what she's going to be like in any situation.'

'How'd you mean?' They were all looking at Reagan now, fascinated: they'd never heard her say so many words in one go.

'Well, take Sarah's so-called best friend, Cerys. Now, I haven't met her, but assuming that she's like I think she is, she'd be the sort of person, in a Japanese POW camp, who'd sleep with the guards to get food, then not share it with the others. Selfish, self-obsessed. Amoral.'

They were all staring at her.

'Go on, then, what about us?'

'I hardly know you.' She didn't want to do this.

'You said five minutes was enough. You've seen all of us for a hell of a lot more than that!' Freddie goaded her.

'Lay off, Freddie,' Tamsin said. 'She doesn't have to if she doesn't want to.'

'See?' Reagan couldn't help herself now. 'Tamsin'd be like the camp mother. She'd be the one who'd sort out the fights and look after the weak ones and worry about everyone. She'd be the lynchpin.'

Tamsin smiled. 'I like that.'

'Sarah would be the vulnerable one. She'd need protecting.'

'From the guards – totally! They'd all fancy her!'

'From everything. From bad news, and infection and the sun – and probably the guards as well,' Reagan went on. Sarah looked a little pained. 'But everyone would want to look after her – she wouldn't be a burden or anything.'

'What about me?' Freddie's bright eyes were challenging. Reagan knew she had to be brave now. This was some sort of friendship test Freddie was setting, and she found herself so wanting to pass.

'You'd sleep with the guards, but you'd share what you got from them,' Reagan told her.

Freddie laughed. 'You're not wrong. And what about you? I suppose you'd be the principled one, would you, the one who stood up to the guards and got shot the second day?'

Reagan smiled broadly. 'I only said I could figure other women out. I never said I had myself sussed.'

They never made it to the bop. Tamsin gulped down the last of the cider so that she had an excuse to go downstairs and get some beer for them. Neil wasn't anywhere in the hall, and she was on her way back upstairs when she saw him, shoulders low, walking towards the street. 'Hiya,' she called. He turned and beamed, then came towards her. 'Listen, I can't make it tonight,' she said. He looked confused. 'I can't be a camp deserter.' That didn't exactly clear it up for him. 'But can I see you tomorrow night? For a drink or something? My room's up there. Kelly. Third floor, room five.'

'Sure,' he said, and she stretched up to kiss him square on the lips. Ooh, there was something about him . . .

They played the *Tenko* game, and Sarah cried some more, and they finished all of Tamsin's biscuits and two of Reagan's Pot Noodles, and they talked and talked, and smoked and got drunk. Several times each girl looked round the room and thought that this was the reason she had come, that this was how she had dreamed it might be. And by the time the three girls went back to their rooms, long after the music had stopped, they were the Tenko Club. Club rules were simple: men, children, work, shopping and chocolates – important, but not *as* important. When they need you, you are there. No giving up. Yes, they were the Tenko Club and they swore, lurching down the corridor, that they always would be.

September 2004, England

There ought to have been a law against driving while you were in tears. It was probably infinitely more dangerous than negotiating the roads after a third glass of wine. It occurred to Freddie that she almost never drove up the A3 *without* crying. The whole landscape, from the hideous modern Guildford cathedral perched above the town to the exit signs for RHS Wisley, its slip road congested with elderly gardeners, driving with totally excessive care and attention, was always blurred for her. She was always leaving Harry behind.

She blew convincingly into a tissue, bit hard on her bottom lip, and switched the radio on. *Woman's Hour*. Listening to Jenni Murray's voice was like eating Galaxy chocolate while you were wearing cashmere socks on a suede sofa. If Freddie won the lottery, she was going to offer Jenni Murray a king's ransom to live with her and read out all the bills and letters, shopping lists and to-dos – think how much nicer life would be.

Jenni Murray was definitely a Tenko mother figure.

She tried to concentrate on the woman talking with passion about the banners of the suffragette movement, but she couldn't stop seeing Harry. He was much braver than her – he had to be – so she didn't cry in front of him. She knew her voice was brittle, unnatural, as she straightened his lapels, and smoothed down the rogue curl that sprang from the widow's peak he had inherited from her. It had earned him the nickname Pugsley, which he had assured her, the first time she'd heard it, shouted across the car park, was no worse than Jugs, or Billy One Ball, or Timmy Tampon – better, probably. She knew he would pull his head away, just as she knew that at home the same gesture would bring him into her shoulder for a hug, their widow's peaks touching. He was tall for his age, but she was taller. She didn't tell him to take his hands out of his pockets, although a master surely would. She knew they were fists.

It was okay for her – she was minutes away from being in the car, where she could cry, and no one would see. Harry had to face a dormitory, a hall, four hundred boys. For the next seven weeks, he wouldn't be anywhere where no one would see. Then she would come to take him home for the oh-so-precious half-term holiday.

Adrian had no idea how much she hated this. By the time he came home this evening she would have cried all her tears. She'd gone to pieces in front of him the first time, and his parents had been there. She'd resented their presence, their need to be fed and entertained, when Harry, who should have been there, wasn't. She'd cried over the dinner she'd cooked.

Clarissa, Adrian's mother, (who would alienate two-thirds of the women in camp and, with a bit of luck, get shot for condescension and insubordination *really* early on) had looked at her with something between disdain and confusion. 'Of course it's hard,' she had said, sounding as though it wasn't, in the least, 'but it's absolutely for the best.' This brooked no disagreement.

'Absolutely,' Charles, Adrian's pompous father, had echoed. They both said 'absolutely' a lot. It made them feel even more right about everything. What the pair of them lacked in intelligence, they more than made up for in dogmatic vehemence. Absolutely insane-making.

'It was the making of me, Freddie, and it will be of him.' Adrian had been nodding too. They looked like a line of those velveteen dogs people put in the back of their cars.

Freddie had wanted to smack them one after the other. She wanted to scream, 'He doesn't need "making", you stupid bastards. I made him already. And he's perfect. And he's eight years old.' But even she recognised the futility of it. It was decided. It had been decided since the midwife had held him up and Adrian had spotted the swollen purple testicles he had never doubted that the baby would possess. Adrian had been to the same school as his father and grandfather before him, and Harold Thomas Adrian Noah, seven pounds eight ounces, was to be no exception.

She couldn't fight them all. Maybe she would have done, but Harry didn't want her to. He wanted to make his father proud, and his grandfather. 'It'll be okay,' he had told her. 'I'll be okay.' And he was. After three years, she and he were used to the agonising parting. On eighteen hideous days they had said goodbye to each other in that hateful car park. It broke her heart that Adrian didn't know what it cost his son. She no longer worried that he didn't know what it cost her.

'Frederica's American.' That was what Clarissa always said, when she was introducing her at some ghastly drinks party or golf club social. Like Sybil Fawlty pointed out that Manuel was from Barcelona. Like 'Frederica's got raging impetigo.' Except that, as far as her mother-in-law was concerned, that complaint was treatable. There was no known cure for being American – unless it was relentless indoctrination and regular use of the word 'absolutely'. Surely she would understand the necessity of public-school education for male children if she were 'one of us'. Clarissa had never understood why Adrian had married a foreigner when it was bound to present so many cultural problems, this inappropriate display being only one. The poor child was called Noah, for heaven's sake. Thank God for the three proper Christian names that preceded it – most entry forms (Oxbridge, Coutts, In and Out Club) would never have enough room for him to include it. She'd insisted on placing the birth announcement in the *Telegraph* herself, with the express purpose of leaving it out, and had been gracious enough to excuse Frederica's unpleasant outburst on reading it as the direct result of a long, tiring labour.

Freddie had always thought, or hoped, it was because she was different from the other girls Adrian knew that he had fallen in love with her. They'd met in the Alps, where Freddie was working for a ski company in Méribel. It was the fifth job she'd had since she graduated from university, and easily the most fun. She shared a flat with four other girls, averaged no more than three hours' sleep a night, and survived on a diet of Rice Krispies and schnapps (which she consumed in legendary quantities with her flatmates in the resort nightclubs each evening), and was having that mythical 'time of her life'. Adrian had come in with a few army buddies, and had seen her before she spotted him. He told her that his friend Stuart had pointed at her and said, 'Now, that's the kind of woman I want to marry.' She'd been standing on a chunky wooden table, singing 'Unbelievable'. Unbelievably badly, he had always laughed. He always used to laugh. He hadn't thought about it for years, as far as she knew. She sometimes wondered if he had only married her because of what Stuart had said.

She'd gone back with him that night to the chalet where he and his mates were staying. They had both been too drunk to do anything, of course. But the next morning, after a cup of coffee, a hot shower and a toothbrush had revived them, my God, they had done it then. Missed a whole day's skiing doing it.

He'd been fantastic-looking then. Taller than her – if only by a couple of inches – and broad. Freddie was big herself – 'statuesque', as Tamsin's mum had once told her to refer to herself, but for years she had just felt huge – and wasn't used to feeling, as little women did, protected and precious in a man's arms. She thought there was a pretty good chance she could have beaten most of the men she had been out with in an arm wrestle, but not Adrian. When she'd come down off the table, and he'd bought her a drink, and they were swaying and watching and getting the feel of each other, he'd put his arms round her waist from behind and his hands had overlapped comfortably. He'd rested his chin on the side of her head, and she had felt suddenly tiny and safe. It was a new and nice sensation. The mates he'd been with that night had called him Red, but that wasn't fair: his hair was coppery, and there were copper flecks to match in his hazel eyes. Tanned from skiing, he looked all sort of burnished and shiny and healthy and big, and Freddie had thought he was delicious.

When he'd taken her home to meet his family, a few months later, she remembered thinking it was no wonder he'd come looking for her that night. They were so stuffy. So false. So cold. She'd been there a whole day, and no one had said anything with any depth or feeling. Weather, golf, food, golf, people from the golf club, golf. His mother had dwelt briefly on some of the more palatable things Adrian had told her about Freddie: that her father had been a serious lawyer in the States and now, retired, lived out on Cape Cod; that Freddie herself had been educated at Oxford, no less (which was impressive without being threatening, since she showed no inclination to use her BA). And she was beautiful. Long and lean and all blonde curls, with that remarkable widow's peak and those extraordinary white teeth that Americans tended to have. Clarissa was particularly vocal about the teeth – Freddie felt like a horse. Charles, having established that Freddie's father was a keen golfer who played several times a week at his club on the Cape, patted her distractedly, then largely ignored her; he was keen to show Adrian the new lob wedge he had won in the spring dinner-dance raffle.

If she hadn't been what she assumed was so completely in love with Adrian, she might have run a mile after that first visit. But she was, and she believed it was him and her against the world, including his parents. They'd giggled hysterically afterwards. He'd parked his vintage Austin Healey next to a lake near his parents' home and taken her face in his huge hands. 'Let's have a closer look at these teeth, shall we?' He pushed his tongue into her mouth and ran it across them, then slid a hand down her thigh and slapped it gently. 'Hmm. Fine flanks. Let's see how she goes, shall we?' They'd had to get out, of course. The interior of the Healey wasn't big enough. He'd made love to her standing up, against the car, one of her feet on the bonnet, whispering horsy terms she'd never heard before, making her giggle even as she concentrated. They'd done it anywhere and everywhere in those days. Freddie thought bed was her least favourite place.

When had he changed sides? When had it become them and him against her?

By the time she got to the M25 *Woman's Hour* had finished. The traffic was heavy as, inexplicably, it always was. She joined the motorway, and sat in the middle lane doing no more than twenty miles an hour. She wasn't in any hurry. She pressed the button and switched from Radio Four to Radio One. She recognised the song – Harry had the album, and he'd been playing it all summer. She turned it up. It felt good to be listening to something he loved. It was hot for September, and she opened the car window to let the breeze in. She felt calmer now.

She didn't hear her mobile phone ring – the music was too loud – but she saw its persistent green flash in the hands-free holder next to the stereo controls. Adrian's office number. Grudgingly, she turned Harry's song down. She hated mobiles. You could never be 'unavailable' any more.

'Hello?'

'Hello, it's me.'

'I know. Caller ID.'

'Of course. How did it go?' He never rang to ask her that.

'Fine.' So she wasn't about to tell him.

'Can you talk?'

She'd thought they already were. 'Yes. Traffic's crummy. I'm going about two miles an hour. What's up?'

She heard him take a deep breath – actually heard him. 'Perhaps it'd better wait until we're home.'

'What?'

'No . . . it's okay.'

Freddie was instantly irritated. 'For goodness sake, Adrian, what's wrong? You've obviously rung about something . . .'

When he spoke next, his voice was louder, and stronger. 'I think you should know that I'm seeing someone. It's become rather serious, actually. I love her, and we want to be together. I wanted to wait until Harry had gone back. I know it's going to be rather complicated . . .' His voice trailed off.

He'd started so well, she thought. You'd think once you'd told your wife you were in love with your lover it wouldn't be that much harder to tell her you wanted a divorce and one or other of you out of the home you shared. But apparently it was.

Silence. She very nearly felt sorry for him. Pandora's box: lid off. Can of worms: opened. Cat: no longer in bag.

'Freddie? Are you there? Freddie?'

More silence.

'Freddie, come on. We have to talk about this—'

'No, Adrian. Apparently *you* have to talk about it. Right now I think you'll find that I *absolutely* don't have to.' And she pushed the red button that cut him off. Her hand was shaking.

She turned the radio on again. The inexplicable jam had cleared, just as inexplicably, and soon she could go at fifty, sixty, then seventy miles per hour. She moved into the fast lane and drove.

It would have been even more unforgivable if she'd

been surprised. She'd known about it, of course. Did a wife ever really not know? She doubted it. It was more a question of whether or not you wanted to know. Because if you did you had to deal with it. And dealing with it was going to be more than 'rather complicated', she feared.

She felt almost bad about hanging up on him. Lousy timing. It had probably been like lancing a boil. Or throwing up after a dodgy prawn. He had probably waited until he couldn't bear any longer not to get it out. She had left Harry maybe an hour ago.

Antonia Melhuish. If she was honest with herself, Freddie had seen the spark flash between them the first time they had met. Antonia had been married to Jonathan, a friend of Adrian's from the army. She was pretty, rather than beautiful. Neat – that's how Freddie always thought of her. Not being able to wash in hot water in camp would have completely freaked her out. She was the kind of woman who never went out without makeup or a belt in her trousers, and whose toenails changed colour in summer to match her outfits. The kind of woman who, years ago, would have made Freddie feel inadequate, unfeminine. Not now. Freddie was more or less happy in her own skin, and that kind of attention to detail seemed vaguely absurd to her. Antonia and Jonathan had never had children, and Freddie had always assumed that was because children would interfere with the neatness: of her figure, her home, her life. But they'd never been close enough for her to ask. Jonathan had moved on to someone messier about three years ago, and now they had a baby. Drunk and miserable at some party, he'd once told her that Antonia always got up out of bed after they had made love and washed herself. He said it made him feel dirty, the idea that she couldn't sleep with something of him on her.

She didn't know how long it had been going on. Probably longer than she imagined. What was that statistic Jenni Murray had told her a few months back? The average extra-marital affair lasted seven years. Maybe theirs had too. There'd been nothing sit-com or *Trisha* show about Freddie finding out – she hadn't pulled a pair of Antonia's knickers out of the washing-machine after she'd washed the sheets, or found receipts for romantic dinners she hadn't eaten when she went through Adrian's suits before she took them to the dry cleaner. In fact, she wasn't domestic enough for either of those, and Adrian was a careful man – he wouldn't have been caught out by something so elementary. She hadn't walked in on them banging away in her bed, or seen their hands clasped, or their ankles entwined under the table at some dinner party. It had been much more subtle. The way he had stopped confiding in her and asking for advice about things at work. He didn't ask how he looked, or whether she loved him. He had stopped leaning on her. The way he made love to her had changed too. Not that he had refused to do it with the lights on, or anything like that.
. . . Freddie wondered if Antonia Melhuish knew that she and Adrian still had sex as frequently as ever.

Perhaps not. And that he was more giving in bed, less interested in himself. He'd always been a great lover – but now he was fantastic. A best-behaviour lover. One day it had all made sense. He didn't need anything from her any more: he was getting it from someone else.

Antonia Melhuish.

And now he wanted to be with her all the time. He wanted to leave Freddie and Harry, and the end-of-terrace house in Shepherd's Bush where they had lived for ten years. He wanted to do it now.

It was funny, but the longer the affair had gone on, the less likely it had seemed that he would leave her. Men didn't leave their wives and children. How many times had she read that in the advice column of a women's magazine? They said all sorts of things about loving the other woman and being understood better and waiting for the right time, but they never went.

Jonathan had left, though, and for a few months Freddie had been afraid. Antonia Melhuish had been all alone in her warehouse in Battersea.

But Adrian had stayed, and they hadn't confronted her, and she had relaxed. Married men don't leave their wives.

Freddie was on the M4 now. She felt light-headed, as if she shouldn't be driving. She pulled off at the service station, and parked in a row of empty spaces. Adrian had put a roadblock in her head, and it was looming huge, dark and impenetrable. He was going to make her deal with it.

Freddie wasn't a great crier. Her father had always said women's tears were manipulative, and she had learned at an early age that they wouldn't get her anywhere with him. Instead she did this dry-crying thing, where she squeezed her eyes shut and felt her lungs tighten, but nothing happened: no appealing tears rolled down her cheeks; there was no snot, no blotchy eyes. It wasn't nearly so satisfying, but it was the best she could do. She put her head on the steering-wheel and closed her eyes. She was exhausted.

This time when the phone rang, it was loud and intrusive in the silent car. She raised her head reluctantly. She wasn't going to talk to him again until she was ready. She had no idea what to say to him.

It wasn't his number on the caller ID – not his mobile, his office or their home number. It wasn't even Antonia Melhuish's. It was a US number.

'Hello?'

'Hello, Freddie?'

'Yes, hello?' It was a lousy line, all fuzzy and far away.

'It's Grace.'

'I can hardly hear you.'

'It's your father, Freddie. I'm afraid I've got some—' The line went dead.

Freddie didn't know the number by heart – she seldom rang it – and had to fumble in her handbag for her diary. She punched it in carefully. This time the line was crystal clear. 'Grace?'

'Oh, Freddie. Thank goodness. It's your father—'

'What? What's happened?'

'He's dead, Freddie.'

It took Tamsin Bernard twenty-five minutes to get from her house to Heston Services, westbound, in her big burgundy people-carrier, and another five to walk across the bridge to the eastbound side. She was too pregnant to go faster. Even at twenty-seven weeks, Tamsin's belly was so low and so vast that it made negotiating the stairs slow and uncomfortable. She paused briefly in front of the Kentucky Fried Chicken concession, remembered that she had left her handbag in the car on the westbound side, then that she was on a mercy dash to her best friend, and pushed open the door to the car park. She squinted into the September sun, looking for Freddie's silver Volvo.

Freddie was leaning against it, with her back to her, smoking a cigarette. Tamsin hadn't seen her do that for a few years. 'Thelma,' she shouted, 'Louise is here. Where are we off to?' Freddie hadn't said why she needed her, just that she did, and where to come. Tamsin hadn't asked. She knew Freddie hated the phone, and that she wouldn't ask if she wasn't desperate – she never did stuff like this.

Freddie turned and smiled at her best friend. It was such a relief to see her. Tamsin smiled back. 'If it's a long way, can you spot me a fiver for some Kentucky first?'

Freddie put out her arms in a gesture of helplessness. 'My dad died, Tamsin.'

'He what? When?'

'Last night. He died in his sleep.'

'How'd you find out?'

'Grace rang me just before I rang you.'

'Grace? Your dad's housekeeper, yeah?'

'Yes. She found him.'

'Christ. Poor woman. Are you all right?'

'I don't know. What do I do, Tams?' Freddie took a long drag on a cigarette.

Tamsin took it away from her and stubbed it out on the ground with the toe of her boot. 'Well, not that, for a start. It won't help, and it'll give you lung cancer and bad breath.'

Freddie rolled her eyes and let Tamsin pull her into her arms, although she was only 5'2" and they must have looked absurd standing together there.

She talked over Tamsin's shoulder. 'I didn't even like the guy.'

'Me neither.'

Freddie laughed. Almost cried. 'He couldn't stand you.'

'Thanks very much.'

'That's okay.'

'So . . .'

'So what?'

'So I haven't seen him in almost two years. He's hardly a part of my life at all. I cannot remember the last time we were together when we didn't row about something, when he didn't make me feel like a failure and a disappointment and a pale shadow of the son he undoubtedly wanted me to be. I don't think he loved me, and I'm not sure I loved him. I moved continents to get away from him. So why am I standing here smoking, for Christ's sake, feeling like someone pulled the rug out from under me?'

Tamsin patted her arm comfortingly. 'Not liking a parent doesn't mean there's no baggage to deal with when they die, Fred. I think it probably means there's more.'

'Baggage? What's with you?'

'Baggage. Stuff. Shit. Feelings. You know what I mean.'

Freddie shrugged.

'Have you told Adrian? Or did you call me because you couldn't get hold of him or something?'

She'd forgotten. She looked at Tamsin's open, lovely face.

'Oh, Tams. There's something else . . .'

The burgundy people-carrier was filthy and smelt of dog. Dog and Kentucky Fried Chicken. Freddie's last revelation had sent Tamsin over the edge, and she was balancing a cardboard box precariously on her ever-decreasing lap, eating chicken dippers as she drove. The silver Volvo was still parked at the service station. 'I think Adrian can chuffing well figure that one out, don't you?' she'd insisted. 'You're coming back with me.'

That was what Freddie had expected, and longed for. She'd been running home to Tamsin, one way or another, for nearly twenty years. The first time they'd barely known each other, really. It had been a few weeks into their first term. Tamsin had had to go home to be her eldest sister's bridesmaid, she said, and it was going to be too grim, all peach taffeta and dodgy dancing, and Freddie just had to come with her, please, please, please. Freddie had abandoned the essay on the Pre-Raphaelite movement she should have been writing and they'd caught the train together on a Friday night. What Tamsin had neglected to mention until after they had changed trains in Reading and it was too late for Freddie to turn back, was that she was one of nine children, seven of them girls, and that Freddie was about to be plunged into cacophonous chaos.

Freddie was an only child. Nothing could have prepared her for what awaited her or, peculiarly, for how it had grabbed her and made her heart sing. The Johnson home in Wiltshire was miles from anywhere; a filthy Land Rover took for ever to negotiate its way down a long, bumpy track that had obviously been incredibly muddy until the frost of the last few days. It was driven, erratically and with much swearing, by Tamsin's eldest sister Anna, the not-prone-to-blushing bride-to-be, who let out a raucous laugh as she recounted each detail of her hen night the previous weekend. She pulled up in front of a vast, dilapidated Queen Anne farmhouse, and two Border collies set upon them boisterously as soon as they got out.

Tamsin's father appeared in the doorway and called the dogs, then saw Tamsin and ran at her, lifted her up and swung her round. 'My darling girl! Welcome home!' Clearly he was overjoyed to see her. Freddie felt self-conscious, foreign, and fairly lonely in this place, which was so unlike any home she had ever had. Then he put Tamsin down and came to her. 'Tams has told us all about you, Freddie. We're so glad you've come.' She, too, was folded into his embrace, and it didn't feel at all strange. 'Come in, come in – your mum's desperate for a hand, Tams. You're not a moment too soon.'

Tamsin's mum, Caroline, was in the kitchen. It was huge, dominated at one end by a black Rayburn, and at the other by a wall of photographs, hanging haphazardly; school photographs, weddings, christenings, graduations, children rolling in grass, standing triumphant on hilltops and laughing on wide winter beaches.

There was a long, scrubbed-pine table in the middle of the room. At one end there were about twenty cream jugs, each with its own arrangement of peach roses, baby's breath and greenery. At the other, Tamsin's mum was bent over a wedding cake, her face set in concentration as she laid a peach rosebud on its top tier. She was short and round, like her daughter (all her daughters, as it turned out), with Tamsin's gleaming dark hair (although she always admitted that hers was now from a bottle). When she saw them in the doorway, she beamed and wiped her hands on her apron. 'You're home, you two!'

It was like being wrapped in a duvet, being there with all of them. That first time, and every time since.

The farmhouse had become Freddie's English refuge, the family her adopted clan, from Anna, now a
mother of three, to George, Tamsin's Down's syndrome brother, who still lived at home with Caroline.
Freddie had always loved being there. Tamsin's dad
had died, and Freddie remembered his funeral as the
only time she had been to the farmhouse and not found
it reverberating with laughter, shouting and Frank
Sinatra. But even then there had been a place for
her with them, and she had felt almost as much a part
of the mourning as they were.

When Tamsin had married Neil she had franchised
her own version of the Wiltshire farmhouse, crammed
into a semi in Ealing, whose walls were painted in a riot
of primary colours while the china was mismatched
and chipped. Now home to her own three babies (she
was carrying number four), a Labrador and Meghan,
the Australian au pair, it rang with the same noises of
her childhood home, although Robbie Williams had
replaced Frank, to Neil and Caroline's despair.

It was still the first place Freddie wanted to be when
anything went wrong. Today was a good day to be
there.

They didn't talk much on the way home. Freddie
could see that Tamsin was angry. Her rosebud mouth
was tight, and her knuckles were white on the wheel. It
was sweet of her to feel so cross with Adrian. Freddie
wondered why she herself didn't. Until Tamsin had
asked about him in the car park she had almost forgotten his call. It had been like a slap in the face,

followed immediately by a punch – the slap had stung, but the punch had obliterated it. Inside her head she kept saying, 'My father is dead. My father is dead.' It didn't sound quite right.

Tamsin's house had off-street parking because Neil had had the front garden tarmacked. Tamsin parked next to Meghan's Fiat Uno, narrowly missing its wing mirror. Driving wasn't her strong suit, and she got appreciably worse when she was pregnant. Only the current baby was at home with Meghan. Flannery – named for Flannery O'Connor, one of Tamsin's heroines of American literature but universally known as Flancase, except by her mother, who always tried to use the full name, and Caroline, who called all her children and grandchildren Poppet, because it was simpler – was holding court outside in a high chair, waving half a banana, having smeared the rest into her hair and clothes. Meghan, in hipster jeans and a micro bikini top (the guards would have been clamouring to sleep with her, but Meghan had principles, and Aussie grit) was next to her in a deck-chair, murmuring encouragement and admonishment while she tried to finish her book. She was devouring Tamsin's paperback collection of the classics.

Tamsin had more books than anyone Freddie had ever known. Literature was her passion. Hence the children's names, and her apparent willingness to condemn her son to a lifetime of saying 'Homer – as in *The Iliad* not Simpson.' Tamsin thought Homer

Bernard a fine name. She was a spectacularly successful secondary-school teacher because her enthusiasm
was contagious. Bookshelves lined practically every
wall and crowded every landing; to the astonishment
of any one who noticed, the books were in meticulous
alphabetical order. Even the children had learned
quickly that to empty the kitchen cupboards or to
dig up the bulbs in the borders was acceptable, but
to mix Marvell and Milton was sacrilege.

'Hiya.' Meghan didn't get up when they came in.

'Hello. And hello, my darling! How's Mummy's
girl?' Tamsin kissed a banana-free patch on Flannery's
forehead.

Freddie tousled the baby's hair, 'Hi, Flancase,' and
was rewarded with a 100-watt grin.

Meghan waved. 'How are you, Freddie?'

Freddie smiled with her lips pressed tightly together.
'Fine, thanks. Great Indian summer, hey?' Quietly
thought: Bloody hell, I *am* English. When did that
happen?

'I've made the salad you like, Tams, the one with the
pecans and that dressing, and there's some ready-to-
bake ciabatta in the larder that just needs bunging in
the oven for ten minutes or so. And a gooseberry fool.
Me and Flancase'll be out of your hair in a few
minutes, won't we, angel?'

Tamsin's head was in the fridge. 'Where are you off
to? I know you told me . . . pregnancy memory . . '

'Music. Bit of Dingle Dangle Scarecrow, which
actually quite rocks, doesn't it, Flan? And then we'll

probably have a coffee. I'll pick up Homer and Willa on the way home.'

'Perfect.'

Now Freddie took in the patio table, which was laid for two with fabric napkins and a vase of gerberas. 'Oh, Tamsin, I'm sorry. You've got someone coming for lunch and now I've messed it up. Look, call me a cab and I'll bugger off.'

'Don't be daft. You're going nowhere. Besides, I've had that Kentucky now – there's some salad going begging.'

'But I'm not really up for company.'

'It's not company, it's Matthew. He's working from home this week, some trillion-page thingy he's got to read, and I said I'd feed him. That's all.' She looked at Freddie sideways. 'I can cancel him, if you like?'

'No. Matthew's fine.'

'He was only saying, at the weekend, actually, that he hadn't seen you and Adrian for ages. He'd love it. You're much better company than I am. These days, I fall asleep after three sips at lunchtime.'

Freddie laughed. 'Shut up.'

'Good, that's settled. You get the cork out of this,' she handed Freddie a bottle of cold sauvignon blanc, 'and I'll get Madam here a bit respectable while Meghan finds out whodunit.'

'Oy,' they heard Meghan shout down the stairs, 'this is bloody Thomas Hardy not Agatha Christie, I'll have you know.'

'Glad to hear it!' Tamsin hoisted Flannery out of the

high chair and slid her to her hip. 'Go on, Freddie, get out there and sit down.'

Freddie opened the bottle, poured herself a big glass, then went out on to the patio, and sat in Meghan's deck-chair. The sun was bright and she pulled her glasses off the top of her head to shield her eyes. She closed them anyway, leaned back against the canvas and let herself be still. She tried to make herself breathe evenly and think nothing.

She didn't hear Matthew come out to join her. He'd eased himself past the enormous three-wheeler buggy at the front door, and Tamsin had ushered him outside while she sorted Flannery out.

For a full minute he just looked at her. At the sun shining on her blonde curls, and her long brown legs with their pink toenails and her familiar face.

Tamsin would be here in a minute. Finally he spoke, went to the deck-chair and touched her shoulder lightly.

'Freddie! I didn't expect to see you here.'

She turned her head, pushed the glasses back on to her head and squinted, and three lines appeared down each side of her nose. 'Hello, sweetheart.' She put out her arms.

He knelt down and put one hand on the arm of the deck-chair to hug her. And even then it was hard not to let the weight of his chest come down onto hers. She smelt of Aromatics Elixir, like she always did.

'I'm crashing, I'm afraid.' And then, 'I just dropped Harry at school.'

His face was concerned. 'Poor you. Was it awful?'

She shrugged, still within his embrace. 'You know.' And it felt as if he did. Childless Matthew.

He hugged her again, then stood up, pulling her with him. 'Seven weeks and counting?'

'Exactly.'

'You look wonderful,' he said.

'You look stressed.' He did. His dark hair was peppery down the sides, these days, and he didn't have any end-of-summer colour. 'I told you you should come with us to Portugal. Or you could have gone with Tams and Neil to France.'

'Christ! You're not recommending that as a cure for stress, surely?' Matthew grimaced. The Bernards and Meghan had gone to Euro Disney in the putrid purple people-carrier.

'Maybe not. But Portugal?'

'Was it wonderful?'

'It would have been more fun with you. I still haven't got over the rejection, actually.'

'Yeah, yeah!'

'Ninety degrees in the shade. Couldn't get Harry away from the pool or Adrian away from the golf course. Could have done with the company.'

'What happened to Tuscany? Every year you say Tuscany.'

'And every year I lose the popular vote.'

'Next year?'

Freddie's face darkened briefly. 'You know what, Matt? Next year I might just get to Tuscany.'

'Then I might just come with you.'

'You're on. Where's Tamsin got to?' She wasn't ready to tell anyone yet about Adrian. Pride? Or was the sentence 'Adrian's having an affair' too difficult? And she didn't know how to tell him about her father. Not after Sarah.

Tamsin told him. She wasn't so careful with Matthew. Which was why he loved her so much. She said it while she put salad into bowls. 'Freddie's dad died yesterday. In his sleep.'

'God.' Matthew put his hand on Freddie's. It felt warm. 'I'm so sorry, Fred. I didn't know . . . Was there . . . He wasn't . . .?'

'He wasn't ill, Matt. Nothing like that. But he was old – eighty-two. I suppose it sounds stupid to say I'm shocked.'

'It's always a shock, I think. Expected or not.' Now Freddie put her own hand on his. Tamsin waddled round the table and stood between them, pulling their heads in towards her bump.

Sarah had been dead for *a little over three years*. It always surprised Freddie when she remembered how long it had been. She could recall vividly when it had been a week, a month, six months, a year. It was always a shock to discover that life carried on. And now it was more than three years. And Sarah had been a wife, not a father.

Much later Matthew took her home, when they'd finished the wine, and three cafetières of strong coffee.

For Matthew and Freddie the garden was warm and the support quietly tangible. For Tamsin, their presence was a good excuse not to do any washing. Homer and Willa had eventually returned with Meghan and Flannery, Matthew and Freddie had listened to them reading while Tamsin grilled sausages and mashed potatoes. Willa, who was six, had leaped gleefully on Freddie, screeching about some playground débâcle she had had with a girl called Phoebe, then demanded that Freddie stay until after bathtime. Homer and Matthew buried their dark heads in a Philip Pullman novel. The *Neighbours* theme tune blared out, and Flannery took off her nappy in the living room.

'Where's Harry?' Willa demanded.

'He's at his school, sweetie.' Willa and Freddie often had this conversation about him.

Willa couldn't grasp why it was necessary to sleep at school when you had been there all day: 'It's much nicer sleeping at home with your mummy and daddy. You should go and get him, Freddie. He's probably really, really sad.' Wise child, Freddie thought.

Homer thought boarding-school sounded great. Largely, Freddie suspected, because of the lack of sisters there. She had heard Homer say his prayers at night: 'Please, God, let the new baby be a boy, and by the way, I didn't mean it when I said I hated Flannery. I just hate her wrecking my stuff, God, and she does it *all* the time. Amen.' Freddie hoped the new baby was a boy for him, too, although she feared slightly for his name.

'Call me,' Tamsin had said, when she left. 'Call me whenever.'

'I know.'

'Adrian home?' Matthew had parked a few houses away from Freddie's in Addison Gardens. There were no lights on in the living room at the front, or upstairs in their bedroom.

'I think so. Unless he's at the driving range.' Or at Antonia Melhuish's. She didn't say that. She still hadn't told Matthew about it.

'Do you want me to come in with you?'

'No need. I'm fine. I've got some figuring out to do, I suppose.'

'Will you go?'

'I guess I'll have to. There'll be things to sort out, won't there?'

Matthew nodded. 'You know who you should call?'

'Reagan. She's good at this stuff. Maybe I will.'

'And Adrian. He'll be there for you?' Matthew wasn't looking at her. 'I will be, too. You know that, don't you?' Now he *was* looking at her. His dear familiar face was kind.

'There is something you could do, Matt.'

'Name it.'

'Could you take me to Harry tomorrow? I need to tell him face to face. And I just need to see him.'

'Of course, but won't Adrian—' He stopped himself. 'Pick you up around ten?'

'I'm sure that'll be fine. I'll call the headmaster first

thing and let him know I'm coming. Thanks, Matt, I appreciate it.' She kissed his cheek lightly. He put his hand to her hair and ruffled it gently.

While she fumbled on the doorstep for her key, he opened the passenger window and leaned across to speak to her. 'Call Reagan!'

She nodded. 'Night.'

And he was gone.

It was November 1988, five months after they had graduated. Reagan was at law school in Chester, at the start of her final year before articles – she'd already been snapped up by a massive, macho corporate City firm in London. When she finished next summer, they were all going to go Interrailing, then get a flat together. Freddie was working in the perfume hall at Harrods, filling time before she flew home for Christmas in Boston. Sarah was working on the local paper in Wales, where her parents still lived, and writing short stories and magazine articles at night in her dad's study. Tamsin had started her PGCE in Nottingham, after spending the summer at home, helping her mum on the farm while her dad was recovering from a mild heart-attack.

They missed each other. When Reagan rang Freddie and told her there was a bop on, the three others found themselves on the platform at Euston, waiting for the train.

Reagan met them gleefully at the station, and they walked arm in arm to where she lived in a tiny terraced house with two relative strangers from the law college. 'One's all right, I suppose,' she said, 'but she'd sleep with the guards for food, and eat it all herself. The other wouldn't make it through the first week.' The others nodded sagely.

Reagan opened a couple of bottles of Bulgarian cabernet sauvignon from Safeway, and they took turns to shower in the tiny avocado bathroom, then congregated in Reagan's double bedroom, giggling in their bras and pants, sharing makeup. Madonna sang tinnily from Reagan's ghetto-blaster beside an old spotted, cracked mirror. Tamsin was dancing, MC Hammer style, to make them laugh. Her knickers were greying, and coming away from the elastic, and her bra was probably two sizes too small. Reagan had no chest at all, just nipples like corks. She pulled on a pair of tiny black knickers, and eyed Tamsin's underwear suspiciously. 'Can we safely assume from the state of those pants that you're not on the pull tonight, Tams?'

'Course not,' Tamsin scoffed.

'Really?' Sometimes, just sometimes, Reagan's voice had an edge to it. 'Still with Neil?'

Freddie answered – she hadn't liked Reagan's tone. 'More than ever, eh, Tams? But it's not going to stop us lot having the flat, is it? You're not quite ready for married bliss yet, are you?'

'She's been ready for that since they had a shared shelf in the fridge in their second year.' Reagan's tone was lighter now. Whatever the moment was, it had passed.

'Neil's got another three or four years before we can think about moving in together,' Tamsin was saying, 'and I've got my teacher training to do, and then a school to find.'

'You've got it all planned, then?'

'Well,' Tamsin giggled, '*I* have. I just hope Neil's thinking the same way . . .'

'He is. He is.' Freddie didn't doubt it.

'What about Sarah?' Reagan nodded towards the bathroom. 'Is she seeing anyone?' They could hear her singing happily above the trickle of the shower.

'I don't think so,' Freddie replied.

Reagan, still naked but for her lacy knickers, was drawing a line of kohl on her top eyelid.

'What about *you*?' Freddie wanted to know. 'You're the one in the fit-to-be-seen pants, smelling of . . . what's that? Chanel?'

Reagan handed her the bottle. 'Graduation present from my gran. Gorgeous, isn't it?'

'Don't change the subject.' Freddie took a swig of the caustic red wine. 'Who's the lucky man tonight?'

She thought Reagan almost blushed.

'No one.'

Tamsin, dressed now, picked up her towel and flicked Reagan with the corner. 'Come on! We know – don't we, Fred? – when you're on the prowl. Who is he?'

Reagan rubbed the red mark on her thigh. 'That hurt . . .' They were still watching her. Sarah had turned the water off now.

'Okay, okay. I suppose if it goes the way I'm planning tonight you'll find out soon enough. He's on my course. Did his degree at Bristol. His name's Matthew Bartholomew and he's lovely. A bit like Tom Cruise, only taller. With brown eyes. And he looks much cleverer. He looks serious, actually, but I don't think he is. He's from Newcastle.'

'Look at her face!' Tamsin said. 'She's gone.' Reagan's face had softened, Freddie saw. She looked really pretty. 'You're a dark horse.'

Reagan shook her head. 'Nothing's happened. I mean, we've barely spoken. It's just that there's something about him. I think I really like him. I suppose it sounds mad – I just have this feeling, you know, that there's some connection between us. Something . . .' Her voice trailed off. She looked at Freddie and Tamsin, who broke the moment by humming Simon Bates's 'Our Tune', heads together, bodies swaying. 'Fuck off.'

'No, really, it doesn't sound weird at all.' Freddie put an arm round her friend's shoulder. 'It sounds . . . sort of beautiful.' She and Tamsin burst into giggles. 'But what I really want to know is, if he's there tonight and you go off with him, can I have your bed?'

The three were still laughing when Sarah came in with a yellow towel round her shoulders and her long dark hair combed out over it. 'What's funny?'

'Nothing.' Reagan didn't want to be laughed at anymore. 'Get a move on, Sarah. It started at eight and it's eight forty five already. These morons are going to be too pissed to dance if we don't get there soon.'

Those bops were all the same – cheap beer, nasty wine, dark rooms filled with sweaty people shouting over the music. Full-on snogging in one corner, a row brewing in another, and at least one person throwing up outside in the nearest bush. Fantastic.

At first they didn't notice that Sarah was missing. Tamsin was trying to repel the advances of some prop forward type who kept 'accidentally' thrusting his pelvis suggestively into her hip, and Freddie was pretty drunk. It was Reagan who saw her. She'd been walking the circuit from bop to bar regularly, concentrating hard on appearing nonchalant, waiting to see him. And eventually, at about half past ten, she did. He was with Sarah. They were standing close together in a corner, and his right arm was raised above both their heads, making a private little world for them. Sarah had to stand on tiptoe to talk into his ear, and when she did, he leaned his head back a little to look into her eyes as he smiled, then bent down to reply, his lips in her hair. Reagan watched them until she saw his hand on her cheek, his mouth move towards hers, and his other arm come down round her back to pull her to him. Then she went back into the bop.

Later that night, Sarah was in her pyjamas, talking dreamily about kissing the most amazing boy. Reagan shot Tamsin and Freddie such a look when Sarah said his name that they were both too frightened to react.

All she ever said to them about it, had said about it in the last fourteen years, the next morning when Sarah had gone to meet him for breakfast, was that Sarah had been in the shower, she hadn't heard a thing, and they must promise faithfully that she never would. And they had.

The answer-machine was flashing insistently. Two new messages. Freddie pushed the button and went to switch on the kettle.

'Freddie?' He had the decency to sound a bit worried. 'It's me, Adrian.' As though this morning's phone call meant he could no longer use the 'me' of intimacy. 'I thought you'd be home by now.' A pause, as though he thought she was at home and not answering, and might do so at the sound of his voice. 'But you're not.' You're floundering, Adrian. A penny dropped. 'I suppose you must be at Tamsin's.' Another pause. 'I hope so. I hope she's helping.' Fuck off. 'I'll be home tonight.' Whose home? 'I hope you'll be there then so that we can talk some more.' Talk at all. 'And Freddie, I'm sorry about this morning.' What did that mean?

The kettle had boiled, and Freddie poured some water over a teabag in a mug.

'Freddie.' This voice was Reagan's. 'I thought you'd be home by now. Tamsin rang about ten minutes ago. Call me. I'm at the office until about ten thirty. I'll be working at home after that. So, whenever you want, just call me.'

★   ★   ★

Her assistant was still working, too. Freddie thought that the woman's voice softened when she gave her name, and wondered what Reagan had told her. 'Freddie Valentine. Oh, yes, I'll put you straight through.'

'Fred? I'm so sorry. About your father and Adrian.' Freddie was grateful, on this occasion, that there was no big pause for her to pour her feelings into. 'What an absolute pisser. Two in one day.' Reagan was always staccato. It used to be from shyness, but in recent years it had been down to efficiency and purpose. Freddie had always imagined that Reagan scared the hell out of any opposing counsel.

'One thing at a time, Fred,' Reagan went on. 'We'll deal with Lord Fauntleroy later.' That was what she had called Adrian since the first time she had seen his flat behind Harvey Nichols, to which he had driven Freddie and her in his Austin Healey, a passing-out present from his parents when he had left Sandhurst. Freddie smiled. Later seemed like a good idea.

'You'll go over, I assume.' Along with everybody else. She wasn't at all sure that that was what she wanted, but Reagan didn't wait for a response. 'Well, I'm coming with you. I'm due some time off, you know.'

Freddie smiled again. Reagan hadn't had a proper holiday in about ten years. She was probably due six months off. 'Reagan—'

'Don't thank me,' Reagan interrupted. She knew perfectly well Freddie hadn't been about to thank her, but now that she had had this idea, made this plan in her own head, she was intent on making it happen. She'd thought it as soon as Tamsin had told her. 'I hear the Cape is great at this time of year. Leaves and all that. Besides, you're crap at all that stuff, and you need me. You can't deny it.' Freddie wouldn't have dared try. 'Shall I book flights for both of us?'

'Do I get to think about it overnight?'

Reagan's smile was almost audible. 'Just overnight. Call me first thing. We're going business class – I've got a zillion air miles and it's about time I spent some.'

Freddie thought she sounded almost excited.

'Talk tomorrow, then?' Reagan said.

'First thing?'

'First thing. Get some sleep.' That was Reagan's formulaic response to traumatic news, just as she would have said, 'Boil water and tear up sheets,' if Freddie had told her she was in labour.

Freddie took her tea and wandered into the living room. She still felt a little like a stranger in it, with its heavy drapes and sea-grass flooring. It was full of her parents-in-law's antiques – for which she was expected to be garrulously grateful, although she had not asked for them – and hung with dull Victorian watercolours. It felt like a Harley Street surgeon's waiting room.

The basement kitchen was *her* place. She had found an architect who would take out the whole back wall and replace it with a glass atrium so that the room was flooded with light on the darkest days. It had huge glass panel doors that slid back so that on warm days the kitchen was in the garden. It had white walls, checked curtains and beech work surfaces, and a dozen black-and-white photographs of Harry, twinkly-eyed and laughing, and lots of primary coloured finger paintings, poems and stories he had made and written. Adrian worried about fingerprints on the glass or the neighbour's cats running amok, and his mother was speechless at the violation of the house ('If one must live in a Victorian terrace, the least one can do is respect the building and its heritage'), but Freddie and Harry loved it.

Upstairs she was always a visitor, a stranger in a strange land. She pulled the cord to the curtains. As they closed, she glimpsed Adrian's back as he locked his car. She left the room quickly; she wanted to be downstairs when he appeared.

She was sitting at the head of the old pine table when he came down the turning staircase. He stood awkwardly on the threshold, hovered nervously, as though he needed permission to be there. He didn't look much like the guy in the bar at Méribel. He was different, not just older. Less. Is that partly my fault? Freddie thought. 'You're home,' she said.

It didn't require an answer, and suddenly he was crying, his face contorted. 'I'm sorry, Freddie. So very sorry.' She almost went to him – he reminded her of Harry. Instead she asked, 'But you did mean it?'

Adrian blew his nose, and rubbed the handkerchief self-consciously across his eyes almost angrily. 'I think so, yes.'

There were a hundred things she might have said.
Had she been such a bad wife, such an unsuitable life
partner? Could she have done things differently?
Could he? But none of them seemed right.

'I mean I don't know,' Adrian was saying now.
To her surprise his indecision was neither flattering
nor irritating. He was only saying what she was
thinking. Could the end of a marriage really be such
a wishy-washy thing? Wouldn't he have had to be
absolutely bloody certain about Antonia Melhuish to
ring her and say what he had, then come home
intending to end something that had lasted years,
produced a child? She thought about Antonia, imagined her listening to this. She probably wouldn't be
thrilled.

'I want to go to bed.' She stood up.

Adrian looked shocked. Was that it? He stepped
aside. 'Of course. You look tired. Can I get you anything?' So careful.

'You can come with me.' As she passed him, she
took his hand and went up the stairs. In their room, she
faced him and let her dress fall off her shoulders, then
stood in her underwear. She wanted to be held, and she
knew she could make him want her. It wasn't about
power. It was about being held.

She was passive as he kissed her, almost gratefully.
She didn't speak as he pushed her back on to the bed
and made love to her gently, as if she was a doll. It
wasn't the orgasm that she was waiting for, although
that came as it always had with him. It was the moment

afterwards, where he lay on her body, squeezing her so tightly it almost hurt, obliterating thought.

Afterwards he lay beside her. His face was a question.

'I know this doesn't change anything.' She answered it.

And then she didn't want to be lying beside him in their bed any more. She got up and walked, naked, across the room to the door. 'I'll sleep in the guest room.'

Adrian said nothing.

When the phone woke her the next morning he was gone. She had slept deeply and because it was in their bedroom it had rung a few times before she surfaced, for a moment she was confused – the light was coming in from behind her, instead of in front. Then she remembered. She wondered if he had taken some clothes. It didn't really matter.

The alarm clock said 8.30 a.m. She never slept that late.

Tamsin sounded concerned. 'Are you okay? You sound a bit spaced out.'

'I just woke up.'

'Is it a bad time? Is Adrian there?'

'Don't think so. He must have gone already.'

'Did you two talk?'

'We had sex.'

'After the talking thing?'

'Instead of the talking thing.'

'O-kay.' Tamsin drew the word out.

'I was too tired to talk, I think. I wanted some comfort. I know that sounds ridiculous.'

'Not ridiculous. A bit sad, maybe.'

'I know. More than a bit sad, actually.'

'What did he say about your dad?'

'I didn't tell him.'

'Now you're scaring me, Freddie.' She sounded it. 'Why not?'

'Because it wasn't his fault, not the timing bit. Not any of it, really. He would have felt so awful, and what would have been the point of that?'

'Christ, Freddie! Your husband is having an affair, for God's sake! He bloody well should feel awful. I don't understand you at all.' She spat out the *at all*. Righteous indignation was one of Tamsin's specialities.

Not that Freddie expected her to understand. Not really. Tamsin had fallen in love with Neil about three months before her nineteenth birthday, and he with her, and they'd been that way ever since, in a not-very-exciting yet spellbinding way: lovers, friends, partners, co-warriors against the rest of the world. Neil was one of those men you couldn't even flirt with – and, God knows, Reagan had tried. Tamsin couldn't be expected to understand a marriage that started off well, then changed. She wouldn't ever get the fact that this new fact, this new direction made her feel relief and even admiration in amongst the undeniable hurt and the anger that Tamsin wanted her to drown in.

'Look, Tams, I know what you mean, I honestly do.'

She'd buy herself some time. 'Maybe it's just that it's been eclipsed by the stuff about Dad. Maybe I can't deal with it all at once. That's what Reagan says, anyway.'

'You've spoken to her then?'

'She rang last night. She says I've got to sort the Dad stuff out first, then deal with Adrian.'

Tamsin made a thoughtful noise.

Freddie went on: 'I mean, I don't know, do I, if the marriage is over? Maybe he's in love with this woman and maybe not. I don't need to sort it all out straight away. I know you probably want me to throw all his clothes out of the window and put paint-stripper on his car.'

Tamsin giggled. 'That'd be a start.'

'But I'm not going to. You know me better than that.'

'I do. It's maddening! I'd have killed Neil by now, not shagged him.'

'I refuse to listen to anything you've got to say about what you'd do to Neil. The whole idea of Neil messing you around is more far-fetched than the episode of *Dallas* where Pam gets kidnapped by aliens and re-appears in the shower.'

'Now I'm hurt. We're not *that* pedestrian, are we?'

'Not pedestrian, no. Absurdly, unutterably, boringly monogamous, yes.'

'Fair point.'

'So leave it alone for the time being, will you? Let me handle it my own way.'

'All right.' Tamsin's tone was grudging, but Freddie knew she was okay. 'So, what other pearls of wisdom did Reagan have to offer?' Tamsin was only a little sarcastic.

'She's coming with me to America.' Freddie hadn't decided until that moment that she was going.

'Me, too.'

'Don't be mad. You're pregnant, for God's sake! And what about the kids and Neil?'

'It was Neil's idea. I'm only twenty-seven weeks. You can fly for way longer than that. Until about thirty-four weeks, I think, if you're well.' Freddie remembered that Tamsin always looked full term from about five months. In shops people would cluck at her, and say, 'Any day now,' and Tamsin would come out muttering angrily, 'Any day now in about three months, you nosy cow!'

'I've got Meghan to look after the kids, and Neil doesn't need looking after,' Tamsin continued. 'Also, as you've pointed out, I need have no concern about Neil's fidelity in my absence. He only likes doing it with fat fecund chicks.'

'Way too much information, Tams.'

'So I'm coming. Can't leave you alone with the Camp Commander for too long, now, can I?'

'You're not just coming 'cos you're jealous?'

'Don't be stupid. I'm coming 'cos there's an Osh Kosh outlet mall on Cape Cod and I'm fresh out of baby dungarees.'

'Tams?'

'Yep?'

'Thank you.' Freddie almost didn't know what to say. She was moved by both of her friends' loyalty.

Luckily Tamsin left no space for sentiment. 'Don't thank me. Just get on the phone to Reagan and tell her she needs enough Virgin miles for three business-class seats. I'm not sitting in steerage with this bloody great bit of carry-on I've got strapped to my front.'

'So, all three of my girls are deserting me?'

She and Matthew were in the car on the M25. For once the traffic was light. Matthew was playing Everything But The Girl on the car stereo, *Baby, The Stars Shine Bright*, his favourite of their albums. Real summer-of-'86 stuff, soulful, melancholic and so evocative.

He'd been listening to it, too loud, the first time she'd gone round after Sarah died. The door had been open, and he'd been sitting at the kitchen table.

'cause I don't like sleeping or watching TV on my own.

So please come on home.

His cheeks were wet, and his eyes were red. She had gone to him, and he had clung to her, half dancing, half rocking, and his shoulders had shaken for the longest time. She had never seen him cry again, even at the funeral, when everyone else was. They were trying to do it quietly and respectfully, but if her husband could hold it together, they probably felt they should be able to, too.

Freddie punched his arm. 'Don't say that – it makes you sound like a pimp!'

'Rubbish. If I'd said "all my bitches" I'd sound like a pimp. Now I just sound like a lonely old man.'

'Old I cannot accept, since you're five months younger than me. Lonely? If you are then it's your own fault. You've still just about got those Tom Cruise looks we all fell for. You're solvent, you haven't got too many foul habits – you're just scared!'

'Damn right I'm scared! All the women out there are predators, aren't they? Single at thirty-five and desperate.'

'You've been reading too many back issues of *FHM*. Being a single woman at thirty-five is perfectly respectable these days.' She hoped it was. 'In fact, they probably wouldn't want to marry you – they'd just want to use you for sex.'

'That I could cope with!'

They fell silent for a while. This was nice. She probably knew Matthew better than she had ever known any man. Parts of him, anyway. It was easy, being here with him.

'Do you mind if I have a cigarette?' He was already taking one out of the packet, and pushed in the lighter on the dashboard.

'Long term, yes, absolutely. Short term, go ahead.'

She leaned in to inhale his smoke. God, she missed cigarettes. The one Tamsin had taken out of her hand yesterday had been the first she'd had since her honeymoon, but it had tasted fantastic. That first hit of nicotine had made her gorgeously dizzy, then smoothly calm. She had felt like a naughty schoolgirl, buying the packet at that service station. And, my God, they'd been so expensive!

'What are you going to do over there?' Matthew asked.

'Well, I suppose there'll be a will, although he and I never talked about it. I assume he's having a funeral. And there's the house. What to do with it. Everybody seems to think I need to go, so I shall.' She smiled.

'I don't think you have to if you don't want to.' He wasn't smiling. 'This is 2004, for goodness sake. Things can be sorted out transatlantically. I don't want you over there if it's going to upset you. There's no point.' He sounded proprietary.

Freddie was thinking about her father. 'It makes me realise how little I knew him. There are three churches in Chatham, and I haven't the first clue which one he'd prefer for his funeral, if a church at all. I don't know if he ever set foot in any of them. When Tamsin's dad died, she knew he wanted "Nearer My God To Thee" played, and his grandchildren kept away, and that Caroline was to wear a yellow dress. And I don't even know if the old goat wanted a funeral at all.'

'Funerals are overrated. Who cares what church, which tear-jerking hymn or which coffin you choose?'

Sarah's had been pale wood, like her bamboo kitchen floor. And there had been roses, palest cream, like the ones in her wedding bouquet, all buds, tied closely together so you couldn't see the greenery. She'd hated lilies, the smell, their long stems and dusty stamens. They had chosen it all, Freddie, Reagan and Tamsin. Matthew wouldn't go with them to the undertaker's.

'You don't have to be there,' he said again.

'I probably need to be there. He was my father.'

Her father had never shown any interest in when she came home or how she got there. She had a credit card, and he paid off the balance each month. He never told her she spent too much, and he never apparently noticed what she spent it on. That Christmas, the one after Sarah had met Matthew at the law-school bop in Chester, she'd been flying home Pan Am, direct into Boston, on 23 December. It had been an expensive ticket: peak time, afternoon flight. It was the only time he had met her at the airport. Perhaps he'd wondered whether she'd taken the previous day's flight, gone via New York, although she never had before, and been blown up over Lockerbie. She had seen him at the barrier at Logan in his long black overcoat, his hands on the rail. He hadn't hugged her even then, even when she had realised what had brought him there. He'd put out a hand and, for a horrible, surreal moment, she thought he might be going to shake hers, but he was reaching for her bag. She had handed it to him, then kissed his cheek, her lips wet on his dry, cold cheek. The driver had dropped her father at his office, then taken her home alone.

*   *   *

'Why no Adrian?'

'He's busy.'

'Golf tournament coming up, is there?'

'Don't be nasty. He does work for a living, Matt. Besides, don't you think two chaperones are enough?'

Her face implored him. Matthew didn't like Adrian, she knew. She needed to tell him what had happened, but they were in Guildford already, and she'd just seen the road sign that meant she was only four miles from Harry. She didn't want to tell him now when they were so close. 'Are you coming in with me?'

'Do you want me to?'

'I know Harry would love to see you. But I also know that a working-class boy like you is likely to get a rash in a place like this.'

'Who'd blame me? I'll just hang around out here and try to act like I own the car rather than stole it, shall I?'

Freddie's shoes crunched on the gravel as she went in.

It was extraordinary how nervous this place still made her feel. Even though she wrote the cheques that kept her son at the school, Freddie always felt vaguely on trial. It was like a bigger, less personal version of Clarissa's bloody drinks dos. The place oozed history and tradition. It occurred to her, as she looked around the panelled room she had been shown into – its walls were a gallery of world-renowned alumni – that her father would have got off on it. He loved all this quintessential English crap. No portrait of Adrian, she noted. It was funny how the more successful a great-grandfather had been the more likely his great-grandson was to be a lazy sod, frittering away the family money on a life of debauchery. Not that Adrian frittered, of course. His parents didn't let him anywhere near their money. He had what the English called 'expectations', which amounted to justification for taking out a spectacularly large mortagage, and hoping the parents, who you never really loved because they sent you away when you were seven, met a painless but premature death before they could spend too much of what was rightfully yours. Christ! Perhaps she'd listened to too many of Neil and Matthew's socialist sermons.

Harry's housemaster ushered him in to the room. Once the door had closed behind him, and he was sure they were alone, he flew at her. 'Mum!' They held each other tightly; her darling boy. It felt like much more than twenty-four hours since she had seen him.

'What are you doing here?' Harry pulled back and straightened his uniform. 'Something's wrong, isn't it? Is it Dad?'

Charley Fairbrother's dad had had a heart-attack and dropped dead, smack in the middle of Michaelmas term. At work, apparently. Charley hit some idiot boy in the lunch queue after he'd said his father had probably been on the job, not at work. What a stupid thing to say. He probably hadn't meant Charley to hear, but he did. Harry remembered that Charley had been almost crying when he hit him, and that he'd got a bloody nose in the fight. But no punishment. Harry hoped it wasn't his dad.

'No, sweetheart, it's not Dad. He's fine. Come and sit down with me.'

Harry let himself be led to the sofa. It was one of those funny ones that looked like the sides were tied on to the back with ropes. He'd never been in this room before. His mum looked okay. Whatever it was, it couldn't be too bad.

'I'm afraid it's your grandfather, Harry.'

'Grandad Sinclair?' Harry looked frightened. I'm making a mess of this, Freddie thought, cross with herself. Just get on with it.

'No, darling, Grandfather Valentine.'

Harry looked mightily relieved, then realised he shouldn't, and rearranged his features back into concern.

'He's died, darling.'

She knew his response was formulaic. One of the benefits of a fantastically expensive education.

'I'm so sorry, Mum.' Harry felt relieved it wasn't someone he had loved.

'Thank you, darling, but you don't need to be too sorry. He was a very old man, and he died peacefully in his bed, asleep, and that's not a bad age or a bad way to do it.'

'Still, though,' he leaned against her shoulder, 'he was your dad.' Out of the mouths of babes.

His mother rested her head on his for a moment,

surreptitiously sniffed for his familiar smell. Too late. One day had given him that institutional trainers and cabbage, slightly sweaty odour he had in common with a million other boys.

'I shall have to go to America, of course.'

Now he was stricken. 'When?'

'Next week, probably.'

'Why?'

'There's a funeral, for a start, and then there'll be the house where he lived – it'll need sorting out. And papers. You know, boring grown-up stuff.'

'Why does it have to be you?'

'There isn't anyone else to do it, sweetheart.'

'Can't I come with you?' He put on the voice he used to use to wheedle favours out of her. Can't I come into your and Dad's bed? Can't I stay up just half an hour longer? Can't we have one more story? Then it had been so much easier to make him happy.

'You can't, my lovely boy. You have to stay here – you know you do.' It made her sad that he didn't try harder.

He knew that was true. 'How long will you be gone?'

'Not long, my love, I promise. I'll be back for half-term.'

'*Half-term*!' It was *ages* away.

'But you and I can speak all the time, and email, and I'll write to you, like always. I'll just be further away.'

'I've got five matches this half of the term. I've been put in the firsts.'

'Darling, that's fabulous! Well done.'

'But you won't see me play.'

'I promise I'll try and get back for one. And Dad will come, I'm sure he will.'

'Do you think so?'

'Absolutely.' As long as they didn't clash with any of his bloody golf tournaments.

Harry's hopeful face stung her. How was it that Adrian had Harry's unswerving love and loyalty when he had done so little to deserve it? He couldn't have been to more than two or three of Harry's matches. Freddie remembered the time he'd shown up unexpectedly. Harry had talked about it for weeks. She hadn't missed one, so her presence on the touchline was as automatic to Harry as his sports master's. She might have been jealous, but since Harry's happiness was what mattered to her, she had bitten it back, tried to be glad that he was there.

He smiled at her now, that wide, toothy smile. He was still her boy.

'Okay. Are you sad, Mum, about your dad?'

Only a child would ask. Adults made assumptions about things like that.

'I don't know, really. Some of the time I didn't like him much, but I don't think, until yesterday when I found out he'd died, that I realised I had all sorts of other feelings about him. And I suppose if I'm sad it's because it's too late now to work things out with him. Do you know what I mean?'

He didn't, of course. He looked confused. How

could he understand? His relationship with her was strong and healthy, and he was a long way from thinking about his relationship with Adrian in any other terms than touchline appearances. She knew that sometimes she tried to make Harry into a grown-up she could talk to – so that he would fill the space Adrian had left when he took his soul out of their marriage. It wasn't fair on her boy.

There was no way she could tell him about the other thing – she wouldn't know how to start. Anyway, he didn't need to know yet. Maybe it would work itself out. Perhaps she'd never have to tell him that she and Adrian weren't together.

The next evening, Freddie was waiting for Adrian when he came in from work. At least, she presumed he had been at work. She had been thinking that she quite often didn't know where he was. Until now.

'We need to talk,' she said.

He looked at her. She couldn't get used to that face – the conciliatory, apologetic, I'm-in-the-wrong face. It didn't suit him.

'Yes, you're right.' He sat down with his hands folded on the table in front of him, like a recalcitrant schoolboy.

'Not about us.' She brushed her hair off her forehead impatiently. 'I've got to go away.'

'Oh, Freddie, is it really that—'

'My dad died.'

'What?'

'My dad died. Grace rang.'

'When?'

'Just after – the other day. On the way back from Harry's school.'

'Christ, Freddie. I'm sorry.'

'I don't know why. What you said is what you said. What you did is what you did.'

'Yeah, but your dad!'

'I know.'

'What was it?'

'A heart-attack. He died in his sleep. It's hardly a tragedy.'

'Oh, Freddie, you sound so hard.'

She felt a sob rise in her throat, but she quelled it. If she cried he would touch her, and she didn't want him to touch her. 'I don't mean to.'

'What will you do?'

'Well, I'm going over there.'

'Soon?'

'Yes. Tamsin and Reagan are coming with me.'

He looked affronted. 'It's all been sorted out, then.'

'Come on, Adrian, it's hardly the right time for you and me to go together. You're not exactly what I need in terms of support right now.'

The guilty look returned. 'No. What about Harry?'

'I told him yesterday.'

'Oh, so I'm the last to know, am I?'

Now she was angry. How dare he?

'Quite frankly, Adrian, you're the person who *deserved* to be last to know.' She walked out of the room.

He followed her up the stairs. 'How long will you be gone?'

'I don't know. As long as it takes.'

'As long as what takes? What have you got to do?'

'I don't know. There'll be a will, and there's the house. Grace will need support. She doesn't have anybody else.'

'And a funeral?'

'Most people have them.' She couldn't keep the sarcasm out of her voice. He sounded like a sulky child.

'Would you like me to come over for that? It's the least I can do.'

'I really wouldn't. I don't see there's any need.'

'What about wanting me there?'

'I don't really want you anywhere near me just now.'

'What will people think?'

'I don't care. There's no one over there who matters to me one jot, apart from Grace. But how very typical of you. If you're that worried about it, why don't you send an enormous ostentatious bouquet? Why don't you have it made in the shape of the words "FATHER-IN-LAW"? We could put it on top of the hearse.'

She was being nasty and she knew it.

She supposed Adrian and her father had been fond of each other, in a strange way. They'd had a lot in common, after all – emotionally buttoned up. She remembered the first time they'd met – her father had been in London on a business trip. She hadn't been going to introduce them, but when Adrian found out he was over he had insisted on coming along. They were meeting, as always, at the Savoy Grill – Freddie didn't think her father had ever eaten anywhere else in London.

She'd resisted Adrian until the last moment. She'd been dressing. She didn't know why she still dressed to please her father but she did. Classic little black dress, not too short, and the pearls he had given her for her twenty-first. Sitting at the dressing-table in the bedroom of her flat she looked in the mirror and didn't recognise the woman gazing back at her – so formal, so preppy, her hair neat. 'Do me up, will you?' she'd asked.

But instead of pulling up the zip, Adrian had slipped his hands into the dress, cupped her breasts and kissed her neck. 'Go on, let me come. I might have an important question to ask him . . .' he had teased.

'Would that be a golfing question, or a legal question? Believe me, those are the only questions he'd be interested in hearing?'

'Suppose I want to ask for his daughter's hand in marriage.'

'Don't you bloody dare!'

'Don't you want to get married?' He had feigned hurt, but all the time he was stroking the side of her breasts, moving closer to her nipples.

'That's not the issue. It's that you would consider asking my father's permission! We're in the *1990s!*'

But the stroking had distracted her altogether. Ten minutes later she had acquiesced. 'You can come, as long as there's no talk of marriage.'

'I thought I just had . . .'

He had followed her instructions as far as *that* subject was concerned.

Funnily enough it had been one of the best nights she had had with her father in the Savoy Grill. There had been a ridiculous amount of conversation about golf – handicaps, courses, clubs – but she'd been able to people-watch during those bits. Her dad had been so relaxed. She hadn't seen him like that since . . . She wasn't sure she'd ever seen him like that. She barely recognised Adrian either – stiffly formal, absolutely correct. If she hadn't known both men better she'd have thought they were trying to put on a show for her.

Afterwards Adrian had gone to get their coats. Her father had nodded and smiled. 'He's the right type for you.'

She must have been mellow that evening. It hadn't occurred to her to remind him that he hadn't the vaguest clue what the right type for her was. She remembered feeling pleased, and proud of herself.

They had parted in the lobby and her father went up to the bedroom he always stayed in.

As they walked out Adrian smirked at her. 'Did I do okay?'

'So it would appear. But you'd do well to remember that it's me and not my father you need to impress.'

He put his arm round her shoulders. 'I find that so much harder to achieve when I'm not naked.'

Looking back now, she felt as if she'd been following

a map and ignoring all the signs. Could she really have signed away her life to a man who was good in bed and played golf just because her father thought he was a good match and she was desperate for his approval?

Now Adrian was looking at her as if he didn't know her. If she was being shrewish and unkind, she thought, it was his fault.

'I'll write to Grace,' was all he said. He turned, with something approaching dignity, and began to leave the room. At the door, he said quietly, 'I'm sorry about your father,' and then he was gone.

September 2004, Boston, USA

Freddie had been eighteen when she had first made this flight into Logan airport, the one that arrived in the late afternoon. It was four months after she had left. The plane braked on the runway and the water in the bay shimmered in the sunshine. The clapboard houses a mile or so away across the water told her she was home. Then it had been cold, and there was snow piled beside them. Now it was warm, and the leaves were still green. But the deep blue sky was the same.

Today the airport was tired-looking, and so were the porters in their grey shirts and peaked caps, touting for trade among the bleary-eyed arrivals. They'd been jolly all the way from Heathrow. Tamsin hadn't flown much, and certainly never in business class. Even Reagan, who hadn't turned right on entering a plane for about ten years, had relaxed and enjoyed Tamsin's experience. Tamsin had paid attention when the non-chalant stewardess pointed out the emergency exits and had even 'taken the opportunity to study the safety card in the seat pocket in front' – until she'd caught Reagan and Freddie chuckling at her. She had looked askance at Reagan when, as soon as the captain had turned off the seatbelt light, Reagan had retired to the loo, then returned having replaced her makeup with a thick layer of moisturising cream. 'I suppose you're going to say no to champagne, ask for still water and retire behind these.' She waved the complimentary eye mask.

Reagan – who had been about to do exactly that – laughed. It was a nice sound that Freddie and Tamsin hadn't heard much in recent years. 'Course not.' She grabbed three glasses from a passing steward, who winked at her, and handed one each to Tamsin and Freddie. 'Cheers! Here's to us. It's a long time since we've done anything like this together.'

And then, because it made them think of her, and because they had fallen into the habit of toasting her when they were together, Freddie said, 'To Sarah.'

'To Sarah,' the others replied.

Tamsin clinked her glass loudly against Reagan's, then Freddie's. 'Here's to Filene's Basement.' The *Rough Guide to Boston*, spine broken at the shopping section, was lying on her tray table.

'Oy!' Freddie only minded a tiny bit. 'This isn't a shopping trip.'

'Sorry, Fred,' Tamsin said sheepishly. 'It must be the heady relief of closing the front door on Neil, Homer, Willa, Flannery and Meghan.'

'And Spot the bloody dog!' Reagan finished.

'The dog's name is Steinbeck, Reagan, as you well know.'

'Aah, they're lovely. Each and every one of them.'

Freddie decided Tamsin shouldn't have any more champagne.

They had eaten the ubiquitous chicken dish and chocolate roulade, and Tamsin had scoffed the box of Godiva cherry liqueurs she had bought in Duty Free. They had watched the inflight movie, and fallen asleep before the end, then woken up and paced the plane, in their droopy blue Virgin socks, waiting to arrive.

Now they had, and now Freddie was subdued. She hadn't been back for years, although she loved this city, because it had meant visiting her father, and she'd devoted too much energy to getting away from him, her huge, terrifying, emotionally barren father. Now, though, he'd won her back. Here she was.

They landed a long way from the terminal, so Freddie sat back and closed her eyes while the plane taxied to its bay. She wondered what Adrian was doing. When you heard that a friend's marriage had gone wrong, it was always a bit shocking. Which was because you hadn't been there, inside it, through the long process that brought a marriage from happy to over. They might wait to tell you, until they could say that they were happy about it, or that it was for the best, or maybe just until they could get the words out without crying. But then you always knew that it hadn't been that quick, and you wondered where the rot had set in, but you could never know. When it was your marriage, it still wasn't obvious. It wasn't the moment when you found out your husband was sleeping with Antonia Melhuish. It wasn't something you woke up and understood. And even when you could admit it was true, that the cracks were so wide they couldn't be filled, you didn't know when it had started.

She remembered the copper-haired army guy of that first night on the mountain. She remembered the man who'd sat in the bathroom with her while she had peed on the stick that had told them Harry was coming. She remembered a man charging around at a picnic with a giggling toddler on his shoulders, and a man helping a little boy bring breakfast in bed, with daffodils in a vase, and soggy cornflakes with too much sugar. And then she remembered the man who had refused to let her keep Harry at home. Who had been gone all day at weekends. Who had never stopped thinking that his stupid mother knew best. Who had never understood that giving comfort wasn't patronising but necessary. For years, those two guys had been the same man. And then the scales had tipped.

You couldn't keep loving a man in the same way. And once you stopped loving him the same way, whatever love there was trickled away.

That was how it felt.

The plane stopped and Reagan took charge. She swept aside the porters, and the three women wheeled their luggage out into the street. It felt good to be outside after all those hours of recycled air. The cab driver she hailed didn't get out of his white cab, just flipped up the boot lid so they could put in their cases. 'There goes his tip,' Tamsin whispered.

'Marriott, Copley Plaza,' Reagan told the man. 'I've booked two rooms. I figured you two would share.' Reagan had always shared with Sarah, if the four had been somewhere together. Tamsin with Freddie, Reagan with Sarah. She must miss her even more than I do, Freddie thought.

It was funny, the way foursomes always comprised the same two pairs. Freddie used to think that Sarah and Reagan had gravitated together because Sarah was the kindest of them, and Reagan the most difficult. At first Reagan had been shy and awkward, but within the security of their friendship this had become something like spikiness, and even bitterness. Sarah was always quicker than either Tamsin or Freddie to make allowances for her, see the good side. Freddie doubted she would still be close to Reagan if it weren't for the groundwork Sarah had put in when they were younger. It was she who had insisted that Reagan was always included.

Sarah had always been Reagan's champion. Freddie remembered one summer evening, a million years ago. They'd been playing softball on Clapham Common – Sarah's firm was in a league, and she had drafted Freddie and Reagan in as last-minute substitutes. It had been one of those hot summer nights when office workers poured out of sweaty offices and filled every inch of green space in the capital. Music and alcohol appeared apparently from nowhere and the air was heavy and close. Glad to be alive nights.

Neil and Matthew were working, although both had

promised to turn up later, and Adrian was off playing golf with some blokes from the office, so it was just the Tenko Club. None of them could remember the last time it had been that way. They had a beery and nostalgic conversation about how much they loved and missed each other in their new busy lives. Tamsin told them she and Neil were thinking of trying for a baby, and Sarah rhapsodised.

'Oooh. How gorgeous. We'll have a baby.'

'*I'll* have a baby!'

'You know what I mean.' Tamsin did.

'I think we should all have one.' Freddie smiled. 'Adrian's mother is on at us anyway, for an heir and a spare. And Matthew is desperate for kids.'

'What am I supposed to do?' Reagan interjected, only half jokingly. 'Head over to the local sperm bank?'

Freddie grimaced. Reagan had been lying on her back, in silence, and, to be honest, Freddie'd almost forgotten she was there. Tamsin wrinkled her nose in reproach, then turned to Reagan.

'I don't think you're quite ready for the turkey-baster method yet, Reags. Blokes drool over you. Look at this lot.'

It was not entirely true. Sarah was the one men drooled over, engagement ring notwithstanding. Which didn't stop Reagan from leaving with one of the softbase team, within the hour, his arm draped possessively round her shoulder. She didn't say good-bye.

'Does she have to do that?' Sarah asked. 'Apart from

anything else, he's my boss's boss. That augurs well for me when it all goes pear-shaped.'

'Don't be daft. Caveat emptor, or something. He looks like a big boy.'

'Do you think that's why Reagan chose him?' Freddie gestured at her own crotch. They all sniggered.

'I mean,' Tamsin added, 'he looks like he can handle himself.'

More peals of laughter. 'If he can handle himself,' Freddie spluttered, 'what does he need Reagan for?'

Now Sarah was shushing them. 'Don't be mean, you two.' She watched Reagan and her boss's boss reach the corner of the common and try hailing a cab. Already he was kissing her. 'That's just Reagan.'

'What do you mean?' Tamsin asked. 'You're always making excuses for her. We're all having a lovely time and she wandered off in the middle of a conversation, copped off with someone you work with, for God's sake, and didn't even say goodnight.'

'A conversation about babies.'

'Yeah, well.' Tamsin kicked at the grass stroppily. 'It's not our fault Reagan can't keep a man. It's no wonder, with that spiky attitude. I don't know why you make so many allowances for her, Sarah.'

'Because that's what you do for your friends.'

'You don't have to do it for us!'

'Don't I?' Sarah's tone of voice had changed. 'What about the fact that these days getting to see you without Neil in tow is nigh on impossible? What about the fact that Adrian never seems to want to get to know us?

What about the fact that you and Freddie are always so down on Reagan?'

This speech – *in vino veritas* – was so unusual for Sarah, that both Freddie and Tamsin sat, open-mouthed on the grass.

'Can't you see that Reagan is envious? And why wouldn't she be? We've all got what we wanted. She's still waiting. If she's spiky, it's because she's defensive. I bet she thinks it's easier to be aggressive than pathetic all the time. And it doesn't help when we all sit around and talk about our wonderful men and all the beautiful babies we're going to have.' She looked from one to the other. Freddie and Tamsin both looked down at the grass, shamefaced.

'I'm sorry to have a go at you, girls, but I'm a little bit pissed, and that makes me brave. I don't like being in the middle all the time. I love you all. And I want you to love each other. Reagan is our friend. She invented the Tenko Club, for God's sake.'

Tamsin smiled. 'Well, not exactly invented . . .'

Sarah picked a handful of grass and threw it at her. 'Shut up!' But she was smiling too. The moment had passed.

Freddie and Tamsin both shuffled over to her on their knees, and cuddled her from each side.

'Sorry, Sarah.'

'Sorry, Sarah.'

Sarah put on her best Joyce Grenfell voice. 'Don't let it happen again!' Just before they pushed her back on the grass and started shoving handfuls of it down her

T-shirt. They were helpless with laughter and covered in grass stains by the time the boys found them.

They'd all been bridesmaids on Sarah's wedding day. They had preened, giggled and helped each other into their satin dresses, high on the emotion of the day and the glass of champagne Sarah's father had sent up to the hotel suite for them. Just before they went down ahead of her, she had handed them each a little Tiffany box, containing a silver Elsa Peretti heart on a chain. Freddie remembered her saying that this was how she had always imagined her biggest best day, being surrounded by her biggest best friends in the world.

Since Sarah had died, Freddie and Tamsin had seen less and less of Reagan, but that had been her choice, not theirs. They had said to each other, more than once, that they felt her withdrawal from them. When they did see her, which was usually after some insistent telephoning – Tamsin had got into the habit of leaving a restaurant name and a time on Reagan's answer-machine, followed by 'Don't even think about not showing up' – things were stiff for the first five minutes, until the three realised they couldn't be bothered to be weird with one another and relaxed. Then it might be months before either of them heard from Reagan again. Tamsin was sometimes cross about it. 'I can't be bothered to make all the running,' she would complain. 'It's not like I've got loads of free time. We're all busy people. If she doesn't want to put the work in, why should we bother?' But Freddie found herself thinking like Sarah – making allowances, worrying about the reason for Reagan's silence, wanting to help. Was it too easy and complacent to assume that Reagan's unhappiness, if that was what kept her away from them, was to do with wanting a life outside the fifteenth floor of her City office block? Looking at Reagan now, checking the three of them in at the hotel's reception desk, Freddie was glad she hadn't given up on her. Suddenly she was happy that she was here.

It was dark outside by the time they found their rooms on the twenty-ninth floor, and Boston twinkled below. Tamsin threw herself on to the nearest queen-sized bed. 'Imagine having this all to myself. No kids, no dog, no biscuit crumbs.'

'You really are gross, Tams, you know that?'

'And me only in the second trimester!' Tamsin complained. She pushed herself up on to her elbows. 'This is nice, though, isn't it?' Freddie nodded. 'How long are we staying here?'

'I don't know. A couple of days? I'm not sure I can face Grace just yet.'

'Don't you think you should let her know you're here?'

'She knows.' Freddie had phoned Grace to say she was flying over.

Grace had sounded grateful. Tearful and grateful. 'I can't tell you how good it'll be to see you again, Freddie,' she had said, and Freddie had felt a stab of guilt. Grace had been wonderful to her – a mother, pretty much – and she had barely spoken to her for years.

Freddie had been almost four when her mother left. She'd gone during the week that Apollo 13 had splashed down in the Pacific. What little memory she had of her was from a photograph and what she had cajoled Grace into telling her when she was a teenager.

There was just the one photograph, as far as Freddie knew – of a young woman, a girl really, with Freddie's widow's peak and big round curls, worn long and parted in the middle like Yoko Ono, hanging in front of her shoulders. She was wearing a maternity dress that ended above her knees, with a huge Paisley print and a Peter Pan collar. The photograph was black and white, but the dress must have been psychedelic. The shoes were clunky, and she looked so young. She hadn't dared ask her father about any other pictures. When she'd read *Jane Eyre*, she had felt a shiver of recognition up her spine – her father was Mr Rochester, brooding, easily angered and a keeper of secrets. But her mother was not locked in the attic. Instead she was long, long gone.

People had tried to draw her on the trauma of her mother's abandonment. Boyfriends sought excuses in it for her rejection of them; teachers looked to it for the key to her detachment. It was textbook, surely. The little girl whose mother ran away must be disturbed. But her mother's departure had been strangely undisturbing for the young Freddie. She had accepted it as one of those things – the tooth fairy comes and takes your tooth from under your pillow; the girl you sit next to in the English class has brown skin; your mother isn't there. After all, she had Grace, lovely Grace, who had come to her father's household the summer after her mother had left and had done all the stuff with her that her own mother might have been doing. They made cookies, read stories and played hide and seek in the big house on Beacon Hill, conspiratorially whispering and putting fingers to lips when they were near her father's study.

What her mother had done to her, and to herself, didn't hit Freddie until she held Harry in her arms on the day he was born, and then it hit her like a hammer, like a freight train.

Harry had been a pretty standard first labour. She had waited at home as long as she could, which irritated Adrian: he had panicked, despite his army training, and was afraid she was going to make a mess on the new carpets. She had pottered around quite happily, and he had followed her with an armful of towels and, mysteriously, a black bin-liner. She'd been almost ready to push by the time she got to hospital – the midwife had said she wished all mothers were as calm as Freddie, who had been disproportionately proud of the compliment. It had all gone along as it should, and Freddie had wondered why Tamsin thought it was so bad. Sure, it was painful, but it was constructive too – it hurt much less if you went along with each wave. When Harry came out, they put him straight on to her chest, and his eyes locked on hers. That was when it had happened. It was like a dam breaking, a thunderclap, an avalanche. Absolute love. The happiest and scariest sensation a woman could experience. Thirty seconds later, the spectre of her missing mother arrived in the room.

Adrian couldn't cope with the tears – he went into the corridor and called Tamsin, who came immediately. She sent him to the car park to walk up and down with Homer strapped to his chest, and went to her friend's rescue. Freddie had cried for ages, clutching Harry, and she remembered Tamsin saying, 'Well, that's been a long time coming.' It had passed, of course. She was too tired, and Harry too all-consuming, for her to dwell on it. She never tried to explain it to Adrian. Clarissa had arrived the next day, with a maternity nurse she had hired without consulting them – 'She would have brought you a bloody wet-nurse if she could have found one,' Tamsin had joked. And the feeling had eventually gone away again.

She never thought that she was missing a mother; there was Grace. It was a father she didn't have.

If her mother had been dead, there would have been photographs of her in Freddie's home, in a wedding dress, in a formal pose, in a hospital bed, proudly holding a newborn for the camera. She would have been spoken of, cried over, and it would have been harder for four-year-old Freddie. But she was just gone. Like the tooth under the pillow just went. And

Freddie had understood, with childish insight, that she couldn't ask her father about it, so she had asked Grace. But Grace hadn't lived there when Rebecca had. She didn't know what had happened between Freddie's mother and her father. She just knew that when Freddie was four, Rebecca had left.

Her mother had been very young, Grace said. Perhaps she hadn't been ready for motherhood, or even to be a wife. No, Grace didn't know where she was. She had just gone, and so had all but one photograph, with the grandparents, memories and stories she might have told.

Tamsin couldn't have borne it – she had always said so: she would have had to get to the bottom of it. Righteous indignation, again. Along with an imagination fed by Daphne du Maurier and the Bronte sisters. It wasn't Freddie's way.

Before she called Grace, Freddie rang home. Adrian answered straight away, sounding tired. She wondered if Antonia was with him. 'It's me, Freddie. I know it's late but you asked me to ring.'

He had dropped her off at the airport. They had talked on the way, but only superficially. She had filled the fridge with ready-made meals from Marks & Spencer, and copied her father's numbers on to a Post-it, which she'd stuck on the noticeboard in the kitchen, next to Harry's football fixtures. He had promised her he wouldn't miss one. She hadn't changed the sheets on their bed, so they would smell of her. She told him where to find the clean ones if he needed them

– for Antonia Melhuish, she meant, although she didn't say it.

He'd winced. 'We've never . . . been together in our bed, Freddie. I wouldn't do that.'

An adulterous husband's code of honour. She had sighed. 'I don't think it matters where you do it, Adrian. It's the doing it at all that I'm struggling with.' Still, now, six thousand miles away, she hoped Antonia Melhuish wasn't neatly naked between her sheets, clean or not.

'I'm glad you called. I wasn't doing anything,' he said now. 'Flight okay?'

'Yes We're just a bit tired now.'

'Of course. You'll call me if you need anything?'

'I'll call.' I do need something: support, commitment, security, trust. I need all of that. I need you still to love me like you loved me in the bar, like you loved me in the field, like you loved me for all those years.

'Goodnight, then.'

'Goodnight.'

Then, of course, she couldn't face calling Grace. They went over the road to the supermarket where they bought some tiny bottles of wine with screw caps, hummus, bread and tomatoes, and had what Tamsin described as a midnight carpet feast in the hotel.

'Very Malory Towers,' Reagan observed.

'You might be up for lobster and an iced margarita,' Tamsin replied, 'but me and Socrates here,' she patted her belly, 'need a nibble and a kip.'

'Socrates? You wouldn't?'

'I might.'

Freddie woke groggily as Tamsin came into the room, armed with Starbucks coffee and chocolate muffins. Reagan was behind her with a couple of Victoria's Secret carrier-bags and a bottle of water. 'We thought you probably needed the sleep. We met in the hallway, both off for some sneaky retail therapy, so we left you to it.'

'What time is it?'

'About ten thirty.'

Freddie groaned, then sat up in bed, propped herself up with two pillows, and took the coffee Tamsin handed her. 'I've got to call Grace.'

'I already have,' Reagan said briskly. 'I've told her we'll be there tomorrow. That'll give you a chance to sort yourself out – and Ivana Trump here a chance to get to Filene's Basement.' She jerked her head at Tamsin, who had pulled from her candy-striped bag a turquoise and red concoction made of netting, which she was holding up across her stomach and balloon breasts.

'Four or five months and I'll be in this . . .' she was saying, almost to herself.

'God help Neil,' Reagan responded. Freddie hid her snigger in her Starbucks paper cup, as Tamsin stuck her tongue out disdainfully.

Later, out in the September sunshine, Reagan put her hand on Freddie's arm. When she spoke her voice was gentler than normal. 'I've got the answer to one question. The funeral is next Tuesday. Grace says he left exact instructions. Hymns and all of that. And he wanted you there. Grace was sure of that too.'

England

Adrian took out his driver, put the ball on the tee, and aimed straight down the eighth fairway. The ball hurtled into the sky and landed about fifteen feet from the green, on a good lie. He was on fire this morning – he'd only dropped one shot, and this new Big Bertha felt good in his hands. He wished he'd got time today for a full eighteen holes, but he'd promised he wouldn't miss Harry's football, and he mustn't. There was just time for these last two holes and a quick pint in the clubhouse. This was always his best hole. He knew how to draw the ball just enough to get it past those trees, and he hardly ever missed.

It was also the hole where he had first bedded Antonia Melhuish. Or perhaps 'bunkered' was a better description. She'd been winding him up that day ever since they'd teed off. He'd wanted her by the second hole, and by the third they'd both noticed that there was no one in front of or behind them. She'd bent over the green with his pitchmark repairer on the fifth hole and he'd seen that she wasn't wearing any knickers under her cotton skirt. He couldn't wait any longer by the time they got to the eighth and, besides, his hard-on was interfering with his game.

She'd sat across his lap, bucking away, his hands lifting her tiny ass, and afterwards she told him she'd never come so quietly or so quickly in her life. He knew he should have felt bad but, Christ, he was only human, after all. That's what he'd told himself. It had been over a year ago, and he still felt turned on and ashamed when he thought of it. He'd got four birdies, and an eagle on the rest of that round.

It had been brewing for months before that. Antonia had made it no secret that she fancied him, even while she was married to Jonathan. She never let him talk about Freddie – or about what they were doing to Freddie. She'd been quite sharp once, when he'd tried. 'I'm not married to Freddie,' she had said. 'I'm not the one cheating. I am free to be had.' So he had had her, three or four times a week ever since.

His second shot landed four feet short of the flag. He was on for a birdie. He shrugged his bag on to a shoulder and strode up to the green.

He'd held out for months. He wished Freddie knew that, but he supposed she wouldn't want details. Antonia had made all the running – God knew what she and that coven, the so-called Tenko Club would have made of her behaviour. She'd sat next to him at dinner parties, running her bare foot up and down his calf – now how could that be so damn sexy, and why was it just that little bit sexier when your wife was sitting on the other side of you, totally oblivious? She'd brushed up against him in the bar at the golf club, in other people's houses. Licked her lips when she was talking to him. He'd been well and truly seduced and, thinking about it, the foreplay had lasted years.

And, God, it was good with her. She had a fantastic little body, permanently tanned, with tiny round brown tits and boyish hips. She was waxed all over, which he found unbelievably erotic, and she liked to go on top, arching her back and mewling so that he could see it. She made him feel twenty-five.

He didn't know how it had gone so far. At the beginning it had been a bit of fun. Lots of men had affairs – half his friends were up to exactly the same thing. They talked about it. They said their wives had put them at the bottom of the list, after the kids. They said they wanted to feel like 'real' men again, not just fathers, providers and handymen. Briggsy and Thompson said they hardly ever slept with their wives any more. Birthdays, anniversaries, maybe the odd Saturday night, if you got them tiddly enough, with the lights off, missionary position. Some were unchivalrous enough to say they were glad to do it with the lights off, now that their nine-stone girl-friends had mysteriously morphed into twelve-stone wives with breasts round their navels and hairy armpits.

That wasn't true of Freddie. They all envied him Freddie. She'd looked after herself – clothed or naked she had hardly changed from the girl he'd married. And she loved sex. In eleven years of marriage he was pretty sure she hadn't refused him once, and often it was her idea. And it wasn't samey and boring, not at all.

So what the hell was he playing at?

Adrian had always done his best thinking on the golf course, but even here he wasn't sure that any of it made sense to him. Antonia assured him it had been his idea, but he couldn't remember when it had come to him, this notion of leaving Freddie for her. On some level he felt he'd been ambushed.

And he couldn't understand Freddie's reaction. His military training had taught him that the number-one rule was to know your enemy, but Freddie had thrown him a real curve ball in taking him to bed like that. No tantrums or ugly recriminations. No crying – not that he'd expected it: he'd only seen her cry a couple of times, on the day Harry was born, and when she had first taken him to prep school. He himself had never made her cry, unless you counted Harry's departure for school, which Freddie probably had. She'd known about Antonia before he'd told her – he'd seen it in her face – and that had scared him. Would he have known if she had had someone else?

Christ, *might* there be someone else?

In his egotism, Adrian felt a rush of fear. It left him as quickly as it had come. She'd always been happy at home, hadn't she? He and Harry had been enough for her. So why hadn't she been enough for him?

His parents would go berserk. His mother would be horrified at having to tell the bridge club there was to be a divorce in the family. They'd probably never accept

Antonia. Although his father had had his peccadilloes, he had always had the sense to keep them at arm's length. Adrian could hear him now: 'For God's sake, boy, dip your wick if you must, but don't forget which side your bread is buttered.' His father was big in mixed metaphors.

He took the flag out, and chose a putter from his Calloway set, set the shot up and hit the ball, true and straight. It caught on the lip of the hole, spun round its edge a few times, rolled away. Damn it. Adrian didn't bother to hole out, nor did he rake the bunker. He shoved the club back into the bag, and marched towards the ninth hole.

A big part of him wished he hadn't said anything. Couldn't he have just gone on this way, loving both of them – whatever that meant – living with Freddie and having fun with Antonia? He hadn't expected to feel this awful, having told her. The words had burst out of him. He wished he could take them back.

And what about Harry? Adrian was horrified to find himself close to tears. He pictured Harry's face when he heard, and cringed. There was no doubt whose side Harry'd be on – they'd always been an exclusive club of two. He'd felt shut out.

And now this thing with her dad. She should be here, sorting things out – she should be fighting for him, shouldn't she, fighting for their marriage, not leaving the field wide open for Antonia. Antonia had wanted to come over last night, but he'd known Freddie would call. Besides, he'd meant what he'd said to her. He'd never slept with Antonia in their house. It might seem a strange place to draw the line in the sand, but drawn it he had, and he hadn't crossed it, not ever.

Anyway, he'd been at Antonia's all afternoon. And now he wasn't entirely sure that it was where he wanted to spend all this time. She had seemed so pleased that he'd told Freddie. Almost crowing. Which he didn't find entirely pleasant.

For the first time since he was nine, Adrian failed to finish a round of golf. He walked across the course, past the clubhouse, and back to his car.

The trouble with Freddie was that she had always thought he had hidden depths, and he was sure he was just as shallow as he at first appeared.

Matthew couldn't concentrate. He'd been sitting at his desk in chambers since lunchtime, staring into space. He'd asked the receptionist not to put through any calls, claiming he needed a couple of hours' intense preparation before some non-existent meeting with a made-up client. He'd tried to read the papers piled on the left-hand side of his desk, but nothing had gone in so he'd given up.

He looked at Sarah's smiling face in the silver frame on his desk. They'd been in Southwold – he'd taken her there for the weekend, surprised her one Friday night, after his first case at his new chambers. They'd been poor for so long – not destitute *La Bohème* poor, more like *Barefoot in the Park* poor. Matthew didn't believe in debt: he'd only ever spent what he had. They'd had their plans – a flat of their own, then a house with room for children – but he wanted to spend this first cheque just on him and her, on the present, not on the future.

They'd stayed at the Swan, in a bright, airy room with a huge double bed. He remembered Sarah giggling in the dining room, saying she felt a fraud among the bejewelled ladies and the fine food. He'd told her she belonged there, but even then he had known it wasn't true. Sarah didn't belong in big diamond studs and a pearl choker. She didn't belong in a fancy dining room. She had been exactly like she was in that photograph: she was sitting outside one of the beach huts along the front – they'd seen one called 'Sarah's Sanctuary' and he'd made her pose in front of it, even though she'd been embarrassed. She was wearing a sweater of his, navy blue with white flecks, and it was huge on her. The wind was blowing her hair, and her face said she felt silly, but her eyes sparkled with love for him. She'd run to him the minute he'd taken the picture, launched herself at him, so that he'd had to thrust the camera into his jacket pocket quickly in order to catch her. He remembered that he had spun around and around with her, stumbling across the pebbles, and then sat her on the groin, and kissed her cold nose, and her warm mouth.

He couldn't remember when he had reached the point when his memories of Sarah didn't hurt so much, when the sharp mushroom cloud of pain had subsided into an ache, when the ache had been preceded by happiness at the thought of something she had done or said. His grief was like the tide going out: at first it had come in waves that crashed around him, taking his breath away, disorienting him, then in ripples that broke smaller and less fierce, and they were further away, and you watched them come up the beach towards you and stop a little shorter each time, bubbling and frothing, but not so wild anymore. Each time you saw more sand, and each time it felt calmer. That was what it felt like.

For weeks after the accident, he had wished she had died in a different way – if she had had to die at all. If she had been ill, perhaps, if he had been able to care for her . . . He knew it was a stupid romantic notion, this vision of him comforting her, having those final chances. He'd have had time to rehearse what he wanted to tell her, and she him.

But that morning, when she had left the house she had known what he felt for her, like she knew she was breathing in and out, like she knew she was late for the bus. She knew because they had rolled towards each other in their bed and held each other as they always did before they got up. Because he had made the mug of tea he always made for her. Because he had watched her brush her hair upside down from the roots like he always watched, loving the curve of her bare spine and the hair's golden sheen. She couldn't have understood it better, because she already understood it perfectly.

It had been so surreal. He was late for work, held up

in the traffic jam caused by her accident. The phone call was so stark. She had been hit by a car. The driver had been trying to read a map and call someone on his mobile at the same time. She'd crossed the road, with London confidence, and he had hit her. He wasn't going that fast. Nothing went that fast in the morning traffic. She had been knocked off her feet and banged her head. If she'd fallen differently she would have been okay. But she didn't fall differently. She fell and she died, before anyone at the bus stop who saw the whole thing happen, could get to her, could touch her with comforting hands, say comforting things to her. She died alone, in the middle of the rush-hour. Everything going muffled after that. Her lying there, when he got to the hospital, already dead. Tidied up by some nurse she'd never met, tidied up for him, as though somehow it would make it easier, no blood, no wound. He'd wanted to see something extraordinary – a gash, or an ugly bruise – but it was like what they always say on television; she looked as if she was sleeping, which was so hard. She looked like she had looked on a thousand mornings in their bed, like she was ignoring the alarm clock and the encroaching sunlight and sleeping. Like she would suddenly squeeze her eyes shut in denial of the day and roll towards him, lay one heavy sleepy arm across him. He would always, always remember that feeling. That violent feeling of standing beside her and realising that he couldn't ever touch her again after he left. He had thought he would never be able to step away from the bed, let the nurses come in and take her away. Because it was the last time. People said it was a good thing, seeing the body, saying goodbye. For him, it had been the most agonising moment. His ribs were sinking into the cavity of his chest and he could barely breathe, suffocated by pain. If he wanted to he could call it up, that feeling, wallow in it. But he had learnt not to.

Now her lovely face reminded him that he had been loved, and that he had loved her. She was his scar. He was disfigured by loss, but it had not killed him, just altered him in a way that would always be obvious to him, and to those who knew him. But he was healing.

And he knew he would love again.

His solitude was a topic for discussion among those around him. It was probably worst at work, where people were less friends than acquaintances. His colleagues had been almost comfortable to start with, with his grief. Everybody had known the right things to say, and the rudiments of giving space, taking away responsibilities and protecting him from too much of their own joy. Those sensibilities had worn off long ago. Now his widower status and the manner of its coming were an embarrassment. They wanted him to be with someone so that they didn't have to worry about him, walk on glass for him, any more. About a year ago one of the assistants had got engaged. He'd been in court, and when he'd come back they'd been drinking champagne. Someone had been out and bought a tray of cream cakes, and the girls were gathered around one desk, laughing. They'd hadn't quite stopped dead in their tracks when he had walked in, but everyone had become subdued. He had forced himself to smile, congratulate her, had even drunk some champagne, but they had all been relieved when he had gone back into his office.

Another of the girls had made a pass at him at the Christmas party. He'd had a few glasses of wine, and he was dancing with a group of them, that silly party dancing. And it felt okay. The girl had been working at chambers for a few weeks, and he'd had no idea that she was interested in him. She was young and pretty, and suddenly she was flirting with him. He'd kept seeing the smooth caramel curve of her breast inside her chiffon top when she leaned forward, and he'd thought maybe he felt something vaguely normal again. When he went to the loo she'd followed him round the corner and kissed him. It felt good at first, and he'd kissed her back. But when she moaned and he felt her tongue exploring, her hips pushing against him, he knew he couldn't do any more. He was scared, and revolted and ashamed, and his arousal dissipated. He had pushed her away and apologised.

That night, he had sat in a cab with his head in his hands, and experienced a rush of irrational rage against Sarah. How could she have left him so young; so fucked up and so young?

Friends had tried to make it okay again. He had learned what to expect when he accepted an invitation to supper, or a sudden spare ticket to a concert or play. There would always be a woman, his age, or thereabouts, single. A girl who'd made an effort to look pretty, and greeted him with an open smile. And Matthew, who had never been any good at being unkind, always smiled and talked to them, asked questions to which he didn't register the answers, and never took a phone number or saw them again.

Tamsin hadn't done that to him. He had practically lived there since Sarah had died, and he adored her. He and Neil had an easy male friendship, the kind that thrived in pubs. They played together on a local unsuccessful Sunday football team, and once in a while, when one of them was starting to feel old, they played a sweaty game of squash at the local sports centre. The kids were great too. Sarah had been Willa's godmother, and Matthew was Flannery's godfather. He remembered holding them as tiny babies in the white lace christening robe Tamsin's mother had used for all of her own children, suited on a Sunday, singing 'He's got the whole world in his hands'. Now they were noisy, demonstrative, messy kids, and he loved them. Tamsin 'lent' them to him sometimes. They would come on a Friday night, with their wheel-along suit-cases and motheaten teddies. They made popcorn in the microwave, and Matthew would watch them while they ate it and danced around his living room to *Top of the Pops*. Then he would tuck them into the guest bed together and read to them ('For ages, much longer than Mummy ever does,' Willa had announced with delight).

Later, downstairs, he would open a bottle of good

red and drink it among the mess of popcorn, colouring books and crayons. One of the things he hated most was that the house stayed unchanged in his absence. No one set foot inside it after he left in the morning, and his was the only key in the lock at night. Sarah had been messy but he wasn't, and after she had died, the house had become spotless and immaculate. He missed the chaos. Homer and Willa brought it back for him. Tamsin had laughed when he'd explained that to her – 'Christ, Matt, if that's what you want, then let's just house-swap once in a while. Neil and I'll come over and revel in the tidiness, and you can decamp to ours and be squalid!' But she had understood.

He slept best on the nights when Homer and Willa were in the room next door, and his favourite bit was when they woke him up – way too early – bouncing on him with giggles and shrieks, and the warmth of their arms round his neck. It was so much better than Radio Four.

Tamsin and Freddie – and Reagan, but less so – had been like mothers, sisters, best friends. They had loved Sarah, too, which helped. They missed her, and they, too, always noticed the gap she had left around any table.

There was a knock at his door. Abby, his PA, opened it just wide enough to put her head through. He picked up a piece of A4 paper that had lain untouched on the desk, looked at it thoughtfully, then at her. 'Yes, Abby?'

'I'm sorry, Matt. I know you don't want to be interrupted . . .'

He smiled. 'What's up?'

'Phone call for you. It's Neil Bernard. Shall I get rid of him?'

'No, no. Put him through. Thanks, Abby.'

She smiled back, looking relieved. She'd only been at the chambers for a couple of months, and Matthew knew she was a bit frightened of him. He probably seemed stern at times.

'Hello, Neil.'

'How are you?'

'Fine. Bored, actually. You?'

'Bored? I should be so lucky. Wall-to-wall women this morning, I'm afraid.'

'Lucky you.'

'You may see it that way, but they're all bloody hormonal.'

'A misogynist obstetrician?'

'Keep that quiet. No, it's the absence of one particular gestating female I'm ringing about.'

'Ah, yes. How are you coping?'

'I'm not. Meghan is. Admirably. I'm just pining.'

'You are one soppy bugger, do you know that? How about a lads' night out?'

'Sounds good.'

'I was thinking a few drinks, maybe a casino, perhaps chat a couple of birds up, finish up at Spearmint Rhino. Something like that?' Matthew joked.

'Yeah, yeah . . .'

'Okay. A curry and a couple of beers round the corner?'

'You're on. Tonight?'

'See you there. Eight?'

'Better make it nine. I've got a private clinic early evening.'

'Traitor.' Matthew had known Neil since he'd thought private medicine was evil. That was a long time.

'Tell that to the mortgage lender.'

Matthew chuckled. 'How are the girls getting on, by the way? Have you spoken to Tamsin?'

'They're okay. Tamsin said she was going to give you a ring, too. Bashing the plastic a bit today in Boston, but heading out to the Cape tomorrow. I bet she'll need another suitcase for all the baby gubbins. As if we didn't have enough already.'

'And Freddie?'

'She's okay.' Tamsin had told him she thought Freddie was dreading going to the house.

'She'll hate going to the house.' She'd dreaded going back when the old man was alive. This could only be more difficult.

Neil sighed. 'Well, the others'll look after her. It's bound to be tough, but it's not like she and her dad were close, is it? I'm sure she'll be fine.'

'I'm surprised Adrian didn't go with her.' He wasn't, but he wanted to hear what Neil thought.

'That wasn't very likely under the circumstances, was it?'

'What circumstances?'

A long pause. 'Oh, fuck,' Neil said.

'What?'

'She didn't tell you.'

'Tell me what?'

'He's leaving her. He's been having an affair, apparently. He told her the same day she found out about her dad.'

'*What?*'

'I know . . . I always thought he was a bit of a git, but I didn't know what a coward he was. He told her on the phone. Bastard.'

It all made sense now. Freddie at Tamsin's that day. Not wanting him to come in when he'd taken her home. The car at the service station. He'd thought it was strange, but he hadn't wanted to push her. Why hadn't she told him? They'd spent all afternoon with Tamsin, who *had* known. He felt a twinge of betrayal. And the next day they'd been together in the car for ages, to and from Harry. Why wouldn't she have told him?

'Matt?'

'I'm here.'

'I've put my foot in my bloody big gob now. I expect she was embarrassed.'

That was bollocks. They'd been through too much together.

'Or maybe she hopes they can sort it out.' Neil was floundering because Matthew wasn't saying anything, and he knew he had shocked him. He also knew he would be in trouble with Tamsin for betraying a confidence. And that was not good.

'Maybe. Poor Freddie.'

'It's lousy timing, although Freddie says he told her before she heard about her dad so it isn't his fault the timing was so bad. Funny how she defends him, isn't it? But, then, I've never been his biggest fan.'

'No.'

The truth was that Adrian had never really gelled in the group. Neil had been the first man on the scene, and he himself had followed three years later. They'd grown up together, pretty much. They liked the same things. They came from the same sort of background. Neil had grown up in a terraced house in Reading, Matthew on a housing estate in Newcastle: they were both hungry for success, ambitious in their chosen careers, eager to build a good future for their families. Matthew always felt that Neil knew what he'd lost when Sarah died – not just the life they already had but the life he had imagined with her, the home, the children, the future that looked a lot like the one Neil was building for Tamsin and himself. It had brought them closer, although Neil left the 'mushy stuff', as he called it, to Tamsin.

Adrian was privileged, and it oozed from his every pore. His parents were landowners and it was generations since his family had had to work for their living, and a public-school education had apparently given him neither ambition nor ability. His insouciance had always been vaguely offensive. Both men remembered meeting Adrian for the first time, about fourteen years ago. The four of them – Neil and Tamsin, Matthew and Sarah – had gone to Méribel to see Freddie, late in the season. They'd scraped together the coach fare on the understanding that Freddie could cadge them cheap beds and lift passes. Tamsin wasn't going to ski, she vowed, but she was content to watch Neil from the bottom of the piste, armed with mugfuls of *chocolat chaud*, the kind with the marshmallows melting on top. Sarah had skied when she was younger, and she was gung-ho to teach the boys, who joked that by the second day they would leave her in their wake.

Freddie had met them off the coach, although it had arrived very late at night. She'd jumped up and down with excitement as they poured shivering through the door, exhausted by the long drive, and queasy with the last, winding climb up the mountain. They'd heard about him before they even got back to her flat. Ex-army officer, terribly handsome. He'd been coming out to see her all through the season whenever he could, and Freddie was sure she was in love with him, which was not something any of them had heard her say before, although there had been plenty of guys.

So perhaps the first man Freddie loved was bound to be a disappointment. Neil and Matthew weren't buying the ex-army machismo, either – the forced loud laugh, the chest that looked either sucked in or puffed out, the continual references to having 'seen action' in the Falklands. It just wasn't what they were into, and they hadn't expected that Freddie would be. Also, she seemed needier and more submissive than any of them had seen her before.

Once they'd had a drink and were beginning to flag, Adrian had led Freddie towards her bedroom, and she had followed demurely, glancing back at them over her shoulder. They had all heard them through the chalet's thin pine door, kissing and falling on to the bed, and had grimaced at each other and busied themselves with sorting out where they would sleep.

That first night, Tamsin had whispered to Neil in the bathroom, while they were brushing their teeth, 'You know the funny thing? He reminds me of her dad.'

Neil had looked quizzically at her. He had never met Freddie's father. 'Not to look at,' Tamsin went on, 'but there's something about him, you know, that makes you think you're seeing what he wants to show you, not what there really is. Do you know what I mean?'

Neil had no idea. He was dizzily tired and all he wanted to do was fall into bed with her and sleep for twelve hours. He shut her up with a toothpaste kiss. 'You think too much.'

'It won't last. Bet ya.'

Next door, already in their sleeping-bags, Sarah had whispered the same thing, in her gentler, Sarah way, to Matthew: 'He doesn't quite fit with us, does he? Like Steve. I know it isn't up to us who she chooses, but I'd so hate it if either of them ended up with people we didn't want to hang around with.'

Steve was the broker Reagan had been going out with that winter. She wasn't skiing, because Steve had taken her to the Caribbean with his stonking bonus. He hadn't made it past Reagan's six-month record, and by the summer she was with a music journalist called Bayley whom she'd met at some concert. He was all right, when he wasn't too stoned, but they'd already learned not to get attached to Reagan's men. You only ever saw them in one season's clothes.

But Freddie and Adrian had lasted all these years. Until now.

After he'd hung up from Neil, who had made him promise he wouldn't drop him in it with Tamsin, Matthew stood up and went over to the window. He hadn't realised it was lunchtime. People were milling about on the grass, clutching cardboard coffee cups. He felt panicky with emotion: part rage at Adrian, part hurt at having been kept in the dark, and the largest part desperate. Desperate to get to Freddie.

He went back to his desk and picked up the phone. 'Abby? Can you get me some details on flights?' He looked quickly at his desk diary, open in front of him. 'Thursday night, Friday morning, to Boston.'

September, Chatham, Cape Cod

Freddie's father's house was on the outskirts of Chatham, the town on the elbow of the crooked arm that was Cape Cod. She had never lived in it – the Beacon Hill townhouse was where she had grown up and she'd been long gone by the time he moved out there permanently in the early 1990s. She'd never had a photograph of it, so Reagan and Tamsin had no idea what to expect when Freddie issued the instruction to turn left, and Reagan stopped the car at the end of a quiet, unmarked road.

Tamsin whistled.

'Wow,' Reagan exclaimed. 'What a gorgeous house!'

Built on three storeys, from traditional clapboard, and painted immaculately primrose yellow, it stood a long way back from the road across a green lawn. There were five broad steps up to a veranda, with a bandstand-like terrace at one end, Adirondack chairs and a swing seat. At the other end of the house there was a tower, three floors high, with a conical, grey-tiled roof atop three perfectly round rooms with windows on all sides. It was surrounded by rhododendron bushes and lush trees. To the left, it was no more than a hundred metres from the ocean, with its own landing stage and a sliver of sandy beach. It *was* beautiful. It didn't look as if it should have belonged to her father. It looked like a house full of love.

'If you get this in the will, can I be your best friend?' asked her best friend.

Reagan punched Tamsin's arm. 'Ssh!'

The front door was open. As they started to walk up the path, a woman appeared in the doorway. When Grace saw Freddie, she opened her arms wide. 'Freddie!' Grace Kramer practically ran at Freddie. She was a slight woman, and Reagan guessed her to be about sixty. She looked as though camp would destroy her straightaway, but she'd probably turn out to be one of the ones who could magic a meal out of nothing and make poultices from herbs. She wore her hair in a sleek silvery bob, and was dressed in grey linen. Her face was kind, but lined, with dark circles under the eyes. She was crying now, and exclaiming in delight, sympathy, sorrow all at once.

'I'm so, so glad to see you!' she was saying, stepping back from Freddie, but keeping tight hold of her arms. There was the faintest trace of an Irish accent. 'Let me look at you!' She sounded as if she was talking to a child. Her own child. 'Too thin,' she pronounced, then pulled Freddie back into her embrace. Then she didn't speak for a moment. Squeezed her eyes shut and hugged. Freddie hugged back.

Eventually they parted, and Grace turned to the others.

'These are my friends, Tamsin and Reagan,' Freddie said.

'Ah, yes.' Evidently she knew exactly who they were.

'They've come with me . . . to help.'

'How kind they are. I'm happy to see you all. Come in, come in . . .' And she was leading them up the steps on to the veranda.

'I'll make us all some tea. You ladies take a seat out here, why don't you?'

'I'll come and help you, Grace,' Freddie said.

Tamsin and Reagan watched as Grace squeezed Freddie's hand, and the two women went into the house, through the screen door.

Tamsin flopped down into one of the wooden chairs. 'I could get used to this,' she said.

Reagan wandered over to where she could see the ocean, and breathed it in deeply. She had always loved the sea. She had grown up in Norfolk and her happiest memories were of climbing the huge shingle bank near her house to perch there, watching the mood of the waves and feeling the salt on her cheeks. Some people watched for a few minutes, then turned back to their lives, but Reagan had always been able to stay for hours.

She hadn't told them yet about resigning because this trip wasn't about her. Her reason for wanting to be here was genuine, she reminded herself. She wanted to help Freddie, and to be with Freddie and Tamsin. The resignation was something apart.

The office hadn't believed her not when she'd put it

in writing, and not when she'd said it, the morning before she left for Boston, calmly and clearly in her boss's office. They'd told her she just needed a sabbatical, that she should take as long as she needed. She wondered what they'd meant by that – whether she really could disappear for six months, then waltz back into the same job, or whether there were limits on what she might need. She suspected the latter.

It had all been rather embarrassing. The managing partner had lost his colour, buzzed on his intercom for the jolly human-resources manager. It reminded her of a conversation she had had with a tutor at university. She'd not done some important essay, and when she'd tried to explain why not, he'd gone all pale and the next thing she knew she'd been sent up to the psychiatric hospital in Summertown, where she'd been tempted to invent a horrific past, just to justify the bus fare and the trouble they'd all gone to, back at college, to avoid having to listen to her. She hadn't, of course.

God knew what they'd thought was wrong – both then and now. Probably that she was pregnant and going off to have an abortion. Or had some ghastly illness. Or maybe just that she was dysfunctional. Which she was, of course. She must be. She earned a six-figure sum, doing something she had once loved and had always been brilliant at. She had a loft apartment, and real art, not an ounce of spare flesh and a wardrobe full of Armani.

And she hated her life. How could she explain that to someone like the human-resources manager, whom she barely knew? How could she explain it to her best friends? She wasn't sure she could explain it to herself. She was afraid that it was all to do with *him*. And maybe even more afraid that it was nothing to do with him.

In the end, she'd been a bit aggressive. She didn't really remember what she'd said: after the human-resources manager arrived there'd been a red mist. But she was pretty sure she'd said they could consider the sabbatical her notice period, and that she wasn't remotely bothered about the bonus she was due to collect at the end of the year, and that she was sure they'd be able to spread her caseload among her peers, who'd just have to pull a few of the macho all-nighters the firm considered a badge of honour and a mark of commitment. Then she'd walked out.

Now she was standing on Freddie's father's veranda, looking at his beach and wondering about stripping off, wading into the blue sea, and not stopping until the water had closed over her head.

The kitchen smelt of cinnamon: sticks of it, tied with plaid ribbon, were hung round the room. There was a bunch above a picture of Freddie, aged about eleven, taken on Boston Common. Freddie looked at herself, saw Harry and felt a pang of longing for him, of connection to him. The swing door shut behind them. Grace busied herself with the kettle and the mugs.

'How are you doing?' Freddie asked. She'd been a

little shocked by Grace. She looked much older than she had when she'd seen her last.

There was a sob behind Grace's answer, and when she turned to face her, fat tears had welled in her eyes. 'Oh, Freddie, it's been hard to be all alone.' Then she added, 'I know you came as quickly as you could, dear . . .'

Freddie hadn't, and felt guilty.

Grace was crying openly now, and for a couple of minutes she couldn't speak. When she did, she said, 'I miss him so much.' That was all.

It was the way she said it, and the sheer misery on her face, that struck Freddie. In an instant she made the shift that a child makes when it sees its parents for the first time through adult eyes. She'd loved him. Of course she had. Why else would she have stayed all these years?

It was so obvious it made Freddie feel stupid. Grace had given up everything for him, a family of her own, a love of her own. She had come with him here from Boston. She hadn't had a chance to build anything for herself that was worth staying there for.

Freddie looked at Grace and saw a woman who'd given the best part of her life in service to her father, a man, Freddie knew, who had been incapable of giving anything back. Certainly he'd never given much back to her.

But as she moved towards her, Grace shook herself, and her composure returned. 'So much to sort out.'

Freddie wasn't to be dissuaded. 'You loved him.' It wasn't a question, or an accusation.

Grace looked at her for a long moment. 'Of course.'

'All this time . . . I never realised. I never thought . . . Poor Grace.'

Grace recognised the pity for what it was, and made up her mind. He should have let her tell Freddie a long time ago. Death made some things complicated, but it made some things suddenly so very simple.

Tamsin bounded in with Freddie's mobile phone – she'd left it in her handbag on the veranda and hadn't heard it ringing. 'It's Harry!'

Freddie grabbed it. 'Hello, darling.'

'Hiya, Mum.'

'How are you, sweetheart?'

'I'm fine. I'm outta there.'

Of course. It was Sunday morning. 'Dad picked me up about half an hour ago. We're going to play golf.' Of course.

'Just the two of you?' She hated herself for asking the question.

Harry sounded surprised. 'Who else?'

'No one – just thought you might have brought a mate or something . . .' Freddie said quickly. It was stupid to think he might have Antonia Melhuish with him. He wouldn't dare!

'No. D'you wanna talk to Dad? He's right here.' Freddie felt the muscles in her stomach and neck relax. He hadn't told Harry anything. Of course not. That wasn't Adrian's style. He'd make the mess and leave her to clean it up. Still, she was grateful he hadn't said anything, even if she knew that was more from cowardice than consideration.

'Don't worry, darling, I can talk to Daddy anytime – tell him I'll call him later.' How easily the lies came when she had to protect Harry. 'I want to hear all about you. How's term? How's the sport?'

She pulled out a chair and sat down at the kitchen table, throwing an apologetic glance at Grace and Tamsin. Grace waved it away, smiling.

Grace and Tamsin glanced at each other.

'Come on,' Grace said, 'I'll show you round.'

'Oh, good – I'm dying for a guided tour.'

They went through the swing door into the lounge, and Tamsin shouted for Reagan, who was still outside.

'What a gorgeous house,' Tamsin exclaimed, as Reagan appeared. 'It looks like a film set.'

The house *was* beautiful. Simply furnished with deep wide sofas in ticking and chintz, polished, deep chestnut floors and modern seascapes on the walls, it was elegant and comfortable – and, Tamsin thought, almost feminine. Not at all what she had pictured for Freddie's father.

'What's with the clocks?' Reagan asked.

'Freddie's father . . . had a passion for them. Wrist-watches, fobs, clocks. He collected them. Takes practically a whole morning to wind them, if you've a mind.'

There were lots: a big wooden grandfather beside the

front door, with an ornamental face; an enormous old railway-station clock mounted on a wall; a pair of delicate carriage clocks strangely incongruous on the shelf above a wood-burning stove. Tamsin gazed round the room, then turned back to Grace and noted the bags under her eyes. She had one of those ageless faces and could have been almost anything between forty and sixty: her body seemed slim and taut, wiry almost. They followed her upstairs.

Tamsin thought of the song 'They'd stopped. Dead. Never to go again. When the old man died.'

'I'm dying to see those turret rooms from the inside – they must be almost completely circular.'

'They are.' Grace pushed open the door and stood back to let Reagan and Tamsin go into one. It was flooded with light, and had a spectacular panoramic view across the beach. Reagan went to the window, apparently silenced by the peace.

Tamsin could see it had been Freddie's father's study. It had a huge old partner's desk in the centre, with chairs facing both in and out of the room. The desk was scrupulously neat, with barely anything on it, although three large grey filing cabinets lined the wall behind. There was little ornamentation except for a couple more clocks and a large, modern-looking oil painting of Freddie at seven or eight. You could tell it had been copied from a photograph, rather than sat for. Freddie was wearing flared jeans, a red T-shirt and a pendant with a miniature 7-Up can as its charm. She had one hand on her hip, while the other pushed a wayward lock of blonde hair behind her ear. The painter had caught the light beautifully – it burnished half of her, and she was squinting slightly, smiling. Around it, in smaller frames, were other photographs of Freddie – as a baby, graduating from Oxford in cap and gown, at her wedding, giggling between Tamsin, Sarah and Reagan. All of us look so young, Tamsin thought. There was one of Freddie holding an infant Harry. But her father wasn't in any of them. 'It's like a shrine, in a funny way,' she said.

'I suppose it is,' Grace said. 'Freddie's never been in here.'

'She should have.' Reagan had been drawn back into the room by Tamsin's exclamation.

Tamsin was thinking how very different she and Freddie were, that there might be a room you had never been into in your parents' home! It was inconceivable.

'Yes, she should. He was so proud of her and all her achievements. So proud,' Grace said.

'He just never told her.' Tamsin knew that Freddie had only ever felt disapproval, disdain and disinterest from her father. Now she wondered. Why should there be such a difference between what he felt and what he showed? And now he was dead, which was a bloody shame because Freddie was going to know, and understand, but she'd have nowhere to go with it, no resolution to chase.

They filed out and Grace shut the door behind them. Perhaps it might be better if Freddie didn't go in there just now, Tamsin thought.

Grace had resumed the tour. 'There are two guest bedrooms along here,' she pointed, 'and they share this bathroom. Upstairs, apart from the master suite, there's another, also with its own bathroom. I'll let you girls figure out who goes where.'

Tamsin looked confused. 'Do you not live in then, Grace?'

'Yes, I do.' She sounded a little jittery. 'There's a fifth bedroom upstairs. I sleep there.' And then she was off down the stairs. 'Have you got much luggage? Perhaps we should get it in. I'll give you a hand, and then I'll see to that tea.'

On the landing, Tamsin and Reagan exchanged a puzzled glance, then followed her.

In the kitchen, Freddie had finished talking to Harry. It had been lovely to hear his voice and his stories about his classmates, his housemaster, and yesterday's match. He sounded happy. Freddie hoped it wasn't pretence – Harry was capable of making himself sound jolly to put her off the scent.

Now she was wandering around, looking at things familiar and strange. There was an Ansel Adams calendar hanging on a hook. She had always loved his black-and-white photographs – so calm and awe-inspiring. She lifted September to look at the October illustration. Her eye was drawn to the only entry for the month, on the tenth: 'Hospital'. One word. Written in red. Curious, but feeling guilty, she turned back to September. This month was busier: golf entered twice

– the second occasion a round he would never play –
some meetings, a supper with friends – and again,
'Hospital'. It featured in August and July. She'd got to
June by the time the others walked in.

'Are you sick, Grace?'

'No.'

'Well . . .' They all watched Freddie's face change.
'Was my father ill?'

'Your father died of a heart-attack, Freddie.'

That was a strange non-answer. Freddie held
Grace's eyes until she looked down. 'Grace . . .' There
was a warning note in her voice.

'Yes. He was ill.'

'What with?'

'He had cancer.' The word fell heavily into the
silence.

Grace pulled out a chair and sat down, her hands
clasped on the table. Tamsin went over to the kettle,
squeezing Freddie's shoulder as she passed, to make
the tea. Reagan moved to help her.

Freddie sat down beside Grace.

'How long?'

Grace took a deep breath. When she spoke she
sounded rehearsed, and she couldn't meet Freddie's
gaze. 'For a year or so. It started like flu, really. He was
so tired all the time, and that was unusual. He always
had so much energy. And he kept having these unbelievable nosebleeds – so much blood. He was losing
weight – and he was a big man, your father – so I
nagged him into going to the doctor. It just didn't feel

right to me, and they found it. It was leukaemia. Acute myeloblastic leukaemia.' She said that slowly and deliberately, pronouncing every syllable carefully. 'It didn't seem too awful at first. They said he needed chemotherapy, a few cycles, and then he had some more tests and things and they said they'd got rid of it.'

Freddie put her head into her hands.

'I begged him to tell you. At first he said he wouldn't until he knew more, and once he did, he claimed it was all over and there was no need. And I think he genuinely believed it *was* over. I did too. We wanted to believe it, I suppose.' She looked desolate.

'So it wasn't over?'

Tamsin understood Freddie's need to know all of it, but it felt like hectoring. This was something that was clearly painful for Grace to talk about, and Freddie was pushing; her tone was harsh.

'No, it wasn't. He found out about three months ago that it was back,' she took a deep breath, 'and that it was terminal. That broke him, really. The first time round, he'd been so sure he could beat it.'

Freddie never understood why people talked about cancer combatively, like you had free will to use against it. It seemed so unfair on the people who had died, as if they hadn't 'fought' enough, had just 'succumbed'. As if they might still be alive, with those who had loved them, if they had only tried a little harder. They said that in the death announcements – 'after a long and courageous battle'. But it was an invidious, aggressive, nasty disease, not an enemy, and if it was going to kill you it would, whether you fought hard against it or not.

'They said it was up to him whether he had any more treatment. It wasn't a question of making him better, just of extending his life. They said, at his age, it might be cruel to put himself through it again. And, my God, the chemotherapy was awful. It made him so ill, so tired. I don't think he could face it again.'

'But he was going to.'

'Oh, yes. I begged him to. I was being selfish, I suppose. I didn't want him to die.' She couldn't have sounded more like a wife if she had tried, Freddie thought. Grace's eyes filled with tears. 'I'm almost glad he died when he did because he didn't have to go through it.' She had taken a tissue from the sleeve of her cardigan, and was dabbing her eyes. 'It happens. Chemotherapy's a big strain on the body. Sometimes they just stop going.'

She stood up, and went to the dresser drawer. From it, she took a wallet of photographs, opened it and pulled one out. She handed it to Freddie. 'This was taken last month. You'll see what I mean, maybe.'

Tamsin and Reagan automatically came across and looked over her shoulders.

Freddie stared at the picture of a man she barely recognised. He was wasted, emaciated, seemed physically to have shrunk. His neck looked so thin, and his Guernsey sweater hung off him, as though it belonged to a much bigger man. His skin was yellowish, and his eyes were sunken. He looked like what he had clearly been: a dying man.

'I was shocked when I saw those pictures – the day I got them back from the developers. I'd been living here with him, you see. I hadn't realised how bad he was.'

Freddie couldn't believe it. All her life he had loomed large, almost mythically big. Strong and powerful. But this man was frail and old. A huge wave of guilt and sadness broke over her. But its undertow was rage.

Grace was still speaking, but now she sounded muffled, as if her voice was coming from far away. 'He didn't die wired up to machines in extraordinary pain, with no dignity, in hospital. He died in his sleep, in his own bed. Peacefully. Like I know he wanted to.'

How can he have been at peace? I didn't know! *I didn't know*! Freddie's brain screamed. Tears rolled down her cheeks.

'He didn't want you to worry,' Grace said. 'Your life wasn't here. You have ties that bind you in England, and it's so far away. He didn't want you to be upset.'

'That's crap!' Freddie's voice was strident.

'Freddie . . .' Reagan reached out to touch her, but Freddie shook her off. She had stood up and was backing away from them.

'I know why – and, believe me, it was never about protecting me. I didn't matter enough for him to want me here. Or he didn't think I deserved to be told. He was punishing me again. I don't know what for. But that's what he was doing.'

Grace went towards her. 'That's not true, Freddie.'

But Freddie was heading for the door. 'It *is* true. It *is*. Don't you try – don't you dare try to tell me anything different,' she spat. And she was gone.

Grace found her on the beach. She was sitting on the sand with her knees hugged to her chest, staring out to sea. Her jaw was set but she had been crying: her face was still wet, and her eyelids were puffy. Grace thought that she looked like the sulky, messed-up teenager she had once been, and felt a sudden ache for that life, and that time – when Freddie's distress had been caused by a bad mark in a test or a crush.

Grace was angry with him. She had loved him, but now she was angry with him for not having fixed this before he left them and leaving her to sort it out. If it could be sorted out. And even if it could, none of them would benefit from it.

'I'm sorry, Grace. I shouldn't have yelled at you like that.' Freddie sounded contrite.

Grace sat down beside her, and put an arm round her shoulders. It wasn't easy – Freddie was a much larger woman – but instantly she relaxed, and laid her head on Grace's shoulder. 'I'm sorry too, sweetie. You shouldn't have found out like that. Believe me, you wouldn't have if it had been up to me.' She followed Freddie's gaze out to sea. 'Perhaps I should have told you anyway. He made me promise not to. But so what?'

'He always was a controlling bastard. I don't know how you stayed with him so long.'

'I loved him.'

'I know you did. But even so . . .'

'And he loved me.'

Freddie didn't grasp her meaning straight away. 'How on earth could you possibly have known that?'

'Because he showed me every day. Told me most days, too.'

Freddie sat up. 'What do you mean?'

'Come on, Freddie. You must have known, really.'

'Known what?'

'About your father and me.'

'What about my father and you?'

'That we loved each other. For God's sake, we've lived in this house for years as man and wife. I thought you knew.'

'Knew how? I've been here as little as possible – you know that.' Somehow, though, Freddie wasn't shocked. It was sort of obvious, when you heard it out loud. After the last revelation, in the house, it seemed strangely unshocking.

'Oh, Grace.'

Grace gave a little shrug.

'Tell me about it.' Freddie wanted to listen. She wanted to know.

'There isn't a great deal to tell, sweetie. I'm not the first nanny or housekeeper to fall in love with the boss. I felt something the first time I met him. He seemed so tragic, deserted by his young wife. You were easy to fall in love with. And him so handsome, so full of life, with all that suppressed energy and something else beneath the surface. I suppose I saw the same things your mother did. It didn't take me long to grasp that he was a difficult man. A real pig sometimes.' She nudged Freddie. 'But you can't choose who you love, can you? And, my God, I loved him. From a distance, for a long time. I don't think he saw me that way at all. He had girlfriends when you were a child. You never knew about them – they were hidden away and none of them ever got close – but I knew. You were about ten, I think, when he first saw me that way. It was Christmas, and we were both a bit lonely and drunk. He was listening to old records and asked me to dance. He danced me right into his bed. Which was a bit of a revelation to both of us.' Grace looked sheepishly at Freddie, who half smiled. 'Sorry, I know he was your father, but . . . well, we found out we were . . . compatible in that department. And that was it, really. There was never anyone else for either of us. We kept it secret sort of, an open secret, while you were living at home, and while we were in Boston. But once we got out here . . . Well, it was his idea. He said he wanted us to be a proper couple.'

'Why didn't you get married?'

'He said he never wanted to be married again.'

'What about you? Surely you would have liked to be married?'

Grace smiled. 'Not really. I have six brothers and sisters and not one stayed married first time round.' She looked hard at Freddie. 'And it hasn't been a walk in the park for you, has it?'

Was it that obvious?

Grace had been at her wedding. It was the only time she'd come to England. Freddie remembered her in a lilac suit and a pillbox hat with one of those veils that didn't conceal anything. She'd been in the background, as she always was, but she'd been so pleased. It seemed funny to think that they'd been together then, Grace and her father. That they had gone back to the Savoy after the wedding and lain together in one big bed, talking about it. It might have made a difference, knowing.

Grace was waiting for an answer. 'Not a walk in the park, no. And I think it's probably over, if I'm honest with myself. Adrian's had an affair – I just found out.'

'Oh. I see.'

'I don't think you do. The affair is largely irrelevant. I think it's about much more than that. I'm not sure I should have married him in the first place.'

'You seemed madly in love with him.'

'Did I?' Funny – Freddie knew that to have been true, yet couldn't imagine it. 'At least Dad was pleased with him.'

'He always said he felt he'd pushed you at him. He was afraid that on some level you'd married Adrian to please him.'

Freddie was taken aback. 'He never said.'

'Not to you, more's the pity, but he said it to me.'

'When?'

'On your wedding day. It was too late by then, of

course – it was so extraordinary, your wedding day. Just like Charles and Di.'

It had been St Margaret's, Westminster, not St Paul's, and there had been only a handful of minor royals present, but Freddie knew what she meant.

'It was so grand, with all the uniforms, and bridesmaids, and those vast flower arrangements, and the cake.'

Adrian's mother had hijacked the day, and Freddie had felt as if she was on a film set. She hadn't known half of the bridesmaids, and Grace was right – the flowers had been absurd. She had a clear recollection of coming up the aisle and scanning the crowd for Sarah and Matthew, Neil and Tamsin, Reagan and whoever was squiring her that summer, and feeling such relief when she spotted them, beaming encouragement at her, and feeling that almost everyone else was a virtual stranger.

'I remember him saying,' Grace went on, 'that the day was everything he had ever wished for you – those things were always stupidly important to him – but that he was afraid Adrian wasn't the one. He whispered to me, "See the way he's looking at her," when you were making your vows, and he was right.'

'What do you mean?'

'Well, he looked nervous, and happy, but he wasn't . . .' Grace struggled to find the right words '. . . he didn't look at you like he would die if you didn't say "I will". No fire.'

'Great.'

'I'm sorry, I'm prattling on. The point is, your father never said anything because he didn't think you'd listen.'

'But he said Adrian was the right type for me.'

'And he always regretted it. He told me Adrian was the right type for him, but not for you. He said you were more like your mother than him. He said she would have been a better judge.' Then she stood up and swept the sand off her trousers. 'Come on – you must be hungry. Let's go and get something to eat.'

Freddie stood up, and they hugged briefly. She looked at Grace, and knew she held the keys that would unlock her father for her. If she wanted her to do so.

They held hands as they walked. 'He did ask me to marry him, once,' Grace confided.

'When?'

'When he knew the cancer had come back. I think he knew he was going to die.'

'And what did you say?'

'I didn't answer. I was still "thinking it over" when he died.' She smiled ruefully, but tears weren't far away either. 'Thought for too long.'

'I hate funerals,' Reagan complained. She was leaning against the bandstand in the small park, smoking a last cigarette before they went along the street into the church.

They'd left the house an hour or so earlier, before the funeral car came for Grace and Freddie. Grace had made the arrangements and was the chief mourner as far as Chatham was concerned. If Freddie hadn't come, she would have ridden in the long black sedan by herself, small, dignified and quiet. Freddie wondered what people had thought about Grace and her father. They wouldn't have known, of course, how it had been between them in Boston, how they had come to know each other. They might have wondered why they weren't married; Grace wore no ring and her surname was Kramer. Freddie didn't imagine that there were many couples in this neat town who weren't married. Had they caused a gentle scandal, a ripple of interest? No wake, Grace had said. He hadn't wanted one. He didn't like people around him at the best of times, and he sure as heck wouldn't have wanted crowds at the house on this day. Not that Freddie knew where 'crowds' of mourners for her father would have come from. She and Harry were the only family he had had, as far as she knew. And Grace, she supposed. Grace had made it clear to the lawyers at the firm and the Beacon Hill neighbours that the funeral was to be private. They had acquiesced easily enough, some muttering about a memorial service at a later date, some acknowledging that this was how a private man who had led a private life would want it to be.

Tamsin was noticing how thin Reagan looked in her black suit. Most people looked skinny to her when she was at this stage of pregnancy – and the rest of the time, for that matter – but Reagan was emaciated. Her chest seemed almost concave. The only black items Tamsin had that she could get into were a pair of cotton leggings and a voluminous T-shirt, which she was wearing now, hopefully redeemed by a black-and-white spotted Armani scarf Reagan had lent her. She tried not to mind that Reagan had been wearing it the previous day as a belt for a pair of unfeasibly small Capri trousers and that now she herself had it knotted around her trunk of a neck. As Freddie would have said, she wouldn't swap lives with Reagan. Although looking down at her feet, swollen and puffy, and then across at Reagan's, slim and stylish in kitten heeled mules, she did wonder.

'I hated my dad's. Mostly because of my mum, I think,' Tamsin said. 'Trying so hard not to cry. And Sarah's was the worst. I only hate the funerals of people I love. Like I only really like the weddings of people I love. If I don't love the people getting matched or despatched, I can take or leave them. Unless they sing that hymn, the one about being in peril on the sea. That always makes me think about Kate Winslet and Leonardo di Caprio and then I cry anyway.'

'You're so shallow.'

'Probably.'

'Do you think Fred's going to be all right?'

'You know Fred. She'll be the picture of composure. It's Grace I'm worried about. She's the one who's just lost someone. I think Freddie lost her father a long time ago, if she ever had him.'

Reagan nodded.

'Hurry up with that fag, will you?'

'Worried you might not get a good seat?'

'Worried I'll be waddling down the aisle behind the coffin, if you don't get a move on.'

Reagan took a last drag, and stubbed out the cigarette with a toe. She pulled the huge black Jackie Onassis sunglasses from the top of her head and reached down to Tamsin, who allowed herself to be pulled up.

'God, I think I need another pee.'

Reagan grimaced. 'You really are human contraception, do you know that?'

'You say the sweetest things.'

They laughed. Their friendship had always thrived and survived because they envied each other's lives only a little, and knew it.

'It's nice to hear you laugh,' Tamsin said.

'It's nice to do it,' Reagan replied. Her tiny shoulders gave the briefest shrug.

Now probably wasn't the time, Tamsin thought briefly, before she went on anyway: 'We haven't heard you do it much lately – or seen you to have the chance of hearing it, for that matter.'

'I know. I'm sorry.'

'You don't need to be sorry.'

'I am, though.'

'You would tell us, wouldn't you, if something was wrong?'

Too soon. Too much. Tamsin practically saw Reagan stiffen.

'Not today, Tams. Today's about Freddie.'

Which was actually just an admission that something *was* wrong.

It would keep.

Tamsin tucked her arm through Reagan's as they walked. 'I'm glad you're here now, and I know Freddie is too.'

Reagan squeezed her hand, grateful that she was letting it go, knowing that was only for now, and they started up the main street towards the church.

Walking towards the church, Tamsin remembered her own wedding. Reagan had seemed so uninterested. It was Sarah who took Tamsin wedding dress shopping and tactfully steered her away from the meringues to the bias cut dresses; Freddie who had organised the riotous hen weekend. If Reagan had been part of a conversation about the impending nuptials at all, she was always the voice of sarcasm and cynicism. 'She's just being Reagan,' was Sarah's constant refrain. 'She's just being jealous,' Freddie's. But it had still hurt a little.

That had lasted up until the day itself. Reagan wouldn't wear a buttonhole, because she said it didn't go with her dress and would make a hole in the silk. Freddie had stood beside Tamsin for a photograph and whispered furiously in her ear – 'If she comes near me, I swear to God I'm going to punch her!'

She had left early, too. Before Tamsin had changed into her going away suit. They weren't 'going away' too far, actually, just to an upmarket pub in the next village for a couple of nights; Neil was a junior doctor, and both time and money were thin on the ground. Reagan hadn't been there to kiss and cheer and scramble for the bouquet Tamsin had thrown over her shoulder.

But when they'd arrived to check in, the girl on reception said they'd been moved to the honeymoon suite, with the four-poster bed believed to have been slept in by Henry VIII on a hunting trip in the year whenever, and the views over the park, and the double bath. When they got up there, a bottle of champagne was chilling in a bucket on the bedside table, next to a huge box of Tamsin's favourite Godiva cherry liqueur chocolates. A note, in Reagan's distinctive spidery scrawl said simply, 'Stay as happy as you are.'

'Stupid girl!' Neil had exclaimed. 'She loves you really, you know.'

That was Reagan all over.

They could have had front-row seats, even with only five minutes to spare. The sparse collection of mourners had hung back, occupying only a couple of rows in the middle. It was a big church, and it looked sad. They were mostly men, with a couple of women. Tamsin guessed they were from the golf club Freddie's father had played at since he had come out to the Cape, or businessmen with whom he might have had dealings. His will was being handled in Boston, Grace had told them. Freddie was going back into the city in a couple of days to see the lawyers.

It didn't look as though anyone else was going to

show up now – the hearse was due to arrive, and the service to start in a couple of minutes. Tamsin tried to get comfortable on the hard pew, and Reagan flicked through the hymn book.

People looked weird in funereal colours all together, just as they did at weddings. They were unfamiliar all in black and equally so in sugared-almond colours, hats and feathers. This was a by-the-book crowd of mourners – no red scarves or yellow buttonholes to denote the passing of someone who would have craved colour and maybe a smile at their funeral. Tamsin's mother had worn a yellow dress to her dad's funeral – the one she had worn for their thirtieth-wedding-an-niversary party the year before. He had loved her in it, she had said. And even more out of it. Very Ma Larkin. She'd made herself, and everyone else, smile at the memory. There was nothing here to conjure a man alive. Just flat black and no smiling. Tamsin hoped it wouldn't take too long. She stroked her bump.

Outside the long black car pulled up outside the church. Freddie loved American churches, with all their symmetry and their white fresh cleanliness. You could imagine them being honestly and swiftly built by wholesome pioneers on sunny, blue-skied days. Grey old English churches were sometimes pret-ty but always cold, and they made you think of primitive, back-breaking stone-cutters, enslaved for decades, driven by fear and piety. That country was old, this one was new, and you somehow felt it most acutely in its churches. There was a memorial outside this one for Chatham's pioneers.

One William Nickerson had come from Norwich, England, in 1637, with his sons and his sons-in-law, and by 1683 they'd bought this place from the Indians, who'd called it Monomoyick, which wasn't quite as catchy, or as quintessentially English, as Chatham.

Then it listed those who had followed, and at the bottom it said, in stern, oxidised capitals: HE WHO HAS NO FEELINGS OF VENERATION FOR HIS PREDECESSORS SHOULD EXPECT NONE FROM THOSE WHO FOLLOW HIM.

She hadn't felt veneration for anyone, let alone her immediate predecessors. Maybe that was one of the things it felt like her father had always held against her.

Behind her, her father's grand coffin was being pulled out of the hearse by the six pall-bearers. It looked incredibly heavy, and she could see them bracing themselves to take its weight. Beside her she felt Grace struggling for control, breathing deliberately, noisily. She reached down and squeezed her hand.

Freddie didn't feel as detached and dispassionate as she had been sure she would but that was probably due to the proximity of her father's body. Did everyone have a vision of the coffin tipping, the lid tilting, the corpse suddenly exposed? Or just her? Over here, of course, open caskets were very much *de rigueur*. She was thankful her father's had been closed. How awful to be staring at a dead body, face arranged into an expression it had never worn in life, hands artfully crossed on a chest that no longer rose and fell with each breath. Gruesome. Still, she looked at the coffin and wondered what her father's body might be wearing today and for ever, and if Grace had put anything into the coffin with him, mummy-style. Bribes to get him over to the right side at the hour of judgement. Mementoes for company in heaven. It was all too ridiculous. She shook herself, suddenly afraid she might cry. Which she would *not*.

Then, across the street, a taxi pulled up. She watched as the door opened, expecting a black-clad stranger. But it was Matthew.

'Matthew.' She hadn't known what a relief it would be to see him. She felt her ribcage sink a little with it. Matthew.

He saw her, and she went to him. He hugged her wordlessly, then pulled back. 'Sorry I'm late. Nearly missed it, didn't I?'

'Late? What are you doing here at all?' She was nearly laughing with the pleasure of seeing him; the pleasure, and that strange relief. 'How did you get here?'

'Cab, plane, cab.'

'I mean, how did you know where we were?'

'Drove down the street looking for the babe with the coffin.' His face became serious. 'I thought you might need me here.' *I hoped you might want me here.*

I do need him here. She'd only just realised it. There was nothing to say except 'Thank you for coming. Thank you.'

He had one of those big leather envelopes with a

shoulder strap that probably shouldn't have passed as cabin baggage but often did if its owner was a stressed-looking executive. He was dragging it out of the back of the cab.

'You're staying?'

'No. It's a day trip!'

She punched his arm lightly. 'How long for?'

'How long do you need me?'

'Indefinitely?' They laughed.

'I can stay a while, if you like.'

'Will you come to Boston with me? See the lawyers, and all that?'

'Course I will.'

She put her hand on his arm. 'Matt, I am *so* glad you're here.'

'I'm glad you're glad. I wondered if I should phone first.'

'Don't be daft. Tams and Reagan are going to be so pleased to see you too.'

As it turned out, only Tamsin beamed when she saw them coming up the aisle arm in arm.

Reagan's heart raced when she saw him. She felt momentarily light-headed, with that peculiar mix of thrill and dread, excitement and horror that she always experienced when she saw him. What is he doing here? she thought, then realised that of course he'd come flying to Freddie's aid. Sir Galahad. Why had he never listened to *her* cry for help?

★   ★   ★

There wasn't much else to look at in the church and, anyway, Tamsin usually found herself staring at the coffin at a funeral, imagining the body inside. Neil said she was macabre. She thought funerals were macabre. Thank God they hadn't gone in for one of those open-coffin jobbies like they had on *Friends* and *Will and Grace*. That was disgusting. She'd never liked Freddie's dad much when he was alive, and didn't think he would have improved with death. Not that she had known him well – she'd only met him a few times – but Tamsin relied on first impressions, and she had never wondered if she had been wrong with that one.

It had been the day of their graduation. Her mum and dad had been at the Radcliffe Camera, proud almost to the point of bursting (literally, in her father's case, in his best suit, which he had bought in his best years, about twenty pounds ago). Tamsin had been able to see them, up in the rafters, from where she had been sitting below, and they were with Neil, whose ceremony was on another day. Her mother had beamed throughout the whole thing, and afterwards, in the bright sunshine, they had taken endless snaps of her in the ermine-trimmed gown. Her parents had had to leave that afternoon, after lunch at Brown's – that was farming for you – and Freddie had begged her to come for dinner that evening with her father. Tamsin hadn't wanted to – she had had celebrations of a different kind planned with Neil, involving a punt and a bottle of champagne – okay then, cava, but who cared if you had bubbles.

But Freddie had pleaded with her: 'Come on, Tams. Remember your sister's wedding?'

'That was three years ago!'

'I know, but there's no deadline on returning a favour, is there? Go punting and shagging with Neil tomorrow. Don't leave me alone with him – *please!*'

So she had gone to the Randolph. 'Where else would my father stay?' Freddie had raised her eyebrows.

'It's the best, isn't it?'

It was very grand. And very dull. Except when it was scary. Which was pretty much every time Freddie's father had opened his mouth. They seemed to spend most of the meal in silence. When Tamsin tried to say things, he looked at her as if she were silly. He clearly resented her being there.

Afterwards, she had berated Freddie: 'Thanks for that. He certainly hadn't bargained on two of us to-night – he made it obvious I wasn't welcome.'

'He's always like that. He's been making me feel surplus to requirements for the last twenty-odd years.'

'Is he always so chatty?'

Freddie had laughed. 'Unless you're talking about golf or law, like I told you.'

'You'd have been better off taking Neil – he can play golf. He says you've got no chance of becoming a consultant unless you can. He's been teaching himself for years. Or Reagan – she's Miss Law.'

'I wanted you. You're my best friend.'

'I don't think he thought much of me.'

'I don't care what he thinks.'

Tamsin had wondered if that was true. Freddie was wearing a dress she had never seen. Her hair was tied back neatly, which it never usually was, and she had on pearl earrings. She looked like Freddie's neat twin sister. It had seemed to Tamsin that what he thought was everything to Freddie.

And she thought he'd been pretty cruel. 'I've never understood why there are two levels in a second-class degree,' he had said. 'Second class is second class.'

'At least I didn't get a third, Dad,' Freddie had defended herself.

'I should hope not, with what these three years have cost.'

'A two-one isn't bad, Mr Valentine.' Tamsin had sprung to Freddie's defence.

'Perhaps. But a little disappointing – after you were made a Scholar at the end of your first year. It implies that your effort dropped away.'

Tamsin waited for Freddie to explode. She would have done, if her parents had dared to speak to her like that, on today of all days. Not that they would, of course. She was the first of their children to graduate from anywhere.

But Freddie didn't say anything. She was staring at her plate, and Tamsin could see she was fighting back tears. When she looked up again, her face was red, and there was a blotchy rash across her chest.

'Still, it's what we do now that counts, isn't it, Mr Valentine? This is just the begining.'

He had looked at her properly for the first time. 'And what are you planning to do, Tamsin?'

'I want to teach.'

'Really?' He had drawn the word out for ages, and that was it. No further interest. He'd gone back to his asparagus with hollandaise. Tamsin caught Freddie's glance and went cross-eyed. Freddie had giggled gratefully.

Afterwards, they went to the Chatham Squire. They changed first, of course, back at the house, and Matthew showered. They drank mugs of coffee on the balcony while they waited for him. No one said much, not even the normal platitudes about it having been a nice service, a good send-off. It was clear Grace didn't want to hear that. She wouldn't go with them: she said she wanted to walk alone on the beach, which Freddie didn't entirely believe. They walked up to the main drag, arm in arm. When they reached the pavement, they split into twos, with Freddie beside Tamsin. 'Come on, you old heifer. They'll stop serving lunch by the time we get there if you don't move it.'

'Heavily pregnant lady here. Show some respect.'

'Rubbish! You were always a slowpoke.' Freddie remembered walking to and from the Radcliffe Camera with Tamsin – who had long since given up the bicycle she had brought to Oxford – day after day, anxious to get back for rowing practice or to the bar, and Tamsin dawdling, talking incessantly. She made the two of them late for more lectures, tutorials, discos and rendezvous than you could count. Was it really more than fifteen years ago? Everything and nothing had changed. She was still talking – although with the baby under her diaphragm, she really didn't have the puff.

Ahead of them, Matthew put his arm through Reagan's, but she held it stiffly, and he felt silly. 'How are you?' he asked.

'I'm fine.' There was no warmth in her voice. Just the brittleness.

'I was surprised you were going to be here. You're always so busy.'

She was instantly defensive. 'Not too busy for my best friends.'

'I didn't mean that, Reagan. It's just that I know you always have a lot on at work. It's great that you could take time off at short notice.'

'I resigned.'

Now he was shocked. Reagan lived for her job. 'What? What do you mean?' His voice was louder.

'Ssh!' she hissed. 'I haven't told them yet.'

'Why not? Has something happened?'

'I don't want to talk about it, not today.' Her tone did not brook dissent.

Matthew was too tired for this. It was Reagan's *modus operandi*. He'd grown used to it over the years, but it wasn't any less draining. She'd let you in on something, and then she'd clam up, so that your interest was piqued, or your concern aroused, and then you were shut out again. Later you were found to have been neglectful or disinterested. It was maddening, and it was childish, and it was worrying, and it was how Reagan had been with him for years.

He'd sometimes thought he understood it. It had been easier, way back. He'd known, in an inadequate male way, that she'd fancied him. She'd flirted with him all those years ago in Chester, and his mates thought she was sexy. One had told him, after she'd been particularly attentive and suggestive with him in the bar, that he was crazy not to take what was being offered to him on a plate. But he'd found it embarrassing, to be honest. She wasn't his type – she was all hard and angular . . . and too . . . *available*, somehow. Even if that did make him a pretty weird twenty-one-year-old. He'd never seen the point of sex for the sake of it. If you didn't care, what was the point? If she was sexy, he couldn't see it, or it was too knowing, too fake for him. He wasn't a prude. And he wasn't the kind of guy who only found one type of woman sexy. He could see Tamsin was sexy. Laugh-in-bed, earthy, no-holds-barred sexy. Anyone could see it from the way she was with Neil. That dirty laugh. Sarah had been sexy, in a ladylike way. That was one of the chief pleasures of it – everyone else saw someone beautiful, but only he saw her being sexy. Eyes glazed with lust, that deep, guttural noise she had made. It was a secret sexiness. Freddie? Well . . . who wouldn't find her sexy? But Reagan? Reagan seemed too desperate.

And he'd never encouraged her. Not once. He'd

been her friend and she had introduced him to Sarah, from whom there'd been no looking back after that first weekend – and his conscience had been clear, even after that night when he had seen Reagan's attitude change towards him. He'd never talked to Sarah about it. Or Tamsin or Freddie. He guessed she hadn't either.

It was the only piece of dishonesty he could remember in his relationship with either Tamsin or Freddie. Or Sarah. And why? He supposed he wanted to protect her. Reagan had always been on the fringes. If you'd asked him ten years ago whether she would be around in a decade, a part of their group, he'd probably have said no.

Especially if they had known what she'd done the night before he married Sarah.

They'd done the hen-and-stag thing the previous week. The stags had been to the same pub they went to most Friday nights and had drunk the usual five pints. The hens had dressed up and gone to Cinderella's, a vast, subterranean glitter-ball hell much frequented by the men of the local police and fire stations. Tamsin had told Neil where they were going to be, and sure enough they had turned up at pub closing time, just about sober enough to be let in as long as Adrian and Neil held Matthew by one elbow each. They had found their girlfriends, or fiancées, dancing to True with members of the emergency services. Tamsin's had been trying to feel her bottom, and she kept putting his hands back on her waist, never once losing the rhythm of the dance. Freddie was deep in conversation with hers, dancing as you would with your uncle at a family wedding. Reagan was having her face gnawed off by some tall guy whose huge hands roamed freely under her top and down her skirt. And Sarah had abandoned her fireman the moment she saw Matthew lolloping towards her, screaming, 'I know this much is true!' She flung her arms round his neck as if she hadn't seen him in weeks. That had been a good night – a dance-in-the-fountain-in-the-park-on-your-way-home-and-tell-everyone-you-really-really-REALLY-love-them type of night.

The eve of the wedding was different. Matt was in a hotel. He'd been to see Sarah, been kissed by her, her mother, her granny, and ever so gently shoved out of the door that had been opened to let in the three boxes of cake, and told not to come back. The Tenko Club had been fussing and giggling together, with curlers in their hair and those weird rubber things between their toes. Sarah's dad was opening pink champagne.

He'd had a quick pizza with his ushers, and gone back to the hotel, pleading an early night and a shirt to iron. He'd actually wanted to be alone. It was such a big thing, getting married, and he'd wanted to think about it without his parents fussing or his mates making light of it. He just wanted some stillness – a moment in the maelstrom.

The knock on the door was unexpected. It was late, and he supposed someone must have forgotten something, or was playing a prank. He opened it warily. It was Reagan. She'd been drinking, and he wondered how she had got there, whether she'd been safe to drive. 'I've come to see you on your last night of freedom . . .' she said, swaying just a little, and slurring.

He didn't want this, but he didn't want to be unkind.

She pushed past him into the room, and the sprung door shut behind her.

When he turned she was too close to him. 'It's your last chance, you see . . .'

He made a valiant attempt to laugh it off. 'Last chance for what, Reagan?'

Now she sat heavily on the bed. It was very soft and sagged – she had to put out a hand to steady herself. Matthew thought how sad she looked.

She recovered her balance, leaned back and fixed him with a lascivious half-smile. 'To have me.'

'Reagan.' His tone was warning, but Reagan had Dutch courage in ample measure and was now condemned to try and finish what she had started. She stood again. When he made no move to go to her, she got up, went across to him and tried to pull his head into a kiss. Her breath smelt of alcohol, and she put her wet, red tongue out, just a little, before their mouths touched, and he was repelled. He held himself stiffly, and pushed her arms away. 'Reagan, please.'

'Matthew, please.' Her voice was smaller now, more imploring, and already her confidence was subsiding. In one last extraordinary move, she pulled up her T-shirt. Her breasts were practically non-existent, mere swells on her chest, with huge, jutting nipples. He couldn't see her face behind the T-shirt, and for a moment he couldn't tear his eyes away from what she was showing him.

Matthew was appalled. This couldn't be happening. He didn't have the first idea what to say to her. How to help her. How to get her out of his room. Gently he pulled the T-shirt down. She was already crying. Now she collapsed into dry sobs of humiliation. 'I'm sorry. I'm so sorry. I'm sorry,' she kept saying, until Matthew couldn't bear to hear it any more and put his arms round her. He was sure, now it was over, this cripplingly cringe-worthy incident, and that it was safe to touch her in the only way he had ever wanted to, with the tenderness of a friend.

'It's always been you – always you, Matthew,' she was saying, into his chest. Whatever he had known about how she had felt, it wasn't this. He hadn't known this. He wouldn't have ignored this. He suddenly felt horribly guilty.

He tried to pull back a little, to talk to her, but she held firm to him, so he spoke over her head. 'It hasn't, you know. It's never been me. Us. There's never been an us. You're being silly. And drunk. And maybe a bit jealous.' He hoped she would look at him, shamefaced, laugh it off. Throw up. Anything.

'I saw you first.'

It wasn't the most mature argument. She sounded like a petulant child.

'And then I saw her, Reagan. There was nothing between you and me, and then I saw her. And it's always been *her*.' He felt cruel, saying it like that, but it had to be best to talk to her simply – to make sure there was never a repeat of this hideous business.

She hadn't said anything else. She had looked at him, through wet eyes, as though he were a stranger, and then she had run out of the room. His impulse had been to stop her – she didn't seem safe – but he made himself let her go. He didn't sleep properly, worrying about whether she had made it home, whether she had said anything to Sarah.

The next morning, when she arrived beside him at the altar, Sarah had wrinkled her nose and whispered lovingly, 'You're all sort of pale grey. Is it nerves? Did you think I might not show up?' Behind her, Reagan had looked at the stone floor.

At the reception he had almost tried to talk to her, but the wedding circus swept him up and kept him moving. Reception line, photographs, meal, speeches . . . Reagan had left long before he and Sarah did, pulling one of his old schoolfriends behind her. He didn't think she'd met his gaze once that day.

By the time he and Sarah were alone, he had lost the will to tell her. There was their long, glorious day to talk about. There was the dress, with its incredibly complicated tiny buttons, to get her out of, and there was married love to make for the first and second time. Then there was the honeymoon, and upgraded seats in the plane paid for by a generous romantic aunt.

Three weeks later Reagan and Tamsin picked them up at the airport, and there was no sign of it. Matthew

wondered if he'd been having some Dickensian nightmare with Reagan appearing as the ghost of something
not done. She was just as she had always been with
him.

There'd only been that one wretched time since, and
now even that was years behind them. He no longer
flattered himself that Reagan's strange unapproachable
moods were anything to do with him. She was an
unhappy person, but he no longer thought of himself
as the reason why.

It was almost a jolly lunch. They ate ribs and lobsters,
giggling at each other in their red plastic bibs, and
drank a few glasses of wine.

'How long are you staying, Matt?' Tamsin asked.

'I can stay for a few days. We just won a pretty big
case, and I've got time off for good behaviour.'

'Good for you!'

'I'm taking my learned friend into Boston with me to
meet with the lawyers,' Freddie said.

'I was going to do that.' Reagan looked upset.

Freddie mentally kicked herself. 'Well, you come
too. Sorry, Reags, I didn't think.'

Tamsin interjected, 'On the other hand you could
stay and keep me company. I'm not going into the city
in this Indian summer heat. I'm staying right here and
wallowing on the beach.'

'Sounds good.' But Reagan's grin was thin-lipped.

When Reagan was at the bar paying the bill, Freddie
smiled gratefully at Tamsin. 'Thanks, mate. Thought

I'd blown it then. I didn't mean for her to feel usurped. It's just . . .'

Tamsin put up her hand. 'I know. No worries. She'll be fine with me. If I can look after a naughty toddler, I can look after Reagan. You two go.'

Reagan needed more cigarettes, and Tamsin said she would go with her – she needed more Reese's Peanut Butter Cups – and that they'd catch up.

Freddie and Matthew put on their sunglasses, and began to saunter back.

'Don't be mad,' Matthew said, 'but Neil let slip about Adrian.'

'I'm not mad. It wasn't a secret.'

'Why didn't you tell me when we drove down to see Harry?'

'Don't know.'

Matthew scanned her face, and let it go. 'You okay about it?'

'Okay about him shagging Antonia Melhuish, or okay about him wanting to set up home with her?'

'Either?'

She laughed. 'Neither.'

They walked on a little.

'Actually, I'm not as upset as I thought I might be. Does that sound weird?'

'Do you mean you were suspicious?'

'Not exactly. I just wasn't surprised. And that's the most significant part. Nothing at home was any different – we were still sleeping together, still saw as much of each other as we used to. All tickety-boo on the surface. That's the thing – our whole life was lived on the surface. There was nothing else and we ignored that. Do you understand?'

Matthew didn't, but he had heard it said. He'd watched enough daytime television after Sarah died.

'And the fact that I didn't notice, that I still can't put my finger on anything – that bothers me more.'

'I don't get it.'

She spoke slowly. 'Because it makes me think that all along, for ages, we've been acting out a happy marriage, not *living* one. And while we weren't noticing, the soul of it disappeared, seeped away.'

'Christ! You're getting deep in your old age.'

She hit his arm. 'Shut up! I'm serious. I've thought about this.'

'Sorry! What are you going to do?'

She sighed. 'I don't know. There's a lot to consider, Harry most of all. I don't know. Hide out here for a while. Hope the answer comes to me, you know?'

She looked at him with her head on one side, and one half of her nose crinkled up.

I have come, he thought. I have come to you.

Boston

Freddie was so glad that Matthew was with her. It struck her that she had never been part of a world like this one. That with all her early promise – the academic achievements, the lofty ambitions and ideals – she had ended up a stranger to this environment. That – strong, resourceful and resilient as she believed herself to be – this world scared her.

How the hell had that happened?

When Harry had been at nursery she'd met a woman who had a little girl in Harry's class. She'd been an attractive prospect, standing out among the Louis Vuitton mums with their blonde highlights, four-wheel drives and whiny voices. Allegra had had wild black hair, and worn geometric, architectural clothes, statement jewellery – a huge chunk of amber, an unpolished knob of turquoise – and always a thick sweep of black eyeliner, lifting at the corners so that she looked arch. She was an astrologer. She'd persuaded Freddie to let her do her chart. Freddie remembered ringing her father to find out what time of day she'd been born, and being surprised at the precision of his answer. Nine fifteen in the morning. She still had the chart somewhere. It said she was a second-half-of-life person. Allegra said that meant she wouldn't fulfil her potential until after she was thirty-five. That was years ago; and she'd been happy then, or busy enough not to think about it, and she had laughed it off. She was fulfilled already, she had thought then. Now she wondered.

She had wanted to be an architect. She remembered that when she was little she had drawn elaborate plans of houses she wanted to live in, childish creations with swimming-pools that had waterslides, and vast playrooms. She spent bus journeys staring at Boston skyscrapers, desperate to know what kept them standing. She could have done it if she'd tried, Freddie was sure. She couldn't blame all of that on Adrian, and she wouldn't lay it at Harry's door. It wasn't her father either. She'd had all the chances, and she'd let them go.

It was a vast meeting room, with a long, highly polished antique table. Freddie counted twenty matching chairs, each upholstered in claret leather. There wasn't a single book in the room, just two spectacular old paintings of Boston on opposite walls. From where she was sitting she could see out of the big picture windows on to the Common. She remembered playing there with Grace.

It had been a happy childhood. It had. Even given that childhood summers were always brighter, warmer and longer, and winters always cosier. The Common had been her garden where she had marked the seasons. She loved it. Like Central Park in New York, it was bordered on all sides by tall buildings, a bustling noisy city. It wasn't as big as Central Park, though, and you could never get away completely from the noise. It changed character as you walked through it. At the entrance, flanked by Beacon Hill and the impossibly shiny and symmetrical state building, it was always thronged with office workers, women in suits and trainers, tourists following the Freedom Trail, ice-creams and balloons, and people with maps looking for Filene's Basement, the world-famous discount store with its ten-dollar wedding dresses. Amphibious military vehicles roared past every twenty minutes, off on their Duck tour of the city, ready to plunge into the Charles River and out again. Her beloved swan boats were on the lake in the middle. And the blue bridge was at the other end of the Common.

In that park she had learned to walk, ride a bike, balance on a skateboard, and kiss. Sanford Goldman, eighth grade, behind the statue of the horse on a hazy August afternoon while their friends lay on the grass a hundred yards away listening to Culture Club and Duran Duran on a tinny tape-recorder. She could see herself out on the grass at every age, the teetering toddler, the energetic child, the self-conscious teen-ager. Back in this room she was suddenly sad about the herself she was in here.

She didn't want to be here. She didn't want to hear any of this. She didn't care. Money was probably the only thing she didn't have to worry about right now. Adrian's parents were rich. Her father must have been pretty comfortable – real estate in Boston and Cape Cod didn't come cheap. All around her there was money. It hadn't bought any of them much happiness, as far as she could see.

She snorted, which brought her back into the moment – and she saw that. Matthew was looking at her.

'What?' he asked.

'I was just thinking to myself what a poor little rich girl I am.'

He was about to answer when the door opened and her father's lawyers came in. They looked like the three ages of lawyer. The first was about a hundred and fifty, so hunched that he was practically folded in half – you could just make out a waistcoat, with a gold fob watch, under his navy pinstripe suit. He carried an elaborate walking-stick, and it took him a good minute to make it from the door to the head of the table. He was followed by a worried-looking middle-aged man with a receding hairline and a large file clasped to his chest. Last in was a woman, whom Freddie deemed about the same age as herself. She was tall, too, with a figure that strained to escape from her sensible, though clearly expensive, taupe suit. Very camp-vamp. She beamed at them, all American white teeth and confidence. 'Katherine Shaw. Good to meet you.' She held out her hand. 'May I introduce Nicholas Lees and George Barker, two of our senior partners. Mr Barker knew your father particularly well, Mrs Sinclair.'

At this Mr Barker began to move in what was almost a quiver. His cloudy eyes were revealed beneath their heavy brows, and Freddie saw that there was still sparkle in them. 'Knew him as well as anyone did.' He chuckled, and held out a thin, dry hand to Freddie. 'I'm sorry to hear of his death, Mrs Sinclair. Condolences and all that.' He waved them aside, and Freddie wondered how much he knew about their appropriateness in her case. 'I worked with him for almost twenty years. Most of the time you were growing up.'

'But we never met.'

'Your father never mixed work and family.' Freddie bristled. He'd never done much family, as far as she recalled.

'But we followed your progress by the pictures of you he always had on his desk – he changed them religiously.' She hadn't known.

The worried man still hadn't spoken, and now he came forward. 'Nicholas Lees. I handled your father's will for him.'

Freddie shook his hand.

'And you must be Mr Sinclair?' This was Katherine Shaw.

Matthew shook his head, with a small smile.

'This is a family friend,' Freddie said. 'Matthew is a lawyer. He kindly offered to come and help me make sense of whatever you're going to tell me.'

Ms Shaw – Freddie was certain she would be a Ms – made no apology for her *faux pas*, and did not look in the least embarrassed. If anything, she was now appraising Matthew. Freddie didn't like her: she was definitely a sleep-with-the-guards type. Maybe for power in the camp rather than food.

Nicholas Lees smiled warmly. 'Shall we all sit down? Have you been offered a cup of coffee?'

She switched off from a lot of it. The thick document in front of her was written in impenetrable legalese, and she didn't try and understand it; she was sure Matthew would translate it for her. She tried to concentrate on the lawyer's monotonous voice, but her gaze often wandered to the window.

He must have sensed he was losing his audience. After about ten minutes, he closed the file in front of him and clasped his hands on top of it. 'Perhaps you would prefer me to summarise the major points?'

Freddie smiled gratefully. 'Please.'

'It is a fairly simple will in real terms, Mrs Sinclair. There are just three main beneficiaries. Yourself, naturally, your son Harry, and Miss Grace Kramer.'

A week ago she might have been surprised to hear Grace's name. And she was surprised her father had thought of Harry. They hadn't known each other very well. Visits you could count on two hands.

'The house in Boston . . .'

'I didn't know he still had a house in Boston.'

'Yes. A sound investment. He bought the property in nineteen sixty-five. I would imagine it has increased in value several times over.'

'The house I grew up in?'

'The same. We have keys, and there have been no tenants in it. He used the property himself on the rare occasions he came into Boston on business, and cleaners went in regularly to keep the place up. Essentially I expect you will find it much as you left it.'

Freddie turned to Matthew and smiled broadly. 'Wow.' He squeezed her hand.

Mr Lees continued: 'As I was saying, the house in Boston comes to you, along with the bulk of your father's estate, much of which is invested. The figures are in this document.' He paused. Matthew resisted the urge to skim through and find out what it might be worth.

'In addition, your father created a trust for Harry. Well, to be accurate, the name of the trust is "Grandchildren of Mr Valentine". Since you are his only child, this means Harry, unless you should have another child in which case the trust would extend to include it. A sensible precaution, given that you are still of – ahem – child-bearing age.'

Freddie felt herself flush, but not as deeply as Mr Lees.

'The bank, myself and Miss Kramer are the trustees, and Mr Valentine left a statement of wishes lodged with the bank detailing his intentions vis-à-vis expenditure from the trust.'

'No Lamborghinis until after college!' Ms Shaw joked.

Freddie was taken aback. 'There's that much?'

'Well, with prudent management, and pending a good performance in the markets,' Mr Lees opened his file, flicked across a couple of pages, 'I believe the current figure stands at about . . . a quarter of a million dollars.'

This was more than Freddie had thought and her head spun. It bought her freedom from Adrian – he could no longer dictate what happened to Harry.

There was more. 'The house in Cape Cod, in Chatham, is left, for the remainder of her life, to your father's housekeeper, the afore-mentioned Miss Kramer. In addition, Mr Valentine made provision – a pension of sorts – for her. On her death, the house will pass to you.'

Freddie nodded. That was right. 'I didn't realise my father had so much money.'

'Well,' this was Katherine Shaw, 'he was a careful man, rather than a terribly wealthy one. He lived modestly, for a man of his means, throughout his life. We tend to find it's a generational thing. These days, we're all about spending, but older people tend to save for the future – if not their own, their children's. They like a bigger safety-net than we're used to.'

She was right, Freddie realised. Patronising, con-descending, and very irritating, but right. Most people she knew were mortgaged to the hilt, with credit cards for every store, and had two or three holidays a year. Future be damned. It looked like her father had had his eye on hers all along.

Now Nicholas Lees spoke mainly to Matthew, and the pair slipped into legal talk. She drank the coffee that had been put in front of her, and thought about the Beacon Hill house. Perhaps they could go there next.

'Miss Kramer will be informed of the arrangements affecting her in writing. That letter will go out this afternoon. One last thing, Mrs Sinclair. I appreciate that this has been rather a lot to take in.' He took an envelope out of his file. 'This letter has been lodged with us for several years. It's from your father. He wanted it to be given to you after his death.' She reached across the table and took it, recognising her father's elaborate handwriting – always in ink, never in biro – 'Frederica'.

'Obviously you'll want to take that with you, and read it in your own time.'

She put it into her bag.

They had given her the keys to the house. It was that simple. It was a ten-minute walk away from the law firm. She remembered wondering, when she was young, why he couldn't come home and have lunch with her, since he was nearby. Beacon Hill was like that: sometimes you had to look closely to see which of the grand buildings were businesses and which dwellings. They were mostly apartments, these days, and the giveaway sign was the bells – three or four for each house.

Number fifty-three. Three broad stone steps led up to the shiny black door. A huge arch surrounded it, set with glass and wrought iron. It was grandeur on a grand scale. Two perfectly manicured miniature pines, planted around their bases with red geraniums, stood guard, and there was only one bell: 'Valentine'.

Matthew followed Freddie inside. There was another door, and then a big hall, with a black-and-white chequered floor, and a large table that cried out for an elaborate vase of tall flowers. Beyond it the staircase swept upwards, with wrought-iron balustrades. The light from the front door and the landing windows above was bright today.

Freddie turned this way and that, taking in the sights of her childhood home. She couldn't believe he hadn't sold it when he'd bought the Cape house, or that she didn't know he hadn't, or that it was now hers. It wasn't completely the same – most of the furniture and paintings she remembered were gone, and there were no clocks – which were all in Chatham – but it felt the same.

They went from room to room, hardly speaking. Freddie, stood in the doorway of her bedroom for ages. She'd forgotten the wallpaper: dense yellow rosebuds with dark green foliage. She remembered she'd had a valance and a quilt to match. The white furniture had long gone, but the wallpaper was going strong. How she had loved that wallpaper.

'If these walls could talk?'

She smacked him playfully. 'They'd have nothing much to say! I wasn't allowed to bring boys up here.'

'And that stopped you?'

'Absolutely.' She made an innocent face. 'That was what the Common was for!'

On the second floor she stopped outside a door. 'I was never allowed in here. This was his office.'

'And you never sneaked in when he was out?'

She smiled. 'I tried, once. My dad was a pretty scary guy, and you needed a lot of guts to disobey a direct command. But I did once. It was locked.'

'Is it now?'

She turned the handle gingerly, and the door swung open. The desk was missing – lots of the books, too. You could see the outline of where pictures had hung on the walls. One painting remained above the fireplace.

'This has to be your mother.'

'I guess so. I never saw it before.'

'I can't believe it. Your father was a piece of work, wasn't he? All this secretive stuff.'

'Tamsin would be so thrilled right now.'

They'd been looking at the oil painting of Freddie the day before, and Tamsin had been incredulous that Freddie had never seen it. 'Why the hell not?'

Even Grace didn't know the answer to that one. 'I don't think he kept it from her exactly, but it was in here and he didn't like people being in his study. Any people, not just Freddie. I wasn't exactly barred from this room, but I wasn't encouraged to come in either. He was a private man, and his space was important to him. What can I tell you?'

Tamsin had harrumphed indignantly.

Freddie had loved the picture of herself and now she was fascinated by this one. She couldn't date it, but it was a formal pose, in evening dress, and the subject was looking sideways, into the middle distance. There was no signature, no date. It was lovely. Not oils this time. This painting was much softer, its colours muted, and the effect almost ethereal.

'Do you think he never stopped loving her?' Matthew asked softly.

'How should I know?' It came out more angrily than she had intended. 'Sorry, Matt. Didn't mean to jump down your throat. It's just that he never told me about it. I wish I knew. I really do.'

'Are you going to read the letter?'

'I suppose so.'

'I don't get you. You wish you knew. He's written a letter. Maybe it'll tell you.'

'And maybe I'll just be disappointed again.'

'You'll never know, will you, unless you read it? Listen, we passed a Starbucks on that last corner. I'm going to go and get us some coffee. And two bits of Rocky Road,' he said.

She smiled. Marshmallows and glacé cherries. Just what the doctor ordered after a will reading and a tour of your childhood home. 'You read it while I'm gone. Yeah?'

'Okay, boss.'

'I'm your lawyer. I'm supposed to instruct you.'

A high-backed leather chair faced the picture. Freddie sat down and pulled the letter from her bag. The envelope was crumpled now, and she smoothed it. It was not a long letter, but she had not expected it would be. That wasn't his style. She could almost hear his voice – he wrote as he had spoken: quickly, with economy.

Dearest Frederica,

You will by now have met with or spoken to my lawyers, and will know my intentions. You and I were not close, and I regret that; any distance was of my making, and although later in my life I recognised this I still felt unable to rectify it. For that I am sorry. You always had scant regard for material things, and I hope you will not think the provisions I have made for you and your son are intended as a substitute; they would not be adequate.

They give you space, freedom and choice, that is all.

There is another choice I feel you should now be permitted to make. It was wrong of me to deny it to you for so long. Your mother lives on Cape Cod. Grace knows where. Please know that I always loved you.

Your father

He had signed with his whole name.

'Bloody hell,' Matthew exclaimed.

'I know.'

The first paragraph made her cry her first tears for him. And for her. What a fool he had been. What a waste.

The last stopped her in her tracks.

She'd never thought of her mother as dead – logic and odds suggested that she wasn't – but she hadn't had any sense of where she was.

She was less than two hours away, and she had been for years: the letter wasn't dated, and he had known. Grace knew too.

The coffee was getting cold. Matthew put Freddie's cardboard cup into her hands. 'How does it make you feel?'

'I don't know.'

'Does it make you want to jump into the car and go there straight away?'

'No.' It didn't.

'Does it make you angry?'

'Not really. I don't know, Matt. It feels . . . weird.'

That must be a bloody great understatement. Matt was like Tamsin. Normal, loving family. His mum was dead now. She'd died eighteen months after Sarah of a heart-attack. It had happened out of the blue, although she'd been a smoker for thirty years. She'd given up in a fit of pique one Budget Day. He'd seen a lot of her, that last year, because of Sarah. She'd nagged him into coming up north for lots of weekends. She'd said she needed him near her to know that he was okay. She'd fed him, and held him while he cried, and listened, and distracted him with stories of his aunts and his reprobate cousins, and his brother's succession of unsuitable girlfriends. She'd come to London, too, cleaned the place, batch-cooked food he never ate. It was she who'd finally dealt with Sarah's stuff. She'd made three piles on the bed. He remembered coming home from work one day and finding them there. One for Humana, one for a dress agency, one of things he had to decide about. The big flowery box with her wedding dress, wrapped in tissue paper, was in that pile.

'You can shout and scream at me all you want, son,' she'd said, 'but this needs to happen. It's time.' Of course he hadn't shouted and screamed at her. He'd let the things go, because they didn't make any difference any more. He'd kept an old T-shirt and a pair of baggy plaid trousers – she'd worn them on Sunday mornings. You could get straight out of bed and go to the newsagents in them, and get straight back in again. *Observer* for him, *Mail* for her, because she loved *You* magazine, even though he told her the paper was a comic, with no brains and no morals.

At first, after his mother died, he blamed himself. It must have been a strain, up and down from Newcastle on the train, coping with him. He'd said to his father that he was sorry. His father had dismissed the apology with his usual brusqueness: 'Rubbish, son. She wouldn't have wished on you what happened to Sarah, not in a million years. But looking after you, after it happened? That was what she was living for.'

Now Matthew asked Freddie, 'So what are you going to do?'

'I don't know.'

'Okay.' He backed off. 'What about the house? Shall we cancel the reservation at the hotel and stay here?'

She looked shocked. 'God, no. I don't think I could

face that. I don't know if I'll be able to stay here again. Certainly not tonight.'

He didn't know what to suggest next.

Freddie did. 'What I want to do right now is go back to the hotel, take a long hot shower, go out to eat, and get very drunk. Up for it?'

'I'm up for it.'

'Let's go.'

Chatham, Cape Cod

'Another lazy day in Paradise!' Tamsin had discovered Lipton's Iced Tea and was drinking gallons of it. She'd just come out on to the veranda with two more tall glasses. Grace was shopping (probably for more Lipton's Iced Tea), and Reagan was sunbathing on the grass. She had taken the patchwork quilt from her bed and spread it out in front of the house. As the day had got warmer she had removed more clothing, and now she was lying there in short shorts and a black bra that looked like a bikini top. It was too warm for Tamsin, who had taken up residence on the swing seat in the shade. They were too far apart to talk and, besides, Tamsin was engrossed in an old copy of *Tender is the Night*. America made her feel very F. Scott Fitzgerald.

'Iced tea! Come and get it while it's cold.'

Reagan had been dozing on her front, but she pulled herself over and sat up.

As she approached, Tamsin said, 'Rather them than me in Boston on a day like today. I wonder how they're getting on?'

'She'll be fine. She's got Matt with her, hasn't she?'

Tamsin looked closely at Reagan, trying to read her

face, although it was hard, with the enormous sun-glasses obscuring it. She'd changed since Matt got here. She was all brittle again. 'What's going on with you, Reagan?'

'What do you mean?'

'Come on. This is me you're talking to. All of this. You being here, for a start. I've never known you take so much time off before, unless you're somewhere exotic with some bloke.'

'Not you as well. That's what Matt said.'

'Well? We've both got a point, haven't we? And what about Matt, while we're on the subject? You've had a gob on you since he arrived. What's that all about? Have the two of you had a fight or something?'

'No, of course not. What would we fight about? When would we have been on our own to do it?'

'So . . . what?'

'I've resigned.'

'You've what?'

'I've resigned.'

'But you love your job!'

'That's what everyone seems to think.'

'We think it because that's the impression you give us. You work all the hours God sends, for goodness' sake.'

'One doesn't necessarily follow the other.'

'No, but you're good at it. You make a small fortune. You're dead important. You've never said—'

'No. Well, you've never asked.'

'That's not fair, Reagan.'

But she didn't back down.

Tamsin sulked quietly for a moment or two, until curiosity got the better of her.

'So? I'm asking now . . .'

Reagan poked out her tongue at her. Tamsin poked back.

'You're right, in a way. I don't hate it. I resigned in a bit of a strop, actually. I asked for some time off and they wouldn't let me have it, so I basically told them they could stuff their job and left.'

'So you might not have really resigned?'

'Oh, I think I probably have. I didn't mince my words. Felt quite good actually.'

'But why, if you weren't unhappy there?'

Reagan sighed. 'Because I'm pretty much unhappy everywhere else.'

Tamsin frowned.

'I want things to change and that seemed like a good place to start.'

'You're not making much sense. If that's the bit that's working, why is it the best place to start? And what other things do you want to change?' Tamsin didn't really believe that Reagan was about to declare a devout wish to marry and have children. That had never been her style, and she wouldn't have patronised her by saying it. She'd never been like her, she knew that much.

Reagan didn't answer.

'What are you unhappy about? You can tell me, Reagan.'

'I'm not sure I can because I don't know. My life. Everything. Nothing.' She hugged herself. 'I thought maybe it was because I was single, that maybe I was a feminist traitor – that all I really wanted was a husband, some kids and a house with a garden.'

'Nothing wrong with that. I hate the assertion that you can't be a feminist and want all that.'

'I agree. But it isn't that. I honestly don't think I'm just waiting for the perfect man to come and rescue me from the glass-ceilinged tower.'

'Really?'

'Really. Besides, I'm a long way from being ready for Prince Charming anyway. I feel . . . sort of barren. Not in a baby-machine way. I feel . . . all dried up. And brittle. And . . . I don't know . . .'

Tamsin couldn't remember Reagan talking like this before.

'Oh, forget it. I'm probably just a bit burnt out. I've been working year in year out ever since I qualified. It's just a mid-thirties, where-am-I-going funk, I expect. And I suppose I just saw this as an opportunity to climb off the merry-go-round. A time-out.' She said it in a terrible American accent, and made a T sign with her hands. Then she was smiling again. 'And you know what? I can afford to take a bit of time off.'

'Absolutely. At least you can do it without having to get pregnant. If I want six months off there has to be a baby at the end of it.'

'Aha – but your work is a calling.'

'Ah, yes. *Goodbye Mr Chips. How Green Was My*

Valley. Dead Poets' Society! You make it sound like the priesthood.'

'It is – it's a vocation. You know that's true.'

'Well, no one goes into it for the money, that's for certain.' Reagan was right: she did love teaching. It was the most satisfying thing she could imagine doing. When you saw a child grasp something, saw the pleasure of knowledge, understanding, achievement go across their face, it was worth the lousy pay and the shocking working conditions a hundred times over. She knew not everyone saw it that way, but she was tremendously glad that she still did. 'And being a lawyer isn't a vocation?' she said.

'What sort of amoral, soulless individual would claim that the law was a vocation?'

'Shut up! You're not all bad.'

'No?'

'Give me a minute. I'll think of a good lawyer!'

'Is this a cue for one of your awful jokes?'

Tamsin had dozens of them, and she was much happier talking on this footing – this was the Reagan she liked best. 'Yeah, yeah. What do you call a ship full of lawyers on the ocean floor?'

'I know.' Reagan pretended boredom, but she was smiling. 'A start.'

'You're a good lawyer, Reagan.'

'How would you know?'

'Because I only have successful friends, that's how.' They both laughed.

Reagan took a long sip of her iced tea, although she'd

rather have had a Diet Coke. I am a good lawyer, she thought to herself. I just don't think I'm a good person.

Later, when the heat had gone out of the day and they were in the kitchen, Reagan said, 'Listen, Tams, no need for everyone to know about my funny five minutes of navel contemplation and self-pity. "This too shall pass." '

'As they say.'

'As who says? Must be Shakespeare. It usually is. If it isn't Oscar Wilde.'

'You're the one with the Shakespearean leanings. But I won't say a word. Camp confidante, remember?'

As Reagan passed her, Tamsin pulled her into a brief, awkward hug. Reagan was stiff for a second, then relaxed into it, and let herself be cuddled, just for once.

Boston

Freddie and Matthew had dinner downtown, in an Italian restaurant behind the Capital Building somewhere. It was the kind of place that still served Mateus Rosé and had a fisherman's net with lurid plastic fish hung on one wall, opposite photographs of obscure 1970s daytime television stars taken with the owner when he still had hair. If it wasn't called Luigi's, it should have been. Freddie kept thinking about the scene in *Lady and the Tramp* when the two dogs sucked the same strand of spaghetti to the strains of 'Bella Notte'. It was warm, fragrant and noisy.

'You know how to show a girl a good time, don't you? A city full of cutting-edge cuisine and you bring me here.'

'Don't be such a snob. Look around you – the place is full of Italians. The food must be fantastic.'

Freddie laughed. 'Okay. Just get him to bring us a carafe of his finest Chianti and a big plate of *carbonara* and promise me we don't have to talk about my father, or my "mother" or Adrian. Tonight it's bollocks to the lot of them. Not one word.'

Matthew crossed his heart and 'zipped' his lips with

two fingers. The carafe arrived, slid expertly on to their table by a waiter sweeping past urgently. Apparently it wasn't optional here. Matthew poured two enormous glasses, and picked his up. 'Deal . . . if you promise me we don't have to talk about old times.' He held his glass towards her. 'Here's to both of us. What's next?'

She looked at him quizzically. 'It's time I moved out of the past and into my future, don't you think?'

They hadn't toasted Sarah. They always did that. For a second, Freddie felt disloyal – but it was up to Matthew, surely.

'That sounds a familiar refrain, my friend. I'll drink to that!' Freddie raised her own glass and took a gulp. 'But what's brought this on? You definitely sound like Tamsin, but you don't sound much like Matt.'

Matthew shrugged. 'I don't know.' He raised his eyebrows, as though he had been startled. He always does that when he's explaining things, Freddie thought. 'Perhaps it's got to do with you lot being away for a while. It made me realise, I'm afraid, that I don't have much life beyond you and Tamsin. And even Reagan. And you're not enough, really, are you? Having you as friends isn't enough.'

He was looking at her in a way that felt momentous, and she didn't know why. She wanted to make him smile, wanted to make the moment smaller, lighter. 'Are you saying you're ditching us?'

Matthew smirked, then winked. 'Ditch the Tenko Club? Never.' He looked vexed now, as though he had more to explain. Freddie didn't want him to have to. It must have cost him enough to get to this point already. She put her hand over his and patted it comfortingly. 'I know what you're saying.'

He caught her hand when she tried to take it back. 'Do you?'

'I think so.'

It was much later when they left. It was cooler now, and Freddie pulled her cardigan round her shoulders and tried to push her arms into the sleeves.

'Wait! Look at you!' Matthew helped her into it, then tucked a stray blonde curl behind her ear.

'Thanks for tonight.' She kissed him on the cheek, then thrust her arm through his and pulled him with her, back towards the hotel.

They were quiet until they got to the eastern edge of the Common by Beacon Hill. This part of the city was bewitching at night, full of history. The Victorian gas-lamps that burned all day only glowed after dark and cast flickering shadows on the rough cobbled pave-ments, red and black. The houses kept their secrets at night, too. Blinds were drawn against the world, to reveal only slivers of light. On the other side of the road the Common looked dark and dangerous, but through the railings Freddie could see a row of trees, their branches hung with fairy-lights.

They walked quickly at first, but then slowed, silently imagining the lives contained within the houses. Matthew stopped outside one: it was on the corner of a street, a four-storey townhouse in grey stone, with grey-green paintwork on its shutters, and a huge dolphin-shaped knocker. A flight of steps led up to the vast front door, and on the second floor one of the rooms jutted out into an ornate pentagonal bay, topped by a verdigris roof and a little filigree balcony. An American flag flew above the door, and the window-boxes on the ground floor were carefully tended. An attic window perched prettily on the roof. It looked like a beloved, moneyed family home.

'I bet that's worth a fair bit,' Freddie commented, seeing him look at it with interest. She noticed that the windows had caught Matthew's eye. In all the rooms where curtains had been closed, their creamy linings illuminated by the gas lamp, the glass panes, not every one, but randomly, abstractly glowed lilac, some darker than others.

'What are they?' Matthew asked.

'I know this.' Freddie smiled, childlike. 'I was paying attention on all those school trips. I love them, too. They're the original panes of glass, made when these houses were built, in the eighteen-somethings – which makes them pretty damn old by American standards. They got the chemicals wrong, you see, when they made them – too much . . .' she trawled in the back of her brain for the answer she knew was there '. . . manganese sulphate, or something like that – never was much good at science. But they got it completely wrong. And over time the glass went purple, and some of the owners kept them. There are quite a lot on the Hill.'

'Pretty, isn't it?'

'It's beautiful. Really beautiful.'

He turned to look at her now, in the gas lamp's glow. Her eyes were bright with the pleasure of telling her story, the story of the lilac glass. She looked about nineteen again.

'You're beautiful,' he said.

She giggled. 'You're mad.' Her tone was light.

But his voice was deep, suddenly serious. 'You are, Freddie.'

Something had changed, in front of the house with the lilac glass. She opened her arms and he came into them, wrapping his round her tightly. Then he pulled back and his hands came up to her face, and held it, tilted up at him, forcing her to look into his eyes, which were still open when he brought his mouth down on hers. His lips were tentative at first, planting little dry kisses on her lips. Then he groaned as her mouth opened and he surrendered to the taste, smell and feel of her. The kiss became hard and passionate. And she kissed him back. And they stood like that for long minutes, under the gas lamp in the street, kissing like lovers.

Freddie felt her body respond to him; her legs trembled, and something unfamiliar radiated out from the pit of her stomach. She wanted to be touched. She wanted him to touch her. She felt him hard against her groin. They were the right height, she thought, as she pressed back, unconsciously starting the rhythm. She wanted him. If they had been inside, if there had been a bed or a sofa . . . she could imagine herself falling on to it with him, pulling aside their clothes, then skin on skin.

He said her name, just once, and that was all it took. 'Freddie.' Matthew's voice was gravelly with wanting her. Matthew. And they weren't outside. They were in the street. And this was Matthew. Her friend. Her friend's husband.

She felt herself coming back from far away. That feeling, when they put you under in the dentist's surgery, and at first you think there's no way you can't count to ten but you don't even get past three and it feels so heavy and so good. But this was in reverse. She was coming back too fast. Bends of the heart.

Freddie pulled away, and saw her own shock reflected in his face. Unconsciously she wiped her fist across her mouth and stepped backwards. 'What was that?'

He stepped towards her, so she stepped backwards again, in some awkward dance, and then he didn't step forward again. 'I'm sorry. I . . .'

'That's okay. Forget about it. We can forget about it, right?'

'Do you want to forget about it?'

She wanted it not to have happened. She felt weak and stupid. What the hell had she been thinking of? 'This can't happen, that's all.'

He said nothing.

Now her tone was imploring. 'This is us, Matt. You and me. We're friends, aren't we?'

His voice was small. 'Always.'

'Always. Exactly. Me too, that's what I want. That's all I want.'

'Are you sure?'

She wasn't sure about anything any more. She was lonely and frightened and sad, and he had felt so good, just then. But it was comfort she needed, not sex. It was the old Matt she needed, not this new one, kissing her like that, making her want him. She couldn't risk it, and she wouldn't.

She started walking, briskly now, back down towards Newbury Street. She had to speak almost over her shoulder: Matthew was standing still on the pavement, watching her. She had to go on explaining. Go on making it all right. 'Let's not confuse this, Matt. We're both lonely. Lonely and a bit drunk. That's all this is. We can get past it.'

Matthew dug his hands into his pockets, and followed her. It took him about five strides to catch up.

'Say something,' she implored.

'I'm sorry. What else do you want me to say?'

'Nothing. No big deal. Crisis over.'

But she lay in bed, with the sheets clutched round her neck, wide awake.

In the next room, Matthew barely breathed. She was through the wall, lying about twelve inches from him but probably further away than she had ever been. He thought about the kisses, and his body betrayed him, and he was hard again, alone in the bed.

At that moment he thought he hated himself.

It wasn't okay at breakfast either. Freddie thought he looked tired, and he hadn't bothered to shave. She wanted to reach out and smooth his hair on the top of his head, where it was barely two inches long and stood up from the night, but she knew she couldn't. They both picked at a muffin, and cradled mugs of coffee, not knowing what to say to each other.

At the next table, a small group of women from Atlanta, long hair curled and sprayed, nails immaculately tipped, noisily plotted a day's sightseeing. Beyond them a skinny grey couple, who looked like those farmers in that famous American painting, ate methodically in silence, looking straight through each other.

Freddie felt depressed again. The free, light mood of the previous evening had been shattered by a moment's mistake and another sleepless night.

Later, when they'd gone up to brush their teeth, Matthew knocked on her door. Freddie opened it and he came awkwardly into the room. The bed was unmade, and Freddie's white nightdress lay discarded across it. Instantly, Matthew felt almost faint with desire again. He shook himself angrily. What the hell was wrong with him? 'I've just called BA and they can get me on to the afternoon flight.'

'Today?'

'Yes. I think it's best I go, don't you? I'm sorry, Freddie, really I am. You're over here dealing with all this stuff, and I show up and make things even more complicated for you, and that makes me feel like an arsehole. I was being selfish and I acted like an idiot, and I'm just going to get out of your space, and let you get on with what you've come to do.'

'I don't want you to go.' Freddie knew that she sounded childish.

'But I have to. It's best. You've got Tamsin and Reagan.'

'I wanted you.' Even as she said it, Freddie knew she shouldn't have. She was being weak, and it wasn't fair.

Matthew shook his head sadly. 'You don't.' Not the way I want you. 'You'll be fine.'

'Will you?'

'Course I will. Come and see me when you get back. It's only a couple of weeks, isn't it?'

'Yeah. You bet.'

He didn't let his body touch her when they hugged goodbye, just his arms. He held himself away from her, and it made her sad. After he had gone, she sat down on her bed, hugging a pillow and wishing she had understood just one part of last night and this morning.

Phone lines between Boston, Logan airport, and Chatham, Cape Cod

'Tamsin? It's Matt.'

'Hiya, Matt! How are you? How's Freddie?'

'She's fine.'

'How did it go yesterday?'

He hesitated. 'It was okay.' He sounded distracted. 'Look, she's on her way back now, and I'm sure she'll tell you all about it when she gets there.'

'Aren't you coming with her?'

'No. I'm on my way to the airport. I'm catching a plane home this afternoon.'

'Has something come up at work?'

'No. It's not that.'

'What's wrong? You sound weird.'

'Oh, Tamsin. I've made a massive mess of everything.'

Tamsin thought she knew where this was going. 'What do you mean you've made a mess of everything?'

'I kissed her.'

She had been right. 'Oh.'

'Is that all you've got to say?'

'What happened?'

'Well, yesterday was pretty tough for her, but we got through it. We went out for dinner – we had a really nice evening. I just felt, you know, close to her, and afterwards we were just walking and . . . then I kissed her.'

'And how did she take it?'

'She kissed me back at first. Then she backed off. She looked completely horrified. I feel like such an idiot.'

'You're not an idiot, but you might be if you're about to run away.'

'Yeah, that's what I'm planning.'

'Are you sure that's the best thing to do? 'Cos I'm not. Why don't you talk it out with her? She's going to be confused, if it came as a bolt out of the blue. She won't know why you did it, or how you feel. Why would you just leave it hanging like that?'

'Because it's not fair. It's not the right time. She's got so much else on her plate. I should never have done it. I'm not going to make it worse by forcing her to deal with it now.'

'You're just afraid.'

'Damn right I am. I'm fucking terrified. I'm scared I've ruined our friendship – and of rejection, or any other scenario you can come up with. I'm pretty much scared to death of all of them.'

'What about reciprocation? Scared of that?'

When he answered, his voice was lower. 'Probably.'

'Look, don't beat yourself up about it, Matt. As far as I can see, it's what you've been wanting to do for months, if not years.'

'So why did I go and blow it by doing it now?'

'Because we're not emotional robots. You did it because it felt right at the time.'

'Not to her, I guess.'

'I'm sure, once she's had a chance to get used to it, she won't be upset.'

'I'm not.'

'Will you call me when you get back?'

'I will. Listen. Don't tell her – she might not want you to know.'

'I can do sensitive. Kept your secret this long, haven't I? I'm sure it'll be fine. Don't worry. Call me soon.'

Talk about bad timing. As she put the phone down, Tamsin shook her head. This had been a long time coming, but he should have picked a better moment.

She remembered the first time he had talked to her about it. It had been Flannery's first summer and she'd been lying on a picnic blanket in the park watching Willa and Homer argue in the sandpit nearby, late one afternoon. Matthew had come straight from work – she couldn't remember where Neil had been, but in those days of new-baby haze, it really only mattered that there was someone to help cart home all the paraphernalia. He had undone his top button, loosened his tie, taken off his black brogues and socks, then flexed his toes. Flannery was asleep, face down between them, and he'd fiddled with the lace trim on her bloomers.

He had talked in general terms, about Sarah, about

how much Sarah would have liked to be here. It was one of the ways they kept her alive, by bringing her with them on trips to the park like this. There should have been another buggy, with Matthew and Sarah's children asleep in it, or playing nearby. Now, though, it wasn't so much with sadness that they said it but fondness.

Then Matthew had stopped speaking. After a pause he had said, 'She'd want me to have somebody else, though, wouldn't she?'

Tamsin's answer was instant, and full of conviction. It wasn't the first time he had asked and her answer was always the same. 'Of course she would.' For emphasis she leaned across Flannery and stroked his arm.

'Do you think she'd mind who it was?'

This was a first. Tamsin was thoughtful for a moment. 'I think she'd prefer a woman.'

They laughed, but when she looked at him she saw that he was still waiting for an answer. 'I don't think she'd put caveats on your happiness. Why are you asking me?'

'Because I think there is someone.'

'Who is it?'

'It's Freddie.'

Afterwards she'd wondered why she felt so surprised. Freddie and he had always been close, the best of friends. It was a relationship none of them had questioned.

And even as she tried to think of what to say to him, she wished it wasn't Freddie because this was going to get messy. Freddie was married, and had been one of Sarah's best friends. She was Tamsin's best friend. It wasn't that it was wrong – that never entered Tamsin's head – it was just that if it had been some pretty young thing from the law firm, someone new, it would have been uncomplicated and straightforward and Matthew, whom she loved, could have got on straight away with living, loving and being happy. And it wasn't going to happen like that. Nothing close.

Then he started to talk about Freddie, what he loved about her, when it had changed. 'It wasn't Thunderbolt City. It wasn't instant. I didn't wake up one morning and think, This is it, she's the woman for me, I love her. It was nothing like that.'

Tamsin said nothing, just let him speak.

'I suppose the truth is that for the first year or two after Sarah died I didn't think in those terms at all. I didn't think about love or romance or sex in the present. I still felt all of those things for Sarah, and I felt frustrated, but I didn't think about it in terms of another person or in the present.

'And the ingredients for loving Freddie were all in place, apart from the physical ones. I've loved her as long as I've loved you, and nearly as long as I loved Sarah. We were friends. I knew how she felt, what she wanted, what she thought about stuff. We've got history, we've got memories. All of that was already there. I don't know when I started to feel different about her physically, when I started to want her. At first I suppose I thought it was just part of the healing process, that I should look at another woman and imagine being with them, and if I thought about Freddie at all it was inevitable that I would start where I felt comfortable, but that nothing would ever come of it, the feelings would go away. But then I realised . . . I never felt them for you.'

'Thanks!' Tamsin interjected.

'Or for Reagan. And the only times I've ever got close with someone at work or friends of friends, those ghastly set-ups, it just hasn't worked for me at all. For ages I felt guilty about it.'

'Not because of Adrian?'

'No, sod him. Because of Sarah. But there was something else. I suppose I felt like I was betraying my friendship with Freddie. She didn't treat me like an ordinary man, like I was just another bloke. I had special privileges. I had a lot of the intimacy of a husband or a lover without being one. She didn't think about it. I remember once we took the kids swimming, and it was a hot day, and she put her top back on without a bra, and it was wet, and . . .' He was shaking his head '. . . she knew I could see her and she didn't care – it just didn't occur to her – but I was seeing her in a different way and I felt bad, almost perverted. It's like I was a voyeur, suddenly, sneaking a peek. So I tried to make it go away but it wouldn't. And the more I thought about it and the further away I got from Sarah, the more I couldn't deny that what I was feeling was real. And it had nothing to do with Sarah, and it had nothing to do with the relationship I'd had with Freddie for the ten years before. It was just about her and me. A man and a woman. I love her, Tamsin.'

He was sitting up now. She stretched across and put her arms round his neck. 'So what are you going to do about it?'

'What can I do? She's married to Adrian. She's happy.'

Tamsin raised her eyebrows.

'She's not unhappy enough to want to do anything about it. And she doesn't think about me that way. And my biggest fear is that she never will. That I'm like her brother or something.'

Tamsin knew he wanted her to say something, but she couldn't: she didn't know what to say.

Chatham, Cape Cod

On the way back, Freddie stopped at Plymouth Rock. It was a bit like the Little Mermaid in Copenhagen – disappointing – where she and Adrian had been on an inordinately expensive weekend trip when Harry was about six months old. She had tried not to think of it as symbolic of anything. Adrian's mother had practically forced her to go. It was frightfully important, she said, to be away from Baby. She always referred to Harry as 'Baby' – not *the* baby, or Harry. Baby needed to realise, she said, that Mummy was not always going to be there. And Freddie always heard, in silent brackets: 'Mummy needs to realise that she's a wife first and stop all that ghastly feeding business.' Weaning at twelve weeks, food at four months, potty-training at a year – that was the correct way, the Sinclair way.

It had been a disaster. She'd missed Harry desperately, and her breasts had ached alarmingly. The only things she remembered about that trip were the longing for her baby, her throbbing breasts, and the tiny little mermaid. And a bad dream she'd had on the Saturday night in which she had returned to find that her infant son had been enrolled at boarding-school. (Which turned out not to be a nightmare so much as a pre-monition, since conversation took that direction shortly after their return.)

Plymouth Rock didn't look like the birthplace of the free world. She sat on a bench and stared at it for a while, behind its bars, beyond its graffiti. When it started to rain, she got back into her car and drove to Chatham.

When she got back Grace was alone. The others had gone out to see the Kennedy compound, she said. Freddie wondered whether Matthew had warned them.

'I got my letter from the lawyers this morning,' Grace said.

'I'm pleased he left you the house. It was your home. It was the right thing to do.'

Grace smiled. 'I couldn't have imagined leaving.'

'You won't have to.'

'On the other hand, I'm not sure I can imagine living here without him. It's a big house to be in all on your own.'

Freddie nodded. 'I had no idea he'd kept the Beacon Hill house.'

'He knew it was worth a lot more than he'd paid for it, but he didn't need the money. He thought you might like to live in it one day.' There was a question in her voice, but Freddie didn't answer it. Grace went on, 'But if not, he knew it would be worth even more by the time you came to sell it.' Again Freddie didn't speak. 'Did you see it?'

'We were there yesterday.'

The two women were quiet. Freddie was fighting to control her anger. Evidently Grace could see it, and she suddenly spoke, fast and quietly, into the silence between them. 'You'll know about your mother, too. We fought about that. We fought about that for years.'

'Why?'

'I felt he should tell you. Particularly after Harry was born. I knew that then, if not before, you would need to know.'

'And do you know?'

Her voice was quiet. 'No.'

'He never told you?' Freddie was incredulous.

'Told me why she left him? No. He would only ever say it wasn't her fault. He said it to me the first time we met when he interviewed me. It seemed so tragic a father left alone with a small daughter. At first I assumed his wife must have died. When I found out she had run away, abandoned you both, I was ready to think all sorts about her. Most people would. But he said, that first day, that he didn't blame her. He said she was too young, that he should never have married her and that he blamed himself far more than he could ever blame her.'

'When did you find out where she was?'

'You were about eighteen. He told me as soon as he knew. It was just before you left for Oxford. He could hardly have told you then, could he, when you were about to embark on an exciting new life on the other side of the Atlantic?'

'How did he find out?'

'She wrote to him.'

'Not to me?'

'She didn't know what you'd been told about her. She was being careful, I think. She didn't want to put a foot wrong as far as you were concerned.'

Freddie snorted. 'Apart from the two she'd put wrong in running away from me when I was four years old.'

'I don't blame you for being angry, Freddie. I know this has all been shocking for you. But if you're honest, what difference does it make that he knew where she was? She wasn't a part of your life.'

'It wasn't his decision to make.'

'But it was, when you were a girl. She went, Freddie, and for years he had no idea where she was. He had no answers for you. And when she reappeared, he panicked. He didn't want you to be upset. He wanted you to go to England, study and be happy. He thought it wouldn't be good for you at that time.'

'Not at that time, maybe. I see that, I suppose. But what about later? I had a right to know.'

'I know you did. That was what I fought him about.'

'Fought and lost.'

'Yes.'

'You could have gone behind his back.'

Grace nodded. 'Perhaps I should have done.' When she looked at Freddie there were tears in her eyes, and Freddie's anger was suddenly tinged with pity. 'Maybe there were a lot of things I should have done differently. Looking back, I can see that I let him make the rules about a lot of things. About your mother, about telling people about us, about the cancer. I don't know what to tell you except that I'm sorry. It's too late now, I know, but I'm sorry.'

Then she said, 'But you moved away, Freddie. Not just physically, and not just from him. You moved away from me. You rejected us both, you know.'

Freddie felt ashamed. It was true. 'So you know where she is?'

'I have an address for her in Provincetown.'

'Have you met her?'

'No.' She sounded hesitant.

'Grace?'

'I never met her but I've seen her. I went up there once. Told your father some story – I knew he'd be furious. It was just after we'd had the letter. I found her, and I watched her for a while – that makes me sound like a stalker. She came out of where she was living then – she's moved since but I have the address. I followed her a bit. Don't forget – I was in love with your father, and she was the woman he'd married. I was curious. A bit jealous, even.'

Freddie was taken aback. She couldn't imagine Grace behaving like that.

'If I'd been braver, I would have spoken to her. But I guess I've never been very brave.'

'Can I have it?'

It was on a piece of paper folded up under the clock on the mantelpiece in the living room. It wasn't her father's handwriting, or Grace's, and she imagined it must be Rebecca's.

'What did the letter say?'

'It's a long time ago. I don't think your father kept it – I don't remember seeing it.'

'But do you remember what it said?'

'It said that she wanted to let him know she was back – we didn't know where from, or I didn't – and that if you ever wanted to know where she was to give you the address.'

'Was that all?'

'I think so.'

'And she never tried to get in touch again?'

'She didn't.' Grace paused. 'But I did. When you graduated, when you were married, when Harry was born, I sent her photographs, just with a little note, letting her know. I never told her where you were, and she never asked. I just wanted her to know something about you.'

Freddie wasn't angry any more. She wasn't so different from Grace, was she? They both did what they had to do to keep the peace, even if it wasn't necessarily what they thought was right.

She stared at the piece of paper in her hands, and wondered what the hell she was going to do.

Tamsin and Reagan were back by the early afternoon. Hyannisport had been disappointingly Kennedy-free, but they had found a great fishmonger and brought back fresh lobster, as well as the timetable for ferries to

Martha's Vineyard and Nantucket. They ate the lobster with melted butter and a glass of white wine, listening open-mouthed to Freddie's catalogue of revelation.

'Coo! It's like *Peyton Place* around here,' Tamsin trumpeted.

'My life the soap opera.'

'So Mummy is alive and well and living in Provincetown, is she?' This was Reagan.

'It's obvious, then, isn't it?' Tamsin said. 'Provincetown is where everyone is gay, isn't it? I was reading about it. She must be gay. That's why she ran away. That's why she ended up there.'

'You can't be serious?' Reagan looked at her in amazement.

'Why not? Let's face it – it would have to have been something apocalyptic to make a mother run away from her own child. Something that turned life on its head. Why not that?'

'You're wasted on teaching – you should be writing.'

'What do you think, Freddie?'

'I don't know what *to* think. Maybe she *is* gay. How would I know? I didn't even know she was alive until yesterday. And she's only been in Provincetown latterly. I don't have a clue where she was in between times.'

Tamsin's imagination was running wild, but she looked at Freddie and decided to keep it to herself for the time being.

'Didn't Grace know anything about her?' Reagan

was asking. 'Like whether she'd had any more children or married again?'

'Don't think so.'

'See? Clearly gay.' Tamsin sounded like Poirot rounding off an investigation. She licked her buttery thumb. 'What else could it be?'

Later, Grace told them her sister in Vermont had asked her to stay for a while and that she wanted to go. Her niece's baby was going to be christened, and she had always said she would go to Waitsfield for that. She needed a bit of a break, too, after the funeral. She said, slightly shyly, that they were welcome to stay while she was gone.

Grace left the next afternoon. Freddie carried one of her bags out to the car, and they hugged. 'Grace? I'm sorry I was like I was.'

Grace held her tightly. 'I'm sorry I didn't treat you properly.' Her shoulders shook, and Freddie realised she was crying. 'I should have fought more for you, for what I thought was right.' Through the car's open window she asked, 'What are you going to do?'

'I don't know, Grace.'

Tamsin came out and waved at the car as it pulled away. She put an arm round Freddie's shoulders. 'What now? Are we off to Provincetown to find Mommie Dearest?'

Freddie laughed. 'God only knows . . .'

★   ★   ★

'Matthew kissed me.'

They were lying on Freddie's bed in their pyjamas.
Reagan had gone to bed an hour or so ago, but Tamsin
had heartburn and Freddie was keeping her company.
They had been watching American sit-coms.

Tamsin knew that already, but she wasn't going to
say so.

'Did he?'

'You don't sound very surprised.'

'I'm not.'

'Why not?' Freddie eyed her suspiciously. 'What do
you know?'

'I don't "know" anything.'

She wasn't sure she believed her.

'Was it nice?'

She smacked Tamsin's thigh. 'That's not the point!'

'Is that a yes or a no?'

'It wasn't nice or not nice. It was . . . weird. He's my
friend. He's Sarah's husband.'

'He's Sarah's widower.'

'But he's still my friend. Our friend. You'd feel
pretty weird if he kissed you.'

'That would be completely different.'

'How?'

'He wouldn't do that to Neil, for a start.'

'But he would to Adrian.'

'Hell, yes. And we'd all be right behind him, cheer-
ing him on.'

Freddie had to smile. She loved Tamsin so much.

'Speaking of Adrian, what are you going to do about

him?' He'd been on the phone again and Tamsin had answered. Even to her, he had sounded a bit desperate. Not that she felt sorry for him, of course. Freddie had waved her hands frantically, and Tamsin had lied for her without a second thought: 'She's not here . . . Of course I'll give her a message . . . I'm sure she'll call you back when she gets home.'

'Ignore him?'

'That's fine, short-term. But it's not really a plan, is it?'

'S'pose not.'

'Do you know if he's still seeing this Antonia Mel-huish?'

'No.'

'And that doesn't bother you?'

'I wouldn't say it doesn't bother me . . .'

'But it isn't eating you up. You aren't thinking about it every minute. Wanting to kill her, kill him, kill them both.'

Freddie realised she wasn't.

'Well, I'd say that was your answer. If it was Neil I'd be dying inside.'

Tamsin had only ever had one evening of jealousy in nearly twenty years. It was after Homer had been born. She'd been a hormonal, lactating banshee and Neil hadn't come home when he'd said he would. Assuming it was an emergency at the hospital, she'd phoned, but they'd said he wasn't there. She remembered sitting on the stairs, staring at the front door, sick with worry. Picturing him with someone else – someone thin and pleasant with a sense of humour and breasts that didn't leak at drinks parties.

He'd come in at eleven o'clock. He'd been at Matthew and Sarah's. He'd had a drink or two, which made him brave enough to say what he'd been rehearsing at their house all evening, which was that he loved her, and he would always love her, but that he was fed up with her treating him like shit because she was tired and concentrating on Homer. On any other day she might have killed him stone dead, but three hours with a mental picture of him in the arms of someone else made her fling herself at him – no mean feat when each of your breasts weighed three stone – and apologise and promise to be better tomorrow.

If Neil had an affair she'd want to die. She might not be the sort of vengeful fiend who cut all the sleeves off suits and poured acid on car bonnets, and it might not be the end, but she knew she'd want to die.

If Freddie couldn't see that her marriage was over, it was only because her head was so full of all this other stuff. To the others, it was obvious.

'What about Matthew?'

'I don't know.'

'Listen, Freddie, I don't know what's going to happen. Maybe you're going to patch things up with Adrian. I hope to God not, but it's your life and no one can tell you what to do with it, even if they know they're right – which I do, incidentally. But whatever, will you think about Matt? I think he kissed you because he genuinely cares about you very much, and I don't think you should disregard that.'

'What are you saying?'

'Just that I know there's a lot going on, and I know you're all over the place, but just, please, think about him.' She couldn't say any more.

England

Adrian lay propped up on pillows in Antonia Melhuish's bedroom. He felt strangely out of place. This was a feminine space: everything was floral, pale and unbelievably neat. She had curtains that looked like frilly knickers, and her kidney-shaped dressing-table had a matching skirt. He was huge and clumsy in here.

She was getting dressed, talking all the time. She was late, and that made her voice faster and faster, until it was a little like a lispy, high-pitched machine-gun in his brain. She was late for the beautician's. He had learned that it took quite a long time to remain so tanned, so blonde, so bald of pussy – she went a couple of times a week. He'd picked her up from there last week. He'd felt out of place there too. It had smelt of seaweed, and was full of loud women talking about men.

She had those nails, too – acrylic, she had told him, fanning her fingers for inspection. Squoval. Whatever that meant. They vaguely frightened him, and actually, they quite hurt when she dug them into his back, which she did quite a lot. He'd been showering after a game of squash at his club last week, and a colleague had noticed the three-inch scratches her talons had left on his shoulder. 'Bloody hell, Ade. Your wife must be quite a tomcat.'

His flash of pride at this acknowledgement of his prowess was extinguished by a torrent of guilt. And a sliver of disappointment. Sex with Antonia wasn't as he had imagined it would be. There was plenty of it – in fact, she was pretty demanding. Selfish, too, he had discovered: the other day he had spent a long time on her, and then, anticipating fair exchange, he had pushed her head downwards. She had sat up, wrinkled her nose and explained that that was something she never did. With anyone. Ever. He had been a little shocked. It didn't tally with the nymphet at the eighth hole.

He suspected it related to her obsession with hygiene and neatness, which bordered, in his view, on abnormal. He wasn't allowed to come to bed unless he had showered, and although early on she had showered with him, which had been fun, increasingly he was despatched to the bathroom alone. She made him feel vaguely as Matron had, which might work on some blokes, but Adrian, perhaps unusually, had found nothing erotic about Matron back then, and still didn't.

Now she had stopped dressing to pull a pillow further up behind his head. 'You'll get the headboard dirty, Adrian.' Perhaps antimacassars would be a good idea.

Freddie was nothing like her. Adrian and she used to fancy each other grubby sometimes. She liked him freshly sweaty after a run. And she would have let him have her across the kitchen sink without thinking twice about the germs it would leave on the granite.

It wasn't just that, although frankly that was depressing. She was talking about lawyers, now. She wanted Adrian to see her 'chap', the man who had apparently got her such a 'fabulous' settlement in her own divorce. She kept saying, 'Adrian, you just don't know a woman until you meet her in court. You think she isn't interested in your money, but just you wait. "Hell hath no fury like a woman scorned." And, besides, who isn't interested in money? She'll take you to the cleaners if you don't protect yourself.'

But didn't he deserve to be taken to the cleaners? He'd had the affair. He watched Antonia's face while she said these things, and noticed that her mouth was pinched. She had these little lines running down her top lip, like she'd been sucking lemons. She looked mean.

Adrian's attitude to money was not unusual among those who had plenty of it. He found conversations about it vulgar, and the undue consideration of it tiresome. Antonia, he feared, felt neither of these things. He had noticed, around the same time he noticed the lines, that when she talked to him about people he didn't know, she gave potted CVs of them, like, 'That's Tony Lewis. Dentist. Drives an Audi TT. I think Jonathan paid for most of it when he had his teeth fixed. Place in Marbella.' Or, 'Sally Smith. Terrible cellulite. Her husband's a partner at Grant Thornton – sold their house last year for £1.25 million.'

He wondered what she would whisper about him. 'Adrian Sinclair. Wife doesn't wax. Worth millions when his parents pop their clogs. Pretty sound bet, apart from unreasonable demands for fellatio.'

'So will you go? At least call him – today.'

He sighed. 'I'll call him.'

'Well done, sweetie.' She kissed his forehead. She was dressed now. 'Right, I'm off. Parking's always a complete nightmare on Saturday mornings so I'll be terribly late.' She was looking at him. 'Unless . . .'

'I'm meeting some of the boys at the golf club this morning. That's in completely the opposite direction.'

'You didn't say.'

'Did I need to?'

Her face was petulant, but she kept her tone light. 'Of course not, darling, but surely an extra ten minutes wouldn't matter, would it?' Wheedling. Freddie never wheedled. 'And you're only going to play nine holes, aren't you?' And, come to think of it, Freddie never minded if he played eighteen, and spent the rest of the afternoon in the nineteenth. Which he had thought was rejection and neglect, but was looking strangely appealing right now.

He threw back the duvet and got out of bed. Antonia pulled his hips towards her, and ground her tiny pelvis into him. 'I'll make it worth your while later,' she said.

Trouble was, he wasn't sure that she could.

Martha's Vineyard

'So, are we going to Martha's Vineyard, or not?' Tamsin was studying the ferry timetable at the breakfast table.

'We can't. We're not over here for a holiday,' Freddie said.

Tamsin and Reagan raised their eyebrows at each other. 'Who says?'

'Wouldn't Neil, for a start?'

'I won't tell him.'

Freddie looked at her doubtfully.

'Okay, so I'd tell him, but he wouldn't mind. As far as he's concerned, I'm only ever in two places. There or not there. Go on. Let's play hooky. You're not ready for the Sicilian-widow thing, and I think we've pretty much exhausted the charms of Chatham. Tell her, Reagan.'

Reagan yawned. 'Abso-bloody-lutely.'

'Is that it?'

'She's a grown-up. I think we two should go to Martha's Vineyard. Just for a couple of days. Stay in one of those inns we picked up the brochures for. The ones with white lace canopies over the beds. We'll ride bikes, walk on the sand, eat lobster. But we can't make Freddie come.'

'And we're not going without her.'

'Stop talking about me like I'm not here.'

'Stop refusing to come.'

'Okay, okay. You win.'

It turned out they would only take bookings for three nights at all the romantic old inns. They almost missed the ferry because Tamsin insisted they stopped at one of the enormous Christmas World stores that dotted the main road through the Cape. Freddie and Reagan couldn't stop laughing – the place was heaving with tat, a million different themes for a tacky Christmas with a soundtrack of nausea-inducing Christmas music.

'They really have this *all year*?' Reagan hooted.

'Oh, yeah. Christmas is big on the Cape.'

'Christmas is crass on the Cape.'

'Shut up!' Tamsin hissed at them. Mrs Christmas at the till, resplendent in a festive apron adorned with a Santa badge that did what appeared to be a Hannibal Lecter impression when you wound it up, was glaring at them. 'I happen to love Christmas.'

'You would – you're a fully paid-up member of the Waltons.'

'You're so rude.'

'Yeah, a bit like this guy . . .' Reagan was holding aloft a plastic Santa who dropped his trousers at the chorus of 'All I Want For Christmas Is You'.

That's when Reagan and Freddie really lost it, and

Tamsin led them out of the shop in disgust. 'I shall come back without you.'

They were just as bad at the drugstore where they stopped to buy a few bottles of mineral water and cans of Coke. The range of pharmaceuticals was extra-ordinary, and Freddie and Reagan giggled at the douche bags, home enema kits and rows of laxatives. 'God almighty! Boots was never this much fun!'

By the time they boarded the ferry, Tamsin was laughing with them. They wheeled their little cases into a booth below the main deck, then went up and outside to watch the ferry pull away from the harbour. The breeze and the sea air felt good on their faces and in their lungs.

'Were you thinking about the Isle of Wight?'

Reagan had been. They'd gone, just the four of them, the summer they graduated from Oxford, straight after finals. They'd been exhausted from the exams and the partying that had followed. Tamsin had been persuaded to leave Neil behind, and Sarah's dad had driven them to Portsmouth.

They had stood on deck and watched the English coastline recede, along with the stress of the last few weeks. The results weren't due for a bit, although the ghastly threat of being called back for a viva, if any of them was on the borderline between degree classes hung over them. They reasoned it could only be Reagan, hovering between a first and a two-one, and she said she'd take the two-one, and they could stuff the viva, although they didn't believe her for a minute. (A month later she got the first they'd all been expecting, nothing borderline about it.) They had felt the acute nostalgia that twenty-one-year-olds feel, but also scared and excited about what lay ahead.

They had had the best time. Sarah had booked them into a B&B, which turned out to be run by Ma Larkin. They were fed a full English every morning, scones with clotted cream at tea-time. The landlady gave them a key – which, she assured them, she didn't do for all her guests: 'You have a fantastic time. You look like good girls to me. I know you'll come in quietly.'

And they had. After the first couple of days the sun had come out, and they had lain in bikinis on the sand, slathered in Ambre Solaire, reading bonkbusters, eating strawberry Mivvis and Fabs, chatting and listening to Freddie's ghetto-blaster. The week had been declared bloke-free – largely to mollify Tamsin and to guarantee Reagan's continued presence, but flirting was allowed. In the evenings they spent an outrageously long time tarting themselves up, then went out – to the fairground, the disco or the pub.

They all remembered it the same way: lots and lots of laughing, dancing, one incident of roadside vomiting, and not a single cross word. They had been golden days. The usual flashpoint – Reagan and Tamsin (Reagan and anyone, let's be honest) – just wasn't there. It was a mixture of relief, euphoria and sadness: they knew they would never be together like that again.

And how right they had been. That autumn they'd

all scattered, and life speeded up, as their parents had always told them it would.

The Tenko Club hadn't been disbanded, and its *lingua franca* lived on – shorthand for describing a new female boss or a male friend's girlfriend. But it had changed. Of course, the thing about golden days was that their brightness in your memory depended on the hue of your present, and Freddie suspected that the three women leaning over the rails of the Martha's Vineyard ferry all saw a slightly different shade.

Martha's Vineyard was good. They didn't sell strawberry Mivvis on the island, and none of them wore bikinis any more – although Tamsin watched Reagan get dressed one morning and lambasted her for still having a six-pack and nipples that pointed in the right direction. And Sarah wasn't there. All of them missed her more than they had in a long time. Because of the Isle of Wight. Because she should be there. They talked about her a lot, too, which they hadn't lately. Not in the context of her death, but about the life they had shared with her. Freddie felt lousy about Matthew, disloyal.

Once, when Reagan wasn't there, Tamsin whispered, 'I know what you're thinking, and it isn't true.'

'What am I thinking, O Wise One?'

'You're thinking you've been unfaithful to Sarah. Or he has. Or most likely both of you have been. And that's bollocks.'

'Is it?'

'Yeah. Our friend died, and that's awful. And she

died young, which is hideous, and wrong, and a waste. But don't you think that's a reminder to us all to make the most of life?'

Reagan had come in and was listening. 'Did you hear that thing on the radio the other day? It was one of those pious thought-for-the-day things. This guy was telling some Buddhist story, which I'm probably going to paraphrase really badly. A teacher tells his student that he has only twenty-four hours to live, and the guy goes home and says all his goodbyes and things, and lies down, pretty miserable, waiting to die. When there's an hour to go, the teacher comes to him and says, "Did you think bad things in the last twenty-three hours?" And the student goes, "No, of course not, I was thinking about dying." And the teacher says, "Did you do bad things in the last twenty-three hours?" and the guy says, "No," and so on. I think the point was that if you live alongside the knowledge of your own death, you live a better life. Shouldn't Sarah's death have taught us that?'

Freddie and Tamsin were stunned into silence. Then Tamsin said, 'Okay, she went into the loo as our friend Reagan, and she has come out as the Dalai Lama . . .'

Freddie snorted. 'I don't think I understood a word of that, Reags.'

'She did get a first, remember.'

'Piss off, you airheads. I don't know why I still spend time with you.'

'Who else'd have you?'

*   *   *

They had been right. What the hell was she doing telling the Buddhist *carpe diem* story? She didn't exactly practise what she preached, did she?

Reagan had been happy in Martha's Vineyard with her friends and, to a degree, she hadn't worried about the world beyond. But something she hadn't noticed before had troubled her. They had talked a lot, about each other, Adrian and Sarah. But in between there had been the general chat – the day-to-day stuff. Tamsin and Freddie had all these other friends, who cropped up in conversation. Neil and Tamsin had friends from the hospital. Tamsin and Freddie had antenatal-class friends, school-gate friends, neighbours. Their lives were full of other people. Not necessarily people they were close to, or who meant more to them than the three of them meant to each other, but cast members, extras in full lives. She didn't have that. She had colleagues, and she had lovers. She wouldn't know her neighbours if they fell through the ceiling of the flat, and she had no friends. How had that happened? How had they gone off and built these complete lives, full of people, while she still had only them? Where had she been when they had taught you how to do that?

'She's so tired all the time. I'm the one who's pregnant, for God's sake, and I can outdo her.'

Reagan had gone to bed before them again and they were sitting in front of the inglenook fireplace. Freddie was drinking Drambuie from the honesty bar. Tamsin was eating the salted almonds.

'Do you think she finds us insufferably dull?'

'No! Do you?'

'I don't know. We must have pretty pedestrian, suburban lives compared to her.'

'Speak for yourself. I've got a philandering husband and I've just come into a small fortune. Dull? *Moi*?'

'You know what I mean.'

'I don't think it's that. I think she's tired because she's depressed.'

'You do?'

'Yes. I feel bad. These last weeks it's been all about me. I know it took her a while to open up to you about the job, and I still haven't had a chance to talk to her about it properly, but it seems to me that she's never been lower.'

'What should we do?'

'I don't know. She's been better here, but I don't know if that's enough. Isn't there a point beyond which people need serious help? Proper help?'

'Do you mean Prozac?'

'I suppose. Or counselling – although I can't see Reagan being up for that.'

'And what do you think is at the root of it all?'

'Well, it's tempting to sit here and diagnose lack of husband and kids. And too patronising. I've never seen her as someone who needs that.'

'Not the kids maybe, but who doesn't need someone to love them? Don't we all need that?'

'I think so.'

'I know so.'

'So why hasn't she found someone?'

'Well, that's the million-dollar question, isn't it?'

'But it can't be just bad luck, can it? I mean, I never get to meet any of the blokes she's seeing, these days, so I can't form an opinion about why none of them are for keeps. You don't either, do you?'

'Hardly ever. I don't think they're around long enough.'

'It must be her.'

'You're right – she pushes them away. I think she's screwed up.'

'Why? You don't reckon there's something serious, do you?'

'Like what?'

'Oh, I don't know. Like she's gay or something.'

'What is it with you and everyone being gay?'

'All right, not gay. But something . . . big that we haven't thought of. Like she's ill, or she's been abused or . . .'

'You want to turn everything into a drama.'

'Sometimes there is one, you know, that isn't created in my head.'

Freddie shook her head. 'Not this time. We'd have had some inkling of it, after all this time.'

'If we'd been looking. You've got to admit, we've marginalised her a bit for the last couple of years.'

'Don't start feeling guilty. You'd probably have given her up altogether, if I hadn't championed her.'

Tamsin nodded. 'That's true. I'm just worried. I do love her.'

'We both do. Even if we're not sure why.'
'But I don't know how to help her.'
'Nor do I. But we've got to wait for her to ask.'
'I can't help thinking it'll be a long wait.'

Ealing

Matthew and Neil sat at their usual table. They had come to this curry house so often that when Flannery had been born the Nepalese owner had sent flowers to Tamsin. They came when babies were born, when cases were won and when patients were saved. It was the first place Matthew had gone to eat after Sarah died. Even before he had felt like venturing out, Neil and Tamsin had gone round with takeaways. The owner had greeted him like the prodigal son the first time he had been in after losing Sarah. He had been so gentle and so sorry.

Now Akash put one tandoori king prawn, one lamb biryani, a mushroom bhajee, two garlic naans and two pints of Tiger beer in front of them. The restaurant was quiet: it was Tuesday night.

'How long now, sir, until the new baby?' He still insisted on 'sir' after all these years, and Neil had stopped trying to dissuade him.

'Just a few more weeks.'

'But your wife is well?'

'Very, thanks, Akash.'

'You are most welcome, sir. Please give her our

regards.' He gave his formal brief bow, and backed away from the table.

'I suppose you've talked to Tamsin,' Matthew observed.

'Yep.'

'So she told you what a dickhead I've been.'

'Yep.' But Neil shook his head.

'She said that?'

'No. You just did.'

'But she thinks I was an idiot.'

'No, she doesn't.'

'Well, I was. Lousy timing. Has Freddie told her about it?'

'Not that she's said.'

'Is that good or bad, do you think?'

'You're asking the wrong bloke, Matt. Affairs of the heart aren't my speciality – you know that. You need Tamsin.'

'She's not here – you'll have to do.'

'Cheers.'

Neil looked at his friend. What Tamsin had said was that Freddie had been in a real state when she got back but hadn't said a word about Matthew, except that he'd had to get back for work. It was driving her mad, she said, but she knew Freddie, and that she'd have to wait for her to talk. It would only make Freddie cross if she discovered that Tamsin already knew. Besides, that stuff with her mum was enough for anyone to deal with.

Matthew knew that, too, he guessed.

'I know I went at it like a bull in a china shop, but it just happened.' Matthew paused. 'No, that isn't true. It was because of everything else. She just seemed so vulnerable, and I wanted her to know that it wasn't all bad. And that I was there for her – as more than just a friend—'

'Mate! She'd just found out her mother was alive and well, living a few miles up the road, and that her father had kept it from her all her life.'

'And that Adrian was messing her around.'

'Exactly! You can see why she wasn't going to be all over you like a rash.'

'I know, I know. What do you think will happen with Adrian?'

'Well, for her sake I hope she gets rid of him, whatever may or may not happen with you and her. Tamsin doesn't think she's been happy with him for a long time.'

'I never liked him. Even before . . .'

'Let's face it – none of us was wild about him. Remember that ski trip?'

Matthew nodded. One morning he and Sarah had been with Freddie and Adrian – Neil had promised to spend the morning shopping with Tamsin – and Sarah had persuaded him he was ready for a black run. Against his better judgement, he had joined them all on a long ski-lift ride to the top of somewhere very very high. He remembered thinking he wouldn't even be able to get off the lift – it looked like a vertical drop. Sarah had been watching him, and had whispered, 'I know you can do it, and if you can't, we'll take the skis off and walk down. Okay?'

He'd got off all right, but after the first terrifying fifty metres, the run still looked like a death trap, narrow and inescapable. He had stopped, and was summoning his nerve. Sarah, a couple of hundred metres ahead, had swished gracefully to a standstill and turned, one pole planted in the ground, to look for him. He put a hand up to ask for more time. Beside him, Freddie was frightened too. He remembered taking a shred of comfort from that – she was an experienced skier and she was still afraid. But Adrian was laughing. Trying to goad and shame her down the slope. 'Come on, you big wimp,' he was saying.

They had both made it down in the end, with little finesse or speed. Sarah had met him at the bottom. 'Well done, darling! My hero,' she had said.

Adrian had turned to Freddie and crowed, 'See? I said you could do it! You big girl's blouse.' Matthew remembered that streak of cruelty. It had seemed nothing at the time – he had put it down to that public-school-educated toughness. But Freddie's hands had been shaking, at the top, and Adrian must have seen how frightened she was. Seen, but not understood. Or cared.

Looking back, it seemed as if, that day, a tone had been set for their marriage. Since then Adrian hadn't seemed to understand her at all.

But Matthew did, or thought he did. At least, he wanted the chance to.

'But she hasn't said what she's going to do?' Neil asked.

'No. Do you know this woman he's gone off with?'

'Tamsin says I do. Apparently we've been to supper with her and her now ex-husband. Can't say I remember her, but Tamsin does. She said she always thought she was conniving.'

Matthew sniggered. 'Your wife is such a drama queen!'

Neil laughed. 'She'd kill you if she heard you say that. She prefers to think she's intuitive.'

'Right.' Matthew was serious again. 'So what does she intuit about me?'

'You want the honest truth?'

'Oh, yeah.'

'She thinks you and Freddie are made for each other. She thinks she's mad for not spotting it before you told her yourself.'

'Really?'

'Really. But she also thinks you've got to give Freddie some space.'

'When did we all start talking like *The Jerry Springer Show*? What the hell is "space" anyway?'

Neil smirked. 'Search me. I just talk the talk, mate. Want another beer?'

'Sure.'

Neil put his hand up and the waiter sprang to attention.

'I don't have much choice, anyway, do I? She's there and I'm here.'

'Exactly. Do as I do. Get some work done. They'll be back soon.'

They both hoped so.

Chatham, Cape Cod

'Do you mind if I stay here while you two go back?' Reagan asked.

Last night they'd agreed to book their flights home in the morning. Freddie was nervous about confronting Adrian, but it was nearly half-term and she was itching to see Harry. And Neil had clearly reached the outer edges of his tolerance about Tamsin's absence. Freddie had answered the telephone to him the other night, and detected a trace of irritation in his usual joke about getting his wife back. He was right – Tamsin should be there, not here.

Reagan's question didn't surprise her. 'We'd need to ask Grace,' she said. 'It's not my house, remember?'

'Can you think of any reason why she wouldn't want me to stay? The house would be safer if I was here, wouldn't it?'

But Freddie was a little worried. 'I'm just not sure it's the best idea.'

'What do you mean?'

'Well, you'd be here on your own, wouldn't you? Wouldn't that get a bit lonely? A bit depressing?'

Reagan shook her head. 'I think it's the best possible

thing I could do. It's exactly what I need, some alone time.'

'I think you need to talk.'

'I don't have anything to say that won't sound ridiculous or self-pitying.'

'I'm sure that's not true.'

'And I don't want to say it out loud. I want to get over it. And the best way I can do that is to be on my own.'

Freddie couldn't help thinking that the fierce streak of independence in Reagan was a large part of what was wrong, but she knew the expression on her friend's face: she wouldn't change her mind.

Chatham, Cape Cod

Tamsin was surprised at how desperate she was to get home. She felt she wouldn't be ready for the new baby until she was there, and she missed the old babies very badly. She and her friends had been dragging their heels a bit since they'd got back from Martha's Vineyard. That had been a blast and she'd really enjoyed herself – as much as a gargantuan woman with swollen ankles and a bladder the size of an eggcup can on a road trip. But now they were back, and had been waiting for Freddie to decide what to do about her mother up the coast. It wasn't Tamsin's style to let her dwell on it, and it had already taken all her reserves of tact and diplomacy.

As soon as she heard Neil's familiar voice on the phone she longed for him.

'When are you coming home?'

'Soon, darling. Things have gone pear-shaped here. And Freddie still needs me.'

'We need you.'

'That's not fair – you don't need me. You've got Meghan. You're working.'

'But it's not the same. This is a family, Tamsin.'

'Well, Freddie's my family too.'

Neil didn't answer and the expensive transatlantic silence lasted several seconds.

'Is that you putting your foot down, then?' she asked.

'Yes, it is. I want you home for half-term. *We* want you home for half-term. You should be home by then anyway, or you'll end up having the baby in the States, and I'll have to get a second mortgage to pay the medical bills.'

'Half-term it is. I wouldn't have stayed any longer than that anyway. I miss you too, you know.'

She could hear his humour returning in the snort of derision that came down the line 'Who are you kidding? You three are living the life of Riley out there – spending your days shopping and eating, forgetting about those of us back here who can't function without you.'

'Now you're being ridiculous. I don't think there's anybody who can't function without Reagan or Freddie.'

'Well, there is someone who can't do it without you. Nothing's right when you're not here. I need you. I don't know what to think about anything. I can't seem to make a decision. And I don't see why I should have to. Tell me the truth. Is Freddie really over there because there's so much to sort out, or is she just running away from what needs sorting out over here?'

'A bit of both, from what I can work out. That doesn't make it invalid, does it?'

'I just think she's being a bit selfish, that's all. You know I love her, but I've got Matt climbing the walls because he thinks he's made a mess of everything, and she's got you over there and I'm climbing the walls right beside him. I suspect that even old Adrian would like to be put in the picture about what's going on. She can't stay there indefinitely.'

'And she's not going to. She'll come back with me. She needs to see Harry. And I'm sure she'll sort things out with Adrian when she's back.'

'What about Matt?'

Tamsin gave a big sigh. 'Matt's a bit more complicated. And Reagan even more so. I don't think she'll come back with us. I'm not sure she'll come back at all.'

Neil was right, she realised. They needed each other to process things. She needed to talk through what was going on with Reagan and Freddie, and she couldn't do it with anyone but him.

'See? You're missing me just as much,' he said.

She couldn't keep anything from him even when she was six thousand miles away.

Gower Peninsula, Wales

When she heard Matthew's car door slam Sarah's mum, Lois, (quiet, but strong: a survivor) came out. 'Hello, my darling boy. How are you?' He was enveloped in her hug.

It wasn't unusual for him to come and see them. Sarah's mother had loved him for loving Sarah, and Sarah's father, Hugh, had recognised himself in the boy Sarah had brought home all those years ago, full of ambition, politics and energy.

They had sold their home in the Mumbles after Sarah died. Her mother said she couldn't bear to be there any more – it was the house Sarah had grown up in and there were too many memories of her. Funny – that was exactly why Matthew *couldn't* sell their house in London. But their new place had a view to soothe the soul, Lois had said. Today the sky was clear, and the peninsula stretched out in front of them. It was always so quiet here.

She bustled him into the house, and put the kettle on.

'Where's Hugh?'

'He's working, my love.' Hugh was with a firm of

auctioneers. 'Won't be back until sixish. Some house clearance, over Cardiff way. You'll stay, won't you? He'd love to see you.'

'I'm not sure.' He'd only decided to come that morning. He hadn't even rung her until he stopped for petrol on the M4. She'd said yes, straight away, that would be grand. He'd bought her a bunch of non-descript flowers from a garage forecourt but she fussed over them as if they were from Paula Pryke.

Sarah had been an only child, and when she'd died, she'd pulled the heart out of Lois and Hugh's life, and all these years later the massive hole was still there. They didn't cry every day. They didn't even talk about her every day. But they thought about her, every day.

At first, there had been no pictures of Sarah in the new house on the Gower. Lois hadn't wanted any. Gradually, though, they had crept in, and now there were lots. It always made him feel breathlessly sad to walk in – but at the same time, being close to them was being close to her.

'Okay.' She'd made the tea, and put out some fruit cake. She was the only woman he had ever known who was never without a homemade fruit cake in the house, which explained why Hugh weighed about twenty stone. 'Come and sit down, my love.'

They went through into the lounge. Everything in it was familiar – the three-piece suite, the coffee table, the paintings – even though the four walls around it had changed. It was comfortable, warm and safe.

'What brings you here, then? Not that it's not nice to

see you, love, but you sounded like you had something on your mind when you called.'

He couldn't fool her. 'I wanted to tell you something.'

'Anything.'

'I think . . .' this was harder than he had thought it would be '. . . I think I'm in love with someone else.' It seemed so disloyal: he was supposed to be in love with their daughter.

Lois had instant tears in her eyes. They came so quickly these days. He didn't remember her crying before – except at their wedding. She looked older, too. There were lines and furrows on her face now, and she seemed more than fifty-nine. She saw that he had spotted the tears, and rubbed them away with her thumbs. 'Don't mind me. Silly old woman. I'm happy for you, darling, I truly am. It's the way it should be. It's time.'

'Really?'

'Sssh. No nonsense. Of course. You didn't need to come all the way out here on your precious Saturday to tell me that.'

'I did, Lois.'

'If it's my blessing you're after, you've always had it. Sarah wouldn't have wanted you to be alone any more than you would have wanted her to be, if it had been the other way round.'

He squeezed her hand across the table.

'Why aren't you with the lucky lady today, instead of eating fruit cake with the old mother-in-law?'

'It's complicated.'

'Love shouldn't be complicated, sweetheart.'

He laughed. 'No, it shouldn't, but it is.'

'Do you want to tell me why?'

'Because it's Freddie I love.'

'Our Freddie?'

'Yes. Does that make a difference to the blessing?'

She was quiet for a moment, then gave a little nod. 'No, I don't think so. But she's still married to Adrian, isn't she?'

'She is. But it's over – at least, I think it is.'

'Because of you?'

'No. He's been having an affair. But I don't think it's even because of that, really. I think it's been over a long while.'

'Sarah always said he wasn't right for her.'

'We all did.'

'How long has this being going on, then?'

'Nothing's going on.'

'But you'd like it to be?'

'Yes. For the longest time, I didn't think there would ever be anyone else. I didn't think I could ever feel that way about anyone after Sarah.'

'But you can.'

'It's not the same. It will never be the same.'

'No. But you can. You should.'

He could, but she couldn't, he thought. And now she was going to lose him, and even though he knew she had meant what she'd said, it probably felt as if a little bit more of Sarah was being lost to her. He got up and put his arm round her shoulders. 'I didn't mean to upset you.'

She sniffed. 'You haven't, Matt. Don't you mind me. You go for it. Freddie's a lovely girl. But promise me you won't stop coming to see me. You promise. You help to keep her alive for me. Will you?'

A tear rolled down his cheek. 'I promise.'

Chatham, Cape Cod

His name was Eric. He looked about thirty; he was very tall. An All American boy. His bleached white-blond hair was curly, and a little too long, and he had an ear cuff on the top edge of his left ear. He looked like a surfer.

She'd noticed him the first time she, Freddie and Tamsin had come into the bar. When they'd all had lunch there after Freddie's dad's funeral, she'd paid the bill and he'd served her. His voice was soft, and his accent was Cape Cod – they said 'Cod' as if it was 'card'. His eyes sparkled. They'd been in a couple of times since, and she had found herself looking out for him. Tonight she was alone.

Freddie and Tamsin were tired, they'd said, and had to pack for their flight tomorrow. She wasn't tired, and she wasn't going anywhere. She was bored. Tamsin was too fat to want to venture far, and Freddie had endless 'stuff' to deal with. Reagan had half hoped she'd want to go up to Provincetown – it sounded like the best place to be – but so far all Freddie had wanted to do was talk about it. So she'd come alone. She hadn't said anything to the others, but she'd hoped she might see him. She'd dressed up a little, nothing sophisticated – which didn't fit with him.

It seemed to have worked. The bar had been quiet, and she'd sat there, drinking vodka and cranberry juice. When he wasn't serving, he leaned against the back wall, where the optics were, and they talked. She liked the way he put both thumbs in his jeans pockets.

He'd worked there on and off since he was twenty-one: his uncle owned it. He came back from wherever he had been whenever he needed money. He did some painting and decorating, too, a bit of gardening. Whatever, he said. And then he travelled. He'd spent the summer surfing in Hawaii. He was still tanned. He wanted to go to New Zealand in the new year, for their summer. Buy an old camper van and drive around South Island. Whatever.

And he'd been to Harvard. His parents had wanted him to do an MBA at MIT. Too many initials for him, he said. He wasn't ready for all that. He was younger than he looked. Too much sun, probably. The lines around his eyes made him look thirty, but he was only twenty-five. When he leaned across the bar she saw freckles across his nose.

She lied about almost everything. Each time he asked her a question she gave the answer she guessed he most wanted to hear. She was thirty-two. She was travelling, passing through. She was a qualified lawyer, but she didn't practise. She wasn't ready, either. She liked surfing. She figured that was pretty safe. How would he know? The only truth she told was about scuba-diving, which she had done and loved.

This was what she always did. She was whatever they wanted her to be. In fifteen years of this she had never met anyone who seemed as if they would like to hear the real truth, so she had never told it. It usually worked. And it did tonight.

When the bar closed, she sat in the corner booth and watched him collect the last few glasses. After he had locked up, they were out in the cool night air.

'Still thirsty?' Without the bar between them, he was suddenly very close. He smelt clean. 'I've got a bottle of Jack Daniel's at home.'

'Sounds good.'

Now they didn't talk. He walked slowly, with a lolloping style. When they got to the bandstand, she stopped, lit a cigarette and offered him one. 'I'll share,' he said, and pulled hers from between her lips. When he had taken a drag, he kissed her.

Home was a couple of rooms on the ground floor of a house. She guessed it was furnished, and that he didn't have much stuff. There was a giant Red Hot Chili Peppers poster above the sofa, and a serious CD player, with a stack of CDs beside it. She put on the only thing she had heard of while he poured them a drink. It wasn't romantic: it was pulsating and loud. Reagan wasn't a George Benson sort of a girl.

She'd forgotten how much stamina fit young men had. He understood, and he didn't make her talk. He let her drink, and then they started. He was very good.

His encore in the shower was among the best – when you were the right height for it, it was hard to beat.

Tamsin had asked her, in drink, Reagan thought, last summer, how many men she'd slept with. She'd knocked ten or so off when she answered twenty-five, and she was glad she had.

'Twenty-five? *Twenty-five?* You're kidding . . .'

'All right, Mrs One-man Woman. We can't all get it right first shag.'

'Believe me, we didn't really get it right until about the fifth shag.' Tamsin had sniggered. 'But don't try and divert me, we're talking about you, you floozy. Twenty-five? Where the hell do you find them?'

It was easy enough. Bars, restaurants, clubs, conferences, boardrooms, once at a petrol station. Finding them was easy.

'Aren't you worried, you know, about—'

'No. I'm promiscuous, not stupid. I make them use condoms.' Nearly always. 'I don't know what the big deal is. Sex is just bits rubbing together, and I don't know why people make such a big thing of it. It's not real intimacy.'

Tamsin had raised her eyebrows quizzically.

'Real intimacy is falling asleep with someone, and waking up still with them.'

'You don't do that?'

'Not if I can help it. Real intimacy is what you say to each other, not what you do to each other's genitals.' She sat forward. 'I mean, would you rather Neil had a quick jump with some nurse in a cupboard after a party, or started meeting that nurse for coffee behind your back, telling her about his feelings? Huh?'

She was right about that, at least. 'But haven't you had that with any of them?' Tamsin asked.

'Not many.'

She'd had it with three, the first two when she was in her twenties. Sarah, Freddie and Tamsin had met them. That was before she got all weird about it. The latest had been a barrister. She never told any of them about him. They'd met at a conference on penal reform at Gleneagles. He was ten years older than her, married with three children. She'd only let it happen because she knew he was never going to leave his wife. She didn't want him to.

He had a little flat in Lincoln's Inn. She slept there with him, once a week or so, for about a year. In all that time, they never had a meal in a restaurant, or went to the theatre, or met each other's anyone. It all happened in the flat. He would cook, sometimes, an omelette or a stir-fry, and open bottles of good red wine. The bed was practically as big as the bedroom. It was black, wrought-iron. They ate in it, drank in it, made love in it and, finally, slept in it. He was called Simon.

One day he drank a whole bottle of the good red wine, cried and told her he loved her. She told him she didn't love him, and she hadn't seen him since. He had broken the rules, and he had had to pay the price.

The reason she never told them – and if she didn't

tell them, who else would she tell? – was because they would ask her why, and she wouldn't know what to say.

Eric was asleep now. He lay on his stomach, with his head on one bent arm, the other resting on the sheet. It was a light sleep, and he kept moving his face against the pillow. She stared at him, trying to figure out what he would want her to do. Would he want to wake and find her there, maybe fuck her again? Would he prefer it if she was gone? Would he want her to curl up and sleep beside him?

She played little games. If he moves, he wants me to stay. She ran a finger up his arm, and he twitched. His eyes opened. That was cheating. She still didn't know. He smiled sleepily. Then he rolled on to his side, and pulled her to him. 'You okay?'

She nodded.

'Not sleepy?'

She shook her head against his chest.

'Wanna go home?'

'Do you want me to go home?'

'I'm easy.'

'I got that!' Keep it light. Keep it light. It felt okay, in his arms.

Still holding her, he said, 'Why'd you tell me all that stuff?'

She stiffened. 'What do you mean?'

'All that stuff about you. It isn't true. This is a small town. Grace is a friend of my aunt. I knew who you were, what you did.'

She didn't speak.

'So why'd you make all that stuff up?'

God, it was too pathetic. 'I've got to go, actually.' How ridiculously English she sounded.

His arms tightened round her. 'You don't have to.'

'Yes, yes, I do.'

He let her go, and she pulled her clothes on quickly.

'I'm sorry,' he said. 'I didn't mean to upset you. I just . . .'

She held up her hand. 'It's fine. I've got to go.'

And she was outside. She knew he was getting out of bed, coming after her, so she ran. And she didn't stop until she got to the bandstand. She sat down heavily on a bench inside it, and waited to catch her breath.

Then she started to sob.

Half-term: England

Neil was waiting at the rail, Flannery on his shoulders when they came through Customs, with Homer and Willa on either side of him. As soon as the sliding doors revealed Tamsin's swollen belly the children wrestled free of their father's grasp and charged at her. She stopped in the middle of the stream of passengers, oblivious to the trolleys unable to pass her, and held them to her. Freddie felt a pang of longing for Harry. Adrian had said they should talk first, that she could pick him up later, and she had grudgingly admitted that he was right – besides, Harry didn't break up until lunchtime. Adrian wasn't there – she hadn't wanted him to come. He would be waiting for her at home.

She watched Tamsin and Neil hug, and couldn't remember ever having been so pleased to see Adrian. Besides, public displays of affection were not very Adrian: he'd have squirmed to watch them, arms tight round each other, kissing deeply. She thought it was lovely. Neil opened his eyes and saw her, took one arm off Tamsin and reached for her too. But Tamsin was too big for that to work, so Freddie settled for a wink and a sort of stroke/pat on the arm.

'Are we glad to see you two.' He grinned. 'Bed's too big without you, babe.' It was one of their songs – Police, 1980s. Just one – they had lots.

'You might not think that after one night with me and this.' Tamsin rubbed her bump ruefully.

'I'll cope.'

The children were full of their news all the way back into London from Heathrow: Homer's latest achievements on the skateboard, explained in excruciating detail; the low-down on Willa's sleepover at Kitty's house the previous Friday, when Kitty's father had come down in his pyjamas at two thirty in the morning and threatened to send them all home if they didn't go straight to sleep; Flannery's fall last night down the last three steps on to the wooden floor, which had resulted in one of the few teeth she had being broken, and making her look, according to her loving father, like a 'village idiot'. Everyone was interrupting, laughing and loud. Freddie let it all wash over her. She was tired from the flight, which had been uncomfortably hot, and at the thought of what lay ahead. When they got to Ealing, she ran a brush through her hair, then put on lipstick and perfume, which made her feel better.

Outside her house, Neil unloaded the suitcase and carried it to the front door. Adrian did not appear, and Neil was clearly not keen to see him. He kissed her quickly, and hurried back to the car. Tamsin wound down the window, and gave her a thumbs-up. 'Call me later. Come for pasta tonight?'

*   *   *

Freddie was fumbling for her keys when Adrian opened the door. About time. The suitcase was between them, so there was no suggestion of physical contact. She followed him into the living room. There, he put his hand on her elbow and bent to kiss her cheek. She let him because it seemed easier than rebuffing him.

'How are you?' His voice was higher than normal, weirdly formal. 'Can I get you anything? A cup of tea?'

She'd been drinking coffee in America – a mug of strong Twining's sounded good. 'Thanks.'

The house was spotless – she had known it would be – as if photographers from *Homes and Gardens* would soon arrive to capture its anodyne perfection. A couple of stiff new invitations were on the mantelpiece. Otherwise it looked exactly as it had when she had left. It was Freddie who had changed.

She followed Adrian downstairs, and sat watching him as he made the tea. She didn't know where to start.

He was the same as he had always been, older perhaps, not an ounce fatter – Adrian associated excess weight with laziness, mental and physical. Their phone conversations had been stilted, as if there was so much to say that actually they couldn't say a word. She had asked about Harry. He had asked after Grace, whom he barely knew, and the weather. They had danced around the ruins of their marriage. Face to face it wasn't going to work either. Freddie wondered about Antonia Melhuish, but only vaguely. That white-hot flash of hurt and indignation had completely gone. She wasn't even curious now.

Adrian cleared his throat. He looked unfamiliar with contrition all over his face. 'Look here, Fred, I think I've made a ghastly mistake. All this Antonia Melhuish business. Some sort of wretched mid-life crisis, I suppose. Horribly self-indulgent, I know, and hurtful, I'm sure. But you being away has given me time to think about what I want, about what's important, and I'm sure now that it's you and Harry. And, well . . . us.'

She didn't respond.

He'd made the tea now, and he put the mug in front of her with something of a flourish. Then he sat down, leaning in eagerly, waiting for her response.

When none came, a fleeting look of bewilderment crossed his face, and he began again: 'So, I'm terribly sorry to have done it, messed you about and all that, but I want things to go back to the way they were before. I want us to put it all behind us, and . . . carry on.'

Freddie wasn't sure whether to laugh or cry. Could he really believe he was saying what she had longed to hear? Or that she was going to fall back into his arms, and his bed, to spend the next twenty years being grateful he'd chosen her over Antonia Melhuish? She enjoyed the power of her silence for another moment or two. Then she asked, 'What about Antonia?'

He sort of snorted. Evidently it was tiresome of her to mention Antonia when he had already explained himself. 'I've told you. A mistake.'

'And does she know this?'

'I shall tell her the moment you agree to take me back, fool that I've been, and give me a second chance.'

That had cost him, she knew. He had never been a man to admit to being a fool, and he was unaccustomed to begging. This was probably the nearest he would ever come to it.

Barely a month after he'd first delivered the news that had shocked her to the core, yet come as no surprise, she was looking at a man she no longer recognised. She felt almost stupid at the thought that she could ever have been in his thrall. She almost couldn't be bothered to be angry with him. It seemed hardly to matter. But then again . . . 'So let me get this straight.' Her voice was quiet, and she was looking him in the eye. 'Antonia Melhuish is sitting at home right now, waiting for you, without the slightest suspicion that you are over here telling me you'll drop her like a hot brick at my say-so.'

He started to speak, but she put up her hand.

'And you, cautious and careful man that you are, just wanted to make sure that this little set-up was going to work out before you gave her the elbow.'

Again he opened his mouth, but she went on: 'So presumably if I say yes we're off upstairs to celebrate with an undeniably good bonk, and then she gets the bullet.' She could swear his eyes had lit up. 'But if I say no, you're back over there before she's even missed you. You'd still get your bonk, am I right?'

Now he seemed downright confused. She could see

him struggling for a response – for a split second too long, although he hadn't stood a chance from the start.

'Off you go, then,' she said. 'With a bit of luck, the bed'll still be warm.'

'Freddie.'

'Don't you dare Freddie me.' She was glad the anger had surfaced at last. 'You weak, selfish, cowardly, prick-obsessed shit.' That was good. Tamsin would have been proud of it. She hadn't been faking it, either: that was what he seemed to her, right now.

Adrian's shock was genuine. He hadn't expected this, and he didn't know what to say next. The easiest explanation was that she was angry. And she had a right to be angry. His father had said she would be. Sexual jealousy was a powerful emotion; he understood that, and she was punishing him – which was probably, no, certainly, to be expected.

She'd come round.

She had to come round.

Now that he was reasonably sure he'd made up his mind, Adrian felt thwarted that things hadn't gone according to plan.

He'd give her time.

He stood up uncertainly. Going back to Antonia's now was not a good idea, so he supposed it would be the club. Not his parents' house. He was in bad odour there. Dad was bound to have told Mother, and she'd be terribly cross. Perhaps he'd ring a friend. He thought about Antonia Melhuish, and her tiny tight ass. God, Freddie was right. He *was* obsessed with his prick. And look what a mess it had got him into.

Freddie was bored with his floundering. She stood up too.

'Right. I suppose I'm throwing you out. I'm here for the whole of half-term week with Harry. Give me a day or two to explain things to him, and then you can come to see him. I'm going back to Boston on Sunday, after I've dropped him back at school, so you can come back here then.'

'What are you going to tell Harry?' He had the decency to sound anxious.

'I'll tell him what I think is best for him.' Freddie knew that sounded pompous. She thought suddenly, guiltily, of Matthew. When she spoke again, her voice was softer. 'Look, Adrian, we both need time to think. I won't tell Harry anything terminal, I promise. Perhaps we can talk again at the end of the week.'

Adrian took the olive twig. 'Okay.' He was unfamiliar with the feeling of fear, but he rather thought he might be experiencing it now. He didn't want her to tell him it was over for ever, and he didn't want her to tell Harry. He figured that leaving now would be his best chance.

Upstairs, he packed a holdall. When he came down she was sitting in the living room. 'I'm sorry, Freddie. I really am.'

She almost smiled. 'No more right now, Adrian. I'll call you.'

He nodded, and left.

It wasn't until the door had shut behind him that she realised he hadn't said he loved her, and he hadn't asked about America.

Matthew lunged across the back of the sofa to grab the phone on its third ring. After a restless night, he'd woken early and gone for a long run. Saturday mornings were always one of the hardest times. He couldn't train himself to sleep here alone, so he was always up, running round the common while everyone who had someone was still curled up in their arms, or making two mugs of tea, or arguing over different sections of the newspaper in bed. That was what he imagined, anyway, as he ran past houses with the curtains closed on all the happy people. He'd been making coffee when he heard the phone ring, and his heart raced faster than it had during the three miles round the common.

'It's me.'

The wrong me. He knew he sounded disappointed. 'Hiya, Tamsin. How are you?'

'Knackered and enormous, thanks for asking. I take it from that lacklustre welcome that she hasn't called but you thought I might be her.'

She always knew everything. 'No. Yes. Sorry, Tams. It *is* lovely to hear you, back on the right side of the pond.'

'She's got things to do, honey. Pick Harry up. Talk
to Adrian.'

'I know.'

'She'll call.'

'Yeah.' He wasn't so sure.

'So, here's the thing. Neil and the au pair from
heaven have taken the kids to the leisure lagoon, I'm
going to bed with Junior for a sleep, and then you're
coming over for supper. Unless you've had a better
offer this fine Saturday evening.'

'Nothing I wouldn't cancel for you.' They both
laughed. She always cheered him up. His mother
would have called her a tonic. She and Neil had been
his steady date on a Saturday night ever since Sarah
died. Them, or a DVD and a curry for one. God, he
was a sad git! 'Seven thirty?'

'See you then. Night-night.' She was stifling a yawn
as she put the phone down.

He took his coffee through to the lounge. It was a
beautiful day. The sun streamed in through the windows so that he could see the dust in the atmosphere.
Where it fell across his legs, which were stretched out
on the coffee table, it was hot, although it had felt
autumnal outside. The Saturday *FT* lay unread on his
lap. He was thinking about Freddie. He hadn't seen her
for two weeks. He would have missed her anyway – he
did when she took her family holiday each summer
with Adrian and Harry. That was always two weeks,
and when she got back she looked so good, tanned
golden by the sun. And she always seemed pleased to

see him. He tried not to think of her and Adrian alone, on holiday. It tortured him, the idea of them together. He rarely saw Adrian touch her, but if he did it was always sexual, always possessive. A hand squeezing her bum or, if he'd been drinking, he might put his hands under her arms to cup her breasts hungrily. He didn't think she minded, although he had scanned her face for traces of displeasure. It was pathetic, he knew, to imagine problems between them. He had a clear memory of a drunken Sunday afternoon in a pub garden, years ago, before Sarah had died. Before they'd even been married, he thought. They'd been all together, the Tenko girls. Drink, sunshine and his sleepy silence had meant they'd all but forgotten he was there too, and they were talking girl talk, about boys. It might have been mildly titillating if he hadn't been a bit drunk and very much in love with Sarah. But he'd never forgotten what Freddie had said. She'd been lying on her back, with one knee bent and the other across it, and she'd been giggling as she confessed, 'He's the best lover I've ever had. He can make me wet from across the room, and he can make me come in about two minutes' flat but he knows how to make it last two hours. And, what's more, he always knows which one I'm in the mood for.' Sarah had shrieked with vicarious embarrassment, and Freddie had laughed at her own boldness.

The conversation had moved on – Reagan had become aware that a couple of guys at a table nearby were listening, and begun telling some elaborate story about a guy she'd met at some conference, and the afternoon had degenerated. Tamsin had even been sick at some point, he thought. But he'd never forgotten what she'd said, and he supposed he'd remembered it every time he'd seen Adrian touch her. He wasn't sure he'd ever known jealousy like this before. It was angry, it was ugly, and it made his stomach ache.

And now he'd probably blown it. What a twat. Talk about rushing in! Shoving his tongue down her throat barely days after she'd found out about Adrian and that woman! *And* her parents. He really couldn't believe how stupid, desperate and clumsy he had been. All the nights he'd lain in bed thinking about that gorgeous liberating moment when he would tell her – show her – how he felt, and that was what he'd come up with: a cheap grope and a snog on a street corner when she was at possibly the most vulnerable point of her life. Well done, Matt. No wonder she hadn't rung him.

Harry was gorgeous. Her gorgeous boy. Guilt, fondness and having missed him made her think he was taller as he walked towards her, a bit broader too. But he felt familiar in her arms, in the brief hug he allowed her in the busy car park, given with the air of nonchalance she knew he did not feel.

Harry had missed her too. Dad was great, in a daddish sort of way. He was fine if you wanted to talk about sport, or stuff like that, but he was rubbish at feelings. Sometimes Harry felt almost like he was older than Dad.

Mum had promised she'd be back for half-term, and he was so glad she was. This was more normal, the two of them.

He threw his bag in the back seat and climbed in beside her, anxious to start the week of freedom.

They talked about school for the first few miles. Freddie knew the questions to ask that would mainline into his psyche, and they were absorbed for a while. It sounded like it had been a good term so far. He'd scored a few goals and tries, his marks were up in maths and science (they were always pretty high in English), and there was a new kid in his form, Michael, whom he seemed to like.

'Where does he live?' she asked.

'With his mother. His parents have split up. She lives in Bath, I think. His dad's some teacher thing, in Oxford. What are they called?'

'A professor?' Harry shook his head. 'A don?' He smiled. 'That's it. A don. Don't they have those in the Godfather, too?'

Freddie smiled. 'Same name. Slightly different job spec.'

Harry shrugged.

'Yeah! Well, that's why he's here. He was at some day school in Oxford, but now that his mum's in Bath they've sent him to school here. His mum says continuity is important for him now.'

The adult words sounded odd coming from Harry and Freddie looked sideways at him. He sounded so matter-of-fact.

He put the radio on. In her absence Adrian had retuned it to Five Live, and it took Harry a couple of minutes to find the white noise he preferred. She turned the volume down a little.

A few minutes later he asked: 'Is Dad at home?'

'No, he's away for a few days. He sent his love and says he'll see you later in the week.' She tried to keep her tone light, and Harry didn't look fazed. It wasn't all that different for him, she realised. Adrian had never lived his life around the school terms the way that she did. Then Freddie almost told him, but the first sentence didn't form properly in her mouth and the moment passed. She went on, quickly, 'How do you fancy going round to Tamsin and Neil's for dinner tonight? We don't have to, if you'd rather stay at home. We could get a video and a pizza, just hang out?'

'No, it'd be cool. I haven't seen Homey since the summer.' She was glad he wanted to go. Somehow, she didn't want to be at home, even with Harry.

She parked near Kensington High Street. On the first day of any holiday McDonald's was a ritual. Freddie sipped a milky coffee while Harry ate a burger and fries, then polished off a giant strawberry milkshake. While Adrian's lack of interest in Cape Cod had spoken volumes, Harry's was almost comforting. She'd been gone. She'd come home. Simple.

He'd outgrown his trainers – '*Already?*' – and they spent an hour in a sports shop choosing an absurdly expensive new pair, then bought a new X box game and a hoodie. Freddie loved being with him. Lastly they bought a big bunch of yellow tulips from the flower stall on the corner by the church for Tamsin, and drove home. When Harry kicked off his shoes and left them on the hall floor where they had fallen, in his eagerness to get to the computer, she didn't call him back to straighten them. She loved his mess in the house.

She gave Tamsin a quick call while she ran a hot bath. 'Still up for feeding us?'

'Absolutely! So long as "us" means you and Harry. How'd it go with Adrian?'

'Tell you later. I've made him go away for most of the week.'

'Good. Give you and Harry some peace and space. Does he know?'

'No. I told him Adrian's got stuff to do, and he's bought it, I think.'

'Well, that's fine for now.'

'What time?'

'Seven thirty?' She heard Tamsin hesitate, as if she was going to say more. 'What?'

'Nothing. Seven thirty.'

It was closer to eight when Freddie parked the Audi outside the Bernards', blocking in Tamsin's car. She'd fallen asleep on her bed, wrapped in a bath sheet, after a long, fragrant bath. She'd woken in the dark to find that Harry had covered her with the counterpane, and she could hear the television in his room. She had roused herself and padded to see him. 'Sorry, sweetheart. Some welcome home.'

'Don't worry, Mum.' He grinned at her. 'Long flight . . . and you *are* getting on a bit!'

'Oy.' She tapped him lightly on the head with the hairbrush she was holding. 'Watch it!'

'I was going to wake you up in a couple of minutes.'

'Well, I woke up by myself, despite my advanced age. Shift yourself. We're due there in ten minutes, and you should shower the *eau-de*-school off yourself before we go.'

She was ready ten minutes before he was. God, she thought, is this pre-teen behaviour? It wasn't long since he'd had to be frogmarched into the bathroom. The water ran for ages. And when he appeared, hair gel was in evidence. She didn't dare say anything, but he looked like Tintin. 'Ready?'

'You look nice, Mum.'

Bless him. Did she? Her hair had dried funny, so she'd just pulled it back and secured it with an elastic. She was wearing jeans and a top she'd bought in Boston. But bless him anyway. 'You don't look so bad yourself. Let's go, or our pasta will be in the dog.'

The jet-lag must have been worse than she'd thought. She hadn't remembered that Matthew would be there. He opened the door to them, with a goldfish bowl of red wine in each hand. He smiled shyly and proffered one, which Freddie took gratefully.

'Hello, you,' he said.

'Hi.' Freddie hated herself for feeling awkward. This was one house where that was never supposed to happen. And he was one person she had never thought it would happen with . . .

'Hey, Matt.' Harry pushed her into the hall, and hugged him briefly, then bounded up the stairs. 'Homey up here?'

'You look great.' Another compliment.

Freddie smoothed her hair. 'Do I? I fell asleep on the bed after a bath and woke up looking like Worzel Gummidge.'

'You look great,' Matthew repeated. Why did women always do that? Did they not know that men only said that when they meant it?

Tamsin bustled into the narrow hallway, offering rescue. 'Hiya, gorgeous. Beautiful flowers. Thanks.' She kissed her. 'Did you get a kip?'

'A couple of hours. You?'

'All morning. Bliss. Then Neil joined me for a couple of hours this afternoon, and Meghan took the kids to Burger King.' She was grinning suggestively.

Freddie held up her hands. 'Too much information.'

'Jealous,' Tamsin declared. She pulled her into the family room, then retreated to the kitchen.

Neil appeared from upstairs with a freshly bathed and powdered Flannery, who obligingly kissed everyone goodnight, with a wet open mouth, before being carted off to bed. Willa was in her pyjamas too, lying on the sofa, thumb in mouth, watching *Stars in their Eyes*. Freddie kissed her. 'Hey, poppet.' Willa waved a brief response.

Freddie moved into the kitchen, where Tamsin was stirring a huge frying-pan of onions, peppers, bacon and garlic. A big bowl of salad was on the table, along with a couple of ciabattas and a saucer of olive oil. She was drinking orange juice from a wine glass.

Matthew had lingered with Willa, watching a traffic warden from Walthamstow transformed into Neil Diamond.

'Everything okay between you and Matt?' Tamsin enquired.

'Why shouldn't it be?'

'Just wondering. So you've sorted things out?'

'Nothing to sort out. Stop asking me. Everything's fine.'

'That's an Adrian "fine", if you don't mind my saying so.'

'I do mind.'

'Okay. Sorry. Enough said.' Tamsin smiled. 'It's just that I'm not about to slave over an absolutely delicious pasta bake if there's going to be dissent among the ranks at the table.'

'There *isn't*!' Freddie said exasperatedly.

'Fine!'

It went away over dinner. Tamsin was a great cook, of the chaotic, and usually drunken Galloping Gourmet school of cookery, and the meal was delicious. Homer and Harry were loud and hilarious. The friendship between the two boys gave Freddie and Tamsin great pleasure. Neil and Matthew egged them on, until

Tamsin made her most disapproving face, and the men moved on to one of their enthralling on-going conversations about the congestion charge and its effect on rush-hour traffic. Freddie let the cotton wool of time change wrap itself around her and listened happily to the others. Adrian wasn't missing from this set-up because he had never really fitted into it.

Eventually Matthew said, 'I'm going to clear up. You three relax.'

'I'll help.' Freddie stood up and started to pile plates. Tamsin and Neil exchanged a glance. Freddie caught it and wrinkled her nose at them.

'Great idea! Come on, Mother,' Neil said, 'you and me and a remote control on the sofa.'

'I'll bring some coffee through in a minute,' Freddie told them.

Matthew felt like a teenager at a dance. He had assumed Freddie would go through with the others to the family room, and now that she hadn't, he was afraid of what she might want to say to him, alone in the kitchen.

'Have you been to see Rebecca?' he asked.

'No.'

'Do you think you will when you go back?'

'You think I should, don't you?'

'There's no "should" about it, Fred. I think you need to.'

'You sound like Tamsin.'

'Tamsin's a wise old bird.'

Freddie smiled. 'And so are you?'

'Not always.' Silence. 'Sorry about Boston, Freddie. I was way out of line.'

Did he mean out of line for kissing her – or out of line for kissing her *then*? Freddie didn't know. 'It's fine.' Oh, God, now she really was starting to sound like Adrian. She wished she could wipe that bloody word out of her vocabulary. She was concentrating on folding napkins that would need to go into the washing-machine anyway and didn't look at him. Matthew put his hand over hers. 'No, Freddie. I mean it. Truly. I don't want it to spoil things.'

She looked up now, into his serious brown eyes. 'It won't. It hasn't. We're friends, Matt. Great friends.'

He gave a tight little smile, but his eyes were sad.

'To prove it, why don't we do something this week?' She wanted to make his eyes smile. 'Harry's going to be here with Homer and the dreaded skateboard on Monday and Tuesday, so I'm Dougie No Mates. What about a sneaky afternoon movie? Or lunch. A gallery?'

Matthew's back was to her now – he was filling the sink with soapy water. ' 'Fraid not. I've got to go to Leicester for work. I'm off on Monday morning.'

She felt a sting of disappointment and, just for a second, wondered whether he was lying. 'For how long?'

His voice sounded strange. 'Couple of days at least. Maybe all week. It's pretty complicated.'

Yes, it bloody well was. Everything was pretty

complicated just now. 'But you'll be back at the weekend?'

'Probably.'

'I'm not flying until Sunday. What about Saturday?'
She flicked the back of his thigh with one of the
napkins. 'Can't wriggle out of it that easily!'

He turned, and this time the smile was wider. 'Okay,
Saturday. You choose what to do.'

'Well, Harry's got to be back for sport at lunchtime,
so say I pick you up at two-ish, and we'll take it from
there?'

'It's a date. Well, not a date!'

They looked at each other and laughed, the tension
broken.

'You silly idiot!' Freddie said.

Later, Matthew lay on the sofa in his house. The light
was off, but he'd flicked on the stereo. He was listening
to U2 in the dark. Slight of hand twist of fate, on a bed
of nails she makes me wait, and I wait without you . . .
He was too wired to sleep. It was like he got a charge
from being with her, and it lasted for hours after she'd
gone. He just kept thinking, Saturday, next Saturday.

Tamsin was rubbing Nivea into her face as she walked
into the bedroom from the landing. She kicked off her
slippers and sat on the edge of the bed, pontificating all
the time. Neil loved this bit of the day: the world,
according to Tamsin. If the television in the corner was
on she would talk over Paxman, ad lib at Parkinson,

shout at newsreaders and politicians. If they were watching a thriller, or a murder mystery, she would exclaim theatrically after ten minutes and write the name of the killer on a piece of paper, which she would hide under the pillows until the end. Then she would produce it triumphantly to prove she had known whodunit all along. She rearranged all the conversations of the evening into headlines and nuggets for him to digest, peppered with predictions, judgements, opinion. He loved her. She was a nightmare, but he loved her. Now, predictably enough, she was talking about Freddie and Matthew.

'They seemed all right, didn't they?' Neil knew he was not supposed to answer. 'I think he's making a Herculean effort not to let on how much it hurt, what happened in Boston. And I don't think she's forgotten it either, but I honestly thought she'd kill me when she got here and found him. Still, she doesn't know what I know, does she? Well, not how much I know. Come to think of it, she doesn't know what there is to know, not really. She knows he kissed her, of course, but she doesn't know what was behind it, does she? Not really. D'you know?'

Neil didn't. Not at all. He knew his head was pounding a bit with all the red wine, and the early start, and the morning spent at the leisure lagoon. And he knew that he wanted to go to sleep. And that, really, when all was said and done, he didn't mind whether Matthew and Freddie were happy together or happy apart as long as they both ended up happy, although he tended to think they might be happier together. But he was wise enough also to know that none of these things would impress his wife. He rolled to her side of the bed, put his head against the small of her back and sniffed Nivea and Euthymol toothpaste appreciatively. She'd been gone too long, and now he just wanted to hold her and go to sleep.

'I think they'll be okay, you know?' She left a gap for his response. 'Neil?' He was asleep, his head against her. When she stood up, he smiled and rolled back to his side of the bed. When she climbed in, he rearranged himself against her, one hand on her belly, across his unborn child.

Tamsin rolled her eyes affectionately. Hopeless. If she'd been the praying type, she'd have said a little one for Freddie and Matthew.

Freddie stood at Harry's bedroom door and looked at him under the Harry Potter duvet, breathing quietly. The early-evening nap, and something else, had taken away any sleepiness, and she was on her way back to bed with a DVD. She'd scanned the shelves, eschewing *Gone with the Wind*, an old favourite, and *When Harry Met Sally*. She'd settled on *Friends*, series Four, episodes 1–4. It was the mashed potatoes and hot chocolate of the DVD world – pure comfort watching. She was glad to be home. America had been a big shock. Grace. Her father's cancer. This business about Rebecca. Reagan. Actually a big shock was an understatement. Distance made clearer how extraordinary the last month had been. Home was familiar. Harry was here. They would have a great week. And Matthew was here. Was that part of it? She hoped she had done the right thing in fixing to see him on Saturday.

Harry turned over, and squinted sleepily into the light that came from behind her. 'Mum?'

'Sorry, honey. Go back to sleep.'

'Love you, Mum.'

She hoped he never became too old or too cool to say that. 'I love you too. Night.'

And they did have a great week. They went to the cinema. They went ice-skating. They did a bit more shopping. One evening, after they had eaten dinner on their laps in front of some incomprehensible reality-TV show to which Harry seemed addicted, she told him about Rebecca. She needed him to understand why she was going back to America – and was anxious that he shouldn't feel deserted. And, on some level, she wanted to see how this revelation impacted on him.

'Wow! That's pretty big!'

'Yes, it is.'

'So why didn't your dad tell you before?'

'I think he was trying to protect me.'

'Why did you need protecting?'

'Because she left when I was very young – too young to remember her. And she wasn't a part of my life. I guess he thought finding out about her might upset everything, you know?'

'I suppose. But you're a grown-up, Mum. You have been for ages. He could have told you before.'

She couldn't argue with that.

'Are you going to see her? Is that why you're going back?'

'I think I have to, don't you?'

'I guess.'

He went quiet for a while, and she wondered if his attention had returned to the television. Then he said, 'I can't imagine not having a mum,' and smiled at her.

On Wednesday morning she rang Adrian and told him he could have Harry on Thursday and Friday. 'I haven't told him anything, so take him to your parents or something, make out like everything's okay.'

Apparently Adrian took this as a positive sign. For once he didn't huff and puff about short notice. In fact, he sounded grateful. 'Okay. Dad and I'll play golf with him at Dad's club. He'd love that. And everything will be fine, Freddie, you'll see.'

Please! She hadn't said anything. She knew she was procrastinating, but she didn't want this week to be about confrontation, decision and momentous events. She wanted it to be a rest from all that.

She left Harry at home with Barbara, the cleaning lady, so she wouldn't have to see Adrian when he picked him up. She told Harry she had to see a lawyer about her father's will. So far, Harry hadn't seemed suspicious: he was too excited about playing a round at his grandfather's club. He'd never been allowed to go there before.

Freddie went to her health club and swam a hundred lengths, slowly and gracefully. Then she sat in the Jacuzzi, head back, eyes closed, and let the warm water bubble around her. She felt more relaxed than she had in ages. She refused to let herself think about Adrian, Matthew, Reagan or her parents. She made her mind empty, and it felt good.

A back, neck and shoulder massage, a pedicure and a facial later, she stood drying her hair in front of the mirror in the changing rooms. Not bad for a thirty-six-year-old, she thought. Not bad at all. Normally she didn't go in for pampering and vanity. Maybe she should do a bit more of it.

And then it was Saturday, and she was driving that hateful drive in the wrong direction. Harry had been quiet last night. They'd all gone to Pizza Express – Neil, Tamsin, Freddie, Harry, Homer and Willa – for an early supper, then Tamsin had taken Willa home, and the rest of them had gone to see some action movie in which the villain had an implausible foreign accent and the hero had time to quip as his life hung in the balance. Harry hadn't said much on the drive home, and he was quiet now. He hadn't even put any music on.

'Mum?' Suddenly she thought she knew what was coming, and felt sick.

'Yes, darling?'

'Are you and Dad going to get a divorce?'

She looked at his face, then at the clock on the dashboard. He had to be back within an hour and she wanted to pull over. Bloody cars. Why did she have to have all these bloody difficult conversations in bloody cars? She felt a flash of irritation – what the hell had Adrian said? It was her own fault, though: she should have talked to Harry before he went off with his father. Did she mean to get her version in first?

'Why would you ask me that?' Crappy response – she knew it even as the words came out.

His face confirmed it. 'Don't ask me a question. I asked you first.'

She needed to stop and face him. 'Hang on a minute.' She indicated left, went off the A3 and into RHS Wisley. She parked in one of the diagonal spots. Old people were milling about in cagoules and sensible shoes.

'Am I allowed to ask what your dad has told you?'

'He hasn't said anything.'

'So why, then?'

He was cross. 'Because I've been home all week, and you and Dad have hardly spoken to each other. Because you went out on purpose when he came to pick me up the other day. Because you've been weird all week. You've been in America for ages, and you're going back tomorrow. I'm not stupid, Mum. I'm not a little kid.'

Clearly he wasn't. Freddie felt foolish. Of course there had been signs that a sensitive child would pick up on. How incredibly naïve and unkind of her not to see that. How selfish.

But he wasn't so cross that he didn't let her put her hand on his. For the first time in ages, she felt tears rising. 'I'm sorry, Mum. Please don't cry. Please!' he implored. But they had started now, and however inappropriate she thought they were, she couldn't hold them back. She struggled for control, biting her lip, and Harry spoke in the gap. 'It'd be okay if you were. Lots of boys' parents are. Michael's fine about it now, about his parents . . .'

He sounded desperate. This was all wrong. Freddie wanted him to cry, or go into a strop, not try to look after her. He was too young for that.

She couldn't believe what a mess she had made of this. She'd had all week to talk to him, and now they were going to have to do it in ten minutes on the way back to school, just before she had to leave him again.

With a huge effort she stopped herself crying. 'Harry, sweetheart, I'm okay. Sorry. So sorry. It's really mean of me to go to pieces on the way back to school. You know how sad I get about leaving you.'

Harry nodded.

'Listen, darling. You're right – I'm sorry, I should have told you. Dad and I are having problems, grown-up problems. They are nothing – *nothing* – whatsoever to do with you, and you must understand that. They are between your dad and me. I don't know what will happen – truly I don't. But it's all come at a bad time for me, with my father dying, and all these things to sort out in America. I can't fix everything all at once, so I've asked your father to give me some space to think about things, and he's agreed.' That sounded plausible to her. Would it to Harry? 'I don't want you to worry about it when you're at school. You need to remember that both of us, your father and I love you very much, and nothing will ever ever change that.' God, she sounded like a bad film. But Harry was nodding, listening. 'And I promise there'll be no more not talking to you. I'll tell you what's happening, I promise. Okay?'

'Okay. I'm sorry I made you cry, Mum.'

She put out her arms and he lay against her shoulder. 'You didn't make me cry, big boy. You – you're the very best bit of my life. Do you hear? You make me happiest.'

He squeezed, and she squeezed back, and they stayed like that for a minute. An elderly couple looked inquisitively through the window and smiled benevolently at them.

Eventually she pulled away and searched his face for reaction. 'You okay?'

He nodded, and the smile was real. She had reassured him, she could tell. He wasn't pretending.

Matthew knew she'd been crying: her eyes were red-rimmed, and her nostrils pink. She looked so vulnerable, and he wanted to touch her. She shrugged off his expression.

'Don't you dare be kind to me,' she said. 'I know that face. I'll start again, and then I won't stop and we'll have a shitty afternoon.'

No, we won't. I'll hold you. 'Okay. Absolutely no kindness whatsoever. Why are you late, you rude cow?'

Freddie burst out laughing. 'From the sublime to the ridiculous!'

'No, really, you are late. I've booked seats at the Electric Cinema. If you don't move your bloomin' ass we'll miss the trailers.'

'And the trailers are the best bit.'

'Exactly! Let's go.'

He wore his glasses in the cinema. They were wire-framed and round, and made him look like a school-boy.

It was comforting to sit beside him, but she wasn't really watching the film. She'd made a mess of things – she could see how selfish it had been to let things slide this week. She had been a wimp. And now she'd left Harry at school, worried about what was happening to his family. It wasn't like her not to put him first.

Afterwards they went to the bar.

'What did you make of that?'

'I wasn't really watching.'

'I know. Boy fell for girl. Girl fell for boy's best friend. Some confusion. Some random violence. Some soul-searching. Some Motown soundtrack. Boy gets girl. There! Now, what is it?'

'It's Harry. He asked me this morning if Adrian and I were getting a divorce. And I cried.'

'What did you tell him?'

'I told him nothing was resolved yet and that we both loved him. Blah-blah-blah.'

'And is that true? About nothing being resolved?'

'I don't know.' She put her face in her hands. 'I'm so confused I can't think straight. I'm so stressed that I feel like I'm permanently on the edge of some terrifying abyss. Like if I breathe out I'll topple over.'

'About Adrian?'

'Not just Adrian. It's everything. I'm so angry with my dad for dying before we sorted anything out. Finding things out after he's gone makes me so frustrated I can't begin to describe it. He never faced anything. We had this horrible, dysfunctional relationship where he found it almost impossible to express any affection for me, but I found a room in his house that's practically a shrine to me. He had this marriage – because in effect that's exactly what it was – with Grace, and I never knew about it. And Grace – she brought me up – was the nearest thing I had to a normal parent and I did the same thing to her that he did to me. As soon as I could I ran like hell from both of them. And look where I ran! Straight into the arms of someone just like him. Another emotionally retarded, domineering man. Somewhere I lost myself – or that's what it feels like – and for the last fifteen years I haven't been me. Leaving Adrian isn't just leaving Adrian, it's leaving the me I was when I was with him. And I'm just so frightened that the other me is gone for ever.'

She looked at him, apparently imploring him to understand.

And in a way he did. When he'd lost Sarah he'd lost himself. He remembered a speech he had heard someone make at a wedding. The speaker had given an analogy for marriage that had stayed with Matthew. The man had been talking about the city of Koblenz in Germany, and about a point where two rivers – the Rhine and another, he couldn't remember which – converged. Apparently at the place they met you could still see their two distinct colours, and after they merged, the colours stayed separate until, further up, they became a new colour. The speaker said that he had always thought of his marriage as being two colours that mixed well and made a more beautiful one. Adrian's colours had muddied Freddie's. That was what she meant. And she was frightened of what might remain when you took them away.

But – like Tamsin, Neil and Reagan – he had known her before Adrian, and he would know her afterwards. She would be fine. She just had to believe it.

'You're in a muddle, that's all. You've got to give yourself time to sort it out. And you can only do that if you stop giving yourself such a hard time about it. You've got nothing to feel guilty about.' He put his arm around her, and she leaned into him. 'It takes time. And you have to find the right place to start.'

'I don't know where that is. Do *you* know?' she asked.

He thought for a bit. 'It has to be your mother. You have to find out what's there, what it tells you about your father. Adrian's not in any position to start throwing his weight around so he can wait. And Harry will be fine.'

'I'm frightened, though.'

'Of your mother?'

'Of what I'll feel about her.'

'That doesn't mean it's right not to find out.'

His mind was working furiously. More than anything he wanted to say he would go with her. Tamsin was back here for good now, and Reagan – well, Reagan didn't feel like the safest pair of hands. He thought about work, and whether he could take more time off. Would he frighten her if he offered? He remembered Boston, and wondered what Tamsin would say.

And then he said it anyway.

'I'll come with you.'

'Don't be daft. You can't – you've got work.'

'You'll need to give me a day or two to square things away, but indispensable-man syndrome is something I've never suffered from. They can manage without me for a while. If I can get a flight I could be there Tuesday or Wednesday – if you want me.' He felt unbelievably nervous.

'I can't ask you to do that,' Freddie said.

'You didn't. Stop worrying and just tell me if you want me to come with you.'

She sat up, apart from him. Yes she did. She did very badly.

'Yes, please. Thank you.'

She said it again, later, when she dropped him off. 'I can't believe how you've all rallied round. I feel so lucky in my friends.'

'We love you. Besides, you all did it for me.'

They hugged briefly. When she pulled back she kissed his cheek, a little too near to his mouth. For an instant, she wanted to kiss him properly, and it surprised her. But he wasn't going to make that mistake again. He opened his passenger door, and the moment passed through it.

Home again, she e-mailed Harry and Adrian.

To: *AdrianSinclair@hotmail.com*
Adrian,
The coast is clear at home. I'm on the Sunday flight back to Boston. We will talk when I'm back. I'm sorry to be vague, but right now that is the best I can do. I'm not trying to punish you.

  Please look after Harry for me. He asked me today if we were getting a divorce. I told him we were having problems but that we both loved him. I know that this much is true. I'd rather you didn't go into details, but I didn't want you to be surprised if he asked you the same when you go down next.

  Freddie

To: *HarrySinclair@hotmail.com*
Dear Harry – I hope the matches went well this afternoon. Daddy has promised to come down and watch you lots while I am in the

States. I'll be home soon, darling, but I know we will speak lots and you can email whenever you like. When we are next together, I promise I'll tell you all about what's been going on over here. It makes *EastEnders* look like *The Waltons*, I can tell you – do you even know what *The Waltons* is?

Please don't worry, Harry. I love you very, very much (and I hope no one is reading this soppy stuff over your shoulder!).

Let me know if you want any CDs sending over!

Mum XX

Half-term: Cape Cod

It was another beautiful afternoon. Reagan had been lying in the dunes for hours. She'd taken a book with her, some weighty tome she'd been meaning to read for years – there'd been a copy on one of Freddie's dad's bookshelves. But she hadn't managed a page. She read the first two paragraphs three times, then gave up and lay back on the blanket she had brought with her.

It wasn't the book. It was her head. For years and years, so long she couldn't remember when it hadn't been true, her head had been full – of work, Matthew, everything – and now it felt as if it had shut itself down. She hadn't listened to the radio since Freddie and Tamsin had gone, or turned on the television.

Every morning she walked into the town, bought that day's food and stopped for coffee, and pancakes smeared with unsalted white butter and real maple syrup, talking to no one unless she had to. She hadn't seen Eric again, and she hoped she wouldn't. It was as if what had happened with him had shaken her awake. She didn't want to do it any more. She wanted to believe she was worth more than that.

Her mobile phone was switched off, shoved into a

drawer. The phone in the house didn't ring. Grace was with her sister, in Vermont, and no one at home or at work, apart from Freddie and Tamsin, knew where she was.

She was sleeping well, waking refreshed and energised, and was eating like a horse. Big plates of pasta and tomato sauce that she made with olive oil and fresh basil, with pine nuts and creamy buffalo mozzarella on top. She was sure she could feel herself getting stronger.

Hunger brought her in from the beach now. She had bought prawns in town this morning, a head of garlic, and some tiny potent chillies. She was going to fry them in butter, eat them with a hunk of bread and a rocket salad, perhaps a glass of oaky chardonnay, then maybe have a nap. A car was parked just down the road. It was duck egg blue, which made it remarkable, and someone was sitting in it, but they didn't get out when she approached the house, and she thought no more of it.

This morning she had hung out some washing – for the first time in for ever: she'd smiled at herself as she'd tied Grace's floral apron, with the deep peg pocket, round her waist. It was probably dry now, fluttering impossibly white on the line at the side of the house. She put down her bag and the blanket, then picked up the wicker basket she had left on the steps up to the veranda.

Coming back, she saw that the pretty car was still there. The driver's door opened, but the occupant was hesitating. Reagan's first reaction was annoyance. A visitor wasn't in her plans today – or any day.

After what felt like an interminable stand-off, a woman got out. She was tall and big. Not amorphous, lumpy big, but large. Large chest, large hips, but still with a waist. She was sort of glamorous, in a Bohemian way, all skimming fabric and shell earrings. A bright scarf was arranged round her shoulders, and her hair was silver. A natural camp leader – you could spot them a mile off.

She walked towards Reagan, and as she did, Reagan was struck. This had to be her. This woman was just like Freddie – she walked like Freddie, erect, graceful. And the nearer she got, the more obvious the resemblance became.

The woman – Rebecca – was looking her up and down, searching her face for clues. She's wondering if I'm Freddie, Reagan thought, and walked forward with the basket on one hip. She'll see I'm not her, that I couldn't be.

When they were about a metre apart, Rebecca's face changed. Disappointment or relief?

Reagan stretched out one hand. 'I'm Reagan.'

'I'm Rebecca.' They shook, awkwardly. 'I'm—'

'Freddie's mother. You had to be.' Reagan struggled for what to say next. 'You look a lot like her.'

Rebecca didn't answer.

'I'm a friend of Freddie's. I came over with her when her father died. To help out. I'm a lawyer, you see . . . and . . .' Her voice died away.

'Is Freddie here?'

'No.' Now she was sure it was disappointment on Rebecca's face. 'She's gone back to England for a week or so to see Harry. It's the half-term holiday at home.'

'I hadn't realised.'

'No.' That, at least, Reagan got. Mothers had this weird calendar thing – they didn't talk in seasons or months, they talked in terms and school holidays. Like you were supposed to know. 'Second week of February?' 'Of course, that's half-term.' For years Reagan had known when these crucial dates were so that she could avoid being anywhere near an airport or a ski resort – the prices were twice as high and they were full of bawling kids and their parents, mothers in unflattering comfortable clothes and fathers weighed down by rucksacks full of toys.

'And Grace?'

Reagan shook her head. 'In Vermont. She went up after the funeral for a break. It's just me here, I'm afraid.'

Rebecca smiled awkwardly. 'I'm sorry. I should have called.'

'Not the easiest call in the world to make, I guess?'

'No . . . I probably shouldn't have come at all – should have waited for her to come to me. If that's what she wanted to do . . .' She was looking at the house now. 'I was just . . . curious. I wanted to see her. Got in the car this morning and ended up here.'

Reagan didn't know what to say.

'Is she . . . is she very upset?' Rebecca asked.

'She's pretty messed up. It's a lot to take in. First of all her father died. Did you know he was ill? She didn't. Found out afterwards, which wasn't nice for her. She was still reeling from that when she found out that the mother she hasn't seen for God knows how long is alive and well and living thirty miles up the road. How do you think she feels? I'd say "upset" was an understatement.' She tried not to barrack, but she was surprised by how angry she felt on Freddie's behalf. 'I'm glad she's not here. And yes, I think you should have waited for her to get in touch with you. You've gone all this time without doing it, so why now?'

Her tone had been harsh, and she expected Rebecca would be upset by it, but the other woman seemed calm. The situation had made Reagan red in the face, and her heart was racing, but Rebecca looked as cool and unflustered as she had walking across the lawn.

'You and she must be very good friends,' Rebecca said.

'We are. Extremely.'

'And you don't want to see her hurt.'

'See her *more* hurt.'

Rebecca's head inclined in acknowledgement of that truth. And then she smiled. 'You're right. I have no business being here. It's best that she isn't. I'll go.'

Reagan nodded formally.

'I'll let you decide whether to tell her I came or not. Clearly you know her best.' There was nothing sarcastic or defensive in the way she said it. 'But if you do mention it, please tell her I'd like to meet her . . . very much. I presume she knows where she can find me.'

Reagan nodded again.

'Thank you, Reagan. I'm sorry, again, to disturb you.' She turned and went back across the lawn. Reagan didn't want to watch her get into the car and drive off. She was embarrassed by the confrontation, surprised by her own involvement, and disturbed by Rebecca's apparent detachment. She went inside, and closed the door behind her.

She'd have to tell Freddie, of course. She looked at the phone, did the quick calculation of time. Then she realised she needn't ring. It would be better to tell her when she got back.

She didn't sleep that afternoon. She lay on the swing seat on the veranda and thought about mothers. It was probably what she had most in common with Freddie. With Tamsin it was all about the mothers. Tamsin was close to her own and had always been certain that motherhood was her true destiny. She had been conditioned to find a mate and repeat the cycle that had treated her so well. Sarah had come from an ordinary family, and had always been a bit of a daddy's girl, but having kids was always part of her plan, and had figured in the dreams the Tenko Club had described to each other late at night.

Reagan had almost envied Freddie for not having a mother. She herself had one, but the connection the others talked about had always eluded and mystified her. She didn't tell her mother things. She wasn't interested in what her mother thought. She wasn't a touchstone, a sounding-board or a refuge. She was a middle-aged woman, and she always had been, who dressed in unflattering shirtwaister dresses and ugly shoes, and had been married to her father since 1959. Before that she'd had no life to speak of. Which wasn't to say that Reagan's father was her life's great passion, or indeed the children of that union. Reagan didn't think her mother had an ounce of passion in her. She had about five facial expressions, at least three of which were almost indistinguishable from each other, and none of which used many muscles. She said things like 'Whatever you think, dear,' and 'I'm not one to interfere.' And she bloody well wasn't. She hadn't interfered once in Reagan's life, hadn't expressed any concern about the plain, shy, bookish schoolgirl; had let her go off to university ill-prepared for the world. She hadn't even murmured when Reagan had emerged, three years later, transformed. When Reagan had taken her first boyfriend home, at twenty-three, and announced that they would be sharing a room, she had acquiesced instantly and moved the towels she had laid out in the guest room. When Reagan had had noisy sex with him well into the night, her mother had risen the next morning with a timid 'Sleep well, dear?'

When shown round Reagan's first flat – one bedroom, in an up-and-coming neighbourhood, which she had paid for herself and decorated in white with Sarah, Freddie and Tamsin's help – she had said it was 'nice'.

When Reagan was made a partner, only the second

woman in her early thirties ever to be invited at her firm, her father had cried, and her mother had said it was 'lovely'. Her mother kept her graduation photograph in an album in the dining room, which was used twice a year.

She didn't 'get' Reagan, and Reagan had given up trying to 'get' her. There was nothing there. In camp, she'd have whinged and wailed herself into catatonia.

When she was younger she had tried to imagine why her mother felt so little about so much. But there was nothing. Her mother was living out a bland, tepid life, and she didn't know that it should make her unhappy and dissatisfied. Over the years, Reagan's irritation had turned to rage, then pity, and settled on nonchalance – sometimes even envy; her mother didn't torture herself.

Freddie had never missed her mother, or so it seemed to Reagan. She was always so blasé about it. 'You can't miss what you never had,' she would say. 'Grace has been great.' She was so independent – Reagan had been dazzled by that when they first met. She had seemed so sussed at eighteen, and so strong. It was attractive and exciting.

She envied Freddie the glamorous story. How much cooler to say that your mother had deserted you as a tiny child than that your mother wore print polyester and meant nothing to you.

Reagan remembered her sense of betrayal when Harry had been born. Freddie had discovered motherhood, and for a while she was just like the others.

Reagan had never wanted children. Never once had that umbilical uterine pull. She was depressed at Harry's arrival. Freddie, Sarah and Tamsin probably thought it was because she wanted a baby too, but they were wrong.

Now she felt jealousy again, gnawing at the corners of her new strength. Rebecca had looked interesting, warm. And now Freddie might get a mother after all.

Cape Cod

Reagan didn't tell her. She meant to: she told herself she had to. But she couldn't do it. Not when Freddie got back and announced that Matthew was coming over.

'Again?' Freddie looked taken aback by her tone, and Reagan tried to soften it. 'Does he not have a job? And all these flights? That's not cheap.' Freddie hadn't thought of that. She felt selfish for the umpteenth time. And then irritated – why was Reagan making her feel so defensive?

'You can talk!' Freddie sounded defensive.

'I'm not working, and I only paid for one return flight. He's back and forth like a yo-yo. It must be driving them mad at his office.'

'But think of the air miles!'

Reagan decided to let it go, and smiled at her friend's attempt at humour.

'What did you get up to while we were gone?' Freddie asked.

'Blissful nothing.' And then the lie was out and it was too late: 'Barely talked to a soul, apart from to buy food and order coffee.'

★   ★   ★

Later, Freddie tried again. 'The real reason Matt's coming back is because he's coming to Provincetown with me.'

Reagan arched her eyebrows.

'With us, I mean, if you'll come too? I'm going to find my mother.'

'Why?'

She had been the first person to ask that question. Everyone else, Matthew, Tamsin, Neil, saw it as necessary. It wasn't 'why' with them – it was 'when'. But Freddie tried to answer. 'Because I need to. I mean, for all these years I haven't known where she was—'

'Yeah, and you've always said you didn't miss her.'

'I didn't know there was anything to miss. And I was happy. But now I know that she's there, I can't really not go, not find out. Surely you understand that?'

Reagan shrugged.

'It will be like an itch I haven't scratched. And it will get worse and worse. I don't know what it will mean, I don't know what it will change. But I have to do it.'

Reagan said nothing.

Freddie couldn't stand her friend's silence. 'Don't you think?'

Reagan's voice was less harsh now. 'I don't know, Freddie. I suppose I understand what you mean about the itch thing, but you've got to ask yourself what it's going to do for you. What can she possibly tell you about why she deserted you that will make it okay, that will make sense to you? Don't you think it might make everything worse? You should think carefully before you meet her, not do it because other people think it's a good idea.'

The 'other people' were clearly Matthew, Tamsin and Neil, and Freddie wondered fleetingly whether Reagan was taking a position. She tried to remind herself that Reagan was her friend too.

She'd thought it might even do Reagan good to be here on her own, and when she'd come out of the house to greet the taxi earlier she had looked fantastic – refreshed, relaxed and softened somehow. Why had talking about Matthew, Tamsin and her mother brought all the scratchiness and resentment to the surface again?

Reagan didn't go with them. She'd woken up with a headache, she claimed, and a run along the beach hadn't blown it away. Freddie wasn't surprised. She'd been funny with Matthew, too. When he arrived he'd tried to kiss her but she'd turned her cheek at the wrong moment and he'd ended up holding her elbow and kissing her ear. She'd rubbed the kiss off in an irritable childish gesture.

'What's with her?' Matthew had said, when they were in the car and had negotiated out of Chatham on the way to Provincetown. It was a beautiful day. The turning leaves were spectacular against a cobalt sky, and the sunshine was warm on their faces.

'God knows! I'm beginning to wonder why she bothered coming here at all.'

Matthew raised an eyebrow.

'That sounds mean, and I'm sorry. I do know why she came – because she's a good friend and a good person, and she wanted to be here for me.' She said that as if she were reading it from a card. 'But, Christ, she can be hard work when she wants to be. It was much easier when Tamsin was here – she's brilliant at jollying Reagan out of herself, and she doesn't take any shit. Reagan's been in a foul mood practically ever since I got back.' Matt tried to be reasonable.

'I think she's got a lot of problems.'

'Well, this is my problem party, and I'll hog the misery if I want to.'

Parking was horrendous in Provincetown. They drove around for ten minutes, and eventually found a space on a street outside an art gallery with two extraordinary seascapes in its window. Both depicted the same view, across a beach out to sea, with a lighthouse on the right-hand shore. One was stormy, so grey and bleak it must be winter; the lighthouse beam pierced the gloom with a shaft of opalescent light. The other was summer: the sea was millpond calm, the foreground beach dotted with sunseekers in fluorescent swimsuits. Both paintings were beautiful, their simplistic style appealing. Freddie looked at them and through them for a few minutes, while Matthew tried to decipher the map. Now that she was here, she wasn't sure she wanted to be.

'As far as I can see, we're on the right street and I reckon if we carry on up there, going left at that dogleg, we'll get to it eventually. It's a good three-quarters of a mile, though. Want me to move the car?'

'We'll never get another space, and the walk'll do me good.'

'Do you want me to come with you?'

'Know what? I really don't. I don't mean to sound all Oates of the Antarctic, but I think I need to do this on my own. Is that okay?'

'Course it is. Whatever you need.'

She squeezed his hand gratefully. 'What are you going to do?'

'Don't worry about me. I'll have a look about – I might go and find out about whale-watching. Not sure it's the right time of year for it, but I could check it out.'

'Don't get picked up, will you?'

'That's a risk you're just going to have to take.' On the pavement he folded her into a hug. 'Okay?'

'I feel a complete wimp now. I want to run away.'

'No, you don't. You're going to do this.' He released her, pressed the address into her hand and pointed her in the direction she needed to take. 'Got my mobile, in case you need me.'

She nodded.

'Got yours?'

She took it out of her pocket and waved it at him. 'Yes, sir. And a clean handkerchief.'

He smacked her ass. 'Get out of here.'

'See you later.'

★   ★   ★

Matthew watched her for a moment or two, then went into the gallery. There were paintings along both walls, and the middle section was given over to sculpture. There were some extraordinary pieces of driftwood, angular and dark, anchored by metal stakes to what looked like hunks of limestone. He thought they were haunting and beautiful, and spent some moments looking at them.

The gallery owner, a middle-aged man in his fifties, balding and overweight, bustled towards him, swaying to the Mexican music playing through speakers in the four corners. 'Are you happy browsing, sir, or may I tell you some more about the works?'

'I was just looking at these sculptures – they're extraordinary.'

'Aren't they?' He looked delighted. 'Made right here in Provincetown from local materials.' Matthew acknowledged him with a nod. Encouraged, he made an expansive gesture. 'Everything you see here has been made by local artists.'

'You obviously have a thriving artistic community.'

'Absolutely.' He looked Matthew up and down. 'Are you over from the UK?'

Matthew felt an unfamiliar nervousness at being a heterosexual man in the minority for once.

'Yes. I'm with a friend. She's gone to visit a relative. I'm waiting for her.' Heavy on the 'she' and the 'her'.

'The paintings in the window . .?' The man nodded.

'These are just lovely. I love the style.'

'Ah, yes. These are very popular with the tourists.'

Did he detect snub in the man's tone? 'I have a few more towards the back of the gallery.' But he smiled as he pointed Matthew towards them.

They were more of the same. A large canvas of a whale-watching ship packed with tourists in colourful cagoules, several smaller pictures made from the beach looking back at the houses that lined the shore. All captured the stark differences between the nature and weather of the cape, and the visitors, with an amazing sense of colour.

Two new customers came in and the gallery owner excused himself.

Matthew decided he liked the picture of the ship enough to wonder how much it cost. He moved forward and peered at the tag pinned beside it: "Whalewatchers", 2002, $2000.

It wasn't the cost that caused the sharp intake of breath. It was the painter's name, typed below. 'Rebecca Valentine'.

It got quiet quite quickly once Freddie had left the bustle of the centre. She passed what looked like the last coffee shop, the crowd evaporated and she was alone on the street. The architecture was fascinating. Lots of the bigger houses, with their wraparound terraces, were bed-and-breakfast 'inns', hand-painted signs waving in the breeze, advertising 'Jacuzzi baths' and 'private sun terraces'. Some were very grand, with weather-vaned glass towers, and elaborate wrought iron. Some were tiny, huddled in between apologetically. Most were immaculate and well loved, although on some the ravages of time and the peninsula weather were apparent.

She got there more quickly than she had expected – she'd been fascinated by the town. Now she lit a cigarette and leaned back against the wall. This house was one of the biggest – tall with grey clapboard. From the street it looked like three different houses, two facing on to the road, with a third between them pushed right back so that it joined up to the back of the other two and formed a courtyard, with tubs of lovingly tended plants and freshly painted white benches. The house in the middle was suspended above the beach by a grey pier. A white picket fence ran the length of all three on the road, and through the side windows Freddie could see that enormous picture windows at the back looked out to sea. The entrance was at the side, off the courtyard. It had a porch, and a welcoming light. She couldn't stop staring at it, and she couldn't go any nearer.

She almost smiled to herself, because Loyd Grossman's voice came into her head: 'Who lives in a house like this?'

She stood there for ten minutes, just staring at it. A passing couple caused her to step back against the low brick wall behind her. They turned, a few yards further along, to watch her, evidently wondering what she was doing. Freddie realised she couldn't stand here all day, but she still couldn't bring herself to go in. Couldn't open the white gate, and go up to the porch and ring the bell.

Maybe Reagan had been right.

Then the door opened. A man and a woman came out, carrying big mugs.

Her mother looked just like her. It was in her height, carriage and colouring – her weight, too, if Freddie hadn't been so careful about what she ate.

This woman was her mother. She didn't notice the man. Her knees trembled, and she felt her cheeks colour.

That is my mother.

She couldn't have avoided being seen, even if she had been trying. Her stance there on the pavement was too blatant.

They were both looking at her, but she could see only her mother's face.

It felt as if they stared at each other for ages, although it was probably only seconds. Freddie tried to read what was in Rebecca's face. She couldn't see shock or surprise. Emotion? Certainly. It wasn't anger. Then Rebecca handed the man her mug and came towards her, just a couple of steps. 'Freddie?'

She couldn't do it. Her mother's movement galvanised her. Shaking her head in pointless denial, Freddie backed away, first walking, then turning and then running. All she knew was that she wanted to run. She ran as fast as she could remember running since she'd been a child, back down the hill, along the street.

She didn't stop running until she got to the last coffee shop she'd passed a few minutes before, and the comfort and anonymity of the crowd closed in on her again.

She sat on the bench outside the coffee shop nursing a cup of hot chocolate and feeling stupid. What a performance. Matthew had come all the way from England for this fiasco, for God's sake. Why had that woman frightened and fascinated her so much? She felt so unlike herself – that was what was so disturbing. It wasn't how Freddie had expected to react. She was strong, and capable; she was emotionally controlled, and she wasn't supposed to feel like this about anything – and especially not about a mother she hadn't seen, or missed, for more than thirty years. Nothing about any of this felt okay.

Rebecca watched her go. 'What can I do?'

The man who had been her best friend for the last fifteen years looked helplessly concerned.

Rebecca took her mug of coffee from him, and went to the bench they had originally been heading for. 'You can come and sit with me.'

They had become friends because they were both failures. Rebecca Valentine, failed wife and mother, had come to Provincetown at the end of her long attempt to run away from herself. Five years later Cosmo Richardson the Third, failed husband and father, had found her. She was serving drinks in a bar. He was buying them.

Her paintings hadn't found a market then, or even a

sympathetic gallery owner. She was renting a couple of rooms, using one as a kitchen-bedroom-lounge, the other as a tiny studio, and working five nights a week to cover her bills.

Cosmo had run away as far as a not very adventurous American without a passport could – he had come from Sacramento, California. He had left behind a scorned wife, and two sons she swore he would never be left alone with again. Her upbringing in Oregon had encouraged her in the belief that homosexuality equalled perversion. He'd felt like a pervert, too: it wasn't long after AIDS. And he was a lawyer. As well as a husband and a father.

Rebecca had laughed when he told her he was a lawyer. 'I'm cursed,' she had said. 'Don't be a lawyer,' she had added. 'Lawyers don't make anything except money, trouble and misery.'

He wasn't a lawyer any more, and he knew he wasn't a pervert either. His relationship with Rebecca was more like a marriage than his own had been. A good marriage.

The waitress and the pervert had talked for hours that first night. She'd taken him back to her room, and let him sleep on the sofa, after she had held him while he cried. They had become the painter and the author, which made it sound a lot easier than it had been. There had been a few lean years, and they had both done other jobs for a long time before they made a living doing what they loved. They weren't rich but they were what other people called comfortable. They called it safe. They owned their home together. They'd bought it at a good price because it had been so dilapidated, and it had taken them a couple of years to get it as it was today. They were spectacularly proud of it.

The front left part was his. He had a sitting room, a big kitchen, and two bedrooms, each with its own bathroom. It was done just his way, with lots of gold and Tiffany glass, which he bought whenever he found it. The back bit, with the spectacular views was hers, of course. The light there was a gift. She had a fabulous studio, plus the other rooms, although Cosmo suspected she slept in the studio on the big day-bed more often than she admitted. He called those periods her 'artistic funks' and she went into them pretty regularly. They rented out the right-hand bit, sometimes for a summer, sometimes for a year, even a week. As long as each tenant was quiet and tolerant, they didn't mind. And they usually were: the intolerant found they couldn't tolerate Provincetown for long.

They'd both been lucky, done well. Rebecca's pictures sold well up and down the Cape, and in a couple of smart places in Boston. Occasionally there were commissions, but mainly she painted what she wanted to paint, and people bought it.

Cosmo wrote children's books. He was the 'creator' – he still loved hearing that – of Chunky Perkins, pocket pop star. A bit of a rip-off of Inch High Private Eye, Chunky was about six inches tall, lived in the jacket pocket of a variety of hapless characters, and had an endearing or irritating habit of popping out and singing at inappropriate times. He looked a bit like Tom Jones, or even Elvis just before the deep-fried Mars Bar years started taking their toll, with a bad rug, and a good heart, and he had a song for every occasion. Cosmo had an encyclopaedic knowledge of pop music, knew the first lines of practically every song that had ever been on the *Billboard* chart, and a vast collection of old forty-fives on vinyl. Chunky was illustrated by an ex-lover – Alexander Webster – whose fit of pique when Cosmo threw him over hadn't extended to turning down the ever-increasing advances the children's books editor offered. His publishers were an old-established house on Beacon Hill, but he hardly ever went there these days – it was all on disk. His agent was negotiating a deal with Nickelodeon, and it seemed Chunky's big break was imminent. Cosmo put almost half of everything he earned into accounts for his sons that they didn't know they had, which ought to help with college. He hadn't seen them for eight years, since their mother had married a redneck, but he still sent cards and gifts on birthdays and at Christmas. He kept a log of them, too, in a leather album, in case his wife hadn't handed them over. He believed, or at least he told himself he believed, that when they were twenty-one they would come to find him, and he thought he might need the album to prove that he had always loved them. It was his what-would-you-grab-if-there-was-a-fire item. That, and a signed photograph of Diana Ross.

If Rebecca had photographs of Freddie, she didn't display them. He had never seen one. And she didn't talk incessantly – as he did about his boys – of her hopes for meeting her daughter. She said she wasn't entitled to. She said she had made her decision when she walked out on Freddie and had to stand by it. He didn't buy that. Not a day went by when he didn't think of his sons and regret that he wasn't with them. Even if the choices he had made and the life he now led were what he needed to do, the regret, guilt and longing for them were still there, and he knew it was the same for Rebecca. As he sat beside her on the bench in the afternoon sun, drinking his coffee, he knew better than most the turmoil she was going through.

Neither of them should have had their children, but what was the point in blaming themselves? He had had his because he had grown up at a time and in a place where it was expected of him, where he had concentrated all his energies on drowning the voices inside his head. She had had hers as part of some escape she thought she was making.

These days, it would all have been so different.

Will was almost eighteen now, Tom just sixteen months younger. Freddie was twice that age, and he had been with Rebecca through the time when she had known Freddie was graduating, marrying, having a child of her own. He had to accept it because he loved her, but he couldn't claim to understand it. As far as he knew she had never once bridged the distance between them: not a letter, not a phone call, not a visit. Which was why he had been so flabbergasted when she had announced that she was going to her ex-husband's funeral. Perhaps when Freddie was in England it had been easier to stay away. But that she should be thirty or so miles away – an hour's drive? It must have been too much.

He had wanted to go with her, but she had said no. She could be so bloody independent sometimes. She'd come back that night and gone straight into her own part of the house. It was an unspoken rule between them that a closed door meant just that, and he had respected her wish to be alone, although all evening he had hoped to hear a knock at his door.

She didn't seem to want to talk about it. A week or so ago she had dressed up and gone out for a couple of hours. He wondered if perhaps she had gone to meet Freddie and, again, he had waited.

Now it seemed that Freddie had come to them. He felt a curious mixture of joy for Rebecca and pure envy. To see his boys walking up that street, looking for him . . . what a sight that would be. Cosmo never let himself think about what they might say to him. In his fantasy they always understood.

She had looked exactly as Rebecca had on the first night he met her. The fashions were different, the hair . . . but essentially she was the same woman. Now the protective part of him was going to make Rebecca talk about it.

Rebecca sighed. 'I suppose she was curious, just like me.'

'Why do you think she didn't talk to you? She'd come all this way.'

'She'll be back. I wasn't brave enough to start a conversation when I went to the funeral, and she's only just found out about me. She needs time.'

'And when she does come back what will you tell her?'

'I suppose I'll tell her whatever she asks me to tell her.'

'And?'

She didn't answer for ages. 'It depends on her.'

She was ready, she thought, for whatever Freddie would throw at her. There would be anger, she was sure, but how curious would her daughter be? Over the years Rebecca had tortured herself many times with the question of whether what she had done was forgivable under any circumstances.

She didn't think of herself as a mother, but they were all around her. It was society's most powerful view of a woman. Plays, books, TV, films, everywhere you looked you saw a lesson in getting it right or wrong. If you got it wrong, the world judged you for ever. It seemed there was no greater crime for a woman than being a bad mother, and she was surely the worst.

She'd thought through the different scenarios. She could have not left. She could have stayed. Or she could have taken Freddie with her – she tried to imagine the life she had had with Freddie in tow. She tried to imagine having stayed. She didn't see how she could have done either of those things and still have arrived at where she was today.

She'd paid a high price for her happiness, but she wasn't sure she could ever sacrifice it. The wound was thirty years old, and it had all but healed. She could go weeks or months now without deep despair settling over her.

Now that he was dead, her loathing and disgust for him had seeped away. It was like the layers of an onion, all the bad they had done to each other. She had done it to Freddie, he had done it to her, and it had been done to him. They were victims and they were perpetrators. Except Freddie. She hadn't asked for any of it.

So Rebecca was ready, all these years later.

She looked down the road where her daughter had run, and hoped it wouldn't be long.

Matthew was waiting for her in a café at the bottom of the hill. 'I'm glad to see you. I seriously think a guy over there was checking me out . . .' he said.

Freddie turned her head, and Matthew tugged at her arm. 'Don't look!'

'Why is it that all straight men think they're attractive to gays? Don't you think heterosexuality oozes off you?'

'Do you?'

'I've never thought about it.' Which wasn't entirely true, she realised, but she wasn't going to tell him that. Enough that he should assume every gay guy in a hundred-metre radius was after him without thinking she was too.

He took a gulp of his beer.

'That looks good, can I have one?'

'Sure.' He beckoned the waitress and ordered, then looked at her and leaned forward over the table. 'Right. Tell me.'

'Nothing much to tell.'

'Did you see her?'

'Yup.'

'And . . .'

'She looks a bit like me.'

'Well, you never looked much like your dad, so I suppose you could have guessed that.'

'I suppose.'

'Did she recognise you?'

'I think so.'

'Right.' Matthew looked like a child intent on a story, open-faced, eager. She could see he cared but she didn't know what to tell him. How could you sit in a café and talk about such complicated feelings over a beer? How could she ever say what she felt about that woman?

She put a hand over Matthew's. 'Listen, Matt . . . I need time to make sense of it all so that I can talk about it in whole sentences. It's too big – you know?' He thought that he did, and he smiled. Just as long as she didn't send him away. She didn't.

They had a couple more beers and watched the strange world walk by. The loving couples, arms round each other, more gay than straight ones, and the New Jersey coach trips of pensioners with their bags of saltwater taffy.

They stayed under the patio heater until their toes and fingers were cold, and then they walked arm in arm along to the other end of the main street, where the car was parked.

There wasn't anyone else in the world that she could do this with, Freddie thought. Reagan and Tamsin wouldn't have let her avoid talking. Adrian would have been intolerant of her desire to be quiet and calm.

Matthew wanted to be whatever she needed him to be. Suddenly she was so grateful to him, so touched by him, and felt so close to him.

They passed what seemed like the last shop just as it was starting to get gloomy. Then, on their right, a path opened out on to a stretch of beach, sheltered by a grassy dune.

'Let's go down there.' She could see a lighthouse beacon beaming through the dusk.

'Aren't you cold?'

She wasn't – there was no wind. It was almost silent away from the bustle, just the ocean lapping on the shore a few metres away.

When she kissed him she could taste his fear and uncertainty. 'Matt?' She held his face in her hands. 'Matt, it's okay.' Even in the grey light, she could see his eyes staring into hers, questioning.

'Is this what you want?'

It was. She pulled his face towards hers again, speaking into it. 'Yes. Please.'

And then he was kissing her back. How strange to be kissing someone who wasn't Adrian, for the first time in more than twelve years. It wasn't like Boston, where she had made herself stop before she even started. It was all new. His responses, his taste, his smell, his lips on hers. She wanted more. She pulled open his coat, and pushed her hands up under his sweater. His T-shirt was tucked in and she yanked at it until she could feel his stomach, soft with downy hair, felt higher until she reached his hard nipples, and then round his back, his smooth shoulders. He was warm and firm. He was pushing her back now so that he could touch her. The moment when his hand cupped her breast, inside her bra, stilled them. The intimacy marked the crossing of a line. But neither of them could stop now. They had time to think better of it, when he laid his coat on the sand, and when they had to pull their boots off to remove their trousers. And when they laughed at themselves, bare-legged in socks. And when they still didn't want to stop, they lay down together, and she unrolled her scarf and threw it over them. Their eyes were open, and she watched him, stunned and delighted, enter her and start to move inside her. And this was different too.

It had been weeks since she'd had sex – a long time for her – and it felt good. Adrian knew exactly how she wanted it, like following a recipe, and many had been the times when she had felt physically satisfied long before she was mentally engaged in making love with him. This was different – every sensation was magnified, new. She realised now that for Matthew it had probably been years. He was trembling.

He said her name, just once into her neck, his breath warm on her cold skin. She held him close.

He came way too soon, but that was okay. She wasn't quite close enough to feel frustrated by it, and somehow it wasn't about that. Sex with Adrian was all about that, and they were very good at it, the two of them. It was the best bit of their marriage, the bit that didn't change, the bit that they used to put everything else right. Freddie knew other women whose sex lives had tailed off altogether – a friend whose husband hadn't been the same since he'd watched her give birth to their child; another who never said no, but who made shopping lists in her head while her husband puffed away on top of her; a woman who hadn't initiated sex for two years. Freddie had admitted once, at a tipsy evening with a few girlfriends, that she and Adrian still did it three or four times a week, and they'd looked at her with incredulous faces, part jealousy, part mistrust. Their attitude had enabled her to think that everything else must be okay too.

This, with Matthew on a damp stretch of sand, in the half-darkness, was different. It took her a minute to grasp that she felt cherished.

When he had caught his breath, he pulled back and his eyes searched her face. 'Sorry.'

She smiled. 'Don't be.'

'Do you want . . .?' He couldn't finish the sentence. Words were obviously harder than deeds.

She rescued him. 'To get dressed before I freeze my ass off – yes!'

It was actually bloody cold now. When Matthew stood up the parts of her that his body had covered were suddenly chilled. They got dressed quickly, without talking, and when they had finished, he pulled up the zipper on Freddie's jacket, straightened her hat and kissed her forehead. She put her arms round him, and they stood still for a minute before he broke away and pulled her towards the road.

In the car they didn't talk for a minute or two, while the heater blasted warm air at their faces. Matthew spoke first. 'I never imagined it would be like that, the first time.'

'I never imagined a first time at all. Did you?'

His expression turned serious, and he was looking at his hands as he answered, 'A hundred times, Freddie.'

She didn't know what to say.

'Look, you must have realised something, after Boston . . .?'

Of course she had, but she hadn't let herself think about it – hadn't had room to think about it. 'We were drunk . . .'

'Don't do that.' His voice was suddenly harsh. 'I wasn't drunk. I'd had enough wine to be brave, that was all. Enough to let me forget that I'd spent months and months pretending I didn't feel this way. Trying to protect you, trying to do the right thing by Adrian and

Sarah and everybloodybody else. Trying to keep you in the box labelled "best friend" because anything else felt so strange. I was so afraid that I'd lose you if I pushed it. I told myself I was waiting for you to come to me – to see me differently. But, Freddie, that moment never came. You never did. You know what the tipping point was?' He didn't wait for an answer. Each word was emphasised. 'I saw I had to risk it. That I couldn't bear to be so close to you and not try. Not any more. So please don't tell me what happened in Boston happened because I was drunk. I tried and I failed. You didn't see me differently.'

Freddie shifted to face him. He wasn't looking at her, so she put her hand up to his face and brought it round. 'I think I just did.'

Pride had set his jaw. 'You think?'

Freddie shut her eyes in exasperation. 'Think is all I can do right now, Matt. I'm not even sure who I am any more. All the things I thought were sure in my life have changed. My father, my mother, Adrian. And now you.'

'I never wanted to make things worse for you.'

'I know. I know you didn't. You haven't.' She pulled him towards her. 'You haven't. You've just got to give me some time. Can you do that?'

'Time I have plenty of.'

'And don't give up on me. Please?'

His smile was sad. 'Never.'

'Thank you.'

They clung to each other.

'I love you, Freddie.'

'I know.' She had always known. It was just that his love had changed and she hadn't noticed. And she wasn't sure whether hers had. It was all happening so fast.

What had happened on the beach had felt good and right. Comfortable and exciting, warm and okay. And in the car it wasn't awkward, even with all this revelation and this new intimacy hanging in the air. The only thing she felt certain of was that she didn't want him to leave her.

'We'd better get going. Reagan will have the search parties out for us,' she said.

'Yeah.'

Matthew wanted to talk to her about Sarah. He wanted to tell her that he knew Sarah wouldn't mind. He wanted to tell her that Sarah had never entered his head, there on the sand, while he was making love to her. But as Sarah hadn't belonged with them there she didn't belong in the car, now. And he was afraid – he felt at this moment that he had her, that Freddie was letting him love her, and he didn't want to do anything to upset this new fragile equilibrium. As he drove, with her hand on his on the gearstick, his heart swelled. He had kissed her, been kissed back. He had touched her, made love to her. He almost couldn't believe it. He wished he had been able to see what he had touched, and he wished that there had been time to be slower, better. But there would be – always, he dared let

himself hope. As long as he didn't blow it now. As long
as he put the tight leash back on his feelings and needs,
and didn't suffocate her with them. He knew he could
do that. He had to.

'Hungry?' Matthew asked, as they drove past the
Chatham sign forty minutes later.

She hadn't been until he mentioned it. Now she was
ravenous. 'God, yes.'

'Shall I go to the shop, pick us up a barbecued
chicken or something? God, I miss curry houses all of a
sudden! Or do you think Reagan's been slaving over a
hot stove all afternoon?'

'I can't see it. Chicken's a great idea. Thanks, Matt.'

She wondered briefly if he was trying to give her a bit
of space, but she figured he hadn't eaten since this
morning either – and time had taught them not to
expect much from Reagan in the culinary line.

He let her get out, and reversed back on to the road.

On the porch Freddie wondered how she looked.
Were her lips red, her cheeks stubble-scratched? Or
was the change in her more subtle? She felt the
dampness of Matthew between her legs. There hadn't
been time to think about contraception, but she was
still taking her pill – it was as automatic to her as
brushing her teeth. Should he have asked? Probably
. . . But it hadn't been that sort of moment. She knew
she sounded like one of those silly girls on daytime
television, but she didn't mind. Their recklessness
made her smile.

She was still smiling when she opened the door and went inside. Reagan was tucked up on the sofa in front of the fire, an open book beside her. She was staring into the flames, hugging her knees, but she jumped up when Freddie came in. 'How are you?' she asked.

'I'm fine. How are you?'

'All right. Lonely here all by myself, actually – glad to see you.' She looked expectantly at the door over Freddie's shoulder. 'Where's Matt?'

Freddie felt herself blush. For God's sake! 'He's gone to get us some dinner.'

Now Reagan was looking at her intently and she wanted to cover her face. She wasn't ready to talk about this yet. She busied herself with taking off her coat and hat, hanging them on the pegs behind the door. 'I could do with a drink. Any wine open?'

But Reagan wasn't distracted. 'What's happened?'

'What do you mean?' That was the best Freddie could do. 'With my mother?' she asked, although she knew exactly what Reagan had meant. That was the trouble with old friends – you couldn't fool them.

'With Matt.'

How could Reagan have picked up on it so quickly? 'Nothing.' It was too quick, too defensive, to fool her.

'I don't believe you.'

'Listen, Reagan, leave it, will you? We kissed each other, that's all.' She didn't know why she was lying. Was she ashamed? 'Moment of weakness. No big deal. Don't say anything, will you? I'm sure he doesn't want to talk about it, and I don't particularly either.'

But Reagan's face was thunderous, her eyes narrowed with rage. Freddie felt jumpy, and a little frightened.

'What about Sarah?'

That was a low blow. It was also the first time Sarah's name had been mentioned since . . .

'What about her? That's hardly fair, Reagan. We just kissed, that's all,' she said again, although she didn't think Reagan believed her.

It was a tense evening. Reagan picked at the food Matthew brought, smoked enough cigarettes to create a fug in the room, and drank several big glasses of wine.

Matthew resented her being there – he wanted Freddie to himself. He wanted to talk about what had happened. Or not talk about it. He had been contented on the way back from Provincetown, relieved. In Chatham, walking from the car to the shop, he had had a rush of delight and punched the air in silent triumph. Now he was increasingly nervous. It was precarious, this new thing with Freddie, and Reagan was a spectre at the feast.

But although she showed no inclination to talk, she wasn't in any hurry to go to bed. It was after one before they all headed for the stairs.

On the landing, Matthew followed Freddie's urgent glance and went into the guest bedroom.

Ten minutes later, Freddie knocked and came in. He was still sitting on the edge of the bed, fully dressed. He had been fighting an urge to tiptoe across the corridor and knock on her door. Now his stomach heaved with a mixture of excitement and relief. She closed the door and leaned against it, one hand on the knob. When she spoke it was a whisper: 'Was it me or could you have cut the air with a knife tonight?'

'It wasn't you. It was Siberia down there.'

'What's wrong with her?'

'Did she ask you anything about today before I came back with the food?'

'I told her we kissed.'

He nodded.

'She's jealous.'

'She's Glenn Close in *Fatal Attraction*.' He laughed, but it sounded nervous, even to him.

'Perhaps I should go and talk to her,' Freddie said.

Perhaps you should get into my bed and stay all night, was what he wanted to say. He bit his tongue hard. 'I wouldn't bother tonight. Let her sleep on it. She'll be fine in the morning. You know how moody she can be.'

Just then they heard a door open above them. Foot-steps padded down the stairs, passed Matthew's door, and went on down to the kitchen.

This made them giggle. Freddie thrust the sleeve of her cardigan into her mouth.

He loved feeling conspiratorial with her, and he wasn't remotely interested in Reagan. He just wanted Freddie to stay with him.

'I'm going to go down and talk to her.'

'Will you come back afterwards?'

'Will you be awake?'

'If you're coming back.'

She wanted to. She wanted him to hold her. She wanted, suddenly, to lie skin on skin with him under the white duvet and hold him while he slept.

'I'll come back.'

He blew her a kiss and she backed out of the room, smiling.

Reagan was sitting at the kitchen table, smoking. She hadn't turned on the lights, but a shaft came through from the hall. The electric numbers on the oven and microwave glowed.

When she saw Freddie, she pushed the cigarette packet to her.

'No, thanks.'

'Doesn't he like you smoking?'

Freddie tried to keep it light. 'I don't like American cigarettes. Too mentholy.'

'I know about you two. You needn't sneak about on the landing like a pair of teenagers.'

Freddie felt the admonishment, even as her hackles rose. 'I wasn't "sneaking about".'

Reagan waved aside her objection. 'Whatever. My point is this. I know about you two.' She took a drink from the whisky tumbler that Freddie hadn't noticed until now. 'But do you know about me and Matt?'

'What about you and Matt?'

'I take it that's a no.'

'What are you talking about, you and Matt?'

'There was a me and Matt. Not lately, of course. You're flavour of the month now.'

Freddie didn't know what to say.

'I used to wonder whether he'd accepted some weird bet to be with all of us. The Tenko Club. You, me, Sarah and Tamsin. Although I can't blame him for leaving Tamsin until last.'

That was unkind – Freddie understood that. It was the only part she did grasp. 'What the hell are you talking about?'

'Well, think about it. First there was Sarah. Well,' she took a long drag on her cigarette, then stubbed it out, 'technically I was first, but then there was Sarah, and then me again. Now you.'

Freddie was getting angry. She was too tired for riddles. 'Look, Reagan, I don't know what you're going on about but I'm knackered. I know you've had a bug up your ass for days. Why don't you stop talking nonsense and tell me exactly what's eating you? Then we can clear the air and I can go to bed.'

Reagan laughed, a hollow, strained sound. 'I'm sorry if I'm keeping you from your bed – or, rather, from his. I thought you should know that the man you're about to sleep with – or have already, for all I know – has slept with two of your best friends.'

'When?'

'Well, Sarah—'

'Not Sarah. I'm asking about you.'

'The night before he got married. Then just after Sarah died.'

'What?' Freddie felt sick.

'You heard me. He'd deny it or try to explain it away. You know, last-minute fling before the wedding, needed a bit of comfort after the funeral. Maybe religious services put him in the mood. I've never had him after a christening, and God knows there've been a few of those, but never say never.'

This was a Reagan Freddie didn't recognise. Moody, yes. Belligerent sometimes. But this was pure bitter malevolence, and she was pouring it like poison into this room, this house, this day. Freddie was shocked, incredulous, almost frightened. She didn't know how this had happened.

She couldn't even think about whether or not she believed her. Instinctively she thought not – but why would Reagan lie? Well, not so much why, but how could she be capable of doing it? And what she had claimed was possible. Reagan was everything Sarah hadn't been. She was angular where Sarah was soft, acerbic where Sarah was gentle, vampish and sexy where Sarah was demure.

She remembered him on top of her this afternoon. She remembered how okay it had felt. She didn't want to hear this now. But Reagan was still talking. 'And, God knows, he wasn't interested in anything lasting between him and me. That was only ever Sarah. He won't want it to last with you either, I shouldn't think. Still, you'll probably go back to Adrian, won't you?' She snorted. 'I suppose you could call it a holiday romance.'

Freddie just stared at her in the dark.

'Don't be angry with me, Freddie.' Reagan drained her drink. 'I only wanted you to know the truth. Sets you free – isn't that what they say?' She stood up. Freddie thought she swayed. She must have drunk a lot of whisky fast. 'So carry on with your little Cape Cod shag-fest. Don't let me bother you.'

Freddie stood up too. 'But you are bothering me, Reagan. I don't know why you're doing this.'

Reagan didn't answer, and Freddie felt an overwhelming need to get away from her. 'I don't want you in my house.' Even as she spoke she couldn't believe she was saying this to Reagan. She felt provoked by the lack of response. In frustration, she said, 'I think it would be best if you left tomorrow.'

But Reagan was on her way up the stairs. Freddie followed her. 'Are you listening to me?'

Reagan tossed a dismissive gesture over her shoulder. 'I heard you.' Then her door slammed.

Freddie looked at Matthew's. She couldn't face him. She went into her own bedroom, shut the door and lay down on the blanket. Reagan's nasty words raced through her mind. She was literally shaking. To have that kind of conversation with anyone would be distressing – but with Reagan, one of her oldest friends . . .

In his own room, Matthew heard Freddie and Reagan moving about, and then the house was quiet. They'd been out of earshot in the kitchen, and he had heard nothing of their conversation, until Freddie had shouted, 'Are you listening to me?' and Reagan had slammed the door.

For an hour he lay tensely awake, willing her to change her mind and come to him. It was more than he could do to go across to her: he was afraid of what he might hear. He slept fitfully, berating himself for being such a coward. It was about four in the morning when he ventured out. He knocked two or three times, gently, on her door. 'Please go away, Matt.' Her voice wasn't angry. 'I can't talk to you now. I'll see you in the morning. Please.'

Tamsin answered the phone on the second ring. She had her feet up on the sofa, with a wedge of walnut layer cake resting on her bump. She'd drawn the curtains and put the television on, and she was thinking of having a nap – after she'd eaten the cake, of course. But who needed *Neighbours* when you had Freddie?

Freddie told her everything, almost in a whisper. 'Do you think it might be true?'

'Of course it isn't true. Don't be ridiculous. But aren't you asking the wrong person? Why do you need to phone me when he's next door?'

'Because I was upset. I'm confused.'

'I understand why you're upset. It sounds like Reagan's flipped. But confused?'

She'd told Tamsin the whole story – seeing Rebecca, what had happened with Matthew on the beach, Reagan's outburst. Tamsin had run through a gamut of emotion: sympathy, delight, anger.

'I don't understand you, Fred. You said it felt right, you and Matt. I don't know what Reagan's problem is, but I truly don't think it has anything to do with either of you.'

After she'd hung up, she didn't feel sleepy any more. The baby was kicking now, anyway. At one point a whole foot poked out of the right-hand side of her belly. She grabbed for the heel. Hello, baby. She's pissing you off, too, is she? Maybe Neil was right – Freddie was putting obstacles in the way of her own happiness. She felt a twinge of annoyance that she wasn't there. She was sure she'd have been able to sort them out.

Freddie had a headache. She didn't think she'd slept at all by the time it was starting to get light outside. She heard Reagan moving about quietly upstairs, but she couldn't bring herself to go to her. At about six thirty a cab stopped outside. Freddie stood hidden behind her curtain and watched Reagan leave. This felt horrible. All of it. Reagan had been one of her best friends for nearly twenty years. It hadn't always been easy, but it had endured. This didn't seem survivable.

She put a big sweater on over her nightshirt, and padded down to the kitchen to make some coffee.

There was a note on the kitchen table with her name on it.

> *Dear Freddie*
> *I am so sorry. I hate myself for last night. I hate myself in general, actually. Tell Matt I'm sorry too.*
> *Reagan*

Matthew came down while she was reading it. He looked terrible. She'd not gone back to him, after she had promised she would. She handed him the note, and made some tea.

'What's she sorry for, apart from the usual?' He was trying to keep his tone light.

'She told me some things.'

'What things?'

'Things about you.'

He stirred his mug, and waited.

'She told me you and she had slept together.'

'When?'

She wasn't looking at his face so she couldn't see his expression, but his voice was loud in the quiet morning. She shut her eyes and the words spilled out. 'Before you met Sarah. The night before you married her. After her funeral.' She couldn't believe she was saying it.

Matthew stood up, the chair legs screeching on the hard floor. 'And you believed her?'

She still didn't look at him.

'Freddie?' He was almost shouting. *'Did you believe her?'*

'No, of course not. Neither did Tamsin.'

'You've talked to Tamsin about this?'

Freddie nodded.

'When did all this happen?'

'When I came down last night, and she was in here. She said it all then.'

'And Tamsin?'

'I called her after I'd gone to bed.'

He was exasperated. 'Why the hell didn't you come in and talk to me?'

'That's what Tamsin said.'

'And she was bloody right. I can't believe you.'

'I'm sorry.'

'You're sorry! That's just great. That's just bloody great, Fred. You really know how to fuck a guy up, don't you? Yesterday was the best day I've had in ages. Years. You felt it too. I know you did. Then I waited and waited and you didn't come – because of this . . .' He shook his head.

Freddie felt ashamed.

They sat in silence for a moment. When Matt spoke again his voice was softer. 'For your information, and not that I can prove it because I can't, but just so you know . . . I have never slept with Reagan. Which is not to say that she hasn't tried. In fact, she told you the times she tried. There was nothing between us in Chester before I met Sarah, except maybe in her head. She did show up the night before I married Sarah, and made an embarrassing, ugly pass at me. She did the same thing after Sarah died, which was in the worst possible taste. Both occasions were excruciating. On neither did I reciprocate, participate or say anything that would give her encouragement or hope. I tried to let her keep her dignity. And I tried to be kind, because she was your friend. And I didn't tell any of you for the same reason. Sarah died having no idea.'

'I'm sorry, Matt. You should have heard her. She was saying such vile stuff.'

'You could have come and got me.'

'I know. *I know.* I'm sorry.'

He put his arm across the table and took her hand. 'Look, what difference does it make? Nothing's changed between us. Not if you believe me. And if you don't, there's no point in any of this.'

'I do. I do believe you.'

'Well, then, nothing's changed, has it?'

Freddie took her hand back.

'What, Freddie?'

Freddie struggled to explain a feeling she didn't understand. 'I didn't believe her. I don't know what's going on with her and right now I don't much care. But what she said, the times she was talking about, put things back into the context they'd fallen out of.'

Matthew was watching her face. 'You're my friend, Matt, one of my oldest friends. You're so important to me. You were married to one of the best friends I ever had. You had this great marriage . . .' Freddie stopped. She didn't know where to go.

'We had this great marriage and then she died. She *died*, Freddie. We all loved her and then she died.'

'And if she hadn't, you'd still be with her.'

He couldn't grapple with that logic. He got up, came round the table and shook her by the shoulders. 'And if, and if, and if. But she *did*, Freddie. And now I love you. That doesn't sound right – it wasn't that simple or that quick. I grieved for a long, long time. And I was in pieces for the longest time. And now I love you. And there's nothing wrong with that. It's just as pure, honest and true as the way I loved her. Why can't you see that?'

She couldn't answer.

His eyes bored into hers. Then he released her and sat down again. 'This is such bullshit, Freddie. All of it. You keep finding excuses. It's Sarah, it's Adrian, it's Harry, it's your dad, it's your mother. It's all such crap. You feel it too, I know you do. Do you think I'd keep forcing my attentions on you like some loser if I didn't know? But I can't wait for ever. I'm a good bloke, but I'm not a total patsy. And if you're expecting me to run away like I did last time, you can forget it. This gets sorted out here and now, Freddie. One of us has to stop and face this. I'm sorry if the timing's bad but you can't hide behind that any more. The time is now. One life, Freddie, and we know better than most that time is precious.'

Reagan had ordered the taxi but given no destination. Now the driver asked, 'Where to?' and she didn't know. 'Is there an airport on the Cape?'

'Yes, ma'am. There's one in Provincetown, about an hour's drive north.'

'Take me there, then.'

'You sure, ma'am?'

'Where do they fly?'

'To Boston mainly.'

'Then I'm sure.'

The airport turned out to be one building. There was a desk, with no conveyor-belts or computers in evidence, just a couple of beige-suited officials, and a Hertz concession where a large St Bernard dog sat sleepily.

There was no plane until the late afternoon, and they wouldn't have confirmation that that flight would be taking off until lunchtime – there was a weather warning. Yesterday's clear sunshine had given way to grey, mizzly fog.

There was no left luggage.

When Reagan stepped outside the building, the taxi had gone. Probably couldn't get away fast enough, Reagan thought. The driver tried a couple of times to talk to her, but she had been rude. Her head was too full for small-talk.

She was hungry, she realised. She'd hardly eaten any dinner last night, and she'd had nothing this morning. One of the beige-suits appeared beside her. 'Can I call you a cab?'

'Where to?'

'Well, I guess if you're set on waiting for that flight into Logan this afternoon, your best bet is to head into Provincetown. It's only four miles away, and it's as good a place as any on the Cape to spend a day.'

She smiled weakly and nodded.

The lady cab driver who arrived twenty minutes later was as wide as she was tall, her body composed of roll on roll – bosom, waist, hips – squeezed into a man's T-shirt and a pair of Levi's. She had a crew-cut, rings on both thumbs and a tattoo on each wrist, but her voice was surprisingly soft. It wasn't a local accent, with its hard, clipped syllables. She sounded more Deep South. 'Are you okay, honey?' she said, after a couple of miles.

Something made Reagan answer, 'No, I'm not.'

'Well, a lot of people say a cabbie's the next best thing to a shrink. Wanna talk about it?'

Reagan looked at the meter. The beige-suit had told her it was a ten-dollar fare into Provincetown and the meter already read six. She didn't think $4 would cover it. 'Not really.' She smiled. 'But thanks. What I do need is a place to spend the day. The weather doesn't look quite right for whale-watching, and there's a limit to the number of coffees I can drink until I need to get back out here for the afternoon flight. I have money. Could you take me somewhere with rooms?'

'That I can do. I'll take you to a great place – it's run by a couple of friends of mine. It's pretty quiet here, out of season midweek – I'm sure they'll fix you up.'

'Thank you.'

It was beautiful, the sort of place you should be with a lover, perched high on a hill, up three flights of wide steps made from railway sleepers.

She sat on the veranda while Tanya went to speak to her friends. She imagined her saying she'd picked up a fruitcake who'd turned up at the airport with no idea of what plane to catch to where. Who looked like she might cry, but didn't want to talk about it.

When they came out, the three of them looked like nurses who'd just heard a terminal diagnosis. Normally Reagan hated pity, but now she felt a shred of comfort. Of course she could stay, they said. No problem. There was coffee and some muffins. No one talked about money.

She smiled gratefully, and took some coffee out on to the veranda. You could only see about ten meters in front of your face, but that was the view she preferred.

What the hell had she done? First the lie by omission, not telling Freddie her mother had been looking for her. Then the hideous, hateful lies about Matthew. They'd been out before she'd known she was speaking, and she had seen pain on Freddie's face but she hadn't stopped. Jealousy had burned like acid in her throat. Reagan, odd one out again. It was like a game of musical chairs where everyone changed position, but she was always the one who didn't get a seat. When she had been speaking, her own pain was the only thing she felt. She'd lost them all now. That much was obvious. They'd all taken a fair amount of crap from her over the years, but this was the end, she was sure. Why would they bother with her now?

And they were the best thing about her life. The only really good thing.

Reagan didn't often cry, but now tears rolled unchecked down her face.

And that was how Rebecca found her.

*   *   *

Rebecca knew the girls who owned the inn. It was a small town, once you took away the tourists, and the inn was only ten doors up from her house. It was the sense of community and acceptance she loved most about it. The girls were gay, but it didn't matter that she wasn't. Although she sometimes wished she was. She wasn't the greatest fan of most men – she'd mostly picked bad ones. She'd gone there for a cup of coffee – the percolator was always on and she wasn't in the mood for painting this morning. The girls knew nothing about her daughter so she had come to listen to the gossip, drink coffee and stop herself watching the street outside home, hoping to see Freddie coming back.

Her pulse beat faster when she recognised Freddie's friend. Maybe Freddie *was* here. Maybe she hadn't left yesterday.

But the girl was alone.

When Reagan looked up and saw her, she was embarrassed by her tears, and wiped her face, vigorously, with her sleeve. 'Hello.'

'What are you doing here?'

'I have absolutely no idea.'

'May I sit?'

Reagan shrugged, so Rebecca sat. 'She came to see me yesterday. Freddie,' Rebecca said.

'I know.'

'Did you tell her I came over the other week?'

'No. Sorry.'

'That's okay.'

The tears started again. 'No, it isn't okay.' And now she was sobbing, harsh, painful sobs that shook her shoulders and contorted her face.

Rebecca moved to kneel by Reagan's chair. She put a hand on her forearm. 'What on earth has happened?'

At first Reagan waved the question away, but when Rebecca didn't move, thus proving that her concern was more than politeness, she said, 'I've been a complete bitch. I've done something unforgivable.'

Rebecca nodded, and stroked Reagan's arm. 'It just so happens I'm the world's leading expert on unforgivable . . .'

Eventually Reagan fell asleep on a red velvet couch in the lounge. Rebecca covered her with a throw and watched her for a while.

Then she took a small black book and her mobile phone out of her bag. 'Freddie?'

'Yes. Who is this?'

'This is Rebecca Valentine.'

Silence.

'I know you were here yesterday.' When Freddie still didn't answer, Rebecca went on: 'I'm not calling about that. I mean, I would have loved it if you'd wanted to come in and talk, but I'm not calling about that.'

'Why are you calling, then?'

'There's a friend of yours here.'

'Reagan.'

'That's right.'

'What's she doing at your house? She doesn't even know where you live. Not exactly.'

'She's not at my place. She's at an inn up the road. I called by and found her.'

'But you don't know her.'

'I met her last week.'

'I don't understand.'

'I came last week to look for you. You were in England. I asked Reagan to tell you I'd been.'

'She didn't.'

'I know. We've talked, she and I. I just thought you should know that she's here. She was planning to take a flight out this afternoon, but from the look of the weather, she isn't going anywhere fast.'

'You came looking for me?'

'Yes. I shouldn't have. I was almost relieved when you weren't there. It was wrong of me. Reagan wasn't slow to point that out, actually. She told me it was your decision when or if to come and find me. And she was right. But, like I said, I thought now you should know that she's here. She's in a terrible state.'

'Why isn't she calling me herself?'

'Because she's afraid it's too late. She thinks what she's said is unforgivable.'

They were both aware of the weird subtext of this conversation. Freddie couldn't quite believe she was hearing her mother's voice.

She was too shocked to be angry, but it felt strange.

'Look, I hope I've done the right thing', Rebecca continued. 'She's at the Point Inn. It's just a bit further up the hill from me, on the right. If you wanted to know.'

Freddie didn't know if she did or not.

'Does she know you're calling me?'

'No. She's asleep. Cried herself out.'

Reagan never cried.

'Right. Well. Thanks.'

Rebecca didn't know what she had expected, but she didn't want to say goodbye. 'You're welcome.'

Freddie hung up.

'That was my mother. She's found Reagan, crying her heart out in some inn in Provincetown. She phoned to say she was worried about her and thought I should know where she was.'

'What?'

'I know.' She put her hand up to stop him speaking. 'Don't ask me.' Then, 'I'm going.'

'Don't.'

'I have to, Matt. I can't leave it like this. What kind of friend would that make me?'

'What kind of friend has she been to you?'

'A dysfunctional one. A nightmare one.'

'You're just running away again.'

'I'm not. I'll be back.' She put her hands on his cheeks. 'I'll be back.'

'What about us?'

She kissed him once, deeply. 'I'm not running away any more, Matt. I just have to do this.'

★   ★   ★

She found the inn easily enough. Reagan wasn't around. She booked a room, and dumped her bag on the bed.

The owners were clearly fascinated by this soap opera playing out in their own backyard. 'You're English too. You must be Reagan's friend.'

Christ, for one buttoned-up woman, she'd certainly made friends quickly here. 'Yes.'

'She's on the beach.'

'In this weather?'

'Best weather for head-clearing. Take the steep steps across the road directly out front, if you want to catch her up.'

Reagan hadn't always been a hundred per cent dysfunctional. She had come round one evening, not long after Harry had been born, straight from work. Freddie thought she looked impossibly glamorous, in an immaculate navy suit and the kind of vertiginous heels Freddie only wore on evenings she knew she wasn't going to have to walk far.

Adrian had been away, and Reagan had recognised the panic and exhaustion in Freddie's voice on the telephone as she had joked that maybe she should have let Clarissa hire a nanny.

'Bollocks! She wouldn't have been a nanny, she'd have been a spy. Give that woman an inch . . . I'll be round. Six-ish.'

Reagan never left the office before nine.

But that night she had arrived, laden with Harvey

Nichols carriers. Handmade pasta with fresh pesto sauce and salad, peach juice and Prosecco from the Fifth floor ('Can't cook, won't cook'), a capacious Anya Hindmarch handbag ('Because I refuse to go out with you if you're carrying one of those grotesque changing bags') and a selection of creams from the Clarins counter ('So you can do something about those dark circles'). Freddie had practically fallen on her with gratitude.

'Just so long as you don't try and make me get all gurgly over junior!'

After they had eaten the meal, drunk the Bellinis, transferred the contents of the grotesque changing bag (a gift from Clarissa), and patted on the cream, Freddie had fallen asleep on the sofa. Harry had started wailing.

And Reagan had put him in his car seat on the leather seats of her Alpha Spider and driven him around West London for an hour and a half, only bringing him back when he was sound asleep. He had slept through that night, and every night afterwards.

It was cold. Was it only yesterday she'd her knickers off down here? The weather changed fast. Now she jammed her hat over her ears and pushed her hands deep into the pockets of her jacket. The wind was sharp, stinging her face.

Reagan was about a hundred yards away, standing at the edge of the foam, staring out to sea. When she was near enough to be heard, Freddie screamed,

'Reagan!' She turned. Five paces nearer. 'Right. I can't believe I'm here, but I am. Matt didn't want me to come, and I'm damn sure Tamsin would have told me to let you stew, but I'm here. This better be good, because I'll tell you, lady, this is your last bloody chance.'

'How did you find me?'

Freddie knew Reagan well enough to grasp that she was fighting the impulse to run and keep running. 'What's that got to do with anything? My mother rang me. Seems that you and she have already met.'

'I'm sorry.'

'For that?'

'For everything.'

'Look, Reagan, I'm here. Make me understand.'

'I can't.'

'Or won't. Has this got something to do with Matt and Sarah?'

Reagan didn't answer.

'Were you in love with one of them?'

Her face gave Freddie the answer.

'Were you in love with Matt? Are you still in love with him?'

'I don't know. I thought I was. For years I thought I was.'

'But now?'

'No. I'm not.'

'What, then?'

Reagan faced her. 'I'm jealous. All right? I'm so jealous I think it could kill me.'

'Jealous of what?'

'Jealous of whom. I'm jealous of you, and I'm jealous of Sarah – at least I was – and I'm even jealous of Tamsin. I thought it was because I wanted Matt. I knew him first, you remember, and he fell in love with her, and that was when it started. Because it showed me that however much I'd changed at university, I still wasn't as good as her.'

'That's ridiculous. Matt falling in love with Sarah had nothing to do with her being better than you. That's not how love works.'

'And how the fuck would I know how love works, Freddie? Hey? Who's ever loved me?' She had beaten her own chest with each word of that last sentence. 'God, Freddie! Did you even know I was jealous of Sarah for dying? Age hasn't wearied her or the years condemned. Huh? How sick is that? She died and got immortalised. Perfect Sarah. Tragic Sarah. Oh, don't get me wrong, I loved her as much as any of you did – maybe even as much as Matt. She rescued me when we were kids. You and Tamsin would never have bothered with me if she hadn't. At the beginning she dragged me along to everything, and I could tell you were just tolerating me. But I wanted to be a part of it.'

'You were.'

'Because of her.'

'Okay.' Freddie was struggling with the force of Reagan's feelings. This stuff was going back decades.

'But do you know what I did the night before after my best friend got married? I tried to sleep with her fiancé. What I told you back at the house – about Matt trying it on with me – wasn't true. It was always me. He never once gave me any encouragement. He didn't even tell Sarah – he didn't want her to be angry with me. And then what did I do? I went round there after she'd died and I made another pass at him. We talked about Sarah, and we both cried, and after he'd finished crying, he went to bed and fell asleep. I got in with him and started kissing him.'

Freddie was horrified.

'And he kissed me back. It's the only time he ever has. He wasn't really awake. He didn't know it was me, he thought I was her. And when he realised I wasn't – I've never seen anyone so angry. He didn't speak to me for months. I didn't see him. He didn't let me apologise. He just said he never wanted it mentioned again. Things aren't the same between us, of course. Something like that doesn't just go away. I made a move on my dead best friend's grieving husband. That's what sort of person I am. Do you have any idea how much I hate myself? I wanted to be you. Or Sarah. Or anyone but myself.'

'This is ridiculous, Reagan.' Freddie was frightened. 'It's madness. How have you let it get so out of hand?'

'I don't know.' She collapsed on to her knees on the sand, and her head fell forward so that her hair hung in front of her face. She was shaking.

Freddie went closer to her. And when she spoke again her voice was calmer.

'I thought if I was this incredible success,' Reagan

went on, 'with my own money and a great career, I wouldn't mind. I thought you lot might even envy me. But you never have – because I've never had anything worth envying. The big job, the fancy flat – they don't count, do they?'

'Of course they don't. But we thought that was what made you happy.'

'You had no idea, you see. And do you know what the most tragic part is? You two aren't just the best friends I've ever had – you're the only friends. You're supposed to see. You're supposed to.'

'You're supposed to show us.' Freddie knelt down and tried to touch her.

Reagan flinched. 'It's all ruined now.'

'Why do you say that?'

'Oh, come on, Freddie! Don't be so bloody Polly-anna – you sound like Sarah. Of course it's ruined. We can't come back from this.'

'Who says?'

'I say.'

'You need help, Reagan, proper help. You're into whatever this is too deeply for us to get you out of it.'

Reagan nodded.

'But it isn't ruined. Do you honestly think we'd still be friends all these years later if you were just the geeky girl from down the hall who Sarah made us hang out with?'

Reagan raised her head and looked at her.

'No way. We're friends all these years later because we still want to be. When you're bad, okay, you're pretty horrible. You can be sulky and spiky and mean. And you've had a pretty good run lately. But when you're good . . . you're funny and generous, bright and loyal. You're here, aren't you?'

'I didn't come here for you. I came for myself.'

'Maybe partly, but you know that's not all true.' She put out a hand to touch Reagan again, and this time she didn't move away. 'This is in your own head, Reagan. It's all in there.' She pointed.

Suddenly Reagan's spikiness had gone. She leaned against Freddie so heavily that Freddie had to struggle to keep her balance, and her sobs took hold of her. Through the noise, the desperate noise, Freddie heard, 'I'm . . . just . . . so . . . unhappy.' She felt like Reagan had finally been stripped bare.

Reagan wouldn't come back straight away. 'I can't face Matt.'

Freddie didn't want to leave her behind. 'I'll talk to him.'

Reagan smiled gratefully. 'I still can't.'

It was amazingly loyal of Matthew never to have told any of them. Freddie had pretty clear memories of his wedding day – she remembered them all together. There was a picture: Matthew in the middle with Sarah, and the three girls round the edge, all beaming. Freddie could see the picture. She kept it on a book-shelf in her living room.

And she remembered the harrowing time just after Sarah had died. They had taken shifts: Tamsin,

Reagan, Freddie and Neil. Drop in, spend time with Matthew, report to the others when you left. One evening she had rung the doorbell. She had been surprised when he smiled. 'Let me guess? Just passing?'

'Of course not,' she had replied. 'I'm on widower-watch this evening.'

He had put a hand on her shoulder and said, 'Well done – admitting you have a problem is the first step to recovery.' They had both laughed.

Those nights were strange. You could be watching television with him, or cooking something in the kitchen, and you'd be talking, or you might be quiet, but suddenly he would be crying silently. You'd turn to look at him, and tears would be welling in his eyes. They'd all gone through it with him. It was on one of those nights that Reagan had done what she'd done. It was pretty appalling. And it spoke volumes about Matthew that he had never said a word.

You could choose, couldn't you, how much you engaged with your friends? When Sarah had died, they had all become almost obsessed with caring for him and for each other. Shock and grief had made them cling together because they could help each other through. His suffering, and their response to it, were acute. Reagan's was chronic: long-term, easy to ignore. Freddie couldn't honestly say it was all Reagan's fault that they hadn't noticed, although she had put up a hell of a smokescreen. Really, they had chosen not to. They hadn't been there for her. If they had, they'd have read the clues, seen the signs. And maybe they wouldn't have got to this point.

In the end, the only one who had offered Reagan protection was Matthew – the one who stood to be most damaged by her.

'Matt will understand.'

'Still, I want to stay here for a couple of days.'

'To do what? If it's just to hide, then . . .'

'Not to hide.'

'I can't make you come back.'

'No.'

'But promise you will?'

'I promise.'

She left Reagan at the Point Inn. She'd had to park down the street, and now she had to pass Rebecca's house to get back to it. Except she couldn't. She walked up to the door and knocked. There was no answer. But as she stood back and tried to walk away, another door, the one on the building nearest the beach, opened.

Rebecca didn't seem surprised to see her. She opened the door wide and stood back against the wall to let her in. Freddie was grateful that she wasn't bothering with small-talk, filling the heavy silence with meaningless platitudes. She went in, pleased to be out of the chill breeze.

Upstairs it was warm. Rebecca had been working – there was a smudge of vermilion on her cheek, a drop on the sleeve of her black smock. It matched the large shawl she wore across the opposite shoulder.

Now that she was here, Freddie didn't know what she had come to say. Rebecca let the silence go on for a moment, and then she spoke. Her voice was gentle. The English accent with which she must have grown up had largely receded, but Freddie caught a hint of it. 'How is your friend?'

'I'm not sure.'

Silence.

'Thank you, though, for calling me. She's going to be staying at the inn for a couple of days.'

'It's good for the soul up there.'

Freddie looked around her at the canvases. 'I like these.'

'Thank you.' She accepted the compliment with a nod.

'Did you always paint?' The first of a million questions she might like to ask.

'No. I didn't start until I came here.' When was that? And why? Freddie didn't know where to start.

So Rebecca did. 'Did he ever tell you why I left?'

'He never told me anything. You just weren't there.'

'You didn't ask?'

'By the time I was old enough to wonder, I wasn't close enough to him to ask.'

'I'm sorry for that.'

Freddie shrugged.

Rebecca smiled. 'You must be a lot like me.'

Freddie squashed the indignant response that sprang up. 'How?'

'It hasn't eaten you up, the not knowing. A lot of

people would have been completely screwed up by it. It would have coloured their whole lives.'

Freddie didn't know why she should tell her, but she found herself saying, 'It screwed me up when my little boy was born.'

Rebecca nodded thoughtfully. 'You couldn't understand how I could have left you.'

'No.'

'But it's made you a better mother.'

'Maybe.'

'Do you have a picture of Harry?' She sounded eager. 'I knew he'd been born, of course, I'd love to see a picture of him.'

Freddie wanted to be angry enough, bitter enough, to say no, to punish Rebecca. Why was she reaching into her bag? Wordlessly she handed Rebecca the soft leather folder she always carried with her. It held three pictures: one of Harry the crinkled newborn, almost obscured by white blankets; one of him as a toddler, framed by her legs, smiling straight to the camera, all blond curls and long eyelashes; and the most recent held a hint of the man Harry would become, no longer unconscious in front of the lens, the slightly affected pose. Still her Harry, though.

Rebecca looked at it for a long time. She put her thumb across one of his faces, stroked it almost imperceptibly, then handed it back to Freddie. 'He's beautiful.'

Was there a break in her voice? Or did Freddie just want there to be? 'You never tried to see him?' *Why? Why? Why?*

'I never tried to see *him*, no.'

The way she said it made Freddie ask, 'You tried to see me?'

'Just once, about a year after I left you.'

Like most of Rebecca's sentences, it left a paragraph unsaid. It was almost unbearable. Freddie didn't know where to go with her questioning or whether to go there at all. Maybe she shouldn't have come. Maybe it would be better never to know. She was all right not knowing. She always had been.

But Rebecca was in front of her. Of course she couldn't walk away. She could only sit here, wondering which of the plasters she should rip off the wounds of her childhood and her adulthood, which scabs to pick to make her bleed. It was so huge that she didn't know where to start.

And infuriatingly, marvellously, Rebecca seemed to know what she was thinking. She was standing now, by the picture window, hugging herself, and when she spoke it was to the sea. 'I'd like to tell you why I left.' There was pride and something like defiance in the set of her graceful shoulders. 'Not because I want forgiveness, or because I think it will all make perfect sense to you, but because it's the beginning.'

She *is* like me, Freddie thought. The beginning is the logical place to start.

Rebecca turned back into the room, and sat, legs tucked beneath her, on the wicker *chaise-longue* opposite Freddie.

'I was nineteen when I met your father, not a very

grown-up nineteen. I'd been in Boston for about five months. I'd come to work for a family my father knew – someone he'd met at university before the war, and stayed friends with over the years. His daughter needed a nanny, mother's help, companion, that sort of thing. She'd had a baby recently, and the birth had gone badly. She was weak and tired. I expect my parents thought it would be good for me, broaden my horizons, and I was desperate to go. Always desperate for something. My life had been so . . . so dull. Safe. Private education, only mixing with the right sort of people, only learning the things a young lady should. I was suffocating.' She looked at Freddie questioningly, and her daughter nodded – that impulse, at least, she understood.

'He came for supper one night. He was a partner at Kitty's husband's law firm. I always ate with them – I wasn't a servant. Kitty and I were good friends by then, and I loved the baby. Your father was good-looking, especially on that first night I met him. He was the boss, of course, and everyone wanted to impress him. He was beautifully dressed, immaculate. I remember his hands – his nails, like he had them done. And he was so much taller than me that I had to bend my head back to look at him. I wasn't used to that, and I liked it. And something happened that first night. It wasn't lust – I'd been at girls' school all my life, I'm not sure I would have quite recognised lust if it had been,' she gave a throaty chuckle, 'but it was something. He looked at me like no one ever had before. Like . . .

like he had to have me. From the first moment he saw me.' She gazed into the middle distance now – remembering, Freddie supposed. She was almost talking to herself. 'I don't think he looked at anyone else all evening. They were all vying for his attention, but he addressed every remark to me. Asked me all sorts of things about myself. He had beautiful eyes. Mysterious. He looked like he'd seen things, you know?

'And then he just went for me. That's the only way I can describe it. It was nothing like wooing or courting. It was like a mission. Flowers, notes, attention. The morning after that first dinner he sent me ten dozen red roses. I didn't know anyone did things like that in real life. Certainly hasn't happened since! I was completely taken over by it. He watched my mouth while I spoke, and made me feel that every sound I made was the most important thing he had ever heard. He took me to the ballet, and the theatre, to fancy restaurants – made me part of those worlds. My parents hadn't lived that way, and if they had, they'd never have included me. He made me feel like I belonged there. We would sit in the best seats at the theatre, and the whole time I knew he was watching me, not the show. Just me. He bought me presents. I was speechless and breathless with the things he did for me. If that sounds implausible, remember that I was little more than a child – a girl with a limited view of life, who had taken her idea of romantic ideals from the books she'd read, heroes like Heathcliff, Jay Gatsby and Maxim de Winter. Men with passion, men with a past, brooding . . .' Her voice trailed away. She stood up and poured herself a glass of whisky from the bottle on the side table. 'I sound like a fool, I know,' Freddie didn't think so, 'but that is exactly how it was.'

She held the bottle towards Freddie, who nodded, and poured a good two inches into another glass.

'Nowadays, a girl like me who wanted her freedom, who wanted escape, excitement – she'd pack a ruck-sack and disappear. I wish I'd been brave enough then, but I wasn't. He seemed like a chance.

'He first kissed me on the Common. In the spring-time. The man in the bespoke suit and the girl in the cheesecloth skirt, there in the park. What a kiss that was, like it had all of himself in it. I'd never been kissed before, not properly, not like that, and if he'd asked me to jump off a cliff with him that morning I would have done it. Instead he asked me to elope with him. Christ, the romance of it. Afterwards I never really knew whether I'd said yes to spite my parents, or because it sounded like an adventure, or just because of that kiss. A week later we were married. I didn't tell a soul.'

She was quiet for a moment. Freddie's head was filled with questions. Where did it happen? How was it? What did you wear? She wanted all the gaps filled in, but she didn't want Rebecca to know it and, more than that, she wanted the story to get to her.

'It would never have worked. How could it? Love's great, if that was what it was, but it ain't enough. There were more than twenty years between us. It was the sixties, and I hadn't lived – I hadn't done a single thing in my life just for myself. Hadn't been drunk, hadn't slept with someone I shouldn't have, let alone someone I should, hadn't lived alone, hadn't got to know myself at all. All I did was swap one submissive life for another. I was a fool.'

She stopped, and Freddie didn't know what to say. This man sounded so little like her father that it was like listening to a book on tape – she hadn't heard anything yet that resonated in her.

'I almost wish I could sit here and tell you that he was a bad husband, that he beat me, or cheated on me, or abused me. Something obvious. I suppose that would make me look better. He wasn't a bad husband, in the way most husbands are judged. But when I married him the spell was broken. Once we'd done it, every-thing changed. Subtly, but definitely. Time – that was the biggest thing. Before then he'd had all the time in the world for me, but he went straight back to work, stayed there all day every day and often long into the evenings. I didn't know where that yearning to be with me had gone. Evaporated. It was like when you're basking in the sun, and then clouds come over – his attention, his time, were gone just like that. I didn't understand. And his lack of time gave me plenty. I didn't have many friends in the States. Kitty was having another baby, and I always knew she didn't approve of what I'd done. My parents hadn't forgiven me. I'd shut them out, and they never met him. I was lonely and confused. Petulant, too, I suppose. I knew he'd lost interest in me, and I didn't understand why.

'I had my first affair when you were about six months old. I remember he said once, after he knew, that he'd never really be sure if you were his or not. But you were. I'd waited to see if having you would swing him back to me. It didn't. So, the affair – well, I'd hardly call it an affair. I slept with the landscape gardener.' She laughed. 'Bit Mellors, I suppose, but my God, his physique!'

Freddie wondered if she'd forgotten who she was talking to, but Rebecca continued, looking straight at her: 'Sorry if this shocks you' – she didn't seem sorry, and Freddie wasn't shocked because she didn't have a maternal image of Rebecca for Rebecca to shatter – 'but I've always been rather keen on sex. After you were born, he didn't take much notice of me . . . and the gardener, well, did.'

Now Freddie smiled. It seemed she and her mother had more in common than she might have thought. If Adrian had ever stopped wanting sex, she knew she'd have been looking elsewhere.

If Rebecca noticed the smile, she didn't acknowledge it. For a moment, Freddie thought of Adrian and Antonia Melhuish.

'I suppose it was wrong of me but, then, the whole thing was wrong, wasn't it? I thought maybe he had someone else too, although he never gave me reason to doubt him. He had plenty of opportunity. I guess it sounds amoral to you, but I thought if he didn't know . . .'

'But he found out?'

'Not until the year I left.'

'It lasted that long?'

'With the gardener? God, no!' Rebecca's voice rose with incredulity. 'There were others. My riding instructor. Pardon the pun. A neighbour's husband – I felt a little bad about that one, but she never found out as far as I knew. A guy I met at some deathly law do. It was only ever sex.' She checked herself. 'That's not true. Sex, yes. I needed it. But I suppose it was also about being held and cherished, if only for a few minutes. He'd given me a hell of a knock, that man. It was the beginning of me getting up from it.'

'So then what?'

'He caught me. He must have known something, that time. He knew where to find me and when.'

Freddie wondered where this was going. 'Did he throw you out?' Was that how it had happened? She glimpsed a new scenario: she didn't want to leave me, he made her go. That would change everything.

Rebecca shook her head. 'He couldn't have kept me away from you, could he? There are laws, courts and rights.'

Freddie was stunned by the way her mother wouldn't hide from her.

'What, then?'

'He let the guy run off – he was no one. He let me pull on my dress. He watched me the whole time. I remember how disgusted he looked, like I was dirty. And then he shouted. He ranted. I'd never heard him do it before. His rage was normally so quiet, so self-contained. There'd been days when I would have given anything for him to rant about something, *anything*, but this was the only time he ever did. He called me an ungrateful whore. He called me faithless, like my mother before me . . .' She let the sentence hang there.

Freddie didn't understand.

Rebecca spoke slowly. 'But he'd never met my mother.'

Freddie was still confused. 'So how . . .'

'Except that he had. That was when I found out that he had.'

Freddie stood up and went to the window. The sea was rougher now than it had been earlier. Waves broke against the beach. She felt sick. 'I don't understand.'

'Neither did I, but he was happy enough to explain it to me. I think he enjoyed it because he could see how much pain it caused me.' Rebecca took a deep breath. Freddie could see that it still hurt to talk about it.

'He'd been in love with her. They'd met during the war. Her father, my grandfather, had been a high sheriff – and your father was stationed in her village. Sounds like a made-for-TV movie, doesn't it? Their eyes met across a ration book. It's almost funny – silk stockings, chocolates, all of that.' This time the chuckle was bitter.

He never talked about the war, Freddie thought suddenly.

'They fell in love, apparently. They were each other's first everything. He wanted to marry her. Believe me, he didn't leave anything out when he told me. Except that he wasn't then who he'd become by the time I met him. I don't suppose he ever talked much to you about where he came from? He certainly didn't with me, not when we met. I suppose I assumed I knew. He'd been poor, raised uneducated, from the wrong background, American. Her father had forbidden it, wouldn't let them see each other. Sounds ridiculous, doesn't it? Sure as hell wouldn't work today. I don't suppose it always worked then, but it did with my mother. He bundled her off to relatives and wouldn't let her come home. He stopped them communicating with each other altogether. Your father never stopped loving her, and he never stopped hating her for letting him go so easily. And I think that happening to him, when he was a young man, dictated and coloured every single thing he ever did in his life afterwards.'

'My God.' It didn't seem adequate.

Rebecca almost smirked. 'Quite a show-stopper, isn't it? My own husband had been in love with my mother more than twenty years before. He'd married me . . . Well, why had he married me? I've had years to think about it. Because I looked like her? Because he was laying a ghost to rest? Because he wanted revenge? Who the hell knows?'

Freddie rubbed her eyes. It was too much. 'How did he know?'

'I think he knew something the first time he met me. I looked very much like her. And he'd asked me all about myself – about my parents, my grandparents, and where I'd grown up . . . and I'd been so flattered that he was interested.' Rebecca snorted.

'And that's why you ran?'

'That's why I ran.'

'Why didn't you take me?'

'I panicked. I was frightened and horrified. So I bolted. I never thought I wasn't coming back to get you. I just knew I had to get away from there – from him – as quickly as possible.'

'Where did you go?'

'Would you believe back to my mother?'

'Did she know?'

'No. He'd changed his name, after the war. Maybe she didn't even remember him. When I got home, I looked long and hard at her for the ghost of lost love, for shadows across her face. There weren't any. Maybe she'd buried it so deep no one could ever have seen it. And maybe it wasn't there. Maybe he'd based his whole life on the kind of lie a woman can tell a man. She married my father before the end of the war. They'd grown up together – their parents were friends. He was a proper English gentleman, Eton, Cambridge, decorated in the war. Respectable, dull, but satisfactory.'

'And you never told her?'

'She was ill by then. Another thing they didn't talk about. She was practically dying, and they hadn't told me. God save me from reserved English families. So much damage is done by living like that. So many secrets. I hope to Christ you aren't raising your son that way. I wanted to tell her – I wanted to spread the hurt a bit. I wanted to know what had happened. I almost couldn't believe it was true. It was hard, when you looked at her, with her perfect, neat hair, her string of pearls – the ones she wore every day of her life, even the last – her cashmere twinset. She didn't look like a woman who could destroy a man's life. She didn't look like she had it in her.'

Rebecca shrugged. 'She was dying. You could see that straight away. She was too thin, her eyes were yellowing and her skin was grey. I couldn't tell her. I didn't tell her. I loved her.'

'What about me? Did you love me?'

For the first time since they had met, Rebecca's shoulders sank and she looked her age. She reached out, then let her hand fall to her side. 'I loved you. Very much.'

'Then why didn't you come back for me? Even if I can understand you going in the first place, why didn't you come back for me?'

'I did. Once.'

Freddie waited.

'Just after my mother died. I got on the next plane that I could.'

'And?'

Rebecca's voice was very quiet. 'I saw you on Boston Common, in front of the house. Next to the swan boats. You were with a young woman. You were wearing a white broderie-anglaise dress and navy blue shoes with little white socks. You looked like an angel. You were laughing fit to bust about something, and the woman was laughing with you. And I started to go to you across the grass. My heart was beating so hard.'

Freddie realised she was holding her breath.

'Then you threw your arms round that woman's neck and kissed her. You said something to each other, and it looked like you were saying, "I love you", and you started walking in the other direction, hand in hand, chatting away.'

'And?'

'I'd lost you. Not even lost you – I'd given you away. You weren't mine any more. You were your father's. You were that woman's. I saw that it would be more selfish to come back into your life than it had been to leave it in the first place. I saw that you were fine. Better than fine.'

'That's not good enough.'

'Not good enough for what?'

'Not good enough for me to forgive you.' Freddie felt desperate. What had she wanted to hear? That Rebecca had been in a coma for thirty-two years, or in prison? Something. Anything.

Now Rebecca risked a touch: she put her hand on Freddie's arm. Freddie didn't snatch it away. 'I'm not asking you to forgive me. I never would. I did what I did. I can't ask for forgiveness – or even understanding. I was a girl, still a girl.'

'You were my mother.'

'I knew I wasn't going to be able to give you the

stability you needed and had where you were. I knew I'd done it all the wrong way round. I knew what I was doing when I left you where you were. And part of knowing that was understanding that you might never forgive me. I've lived with that all these years. I understand what I did. And for a long time I thought it might kill me. But it didn't. I lived, and you lived. And you've been happy, I hope. I forgave myself, Freddie, a long time ago.'

White-hot anger exploded in Freddie's brain. 'You did what?' She pulled away her arm roughly. She could hardly believe Rebecca had said that to her.

'Maybe that didn't come out right—'

But Freddie wasn't going to give her the chance to rephrase. She heard herself shouting, raw, sarcastic: 'Well, good for you, Mum. You forgave yourself! How very new age of you! Thanks for sharing! You saw me laughing in a park, and that gave you the right to walk away from me for the rest of my life without a backward glance and forgive yourself.'

'It wasn't like that.'

Now it was almost a scream. 'It was *exactly* like that!' Freddie grabbed her coat and bag from the banister where Rebecca had left them.

'Don't go.' Against Freddie's mounting hysteria, Rebecca's quiet plea.

Freddie looked closely at her mother's face, and spat words at it: 'Tough shit, Mum. It's my turn to walk away. After all, you're happy now. You don't need me. You're better off without me.'

She slammed the door behind her, harder than she had ever slammed one before.

Upstairs, Rebecca downed her whisky, then pulled her shawl tightly round her. She sat down in the wicker chair, and watched the storm brewing.

Outside, in her car, Freddie laid her head on the steering-wheel, and sobbed for a long time. Then she drove back to Matthew, and this time she told him everything. She told him about Reagan, and about Rebecca, and her father. And she cried almost the whole time.

Later, they fell asleep on her bed, fully clothed.

Sometime in the middle of the night they woke up cold and uncomfortable, shucked off their clothes and climbed under the counterpane. Matt just spooned her. Before she went back to sleep, she reached one hand behind her, and stroked Matthew's cheek. 'Thank you.'

'Come back with me.'

It was the next morning, and although he'd tried, he couldn't extend this trip. He had to be back for a Friday meeting, and he had sensed trouble when he had attempted to back out if it. Then he'd tried to get a red-eye on Thursday – go straight from the airport – but the planes were full, so he had to go tomorrow. He hated to leave her. This morning she looked like a Victorian invalid – her eyes were puffed with crying and sunk in a pale face.

She had smiled gratefully at him when he had taken her a cup of coffee, but she had shaken her head. 'I can't. This isn't over. Besides, Reagan's still here.'

He'd put out his hand to touch her face, and she had caught it, kissed the palm. 'Then I'll come back,' he said.

'No. Enough. I'll be home soon.'

'Not soon enough.'

'You'll get the sack.'

'They wouldn't dare.'

'You'll get a deep-vein thrombosis.'

'I'll wear those funny socks. I'll come back.'

'Grace'll be home this week. And I daresay a shame-faced Reagan will appear at some point.'

'And how will that help?'

'I don't know. Might encourage me to come out from up my own ass.'

'Stop it, Fred. This is big. It's allowed to be big.'

'I don't want any of it.'

'You don't get to choose, I'm afraid.'

'Let me drive you to the airport, at least. I need some city. I promised Harry some trainers from Niketown – you can post them when you get home.'

'You know how to show a guy a good time.'

'I haven't even started!'

Boston

Being in Boston made the other stuff recede. They just enjoyed being together. Once, in the afternoon, as they walked along the street, holding hands, it struck her how easily it had happened. This was okay, after all. This was good.

Then they were outside the lilac-glass house again. Inside a party was in full swing, and the windows were dressed with white lights. People in evening dress were drinking champagne, while a waiter, in starched white, handed round canapés on a silver tray. Matthew put his arm round Freddie. 'Do you remember?'

'Of course I remember.'

Already a couple's shorthand.

'It's a bit like us, this house, isn't it?' Freddie mused.

He smiled his sideways smile at her. 'And how do you figure that, exactly?' His tone was nursery-school teacher.

She nudged him gently in the ribs. 'Something went wrong, didn't it, when they made those windows? Like it all went wrong for me in September.' September seemed for ever ago. 'But it turned out to be so right. So beautiful.'

He loved that, and he was starting to believe he might get his happy ending. With her. So he kissed her again outside the lilac-glass house, but it was so different from the last time. He kissed her mouth, muttering into it that she was crazy and he loved her being crazy, and that he just loved her, full stop, and she kissed him back, with all of herself.

He was almost instantly hard against her thigh, and she put her hand down, between them, to reach for him.

But Matthew groaned. 'Oh no you don't. Not another al-fresco job. I don't think I could manage it in this cold, anyway, even if you are the most exciting woman on the planet. You and I are going to find us a bed.' He turned away from the lilac-glass house, and they started down the street, walking as fast as they dared, clinging together on the icy pavement.

It actually took them a while to get to the bed, but as soon as the hotel-room door was closed, they were pulling off each other's clothes. When Freddie was naked, Matthew held her at arms' length by both hands, turning her body this way and that, like in a courtly dance, in the lamplight. Then he turned her round, and kissed her neck, down her spine and back up, until she shuddered with longing. He pushed her into the upholstered chair by the window and stroked and kissed every inch of her. Each time she tried to touch him he brushed away her hands, so she arched her back and surrendered to him. She felt like a piece of fine porcelain, beautiful and precious.

When she couldn't stand it any more, she pushed herself against him, and, caught off guard, he fell back on to the carpet. She straddled him, kissing him passionately. Now she didn't want him to be gentle.

But he was.

He had forgotten how much he wanted to make it all right for her, after the beach, how he had remonstrated with himself for being too fast, too clumsy, and she had forgotten that it had been like that on the beach, and forgotten that anyone else had ever known just exactly how to, and in a stupid, wonderful way, it was like the first time for both of them.

He half carried her now, to the big soft bed. It took the longest time, and it was perfect. They ended sitting up, her across his lap, their legs stretched out behind each other, holding each other tightly, barely moving, barely tilting their hips, tipping each other so quietly over the edge into something so perfect and so close and so loving that Freddie felt tears in her eyes. When she looked at Matthew he was crying too.

Eventually Freddie got cramp in her left hip. She tipped Matthew's face in her hands and kissed his lips, wiping his wet cheeks with her thumbs. Then they lay down, and held hands under the duvet.

'Wow.'

'Wow indeed.'

'Wanna do it again?'

'You might have to give me a minute.' Matthew sounded a little worried.

'I'm kidding.' She was giggling now, and he loved the sound of it.

Freddie stretched out, and turned so that she was curled into him. Her bottom nestled in his lap, and he thrust at her once, twice, playfully. She reached behind and slapped him gently.

'Who's kidding now, then?'

They were quiet for a while, listening to each other breathe, tuned in to how they felt in the other's arms, how they smelt, how they fit.

As Matthew was falling asleep she said, to herself as much as to him, in sleep as much as in wakefulness, 'I love you.'

England

What was that Bernard Manning-esque joke? It went something like 'Doctor, doctor, I think my wife's dead.' 'What makes you think that?' 'Well, the sex is the same but the ironing's piling up!'

The sex was most definitely *not* the same, that was for sure, but by God the house was in a state. Mrs Harper – only Freddie and Harry were allowed to call her Barbara – had had a hip replacement straight after half-term, and would be convalescing indefinitely. She was also very angry with Adrian, who had always found her formidable anyway. She had one of those bosoms that had spread into a shelf, and she folded her arms Les Dawson-style under it whenever she spoke to him. By mutual agreement, this had happened infrequently in the decade or so that she had been cleaning for them. If Freddie didn't come back, he was sure Mrs Harper wouldn't either. The whole place was looking a bit *Withnail and I*. A pile of ominous-looking post teetered on the hall table, and the plants were dusty. This morning he hadn't been able to find any clean socks, and an epic voyage with an armful of washing to the utility room had been thwarted by the empty bottle of washing liquid, if not by the almost incomprehensible symbols on the washing-machine.

Back upstairs, he had borrowed a pair of sports socks from Harry's drawer, but they were too small.

He was fed up with the ridiculous limbo in which Freddie was making them live. She should come home. There was really no need for her to stay in America. Or to stay away from him. He'd confessed all about Antonia Melhuish and he'd ended it. What more did she want? A man was entitled to one transgression, wasn't he? He had friends who'd had affair after affair and they still had clean socks.

No, it was intolerable.

He'd been lying low for a few days. An empty bottle of twelve-year-old malt was evidence of this. Now it was time for action. A flame of the old military discipline flickered within him. He'd start by finding help. Then he'd get hold of Freddie and have it out with her, once and for all. Get her back here where she belonged. Then he might go into the office.

Feeling better, he took the *Yellow Pages* down from the shelf. Domestic help – cleaning agencies . . .

The phone rang as he was reaching for the receiver. Irritated, he answered: 'Yes?'

'Is that Adrian Sinclair?'

'It is.'

'This is Clive Dunmore, Harry's housemaster.'

'Yes?' Adrian remembered him as a mousy man who didn't even look as if he could have broken up a decent fight among the first-formers. He ran the chess club, and had one of those ludicrous fish symbols on the back of his car.

'I'm afraid I have worrying news. We think Harry has run away.'

'Run away? What do you mean "we think"?'

'He hasn't been seen since last night at lights out. None of the other boys appears to have any idea where he is. The grounds are being searched, but so far there is no evidence that they are here – another boy is missing too.'

'Who?'

'A new boy. Michael Wilson? He and Harry have become quite close this term.'

'Yes. He's spoken about him.' Adrian didn't quite feel panic – Harry was a tough kid – but he felt distinctly worried.

'We've just spoken to Michael's mother and she hasn't heard anything. We wondered—'

'Of course not. I would have let you know. Has anything happened at school? A fight or some lousy marks, or anything?'

'Nothing out of the ordinary. We've spoken to all his masters, and the staff are still talking to the boys, but so far nothing. We wondered . . . is anything happening at home that might—'

'What do you mean?' Adrian knew exactly, of course, but the whole tack of the conversation was making him queasy.

'Well, we know that Michael's parents have recently separated. Indeed, he came to us as a direct result of it.'

Adrian pre-empted his unspoken question – put them both out of their misery. 'My wife has been abroad a great deal this term. Her father, who lived in the States, died in September, and his estate and affairs have taken up a great deal of her time. But she was with the family for half-term. Harry was fine when she went back.' He was buggered if he was going to discuss his private business with this little man. The Sinclairs did not go in for public laundering of dirty linen. Besides, it was nothing like that for them.

'So, is Mrs Sinclair currently away?'

'Yes, she is.' Adrian let his impatience show. 'So what's to be done? How are we going to find them? Have you called the police?'

'We have. An officer is on his way over. He wanted to know how much money we thought the boys had.'

'I haven't a clue. Don't you control that?'

'Tuck-shop money, yes, of course. And they aren't supposed to keep cash at school but—'

'Then I'm sure he didn't have much. They can't have got far.'

'I hope not.'

'I suppose I'd better stay here. I'll make a few calls.'

'I'm sure that's for the best.'

'You'll ring again as soon as you have news?'

'Of course.'

Adrian hung up without saying goodbye. Christ! This was just what he needed. He glanced at his watch. Thank God. He couldn't sanction calling Freddie now, in the middle of the night. With a bit of luck Harry would turn up before she woke.

He went to the front door and stepped out into the street. He looked up and down in both directions, hoping against logic to see a small figure hurrying his way. It was bitterly cold – the temperature must have dropped five degrees since yesterday. He shuddered involuntarily. Somewhere Harry was out in this.

He went back inside, and thought briefly again of phoning Freddie, but fear of her reaction countered his need for support. She was the strong one. She always made everything work. The washing-machine and Harry.

Guilt was unfamiliar to Adrian. He hadn't felt it the whole time he'd been with Antonia, but now it stabbed him through the heart. Harry had run away because of what he'd done. He and this Michael kid must have done a number on each other, and whatever this was, a cry for help or a protest, it was Adrian's fault.

He went back to the phone and pressed Tamsin's number on autodial. She answered. He could hear breakfast in the background, Meghan cajoling Flannery, Willa and Homer chatting.

'Tamsin? It's Adrian.' He didn't wait for acknowledgement. 'Harry's run away from school. Have you heard anything?'

'Shit.' The room behind her went quiet. 'No. Course not.'

'Can you think of anywhere he might be?'

Tamsin was silent for a few seconds. 'No, but I'll ask Homer. Hang on a second.'

The line went dead – she must have put her hand
over the receiver.

Adrian was aware of his every heartbeat. He felt
short of breath.

Tamsin's voice again. 'He didn't say a word to
Homer when he was back at half-term.'

'Okay.'

'Have you told Freddie?'

'No. She'll be in bed.'

'She'll want to know.'

'I don't—'

Tamsin interrupted him, her tone fierce: 'Don't be
such a coward. You've got to tell her.'

She always made him feel so bloody defensive. She'd
been doing it for as long as he had known her. Everything she ever said to him screamed, 'I know her better
than you do. I know what she'd want better than you
would. I love her better than you do.' It had stopped
them ever being friends.

She was in full flow now: 'And, what's more, you've
got to get her on a flight first. She'll want to be here.'

'I hardly think that's necessary.'

Tamsin saw red.

'And the fact that you can't see immediately that that
is exactly what Freddie would want and needs is
precisely the reason that your marriage is in the state
it's in.'

He was shocked and indignant. But as he spluttered into a retort, she interrupted him again: 'I'll
give you half an hour. Then I'm calling her myself.

Do the right thing, Adrian, for Christ's sake.' She hung up.

Ten minutes later, Freddie rang Tamsin. All she said was 'Oh, my God.'

It was all she needed to say. Tamsin had been pacing up and down the kitchen since she'd hung up on Adrian. She'd felt panic and fear, and she'd thought the unforgivable Thank-God-it-isn't-one-of-mine that occurs to all mothers when something bad happens to someone else's child. She'd drunk the tea Meghan had made for her, so she was ready for the call. Her voice was soft, gentle and as calm as she could make it. 'It's okay, Freddie. He's going to be fine, I promise. He's with his mate. There's safety in numbers. They'll look after each other. They won't have done anything stupid, I'm sure. I know Harry.'

It was cold, grey and drizzling, and she didn't feel anything like as confident as she sounded.

'Do you think?' It was a little girl's voice; a little girl's question.

'I absolutely do.' Tamsin bustled her on to the practicalities: 'Did Adrian sort out a flight?'

'Yes. I suppose I've got you to thank for that.'

'He probably wasn't thinking straight. But he did it?'

'Yes. I'm on the first flight out this morning. It's a couple of hours' drive, and that ridiculously long check-in, of course, so I'll have to go soon. Thank Christ he phoned. If he'd waited until the morning I'd have lost so much time.'

Silently Tamsin rested her case. 'What's he doing?'

'Well, he's spoken to a police officer – they're at the school now. They've told him to sit tight in case Harry gets in touch. And the school's given the police all the information they had . . . what he might be wearing . . .' Freddie's voice broke. 'Oh, Tamsin.'

'They'll find him. Freddie?' Her voice was firm. '*They'll find him.*'

It was cold. He was wearing a vest, a T-shirt, a hoodie, and his lightweights under his coat, but it was still freezing. His beanie was pulled down over his ears, but he'd forgotten his gloves, and his fingers were stiff with cold. He looked at Michael, beside him in the bus shelter. His nose was red, but he was still asleep. How could he sleep when it was so cold? He shoved him with his shoulder. Maybe when he woke up Michael would tell him where they were going.

It had been exciting last night, waiting until lights out, getting dressed under the covers. He'd felt a bit *Mission Impossible*, getting out of the grounds, and it had been fantastic when they'd arrived undetected in the outside world. They'd run as fast as they could through a field, whooping when they dared. Free.

But then Michael had made him keep walking. They had to get as far away as they could, he said, before they were missed. He talked about patrol cars and sniffer dogs, which kept Harry going.

Michael kept saying, 'That'll show them they can't just fuck up my life and get away with it.' He said that a lot. Then he'd look at Harry and add, 'Or yours,' with emphasis. Michael wanted morning to come faster so that his parents, in their separate houses, could start worrying and feeling bad.

Harry was glad his mum was away. They wouldn't tell her, surely. He didn't want her to feel bad. But Michael was right: parents had to understand they couldn't just think about themselves. Michael said he'd overheard his mother having a fight with her mother about it. His grandmother had said that his parents were 'volunteers', that Michael was the only true 'victim'. Harry thought Michael liked that word. He wasn't sure what he meant, but he supposed his friend must be right. If his own parents wanted to 'fuck up' their own lives, that was up to them, but he was the 'victim', and this was going to show them. He just hadn't expected it to be so cold.

Matthew was going out of the door when he heard the phone. He was already late. His voice sounded impatient.

'It's me, Matt.'

'Freddie!' She sounded wretched. 'What's the matter?'

He didn't have the same time to rehearse comfort for her. Fear clenched his gut. 'Oh, my poor Freddie. Poor Harry. Do you know why?'

'I think so. It's my fault, I'm sure of it.'

'For God's sake, you can't be sure of anything. Even assuming it is to do with you and Adrian, that's not your bloody fault, is it?'

He could hear that she was crying, and that killed him – she was crying and he couldn't hold her. 'That's not what's important, anyway, at the moment. The only thing that matters is finding him. And they will. They have to.'

'Why won't you tell me?'

'Stop whingeing!'

'No.' Harry had had enough. He was hungry, not to mention freezing, and he was starting to be frightened. Really scared. He didn't know where they were, or where they were going. He hadn't recognised anything for a couple of miles. It was overwhelming.

'Shut up, Harry.' He didn't recognise this Michael, either. Before, at school, it had felt like they were equals, friends. But now, out here, it was like Michael thought he was in charge. And he was weird, too, all this stuff he was saying. For the last hour or so, as they trudged along the lane, Harry had begun to think that Michael didn't have a plan. Now he wouldn't answer.

He looked at his watch. It wasn't far off lunchtime. They hadn't had anything since supper, except the KitKats they'd stuffed into their pockets. And a bottle of Coke between them. In his back pocket he had a ten-pound note. There was a garage with a shop across the road, and he had said that he was going to go in and buy some crisps. He was hoping to linger a while and warm up. But Michael had this mad look in his eyes and said he couldn't because they couldn't risk being spotted. Harry thought that was a bit overdramatic. He thought about Mr Dunmore, and the other teachers. They'd have noticed they were gone by seven thirty, eight at the latest. So as far as school was concerned they'd been missing for four hours. He wondered what was happening. Fear of being out here on their own in the cold vied with fear of what would happen when they were discovered. The latter was winning.

Now Michael sat down heavily on a bench. Suddenly, horribly, he was crying, sniffing, rubbing his eyes, humiliated by his tears. 'I don't know where we're going,' he admitted. 'I don't have anywhere to go.'

Harry didn't know what to say. He felt betrayed, but he also felt a rush of sympathy for Michael, and recognised that whatever was happening with his own mum and dad, it wasn't the same. He just didn't feel that sense of abandonment. He didn't feel he had nowhere to go.

And the balance of power shifted. Harry's confidence, which had deserted him some time during that long cold night in the bus shelter, flooded back.

Studiously ignoring Michael's tears, in the prep-school way, he said, 'Stay here a minute.' He crossed the road and went up to the garage shop. There was a queue of busy-looking people, all men, and no one looked at him. There was one of those machines where you served yourself with hot drinks, and he carefully made two cups of hot chocolate. Then he picked up a slab of milk chocolate, and a couple of sandwiches, adding up the prices as he went along. There was phone money in the change, and by the time he got back outside the warmth in the shop had brought feeling back to his toes and fingers.

On the bench, Michael had stopped crying, but was still slumped against its back, chin buried in his coat. He took the hot drink wordlessly, and ate a sandwich in record time.

Harry spoke. 'We'd better call someone.' Michael nodded without looking at him.

'Matthew?' He could only remember two numbers, apart from home. Tamsin hadn't answered; and his despair amplified when he heard the machine pick up the call. Then there was Matthew's mobile – he knew the number because Matthew had lent it to him a few times. Mum wouldn't let him have one of his own. They weren't allowed at school anyway. He dialled again, looking anxiously at Michael, who still hadn't moved. At least he was sipping from his cup.

Matthew's PA was sitting opposite him in his office, filling an A4 pad with shorthand. 'Is that you, Harry?'

'Yes.'

'Thank God.' Matthew exhaled with relief. He looked at the clock above his PA's head. Freddie was still in the air. Poor thing – she'd be in hell. 'Where are you?'

Harry gave the name of the village, and the number of the phone box he was calling from, and Matthew told him to stay put while he called the school and Adrian.

Five minutes later he rang back. 'Are you okay, mate?'

'I'm cold and tired and hungry, but I'm okay.'

'What happened?'

'We ran away, me and Michael.'

'Is Michael with you now?'

'He's outside on a bench. He's pretty upset.'

'You're about twelve miles from school. They're on their way now. Your dad, too.'

Harry wasn't frightened now of what they would do or say. He was just glad it was over.

'What about Mum?'

'She's on a plane. I've texted her. She'll get it the minute she lands. She's in a terrible state, Harry. You've scared the hell out of her.' Matthew couldn't help saying that.

'I know. I'm sorry.'

Matthew heard the tremble in Harry's voice. 'She'll be okay, Harry, once she lands and gets the message.'

Harry didn't speak.

'Your dad'll be there soon, mate.'

'He'll go mad.'

'No, he won't.'

'He will. He'll go on about letting him down, not behaving like a Sinclair should. All of that stuff.'

Matthew knew there was no point in denying it. He could hear Adrian's plummy tones doing exactly that – in fact, he already had. When he had called just now, Adrian had voiced about thirty seconds of normal parental relief before he'd been saying exactly what

Harry was expecting. Matthew had been glad he was on the phone to him, not looking right at him – he feared it would have been impossible not to punch him on his aristocratic Roman nose. It was Freddie Harry needed.

He wanted to keep Harry on the phone until help came – he sensed Harry needed to talk. 'Want to tell me about it, Harry?'

'Not really.' Then, 'I don't mean to be rude . . .'

'Don't worry.' Matthew felt useless, but he chatted about the cold, about how nice it would be to have a warm shower and get some clean clothes on, while Harry muttered, 'Yes,' and 'No,' and didn't volunteer anything.

After a couple of minutes, Harry interrupted 'Mr Dunmore's here.'

'Okay, you hang up. Harry?'

'Yes?'

'Don't worry. Your mum will be there soon.'

Then Harry was gone.

Abby was looking at Matthew inquisitively.

'That was a friend's son, Harry. He'd run away from school,' he told her. 'He's okay now. His housemaster just arrived.'

'Why did he call you?'

'I don't know.'

But he did. He knew that Adrian was emotionally inadequate.

Harry had weaned himself just like Freddie had.

Freddie wanted to believe she didn't need it from anyone else, that intimate support. He hoped Harry wasn't damaged the same way.

When he looked up again, Abby was still watching him. 'Are you okay?' she asked. She meant well. When he didn't answer straight away she stood up. 'Why don't we leave this for a few minutes? I'll go and get on with the bits you've already given me for ten minutes.'

What he really wanted was a cup of tea but, these days, he couldn't ask for it. There was a kitchen that did not discriminate between the ranks, full of gleaming stainless steel, and a fridge full of lunches from home for those slavishly following diets that restaurants and cafés didn't cater for. 'Thanks, Abby. I think I'll go and grab some tea. Can I get you something?'

'No, thanks.'

She'd had some coffee twenty minutes earlier with the senior partner's PA, Jessica. Jessica had been pumping her for information about Matthew. 'Come on – he's been on a different planet for weeks. What gives?'

Abby was loyal, but even she couldn't pretend Jessica was wrong. 'I don't know.'

Jessica looked unimpressed. As Abby was aware, because Jessica had told her, she knew what *her* boss had bought for his wife's birthday, not to mention how much it cost, his collar size, that he liked his shirts lightly starched, and that he wasn't always alone when he stayed overnight at his club working on 'big cases'. 'Money, or a woman, or both,' she opened. 'Has to be.'

Jessica watched too much television, and read too many of those magazines with photographs of Hollywood stars and their cellulite. Abby thought she came in every day determined to pretend she worked in the same law firm as Ally McBeal.

'I really don't know.' Abby had put the milk back in the fridge and slammed it to indicate that the discussion was over.

At which point, Jessica delivered her *coup de foudre*. 'Well, he wants to watch it. Blake's on to him. I heard him say so the other day. Matthew dumped a load of work on someone and buggered off at short notice a few weeks ago. Blake reckons he hasn't had his eye on the ball since. He said they were carrying him.'

Abby watched him going down the corridor towards the kitchen. She knew Jessica was right – he wasn't 'firing on all cylinders', or 'playing with a full pack', or whatever silly phrase you wanted to use, and she was worried. About him, yes, although whatever romantic ideas Abby might have had about her handsome widowed boss had dissipated under his stern, uncommunicative gaze. But also about herself: if he was in trouble at work, so was she. And she'd promised her flatmates she'd go on that two-week holiday in Crete with them . . .

In the kitchen, Matthew couldn't keep still while the kettle boiled. He paced up and down, looking at but not reading the notices on the board, opening the fridge, jiggling the change in his pocket.

Freddie would be landing in an hour or so. He wanted to go to the airport. He wanted to go so badly that it was almost unbearable.

But he couldn't. He couldn't because he was snowed under with work. And he couldn't because he knew his boss had noticed the change in him. And he couldn't because he wasn't sure she would want him to. And he couldn't because Harry wasn't his son. He was Freddie's and Adrian's son.

He just couldn't.

The kettle boiled, and he poured water on to the tea bag.

It was like a stitch. But he couldn't go.

The plane was early. The flight had lasted for ever. Freddie had refused food, headphones, a complimentary copy of the newspaper. She hadn't been out of her seat once. She was afraid if she spoke or moved she would explode. She had sat for the entire six hours staring at her hands, or out of the window at the grey nothingness, or at the stitching on the seat in front of her. The middle-aged businesswoman beside her tried a couple of times to engage her in conversation, but she gave the briefest response. She couldn't talk. Not when this was happening. The woman gave up and watched the movie.

She was concentrating on holding at a distance the images in her head that would kill her: Harry lost, Harry hurt, Harry frightened, Harry dead. She was rehearsing things to say, and she was trying desperately to remember how he smelt when you held him.

When they came in to land, the soft rock that Virgin piped through all its aircrafts jolted her back to reality. She hadn't even noticed the plane banking or descending. The television screen on the seatback flashed the time and the temperature. It said seven degrees. Freddie wrapped her own cardigan tightly around her. She switched on her mobile as soon as the wheels hit the tarmac, hiding it by her side, turning the volume right down. One message received: 'HE'S SAFE. MATT X.'

They turned off the seatbelt sign, but for a minute Freddie couldn't stand up. She'd lost her legs.

She had two voicemails. Adrian had called to say he would meet her at home with Harry, and Tamsin, in the manner of Stevie Wonder, just to say she loved her. Matt must have told her Harry was safe.

She didn't have any luggage – she'd shoved a few things into a bag and come. The arrivals hall was crowded with people. Her eyes scanned them and she realised she was looking for Matthew. But he wasn't there. Disappointment flashed through her, but her eyes alighted on a sign with her name on it, and she marched towards the driver holding it. Adrian must have sent him. At least he'd thought of it.

All that mattered now, though, was getting to Harry.

If he'd looked bigger to her when she'd picked him up for half-term, now he looked little again, vulnerable and frightened. When she went into the room he flew at her, and let her hold him for the longest time, smoothing his hair and murmuring into his ear. When she felt the panic go out of him, and his heartbeat had slowed, she pulled back and spoke straight into his face, holding his shoulders with both hands. 'Promise me you'll never do anything like that ever again.' She couldn't help giving him a little shake, but then she pulled him back into her arms and spoke over his head. 'I was so frightened, Harry, so frightened. What if . . .?' She didn't finish the sentence, just clung to him.

She sent Harry for a shower while she made him a bacon sandwich. Adrian didn't have much else in – it was a bachelor's fridge.

He was almost too tired to chew, his eyes sunk in his face. He ate, slowly, one round, but was defeated by the second. He'd been awake all night, and he needed to sleep. His eyes closed almost as soon as he lay down on his bed. When she got to the door, he muttered, 'Sorry, Mum.'

She went back to him and stroked his cheek. 'You sleep. We'll talk later.'

Adrian had opened a bottle of wine, and she took the glass he offered her. She was tired too. It had been a hell of a day. She kicked off her shoes and sat down on the biggest sofa. Adrian sat opposite.

'What a mess,' she murmured.

'I know. I'm sorry.'

He didn't sound himself, and she felt a rush of sympathy. He loved his son, she knew that. They'd gone through it differently and separately, but they'd both gone through it.

'It must have been awful, sitting on that plane.'

'It was. Must have been grim for you, too, having to tell me.'

'I wouldn't have done – not very brave, I suppose – but Tamsin made me.' He smiled wryly.

'She was right. I'd have hated not knowing. I'm his mum.'

Adrian looked almost shamefaced.

She took a deep breath and a gulp of wine. 'We need to sort this out.'

'Freddie—'

She put up a hand. 'Let me speak, Adrian, please. I've got it all in my head and I need to say it.'

He stood up, went to the window and looked out at the garden. She took a deep breath. 'I'm sorry if this sounds harsh, but I think straight out is the best way to say it. I just don't want to be married to you any more.' She couldn't see his face, so she couldn't evaluate his reaction. 'It hasn't been right for a long time. It's not Antonia Melhuish. I believe we could have come through that, if it was only that.' Although, as she said it, she knew it could never have been only that. 'It goes much deeper than an affair. We're not happy together, you and I. We don't want the same things. We don't see things the same way. We're not a couple. A couple who are going to stay married need to be best friends. They need to feel things the same. We don't.'

'I never thought we wanted to live in each other's pockets.'

'I don't mean that. Of course not. But at the end of the day, the two of us should want the same things.'

'I don't understand.'

Confusion and frustration were etched on his face when he turned to her. 'I don't want to spend the rest of my life living this way.' She had to explain it to him. 'I won't. I want more. I deserve more.'

'Is there someone else?'

'That hasn't got anything more to do with it than Antonia Melhuish had, but yes, there is.'

Now his expression turned to shock and anger. She wouldn't have lied to him, but she wished he hadn't asked.

'Who the hell is it?' When she didn't answer, his eyes scanned the room as he thought. Then they widened. 'Matthew! That bastard!'

'Adrian—'

'I see now. How long has this been going on? You mean you let me go on and on apologising for Antonia, berating myself for being so stupid, and all the time—'

'Keep your voice down. Harry's had quite enough for one day.'

'Harry! It all makes perfect sense. Matthew's been worming his way into my son's affections – for God's sake, Freddie, he even called him first when he ran away.'

Adrian was really angry now. He saw things simply, she realised: you were sleeping with your spouse or you were sleeping with someone else.

'I mean I'm sorry the bloke's wife died, but that doesn't mean he can help himself to someone else's.'

He was getting louder again, and Freddie was genuinely afraid that he would wake Harry up. And she wanted to tell him herself, not have him hear it from the top of the stairs being screamed in some wretched row.

She went as close to Adrian as she could get, and hissed, 'Shut up! If you wake Harry, I'll kill you!'

The venom in her voice silenced him, and broke the spell of his rage. He dropped into the nearest armchair.

'Matthew has nothing to do with you and me. He didn't come after me – he couldn't help himself. I'm not something to be given or taken. What happened has happened since you told me – if you remember – that this marriage was over.'

'I told you I'd made a mistake. You didn't have to get even!'

She didn't know how to get through to him. His lack of comprehension was stunning. 'I wasn't trying to get even with you, Adrian.' She got down on her knees in front of his chair, and made her voice slow and calm. 'Can't you just listen, and think about what I'm saying?'

He nodded.

'This isn't about Matthew and it isn't about Antonia. This is about us. Don't you see that if we were in love with each other, there wouldn't be any Matthew or Antonia? There wouldn't be room. We wouldn't see them.'

'I'm not in love with Antonia.'

'And you're not in love with me.'

'How the hell can you say that?'

'Because if you were I'd feel it, Adrian, and I haven't felt it for a long time.'

'You're just making excuses. You haven't got the guts to tell me you don't love me, so you're trying to make out that I don't love you.'

'Okay, Adrian. I don't love you.'

'You do.'

'No, I don't.'

He didn't answer this time. His shoulders dropped.

'I did, but I probably should never have married you,' Freddie added.

'How can you say that? We've been happy. We have Harry.'

'And we'll both always have Harry.'

'Are you going to take him away from me?'

'I wouldn't do that.'

She sensed that he was really listening now. 'But I am going to take him away from that school.'

He started to speak, but she interrupted him: 'I am, Adrian. I should never have agreed to send him there – I have hated it, and so has he.'

'You can't do that.'

'I can, Adrian. Don't push me on that point.'

He hesitated. She knew he was figuring it out. She might take Harry to America.

'Listen,' Adrian said, 'I feel just as bad as you do about him running away, but surely it was us, not the school, that made him do it.'

'Do you think he'd have run away from home?'

'I don't suppose so,' Adrian conceded.

She could have said that the school was part of what had damaged Adrian. She could have said that what she had learned about her father had made her all the more determined not to turn Harry into someone who couldn't express emotion. But she didn't need to: she could see that she had won, or at least that she had made him believe her, about Harry and about them, if not about Matthew.

He would probably reinvent it. She knew Clarissa and Charles would. 'Should never have married a foreigner,' one would say. 'Absolutely,' the other would reply, and they would nod as they did, and write her off as a bad job.

But she would have Harry, and she would have Matthew, and she would have herself.

Harry had only ever flown in Europe, so the televisions in the seatbacks in the Virgin economy section were a source of great excitement. When he found out you could play Nintendo on them, his cup ran over. 'This is so cool.' He looked at his watch. 'I should be in physics now.' He pretended to vomit, rolling his eyes, and sticking an index finger into his mouth.

'I should probably think about home-schooling, just for the trip.'

'Yeah, right, Mum. Know much about physics, do you?' He was delighted.

'Don't be cheeky!'

Children of Harry's age made fascinating travel companions. But Freddie could remember his first flight when he was about eighteen months. They'd booked a fortnight in the sun. After three hours with Harry suspended from the add-on seatbelt secured round her waist, kicking the seat in front, screaming his head off and spraying organic breadstick crumbs around the cabin, she had felt more in need of a month at a Himalayan retreat. Adrian had read the *Telegraph* throughout, from the relative safety of the seat across the aisle, and tried, she thought, to look as though he were travelling alone. A dozen pairs of eyes bored a hole in her head from the seats behind. For the next few years they'd stuck with Devon and Norfolk. And once Harry was old enough they had begun their annual pilgrimage to wherever there was a good golf course.

But now Harry seemed perfectly happy. He had played with his seat for a full ten minutes, pushing the recline and reset buttons, then fiddled with the light. He summoned the stewardess for no apparent reason, and established that he could, if he wanted to, get all the audio and visual channels, including the PG film and a rather heavy classical-music channel. He drank two Cokes and ate his and Freddie's minuscule bags of nibbles.

Then he studied the inflight safety card in morbid detail, plugged himself in, sat back and was lost in some computer game.

Three hours in, he'd finally taken off his headset. 'I can't believe you never brought me before.'

'I should have done. I'm sorry.'

'I didn't mean that. I suppose I was too young before, but I think I'm going to like it over there. I mean, like seeing where you grew up and stuff. It'll be weird.'

'Good weird?'

'Good weird.'

'Good weird' just about summed it up.

When the stewardess brought lunch, Freddie had a little bottle of red wine. It made her feel sleepy, and she drifted for a while, comforted by Harry's presence beside her. It was like when you had a really bad headache, took something, slept and woke up with it gone. It felt so spectacularly good not to have it. This felt like that.

'Harry? Can we have a talk?'

'Course.' He nestled into the side of his chair, facing her. 'Tamsin said you'd talk to me when you were ready.'

'She did, did she?' She ruffled his hair. 'When did you get so grown-up?'

He shook away her hand. 'Get off.' Then, 'Me first. I'm sorry about running away. There was nothing grown-up about that. I never wanted to do it, really. It was Michael. I'm not saying he made me – that would be pathetic – but I wouldn't have done it if he hadn't. That sounds pathetic too. I'm saying I know it was wrong. I won't do it again.'

'Would you like not to go back to that school?'

'Not ever?' His face gave her the answer.

'Not ever.'

She should have put her foot down years ago. The woman who had let Adrian and his bloody parents send her son away had vanished as quickly as she had appeared. This felt good.

'Where would I go instead?'

'Well, that would be up to you, to a point. We could look at day schools around home. You could even go with Homer.'

'To the state school?'

'Would that be a problem for you?'

'No. It would be brilliant. But what about Dad?'

'Dad would take some convincing . . . but . . .'

'What about you and him?'

'Ah.' He wanted to hear it all. 'Those problems I told you about?' He nodded. 'We can't fix them, sweetheart. Dad and I aren't going to be together any more.'

'You're getting a divorce.'

'Eventually we will. Yes. I'm sorry.'

'Are you unhappy about it?'

God! Paxman, eat your heart out on the difficult questions. 'Yes, of course. We both are. No one wants to be divorced, Harry. When you get married, you make promises, and you believe you will stay married. And if it doesn't work – and there are a thousand different reasons why marriages don't – you feel like you've failed. And if there are children in that marriage, you feel it much more – you've failed yourself, each other and your kids. Failarama.'

'Why didn't yours work?'

'It's complicated, sweetheart. You really are too young to understand quite how complicated.' That answer didn't satisfy either of them.

'I don't love Dad any more', Freddie said. 'Not that way – not the way you're supposed to.' That was simple enough.

'Does he love you?'

'Not in the right way.'

'Do, you love other people, both of you?'

This was where she had to be careful. She hadn't assumed he would make that jump so fast.

'I don't know about Dad, sweetheart, but that's a conversation you can have with him. I love someone else now, yes. But you need to know that the two things have nothing to do with each other. It isn't this other person's fault that I don't love Dad any more.'

Harry was quiet for a moment. 'Is it Matthew?'

Was she the only person on the bloody planet who hadn't seen this coming? Even her own son appeared to have wised up before her. 'What makes you ask that?'

'I'd like it to be Matthew.'

'Why?'

'You shouldn't be on your own, either of you. Matthew needs someone new. He's been sad since Sarah died. And if it was Matthew you fell in love with I wouldn't have to get used to someone else. I'm already used to him. I like Matthew. He's cool.'

And there you go. Harry, her little boy, had distilled

the *angst* of the last three months into a few simple sentences. She wanted to hug him. 'It is Matthew.'

Harry nodded sagely, letting the information roll around for a second or two.

'Cool.'

Adrian had looked frightened when she told him she was taking Harry back to the US with her.

'How long for?'

She had no interest in hurting him, not now.

'We'll be back for Christmas.'

'And what then?'

'I don't know, Adrian. I need time to think about it.'

'But you might go back? You might live there?'

'I suppose so. I've got the house, anyway. I need to rethink everything about my life. But I don't feel like I have a home, just now. Not a physical place that feels like home, anyway. England isn't where I'm from, and America isn't where I've been. I feel misplaced. But home is Harry, and . . .'

'Matthew.'

Freddie nodded. 'I think he will be.'

Adrian's jaw set defensively.

'He'll never be Harry's father.'

'Of course he won't. He wouldn't try. Wherever we end up, Harry will always be your son. I would never try and keep you apart. I don't want to hurt either of you. He loves you.'

'And I love him.'

'I know.'

She didn't say what Tamsin might have said. That he hadn't made much of an effort to see Harry when he was an hour down the road. She didn't want to score points. She had loved him once.

'What about us?'

That startled her.

'I mean,' he added, 'have you been to see a lawyer? Should we do that?'

'Yes, we should.'

He flinched.

'Adrian! What's the point? It's over. We need to move on. Both of us. And we can't do that while we're still married.'

He was shaking his head. 'It's just that you sound so unsure about everything else. But as soon as I mention that, you're certain. Yup. Divorce. Definitely.' He looked into her face.

'Have I been that dreadful to be married to?'

There was nowhere for this conversation to go. Freddie put her hand on his arm.

'Not dreadful, Adrian. No.' Took a deep breath. 'Just not enough. Not right. I'm sorry.'

He covered her hand with his own, and nodded. 'Okay then.'

Grace was home, and so was Reagan. They came together down the front steps of the house as their taxi pulled up. Reagan clung to Freddie for a moment, then said, 'Good to see you, Harry.' She was looking at Freddie over his head – she knew how good: Freddie had left a message at the Point Inn from Logan last week.

'You remember Grace, Harry?'

'Of course he doesn't. He hasn't seen me in years.' Grace smiled at him.

Harry shrugged politely. 'Sorry!'

'Rubbish! What have you to be sorry for? Now, come on in with me, and let's get you something to eat – plane food isn't up to much, is it?' The two ambled towards the house.

Reagan shivered and Freddie put an arm round her shoulders. 'How have you been?'

'Okay.'

'Really?'

'Better, anyway.'

'What are you going to do?'

'I'm still not sure. I think I'm going home to England for Christmas, sort out a few things there.'

'You'll be welcome. I've talked to Matt and Tamsin. No one's angry with you.'

Matthew was too happy to be angry with anyone. Tamsin had been harder to convince. 'I can't believe she did that to you.' She'd taken some talking round.

Reagan smiled. 'Thanks. How did you pull that one off?'

'They just want you to get some help. No one wants you to be unhappy.'

'I'm going to.'

'To be honest, Tamsin and I feel bad that we didn't make you sooner.'

'You shouldn't. How's Matt?'

'He's great.' Freddie took a deep breath. 'Look, Reagan, you should know—' Reagan put her hand up to stop her.

'You two should be together. I'm glad. Really.'

'Good, because he's coming back.'

'Again?' But this time she was joking.

'What can I say? He can't stay away from me!'

'Even if it gets him fired?'

'That's sort of the point. Although I don't think they'd be stupid enough to fire him. I'm not even sure they *can* fire him. We're having a serious think about moving here for a while. I've taken Harry out of school – he and I have American passports – we've got the Boston house. It might be a good place for us to be while we all get used to everything.'

'Funny you should say that, I was thinking the same thing. I really love it in Provincetown. I feel like I could make friends there – the first friends I've made since . . . you lot, really.'

'That's great. Who are they?'

'Well, the girls who run the inn have been so kind to me. And they know a lot of people in town. And . . .' Freddie almost knew what she was going to say before she said it. '. . . I've been spending a bit of time with Rebecca.'

'You have?'

'Yes. Don't be mad. We don't talk about you. I bit her head off, that first time, when she came looking for you in Chatham.'

'I'm not mad. You can talk to whoever you like.'

'She's nice, Fred. She reminds me of you in a lot of ways.'

Freddie knew. 'We had a horrible time the last time I saw her. I said some nasty things.'

'She was so worried when we got the message about Harry.'

'Well, Harry's fine.'

'Thank God.'

'So you'd stay in Provincetown?'

'I don't know – I haven't really thought. I just think I need to be somewhere else for a while, you know. Cosmo and Rebecca have these rooms at the house that they rent out.' Freddie rolled the idea around her head and it felt okay.

Grace had been thinking about her future, too. 'I wanted to ask you what you thought.' She wanted to open the Cape Cod house to paying guests. She said she'd been looking after people all her life, and she wanted to stay where she was, but she couldn't imagine rattling around in it by herself, and this seemed like the perfect solution. She could be open when she wanted, and closed if she preferred to be alone.

'I think it's a brilliant idea.'

Grace smiled properly for the first time since Freddie had arrived.

The plan started as a random thought, as she fell asleep one night. When Freddie woke up, it persisted. She talked it over on the telephone with Matthew, and he thought it was a good idea. 'Will they do it, darling, do you think?'

'I don't know, but if I don't ask I'll never know. They both love me. Let's find out.'

'Don't you want to wait until I get there in a few days? I could come with you.'

But she didn't.

'Will you come somewhere with me?' Freddie had asked Grace. Grace had said yes without asking where – she must have known.

She told Rebecca they would meet her on neutral ground and suggested the coffee shop at the end of a row of stores at a right angle to the beach. There was a deck, down a couple of steps, which fronted on to the sand. She and Grace took their coffee out to where four or five weatherbeaten picnic benches stood. They were all empty, and Freddie headed for the middle one. As she sat down, she noticed the sign that hung on the fence that separated them from the beach. Cartoon-style, it was a picture of Planet Earth, bright green and blue, and the slogan encouraged you to deal respon-sibly with your litter: 'LOVE YOUR MOTHER.'

It was cold, but it wasn't windy, and when you sat still, the sun was warm.

'Are you all right, Gracie?'

Grace smiled. 'You haven't called me that in a long time.'

Freddie hoped bringing Grace here wasn't the latest in a long list of selfish acts, all designed to make herself feel better. She wanted this to be good for all of them, even Rebecca. 'Haven't I?'

'No – you used to call me Gracie all the time when you were a little girl.'

A small group walked across the beach. It looked like three generations of one family – a grandmother, a mother, and a young child, almost completely obscured by a hat and a scarf. The adults each held one of the child's hands and swung him or her between them every few steps. Freddie could hear the little one's delighted laughter.

'Hello.'

It was Rebecca, and she'd come alone. She was wearing the most spectacular coat: tapestry, in jewel-bright colours, with an enormous purple fake-fur trim at the neck. With it, she had on a purple beret at just the right angle. She looked beautiful. Freddie noticed Grace look down at her own grey coat: it was expensive, and beautifully tailored, but it wasn't purple tapestry. She wondered if Grace's first thought had been the same as hers: how can a man love two such different women? Then Antonia Melhuish jumped into her head, followed by Sarah. 'Thanks for coming.' She stood up, oddly formal.

'As if I wouldn't.' Rebecca turned to Grace and held out her hand. 'You must be Grace. I'm so happy to meet you at last.' They shook hands.

'I'll get you something to drink. What would you like?'

'Tea, please. No milk or sugar. Earl Grey, if they have it.'

Freddie went inside. She could see the two women through the coffee shop's window as she waited for the tea, but not whether they were talking to each other. When she got back, she put down the tea and sat opposite them. Then she began to talk.

'We're all part of a puzzle, us three. To an extent we've all lived with missing pieces, all these years, and I think we've all been the worse for it. We've lived our lives a certain way because those pieces aren't there – I know I have. My father is dead, so we can't finish the puzzle, but we can put in the pieces we all have. I have pieces of your puzzles, and you both have pieces of mine, and of each other's. We can tell each other the story of my father. I don't know about you, but I need to do that. We can't get back the life that's gone, but I've spent a lot of time thinking about it, and if we don't do this – if *I* don't do this it's going to go on affecting the way I live, and I don't want that. So I want this. And if you don't want it for yourselves, I'd like you to do it for me.'

She looked from one to the other. Grace nodded wordlessly.

Rebecca spoke first: 'I think you're right.'

'Okay.' Freddie looked down at her hands, clasped together on the table, and the trace of her lipstick on the rim of the white mug. 'My father, Thomas Valentine, was born in November 1921. I don't know a thing about his childhood except what Rebecca has told me, and I don't think she knew much more than I did.'

'That wasn't his real name.' This was Grace. 'He changed it after the war.'

Freddie felt a tremendous sense of relief – they knew, between them, and they were going to share it. This was going to work. 'Why?'

'The Thomas was his own, the Valentine was the name of a commanding officer he came across in the army. He thought it was a better name. His name was Thomas Jacob.'

Freddie nodded at her – she didn't want to interrupt any more: she wanted to hear what Grace knew. 'I think he had a happy enough childhood, at the beginning. He had two younger brothers. His father owned a general store in a small town in Maine. I can't remember the name, but I would if I saw a map. We never went there.' She shook her head at her own digression. 'He went to school – he sounded like a pretty normal boy. He didn't have any pictures of himself as a child, but he said he was big, never had any trouble with bullies or anything like that, and good at sports. Things didn't start to go wrong until he was a teenager. They had a lot of bad luck then. One night there was a fire, which put the store out of business, and killed his brothers. They were upstairs – they couldn't get to them. He remembered trying to. But it was too hot – the fire had taken hold. He couldn't get to them. But he saw one at the window, before the smoke got to him, I guess, banging, trying to break the glass. He said he could see his mouth moving, but he couldn't hear what he was saying. He had nightmares about that all his life.

'He never talked about it, but I always thought it must have damaged him. I think it hardened him. By then, of course, it was the Depression, and although things were better on the east coast than they were in other places – California and the Dust Bowl and all that – there wasn't a lot of money around. His father couldn't get the business up and running again, and Tom had to drop out of school. I don't know the exact order of things, but his father drank, and things got very bad between him and Tom's mother. He said she never got over losing her boys.

'He once told me that he would have thought losing two would bring her closer to the one who'd survived, but he always felt she pushed him away. Almost like she held his survival against him. I know it sounds odd, but you do hear of things like that, don't you? Grief is a strange thing.

'He had a strange memory of that time – I guess some things got blocked out. He did remember drunken rages and violent episodes, but he said they were sporadic. Most of the time he said the three of them just lived miserable grey lives.

'So the war was a relief, in a way. He told me he used to watch the newsreels at the movies, watch the soldiers at war in Europe and Africa, and pray for America's war to start. He remembered hearing the news about Pearl Harbor on the radio and thinking he was probably the only twenty-year-old male in America who was glad about it. It was his way out. He couldn't wait to leave, and he said he never went home. His mother died during the war, and his father just stopped writing to him.

'Ironically, he had a quiet war. It's not fair, really, when you think about it. So many young men who didn't want to be there were getting killed, while he was desperate to be in the thick of it but got assigned to some pedestrian job. He told me he never fired a gun after basic training, not in the whole war. He was never bombed or even frightened. Not by the war, anyway.'

'That bothered me for years,' Rebecca put in, 'thinking about him stationed in the village where my mother had grown up. It was such a sleepy place. I still can't imagine it swarming with GIs.'

Grace looked at Freddie quizzically.

'This is where I come in,' Rebecca went on. 'I don't know much about his war, but I know a lot about where he spent it. I was brought up there.'

Bewilderment crossed Grace's face, but she didn't ask.

'Salisbury Plain – that's where they all were. When I was growing up, it was somewhere to take our bikes. It's where Stonehenge is. When I was a girl you could still get at it, but now it's cordoned off. Back then you could lean your bike against the stones and climb up on them. We used to go there in summer, me and my friend.

'It was a chocolate-box village. You could only get to

the houses on the main street by crossing little bridges –
a stream ran through it. We had a church, a post office,
three pubs and a school. Not that I went there, of
course. I went to a private girls' school in Salisbury, an
endless bumpy bus journey away. I used to spend all
my pocket money on barley sugar because it stopped
you feeling sick. We lived in the house my mother had
lived in all her life. It was the biggest in the village – only
the rectory came close. It was Georgian, all symmetry
and immaculate white rendering with huge windows. It
was full of antiques, and big ugly paintings. My mother
always used to say that it hadn't changed since she was
a child – but I never knew whether she thought it was a
good thing or not.

'Her childhood was just as restricted and regimented
as mine, and she must have hated it as I did, but it
didn't stop her doing it to me. What is it they say about
the sins of the fathers? If she had ever given me a hint of
what must have happened in the war . . . but she never
did.'

'What did happen?' Grace interjected.

'My mother and Thomas fell in love.'

Grace was evidently shocked: her eyes moved
rapidly as she struggled to come to terms with what
Rebecca had said.

'So you never knew?' Rebecca asked her.

'No, I didn't.'

'Why did you think I left?'

'Wait a minute,' Freddie interrupted. 'What else do
you know about them?'

'Only what I told you that time when you came to the studio.' Rebecca looked again at Grace. 'I told Freddie what he told me. He found me in bed with a lover, and exploded, called me all sorts of names, then said I was just like my mother.'

'And before that you hadn't known they knew each other?'

'Of course not. He'd known, probably from the first time he met me, who I was, but he never said a word. He couldn't, could he? But he told me then. And how!'

'What happened?'

'My mother's parents sent her away, split them up. He wasn't good enough. He was American, he wasn't an officer, he didn't have money.'

'And that was that?'

'Apparently so. I think he hated her for letting it happen.'

'Would she have had any choice?'

'Of course.' This was Freddie. 'It was the twentieth century, for God's sake, not ye olden days. If she'd wanted to, she could have fought for him.'

'So she never really loved him?'

'That's a piece of the puzzle none of us will ever find,' Rebecca said. 'I wish I'd had the guts to ask her. But at the time I couldn't bear to think about them together.'

'And your mother's dead?'

'She died soon after I left Thomas. And I never spoke with my father about it. He probably never knew.'

'But you knew your mother. What do you think?'

'I think she can't have loved him. If she had, it would have shown up somewhere in how she was for the rest of her life. It marks you, something like that, doesn't it? It leaves a thumbprint, a footstep, in the map of who you become.'

Grace nodded. 'She left marks on *him*.'

'Exactly.' Rebecca looked at Grace with something like surprise. 'And look at the repercussions.'

'Are you saying . . .' Grace was struggling '. . . are you saying he married you . . . for *revenge*?'

'That, or to replace her. To try and make me like her. And I don't know which would have been worse, to tell you the truth.'

'If it had been revenge, surely he would have wanted to make sure your mother knew.'

'She never knew?' Freddie asked.

'I don't think so – I never told her. And he'd changed his name, hadn't he? They didn't come to our wedding so they never met. My parents never wanted to meet him – they were so angry with me.'

'And when you found out?' Grace asked.

'Like I told Freddie. She was dying.'

'And you didn't say *anything*?'

'I didn't ask her straight out. I tried to get her to tell me. I spent hours beside her bed. I asked her about her childhood, about my father – I gave her every chance to tell me. But she didn't.'

'She can't have loved him,' Grace said. 'She didn't tell you because it wasn't a part of her soul.'

'You don't know that.' Part of Freddie wanted to believe that she had. The Tamsin part, the part that still believed in heartbreaking, unrequited love. It made her ache for her father, to think that his whole life had been turned by something that might not have meant as much to Rebecca's mother.

'He never told me. He could have told me. He *should* have told me.'

'He should have told all of us.'

'What happened to him at the end of the war?' Freddie asked.

'He came back to the States. Like I said, he never went back to Maine. He went to Washington and reinvented himself there, with that guy's name. He was obsessed with success, driven. I don't think he did a single thing that wouldn't have bettered him. He worked, went to night school, qualified. Of course, once he'd done all that, he had to move. America isn't so different from England – certainly wasn't in the 1950s. Work and achievement weren't enough for a career in law back then – you needed the right background. So in the 1950s he came back to Boston.'

'And made it all up.'

'Exactly. It was all a big lie.'

'It's weird,' Rebecca said. 'Losing my mother was responsible for all his success. It was like he was obsessed with making himself into the kind of guy she would have been allowed to marry, even though he couldn't have her.'

'And you were the next best thing?' Freddie suggested.

'I used to think it was that. He was so cruel at the end. But we were happy, at first. I guess he was just fucked up. I don't think he knew what he was doing when he met me. All his energy and time had gone into making himself this big-shot lawyer, with cash in the bank and a big house on Beacon Hill. Getting respect. Knowing all the right people. But I don't think he'd ever fixed himself.'

'Rebecca's right. He was a broken man when I met him. And I never really fixed him.' Grace smiled weakly. 'I fixed the part of him that wanted to be loved for himself. I think I did that. Even if he didn't tell me everything, I'll always believe that we had real love.'

'You did, Grace,' Freddie said.

'But I never fixed the other part. I never made him a good father.'

Both women looked at Freddie, whose cheeks were burning.

'He loved you, but he wasn't a good father,' Grace added.

'Why?' Rebecca asked Grace. 'He loved her when she was born. I could see it.'

Rebecca thought of the big man holding the tiny baby. He'd planted a brief kiss on the top of her own head, her hair still damp from the exertion of delivery, and gone straight over to the basket. Freddie had practically fitted into one of his hands. Rebecca remembered the downy hair, and the little fists thrashing at the air. And the wonder on his face.

'He never told me about his childhood, about his brothers and everything, until he knew he was dying. If he had I might have understood him better,' Rebecca said.

'And that was why you went, because you found out about your mother?'

'Yeah. We hadn't been happy for a long time. I wanted to go. But when I found that out, I had to.'

'Where did you go?' Freddie asked.

'Like I said, back to England at first, but that didn't solve anything – I couldn't have stayed there. So I came back to Boston. That was when I first saw you, Grace. He must have hired you almost straight away – he knew I'd never come back to him.'

'He thought you might come back for Freddie,' Grace said.

'I did. I told her. Just once. I saw the two of you on the Common.'

Freddie squeezed Grace's hand briefly.

'It wasn't just that you two seemed so happy,' Rebecca went on. 'I wasn't jealous, or anything. Just incredibly sad. And I knew I wasn't any good. I wasn't sure I ever would be. But I certainly wasn't then.'

'Where did you go?'

'Everywhere. Anywhere. It was a bit of a voyage of self-destruction. I broke myself right down before I could start building myself back up. I got the freedom I'd wanted – and I used it, believe me. I took a lot of drugs, I drank, I put myself in dangerous situations in dangerous places. It sounds romantic, and you think you've seen it in films, but you haven't. The worst bits were awful. Rock bottom. I was chasing oblivion, I think.'

'And I was raising your daughter.' Grace's voice wasn't angry or judgemental. She was just maintaining the time line.

'Thank you.' Now Rebecca took Grace's hand. 'Thank you. I knew before I went that she was going to be okay.'

'I was more than okay. Grace was great.' Freddie felt a surge of loyalty. But now it was no longer balanced with rage. Just sadness, and regret.

A couple came out on to the deck with mugs of something, saw what was happening, and went back inside.

Rebecca laughed her noisy laugh, and wiped her eyes. 'We must look like a bunch of lunatics.'

'And aren't we?' Grace was smiling too. 'What saved you?' she asked.

'*Who* saved me. I came back to the east coast, some time. Can't even remember how or why. I knew I couldn't come near you, Freddie, and I found myself at the docks, and rather than throw myself in I took a boat, and it brought me here. I got clean, I got a job and eventually I met Cosmo.'

'The guy you live with?'

'Yeah.'

'Have you and he got a family?' Grace's question sounded almost too polite. Dinner party chat, in the middle of all of this.

Rebecca laughed again. 'Cosmo and me? No. He's gay. There is no Cosmo and me, except that we're best friends.'

'So there's never been anyone else.'

'No. No husband, no children.' Rebecca's voice was serious again. 'Call it my penance. Or a rare bit of self-knowledge.'

'Or another tragedy,' Grace said.

They were all silent for a minute.

'Did you get the pictures I sent?' she asked Rebecca.

'Every one. And I thank you for that.'

'I need to walk,' Grace said.

The three women stood up and moved on to the beach.

'Do you feel like you've put your puzzle together, Freddie?'

'As much as I can.'

'And?'

'What do you feel?'

'I don't feel angry any more, except maybe with him.'

They walked on.

'I can never make peace with him now.'

'He died loving you. There was a sort of peace in that for him.'

'And I'll have to make that mine too.'

'All these wasted years, for all of us.'

'They haven't been wasted for me,' Grace interrupted. 'I had you, I had him. I only wish I could have understood better.'

'I wish we all could have done.'

★   ★   ★

Later, Rebecca walked Grace and Freddie to Freddie's car. Freddie watched as the other two women said goodbye. They held each other's hands for a few seconds. 'I haven't said I'm sorry for your loss,' Rebecca said.

'Thank you.'

Freddie tried to read the look that passed between them, but she couldn't.

Rebecca came round to her side of the car. 'What are your plans?' she asked.

'I'm only just beginning to work them out.'

Rebecca nodded.

'I'll call.' Freddie realised as she said it that she would.

'I'll be here.'

Freddie almost kissed her, but not yet.

Rebecca stood in the road and watched the car until it disappeared from view, then turned and walked up the hill towards home.

Cosmo was waiting. He opened the door and put his arms round her. 'Better?'

'Better, Cos.'

A couple of days later Matthew arrived. That night she found him in her bed, reading a book he'd taken from the shelves. He looked up as she came in and she ran over to him. She loved this straightforward man who wore his emotions on his sleeve and held nothing back. Who had no secrets. She'd been look-ing for him all of her life, but it had taken so long to realise it. 'I'm sorry I hid from you for so long,' she said softly, into his chest.

'You only hid because you knew I'd find you.' He kissed her neck.

'And thank God you did.'

'You remember the picture in the office on Beacon Hill?'

Freddie had been thinking about the same thing. 'It must be Rebecca's mother, not Rebecca.'

Grace nodded. 'Imagine how Rebecca must have felt when she realised. Poor thing.'

'Grace!' Freddie was surprised to hear Grace defend her mother.

'She was barely more than a girl herself. And that was a shocking thing to learn – maybe even more shocking than you and I can imagine, Freddie. Ask yourself what you would have done.'

'I wouldn't have left *me* behind.'

'You can't say that.'

'Can't I?'

'No. You can't. She was all alone. You heard her say she didn't have friends she could turn to. The man she had loved had betrayed her in just about the most awful way I can imagine. And her family – they were no better, were they? I understand exactly why she ran.'

'You've never had a child, though, Grace.' She regretted saying it the moment it had come out of her mouth.

Grace looked down at her hands, folded in her lap. 'No, Freddie. You're right.'

'I'm sorry, Grace.'

'Why? You're right. I never had a child. I can't know, then, can I?'

'Did you and my father ever talk about it?'

'He knew I wanted one. It just never happened.'

'Didn't you get treatment or something?'

'Times were different, you know that. Besides, I don't think your father could have gone through it – he was a very private man.'

'And look where that's got all of us.'

'It's how he was, Freddie.'

'But you did want kids with him?'

'Of course I did. But I don't want to leave you with the impression that it destroyed our lives, not being able to have them. We had you.'

'*You* had me.'

'He did too. He was so proud of you, Freddie.'

They were quiet until they drove into Chatham. Then Freddie asked, 'You want me to forgive her, don't you?'

'I think it would help.'

'Help who?'

'All of us, but especially you.'

When she got back, Reagan was out and Harry in the garden.

'I'm going to lie down for a while,' Grace said.

'Thanks for coming today.'

'You're welcome.'

'Did it upset you, seeing her?'

'It didn't. What happened between them was such a long time ago. I feel like you said – like some of my questions, some I didn't even know I was carrying around with me, have been answered. And I liked her. I didn't necessarily expect to, but I did.' She sounded surprised.

I like her too, Freddie thought.

She poured herself a glass of milk, and thought about calling Matt or Tamsin. Decided against it for now. She wandered around the house for a while, then found herself in her father's study. She couldn't quite shake the feeling that she was doing something wrong in opening the door and going in. It didn't have a lock so she could have gone in any time she wanted. Maybe everything about her father had been like that – she could have had it if she had wanted it. It made her feel unutterably sad.

She looked at all the pictures of herself. You wouldn't have all those if you didn't love a person, would you? There was nothing public about this room. It was where he had sat, on his own, thinking about his life and gazing at pictures of his daughter.

She was starting to believe what Grace had told her. That he was proud of her. That he had loved her. She just wondered why he had never succeeded in letting her know it. Why he had never tried. She looked at the picture of her holding a tiny Harry. She told Harry she loved him every time they spoke. She was sure he felt it, too, like armour against the world. Didn't she tell him again and again that no one in his life would ever, ever love him like she did, as much as she did? And wasn't that true?

If it wasn't her father who had taught her the importance of letting your child know that you loved it – and it couldn't have been Rebecca – so it must have been Grace. Grace and Tamsin. She felt suddenly overwhelmed with gratitude that she had them in her life.

From the window of her father's study she could see Harry. Grace had got hold of a bike from somewhere, and he'd built an assault course in the front garden, with planks of wood and bricks. He was bunny-hopping his bike across a row of tin cans.

She hadn't seen this self-sufficient child before. At school he was always surrounded by a gang of boys. At home there was always her, determined to cram quality into precious chunks of time. And Adrian. Here he was different. He hadn't once said he was bored, spoken of missing people. He chatted to Grace, and Reagan, her and Matthew, like an adult sometimes. He was sleeping twelve-hour nights, and eating like a horse. And he wanted to be outside all the time. When he couldn't persuade one of them – most often Reagan – to do something with him, he was happy alone, mastering this cycle route, building bonfires. Grace had shown him how to toast marshmallows on skewers, sandwiching them at exactly the right moment of melting stickiness between crackers with a square of dark chocolate. Watching the two of them huddled conspiratorially over the fire, watching him outside now, she felt calm and confident about him for the first time in years. For the first time since he was a baby she felt certain she was doing the right thing. She felt as though she had rescued him. And it struck her how strange it was that doing what was right for her had turned out to be doing the right thing for him. If only all parents understood that.

At supper that night she hugged Grace. 'You're right about Rebecca. I don't want to be like my father. I don't want to be unforgiving and remote. I don't want to lose the people I love.'

Grace patted her arm and smiled.

Thanksgiving

The telephone rang early enough to be almost frightening. Freddie picked up the receiver, grabbed her dressing-gown from the end of the bed and pulled it on.

'Freddie?'

'Tamsin? What's happened?'

'He's here, Freddie.'

'Oh . . . It's a boy!'

'Willoughby.'

'Willoughby.' Freddie trawled through her literary memory, but Tamsin interrupted her thought process.

'You know, Jane Austen.' She sounded mildly impatient.

'Of course!' Freddie didn't have the first clue, but so what? Willoughby. She liked it. Let's face it, it could have been so much worse. At least this child would be Will – oh dear, Willa and Will. They sounded like characters in a primary-school reading scheme. Still, better than poor old Homer and Flannery. 'When was he born?'

'Eleven forty-seven last night. I did call but you weren't in, and I didn't want to leave a message. I've been dying to talk to you all morning, and this is the earliest I dared wake you up.'

'A Thanksgiving baby!'

'I suppose so – I hadn't thought of that.'

'It's fantastic! Hang on, where are you calling from?'

'Home. Went in last night, popped him out, home for breakfast. Flannery didn't even know I'd gone, so she was rather bewildered by the sight of the baby when she woke up.'

'Is that a good idea, coming straight home? Wouldn't you get more of a rest if you stayed in for a bit?'

'Rubbish! I'd much rather be here. Hospital wards are so disgusting, these days. Bring back Matron, I say. Besides, I've got Meghan, and Neil'll take a few days off. I'm not even sure I had the option, to be honest. No stitches, no tears, no drugs – unless you count the large glass of red wine I drank with last night's supper, and a few puffs of good old gas and air. The midwife had a quick look at him and packed us off.'

'Sounds a bit perfunctory.'

'Well, this isn't the nineteen fifties. No month in a sanatorium for us modern mothers.'

'And how was it?'

'Grim. Hurt like hell, zero dignity – you know the form. I feel a bit Amazonian, actually. A bit Xena the Warrior Princess. And I love that bit, five minutes later, where you think, That wasn't so bad, I could do it again!'

'Not *again*, surely!'

'Well, maybe not – but who knows? Perhaps I won't mention it to Neil just yet, anyway.'

'Poor Neil. How is he?'

'Like he always is. Completely overexcited. Treating me like Joan of Arc.'

'I wish I was there.'

'So do I. It's only a couple of weeks, though, isn't it? I'll get Meghan to e-mail you a picture – she's good at stuff like that.'

'What does he look like?'

'Not what, who! He's heaven in a sleepsuit. He's the spitting image of Homer when he was born – or, rather, how Homer might have looked without the ventouse effect!'

Freddie laughed. 'Oh, God, yes, I remember his poor little head.'

'Your face! You thought it was going to be perma-nent! Like we had an alien in the gene pool.'

'I'm so happy for you, Tams. Congratulations – big, big congratulations! I'm going to go to FAO Schwartz and buy him the biggest teddy bear they have.'

'Don't you bloody dare! Neil says if one more stuffed animal comes into this house he's going to leave us.'

'As if.'

'And you'd never get it through airport security.'

'Okay, then, a little one. We'll smuggle it past Oberführer Bernard. The poor boy has to have some-thing of his own. Where is he now?'

'Here. I'm making a rod for my own back, as Mum

would say. He's spark out on his mother's ample bosom. I think he's waking up, actually.'

On cue, baby Willoughby's reedy newborn cry came down the line.

'Oooh! I can hear him. Hello, Willoughby!'

'Hang on a minute – I want to hear all about you. Let me just plug him on.'

For a moment Freddie listened while Tamsin muttered to her baby as he latched on to her breast, her voice melodic and soothing. She was so good at it, and it wasn't just practice. Freddie had needed two hands, a sausage-shaped cushion and full concentration to feed Harry, and in the first week, more often than not, it had resulted in tears and a phone call to the health visitor. She could see Tamsin now, phone tucked under one ear, Willoughby's tiny head in one hand, the other at her buttons. She had always made it look so easy. Then she was back. 'Okay. Now dish.'

'I don't know where to start.'

'Matthew! Where else? What's happening with him?'

'There's plenty else! My father, my mother, all this stuff we've got to sort out—'

'That's all the past. Matthew's the future. That's why he's more important.'

Freddie loved Tamsin's way of cutting to the chase. She was right, she supposed, if not to dismiss the rest, then at least to prioritise. 'And you're certain of that, are you?'

'Absolutely. Since before either of you probably.'

'Really?'

'Really! Now, stop teasing and tell me. Where is he?'

For an instant, Freddie felt about sixteen. She giggled. 'He's upstairs asleep in my bed right now.'

'No, he's not!' Matthew was behind her, stooping to kiss the back of her neck. 'Who could sleep with all this squealing going on? That you, Tams?' He leaned around to hear his friend's voice.

'She's had the baby, a little boy, born last night – a Thanksgiving baby. They're all fine!' Freddie flashed him the headlines.

'That's brilliant!' Matthew beamed.

'Pass him the phone,' Tamsin requested. Freddie put up her hand to cup Matthew's face and pulled it round, so that the receiver was in the middle and they could both hear. 'It *is* brilliant, and he's gorgeous, and you'll see him when you come home, but could you get lost now? I want to talk about you to Freddie!'

Matthew laughed. 'I'll make some tea. I love you, both of you – all of you.'

Freddie watched him go down the stairs, rubbing his bedhead sleepily. 'Very subtle!'

'We're too far gone for subtle, Fred. Right, carry on.'

Freddie climbed back into bed with the phone, and pulled up the duvet under her chin. Tamsin on the end of the line was an emotional hot water bottle, and she sank back against the pillows to talk to her best friend. 'I feel like a kid.'

'Fine. How does he feel?'

'Are you being sincere or pervy?'

'Depends what you want to share . . .'

'He feels fantastic. Really. It's clicked, it's just clicked.'

'That's brilliant.'

'Why don't you sound surprised?'

'The only surprise as far as I'm concerned is that it took so long.'

'He says he's felt this way about me for ages, and I just didn't see it. Did all of you, then?'

'Well, I don't know about all of us. I did, of course, but I'm a deeply intuitive individual,' she laughed, 'who knows the two of you better than anyone else alive, I suppose. Then again, Neil saw it, and he's about as intuitive as a potato.'

'That's not true! I can't believe it.'

'Come on! I reckon you didn't let yourself see or feel it. That's all. You were wrapped up in Adrian and not wanted to walk out of that marriage, weren't you? He's done you the biggest favour, if you think about it, forcing your hand with that woman. What's the state of play, by the way?'

Freddie didn't want to think about Adrian. He didn't belong in her consciousness among all this happiness. 'Don't know.'

'You'll divorce him?'

'We'll divorce each other, I suppose. I haven't really thought about that yet. The legal bit seems irrelevant when you've got the important stuff sorted out, doesn't it?'

'You'll have to think about it soon.'

'I know.'

'How's Harry?'

'Okay. Brilliant. He's coped brilliantly. Kids are amazing, aren't they?'

She swore she could see Tamsin looking down at the top of Willoughby Bernard's tiny head as she replied, so softly, 'They are.'

'I mean, he's taken all the Matt business in his stride. It's like nothing has changed between them, but I suppose they were close before. As for the Adrian stuff, so far so good. He seems fine.'

'He will be fine.'

'I know. We're so relieved.'

'So we're a we, are we?'

'Oh, yeah. We're a we. We're more a we than I think I've ever been. If you know what I mean.'

'I know.'

They were quiet, long distance, but then Tamsin squealed girlishly into the phone. 'I'm so jealous, all that new-romance stuff. I love Neil more than life, but there's no feeling in the world like a new love. You lucky cow!'

Freddie hugged herself. 'I know! Oh, Tams, it's like someone just switched all the lights on. It's not like I'm with my friend at all. Except of course it is. I'm with my friend, my great friend, but it isn't weird at all, you know. It's like my great friend is suddenly this incredibly sexy, gorgeous, funny, fantastic—'

'He was always all of that.'

'But it was different. I love him.'

'And he loves you.'

'When *did* you know?'

'For sure? After you had dinner in Boston that night. He told me then. I mean, I'd suspected for ages – years, really. But he let me in on it then. That hurt him so badly.'

'I know. I was confused.'

'He knows. He was so angry with himself for his lousy timing. He was afraid he'd blown it for ever.'

'Why didn't you tell me?'

'Freddie!'

'I know, I know. I suppose I still didn't want to think about it. The timing had to be right.'

'And it's right now?'

'Its hard to imagine anything being more right.'

Matthew pushed open the bedroom door, carrying two mugs of tea.

'I like the sound of that.'

Freddie could hear Willoughby stirring. That boy was already showing signs of an epic sense of timing.

'Oops. Looks like I've got a demanding man to deal with.' Tamsin was feeding Freddie a line. The comedy duo hadn't lost its touch down the years.

'Me too.'

'Love you, miss you, see you soon.'

'Love you, miss you, see you soon too.'

They airkissed loudly into the phone and hung up.

'You too what?' Matt had undone his dressing-gown, and was preparing to climb back in beside her.

Freddie felt a jolt of pure lust, and reached for him.

'She's got a demanding man to deal with. I said I had one too.'

'Too right.' He spoke into her open mouth, and then he was kissing her, and touching her, and she was lost again in the new miracle that was the two of them.

Later that morning, Matthew went out on his own. He was trying not to crowd Freddie and Harry. Especially Harry. Big things were happening for him, and he needed his mum to himself. And now Matt was the one who got to climb into bed beside her, hold her while she fell asleep. He still almost couldn't believe it. His pulse raced when she came into a room. He wanted her all the time, but now he could feel himself starting to relax. He was no longer in such a hurry, because he believed he had forever, and it felt so good.

Today he had said he would do some supermarket shopping. Grace had protested, and Freddie and Harry had said that he should go with them on an ocean walk, but he was happy. Reagan had gone out running earlier and wasn't back yet. Freddie was still coming round with a mug of coffee and he'd left, kissing the top of her lovely head. They'd gone back to sleep after Tamsin's call, and the lie-in had left them both fuggy.

Half a mile up the road he spotted Reagan on the main street, pulled alongside her and wound down the window.

'Hey!'

'Hey yourself.' She came over and leaned in.

'Christ, it's cold. Do you want me to drop you off at home?'

'You're going the wrong way.'

'I could turn around.' He smiled. 'Seriously. You're not running.'

'I have been. I'm just resting.' Reagan's nose was red, and her breath was coming in clouds. 'Where are you off to, anyway? And where are the rest of the Waltons?' It was a Reagan thing to say, but there was a new tone to it. It didn't sound vicious.

Matthew started to answer her, but she had seen something out of his window, across the street, and she wasn't listening. He turned and saw the barman from the Squires.

'Earth to Reagan.'

'Sorry. Look, Matt, I've got to go. Thanks for the offer. I'll see you later, yeah?'

'Eric!'

He turned, saw her, and stopped.

'Hi.'

'Hi.'

It really was cold. Eric's hands were buried in his pockets, and his beanie was pulled down low across his forehead. He shuffled from foot to foot. 'How have you been?'

'I'm sorry.' She blurted it out, and didn't know what to say next.

'*I'm* sorry.' She hadn't expected that response. 'I shouldn't have pushed you. It was none of my damn business. You didn't owe me anything.'

'No. You were right. I was lying.'

Eric shrugged. Reagan wanted to make him understand.

'I was really screwed up.'

'Was?'

She smiled ruefully. 'Probably still am. But I'm getting better.'

'I'm glad.' Did he look nervous?

'I just wanted to apologise for running off like that.'

'It's okay.'

They were silent for a few seconds, looking at each other. But it was too cold to stay that way for long.

'I'm opening up. Do you want to come in for a coffee?'

Reagan looked down at her feet, and nodded to herself for a moment. Then she said, 'No. But thanks, Eric.'

He wasn't the answer. He was nice, sexy and nice; he was the sort of guy she could lose herself in quite easily. But he wasn't the answer.

He shrugged again. 'So I'll see you around?'

'Maybe.' She started running again. Ten yards down the street, she turned without stopping. Eric was watching her.

'Maybe.' She shouted it this time, and he smiled his open, sexy smile at her, before he turned and walked away.

Freddie saw Rebecca once more before she flew home. She wanted her to meet Matthew. She didn't even really understand why.

'Where's it going, then, this thing with your mother?' Matthew asked on the way.

'Well, I don't know that I'm ever going to see her as a mother. In a funny way, this whole autumn has made me think of Grace more in that way. With Rebecca, it's just biological. I'm not angry now, and I feel as if I understand as much as I ever will. By which I mean that I understand why she did it, but at the same time, even after everything, I know I couldn't. There's nothing that could make me leave Harry. But mothers are people, aren't they? I'm that kind of mother, she's another kind. And Grace is maybe the best kind. With Harry, you know, it's uterine. It's physical. I got a mother's love from Grace because she had it to give and no one of her own to give it to. We're all different. My love for Harry doesn't appear to have anything to do with his father. Grace's and Rebecca's love for me was intimately connected. Grace gave it as a part of that and Rebecca withdrew it because of that.'

Matthew smiled at her. 'Is it really that simple?'

'"Simple" isn't the word I'd use.' She almost laughed. 'But I think it's clear. And it's okay. I feel freed from the compulsion to repeat the sins of my parents in my own life.'

'You were never doing that with Harry.'

'Not with Harry, no, but with my father – I never tried to get closer to him. It was like this stupid game. When he withdrew from me I learned to withdraw right back – from him *and* Grace. Look how easily I walked away from all that. And Rebecca. Don't you think that if I'd bugged him, nagged him, not let him get away with it, he might have told me where she was years ago? Even Adrian. That marriage went wrong long ago. Not dramatically wrong, just sour. I neither fixed it nor walked away from it. Mine's been a classic life half lived. I've stuffed up all the major relationships in my life and I didn't even realise I was doing it.'

'No, you didn't. Look at Harry. Look at Tamsin, Sarah and Reagan. Those are fully functioning, healthy, emotionally connected relationships. Look at me . . .'

She put her hand on his knee. 'You're a case in point. I'd have blown that too, if you hadn't been so persistent.'

'Persistent! What an awful word.'

'You know what I mean.'

He smiled. 'I was never going to go anywhere else.'

'Never?'

'Well, okay. Not never. But you had a while yet to get me to chase you.'

'Was that what I did?' She gave him a sly sideways look, but her eyes were sparkling.

He raised his eyebrows warningly at her, but he twinkled right back.

Cosmo was there. 'I hope you don't mind, but I couldn't bear not to meet you.' Freddie put out her hand to shake his, but he pulled her into a brief embrace.

'Sorry, I just feel like a hug is more appropriate.'

'Cosmo!' Rebecca shot him a warning glance, but Freddie hadn't minded.

After all, Cosmo was another piece of the puzzle.

'You're so much like your mother.'

Rebecca was fast: 'Only to look at.'

Freddie wasn't so sure about that as she might once have been. 'I hope I look half as good when I'm your age.'

'Bound to,' Cosmo assured her. 'It's in the genes. Look at those cheekbones!' He was quite possibly the campest guy she had ever met, but she couldn't help warming to him. At the same time she wondered how he had ever pulled off living as a straight. What priest in his right mind would have married him to a woman?

'This is Matthew.' She pulled his hand, and he came forward to stand beside her.

'He's my Cosmo,' Freddie said. Then, realising the implications of that, she leaned in to Rebecca and almost whispered, 'Except he's straight.'

'Shame! Doesn't mean he can't help me open a bottle and get some glasses, though, does it?' Cosmo led Matthew off into the kitchen.

Alone, the two women sat down.

'Not the guy in the wedding photographs?' Rebecca was smiling at her.

'He was married to one of my best friends. Sarah died in a car accident three years ago. Matt and I stayed close friends, and now we've become much more.' It was the first time she had said it out loud. And it was to Rebecca that she had said it.

'I'm happy for you.'

'Thanks. I'm happy for me too.'

The next remark came out before it had formed properly in her head. 'I wish you weren't alone.'

Rebecca smiled indulgently. 'I'm not alone, Freddie. Cosmo is all the companion a husband would be, and more. We have friends, lots of friends. I have my work . . .'

'But—'

'And I have lovers when I want them. Sorry to be shocking. Of course, that ready supply might dry up a bit as I get older,' she chuckled, 'but I expect my interest will dwindle too. At least, I hope so.'

'And it's not because of me and my father?'

'Not entirely. It was, for a long time, but now it's how I like it. Truly.'

Cosmo and Matt were back with the wine. Matt looked faintly amused.

'Now, people,' Cosmo was saying, 'are you staying on the Cape for Christmas? Don't look at me like that, Rebecca darling' – he couldn't see her face, but it was obvious he knew the expression she was wearing – 'I'm not asking them to move in. I know you say softly, softly, but I say fuck it, you're only here once and you're a long time dead, if you know what I mean.'

Finally Freddie did.

'And if they're on the Cape for Christmas, they just have, *have*, HAVE to come to the party. We have it every year. It's legend, believe me.' He drew out the word into LEDGE-END. Matt didn't doubt that it was.

Freddie had to laugh. He was contagious. 'I do believe you, Cosmo, but we're not.' She looked at Rebecca. 'I've got to go home, or they'll think I've emigrated. We've got things to sort out there. Besides, it *is* home.'

'Shame. But you'll be back.'

Freddie rather thought she would.

'Your friend Reagan?' Rebecca was leaning through the car window, which Freddie had wound down so that she could wave. 'She's going to be fine.'

'I'm glad. She's lucky to have you on her side.'

'Thank you.'

Freddie almost kissed her.

As the car drove away Cosmo put his arm around Rebecca's shoulders. 'Ah, Mama, didn't our little girl grow up beautiful?' He was playing a role in some 1950s sit-com.

She punched him in the stomach, but then let him hug her. 'I may never be able to say that I'm proud of her, but I'm pretty sure I'm proud to know her.'

And that was good enough.

'Do you wish we were staying here for Christmas?' Matthew asked, as they drove.

'No. We need to be at home. I haven't seen that gorgeous baby, and Harry needs to see Adrian. You'll see your dad, and Sarah's parents.'

'I thought we might go together.'

Freddie smiled. 'We might just.' Then, 'But I want Grace with us for Christmas.'

'Have you asked her?'

'No, but I'm going to. Tonight, maybe. The flights are probably filling up.'

'Do you think she'll come?'

'Yes. We're back where we were, she and I. And she adores Harry.'

London: Christmas Day

It wasn't exactly a Norman Rockwell painting, but it was pretty close. The turkey was enormous and golden. Tamsin had cooked it overnight in her battered 1950s Aga and driven over with it clutched on her lap, shouting at Neil to take the corners gently. Freddie looked around the table. The kids had peeled the Brussels sprouts, which she was afraid were going to present an interesting taste and texture, since Homer's were barely touched and Willa's whittled down to their palest green hearts. Flannery had been sampling Quality Street all morning, and was sporting a raffish chocolate goatee, which had been imprinted on tiny Willoughby in a Christmas kiss. He was watching, bush baby eyed, from his bouncing chair, which was perched illegally on one of Freddie's beech work surfaces. He was wearing a beanie disguised as a Christmas pudding, and a body suit that declared he was his 'Mummy's Little Christmas Cracker', but fortunately he was oblivious to that humiliation.

Tamsin was asleep sitting up on the sofa. Her hands were resting on her waterbed of a tummy, and an untouched glass of champagne stood beside her. Neil was helping Meghan to set the table, and every time he passed Tamsin he slowed down to look at or touch her. He was always like this when she'd had a baby. As if he couldn't believe she was so clever, strong and brave. As if he couldn't believe he was lucky enough to have her.

Freddie remembered going to see Tamsin in hospital after Homer had been born. It was all so new to them both then, Freddie with an impractically big bunch of gladioli ('Cos I'm so glad') and a contraband bottle of Bailey's, Tamsin in an enormous white Laura Ashley nightie, weeping and giggling at the two nipple-height wet patches spreading across it, Homer absurdly small, red and cross, with a cone head, rudely bruised at both temples. Tamsin had watched Freddie's face as she had peered into the plastic box. 'Yes, it *is* only temporary. Poor little bugger – it got a bit *All Creatures Great and Small* in the end. That'll be my incredible snake hips, making things difficult.' She snorted, laughed a bit more, cried again.

Freddie had folded her into a huge hug.

'Careful! I've got the Bayeux Tapestry going on down there, and it isn't half throbbing.'

'Yuck.'

'Oh, yeah. Yuck doesn't do it justice, believe me.'

Freddie had been a few months pregnant with Harry – she was trying not to think about that side of it. 'He's gorgeous.'

'He's funny-looking.'

'Tams!'

Tamsin had grinned then. 'All right, he's more than

gorgeous. He's fanbloodytastic. And I'm a big fat genius.'

'You are.'

'And you're a godmother.'

'Really?'

'Who else would we ask?'

'Reagan and Sarah?'

'There'll be more babies for them. You first. He's going to need all the help he can get and you've got to promise to be the debauched, amoral godparent. Neil is insisting on his brother and my brother for god-fathers, and they'll be no fun.'

'He'll need all the help he can get because you're calling him Homer, not because he's getting serious godfathers. Will there be an opportunity to object at the font? You know, renounce the devil and all his works, plus the name Homer?'

'No, there will not be. It's an epic name.'

'And he'll have an epic struggle with it. A mother less than a day and already an abusive parent!'

But Freddie had been so happy and proud that day six weeks later when she held Homer as the doddery old vicar poured an eggcup's worth of cold water down his little ruched neck and he had howled.

And Reagan and Sarah had had their turn, Sarah with Willa, and Reagan, just last year, with Flannery. All three of them, Tamsin, Sarah and Reagan, had been godmothers to Harry – Freddie flouted tradition – even though Adrian had called them the three witches and muttered all day about toil, trouble and eye of newt. No one had taken the slightest bit of notice of him, or of the chinless wonder from Sandhurst he had been permitted as sole godfather. It had been another of the golden days they had all shared, and another of the silken ties that bound them together.

Before she had fallen asleep, Tamsin had been sitting with Freddie, watching Matthew and Neil trying to build the wooden shop Santa had rather thoughtlessly chosen for Flannery. They were hopeless, laughing, and Flannery was between them, brandishing a toy hammer, which she banged on their heads in turn, until Matthew caught her up in his arms and tickled her until she roared.

'Can you keep a secret?' she whispered.

'Almost certainly not,' Freddie acknowledged.

'We're going to get you two to be godparents to Willoughby.'

Freddie looked at her.

'Together, you know. Like a couple.' She looked so pleased with herself that Freddie was touched. 'Neil's going to ask Matthew later.'

'Can we do it twice?'

'Don't see why not. What do you say?' Tamsin asked.

'I say thank you. We'd love it.'

Answering for Matthew. *We*'d love it. *We*'d be so happy. We *are* so happy. *We*. It felt good.

Tamsin was smiling like a Cheshire cat. 'All the people I love are happy.'

'Getting there.'

There were tears, suddenly, in Tamsin's eyes. She rubbed them away. 'Bloody hormones.'

'Can *you* keep a secret?' Now it was Freddie's turn. 'Most definitely.'

'We're going to try for a baby.'

On their last morning on the Cape, Matthew had been lying in bed, propped up on pillows, watching her get dressed. She loved how he looked at her. His face was proprietary, proud, lustful. They'd made love for hours the night before, until she was dizzy with it. The house had been quiet – Reagan and Grace had taken a reluctant Harry Christmas shopping – and they'd played, cooked a meal together in the kitchen, then watched television. They'd started on the sofa downstairs, like a pair of teenagers, ended up in bed via the shower and even the stairs – a new and not entirely comfortable idea for both of them. Post-sex sleep was just so good, and she had felt so lazy when the grey wintry sun had woken them. But now she was up, and Matthew was languorous. She threw last night's T-shirt at him. 'Get up, lazybones, and stop looking at me like that.'

He'd swung his legs out of the bed and come across the carpet, naked, to sweep her into a hug. 'I'm never *ever* going to stop looking at you like that.'

'Okay.'

He followed her into the bathroom, dragged on a dressing-gown while she looked at herself in the mirror, then put his arms round her waist and they gazed at the new tableau of Matthew and Freddie. Freddie caught sight of the round foil packet of little pink pills in her sponge-bag, and felt a stab of panic. 'Shit! I forgot to take one yesterday.'

He was still looking at them both in the mirror, grinning.

'Good,' he said.

'Good how?'

'Just good. Throw them away.'

'Matt—'

'Freddie.'

'Just like that?'

'Just like that.'

She had laughed then, and tossed the packet over her shoulder. It hit the shower door and fell to the floor. But they stayed like that, for a few moments, smiling broadly at each other in the mirror, understanding.

'Oooh!' Tamsin squealed now, and the boys looked up.

'What are you two talking about?'

'Never you mind. Just get on with the shop before Flannery's too big to play in it.'

Matthew winked at her.

Reagan and Harry were out. The week before, Reagan had been despatched to buy Harry his heart's desire, a mountain bike. Freddie knew nothing about them, and had judged Reagan the better shopper. The result had obviously thrilled Harry, who had gasped, almost like the little boy he had been so recently, when he'd seen it, beribboned, in the front hall that morning, tied to a very long piece of string that began at the foot of his bed. He'd pronounced it 'well cool'. Reagan had cycled over in full Lycra – 'Christmas morning! What a fantastic time to cycle – the streets were practically deserted so I didn't have to swear once' – and the two had gone off to work up an appetite for their Christmas dinner. Harry thought Reagan was the bee's knees. Freddie said so to Tamsin. 'I'm afraid it might be the beginning of a little crush . . .'

'I wouldn't be afraid. It'll do Reagan good. It's *Reagan's* little crushes we need to worry about, not the ones people have on her.'

'You're mean.'

'You know I love her really. Even if she is a bunny-boiler.'

'Tamsin!'

Adrian had rung at breakfast time. Freddie had answered.

'Merry Christmas,' he had said.

'And to you too.' It was the first Christmas they hadn't spent together since they'd met all those years ago. Freddie almost felt sorry for him. He was with his parents, which was a Yuletide sentence. There would be church, sherry with the desiccated neighbours and a stiffly formal lunch served in the vast cold dining room. All the while his mother would be issuing a lengthy diatribe against her and probably Adrian too. At least tomorrow he would have Harry. 'If you're sure it's okay with you,' he had said.

'Of course.' She had wanted to reassure him. 'Harry wouldn't have it any other way. You're his dad. Of course you must spend some of Christmas together.' And she'd added, 'I wouldn't have it any other way, either, Adrian.'

Something in the way he had sounded grateful hurt her. He hadn't left her. They'd left each other. She didn't want to go back, even though she knew he did, and probably always would.

She'd spoken to Rebecca earlier, too, before the hordes had descended on them. She had known, somehow, that she would ring.

It was late on Christmas Eve, or rather early on Christmas Day, on the Cape. 'Can you hear me? Freddie?' And she could, but only just. There was a loud beat in the background, and she heard fireworks going off intermittently, and screaming laughter. 'Cosmo's having a Christmas Eve *Mardi Gras*. I swear to God I'm the only straight person here. And practically the only one who isn't dressed up like a member of the Village People.'

Freddie laughed.

'I've escaped to my studio for five minutes. I'm getting too old for all this!'

'Rubbish.' Even Freddie knew *that* wasn't true.

She heard a door slam, and then it was quieter. It sounded as if Rebecca had sat down. 'I wanted to wish you a merry Christmas, Freddie.'

'I'm glad you called.'

'And a happy new year.'

'Thank you.'

She wanted to ask her mother to come to England and meet Harry. To get to know her, be with her.

And she would. But not now. For now it was enough that Rebecca had called, that she was at the other end of the line, on the other side of the Atlantic, wishing her a merry Christmas. They left the line open and silent for a moment, full of things they couldn't say, and probably didn't need to yet.

'Merry Christmas, Rebecca.'

'Reagan's an awesome rider, Mum! You never said.'

Freddie flashed a warning glance at Tamsin, who stifled a giggle.

'I can't believe you two are the same age!' Harry went on.

'All right, Harry.' This was Neil. 'That sort of re- mark doesn't go down too well with women.'

'Too right. You're talking about me as well, Harry, don't forget.' Tamsin was breastfeeding Willoughby on the sofa, which Harry found excruciatingly embar- rassing. He acknowledged that she had spoken with a slight tilt of his head.

He coloured, and smirked at his mother. 'You know what I mean.'

Reagan's cheeks were flushed, eyes bright from the ride. She looked pretty, and lighter, too, somehow. She beamed at Matthew as he handed her a glass of champagne. Freddie remembered something she'd said on the Cape to both of them just before she'd left. She'd hugged Freddie, then turned to Matthew. 'It wasn't really about you, after all.'

Matthew had shrugged diffidently.

'It was about me, and what you represented. I think that was it.' She said it like a student who had unravelled a complex problem.

He'd smiled then. 'Don't tell me the spell's been broken!'

And Reagan had punched his arm, quite hard. 'Yep, I think the drug's worn off.' She looked him up and down appraisingly. 'You look . . . kind of ordinary to me now . . . to be perfectly honest.'

They'd all laughed. Then Matt had hugged her and she had left.

Freddie still didn't know whether she had truly meant it, or whether she had said it to let them all off the hook. But looking at her now, she could believe it was true.

Lunch was served. Matthew stood at the head of the table and carved, while everyone else handed round serving dishes, and helped each other. The children pulled crackers and yelled out the jokes, Homer and Harry embellishing them *sotto voce*. Grace had to be made to stop cutting up Flannery's food and sit down, and Meghan's mobile rang from Sydney just when Neil was about to make a toast, and Tamsin rocked Willoughby in the crook of one arm to get him to sleep, which seemed unlikely amid the cacophony, and Freddie just watched them all, and smiled. Now Neil was calling them all to attention, with a knife on the side of his glass. Even Flannery was briefly stilled.

'I'd like to make a toast. Merry Christmas, one and all. To the chefs, to the bottle-washers and, most of all, to the members of the Tenko Club, and to those of us lucky enough to love them.'

Which, rather typically of Neil, was just about perfect.

I would like to thank (and hug) the following people:

For their support and their Herculean efforts on my behalf, which are appreciated beyond words, Sue Fletcher and all the brilliant people who work with her at Hodder & Stoughton, and Stephanie Cabot and her lovely team at William Morris.

For their Eskimo and butterfly kisses, Tallulah and Ottilie.

For their friendship, their tolerance, and their continuing willingness to tell me great stories, Tim Barker, Peter and Suzanne Cluff, Will Norris, Kate Osborne, Nick and Nicky Spence, and, once again, the Reading Groupettes, Nicola, Maura, Jenny and Kathryn.

And, as ever, Mum and Dad, without whom . . .

Host Your Reading Group at

SUTTER HOME.

Winery's Victorian Inn Sweepstakes

... and enjoy bestselling author Elizabeth Noble's heartwarming books with friends

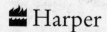

Host Your Reading Group at Sutter Home Winery's Victorian Inn Sweepstakes

OFFICIAL RULES

1. NO PURCHASE OR PAYMENT NECESSARY TO ENTER OR WIN. VOID WHERE PROHIBITED OR RESTRICTED BY LAW, INCLUDING ALASKA, CALIFORNIA, COLORADO, HAWAII, RHODE ISLAND, UTAH, PUERTO RICO AND ALL U.S. TERRITORIES AND POSSESSIONS. Sweepstakes begins January 1, 2006 and ends on June 30, 2006.

2. Eligibility. Sweepstakes open to all legal residents of the United States (excluding Alaska, California, Colorado, Hawaii, Rhode Island, Utah, Puerto Rico and all U.S. territories and possessions) ages 21 and older at time of entry. Employees of HarperCollins Publishers("HarperCollins"), Sutter Home Winery ("Sutter Home")(collectively, "Sponsors"), members of employees immediate families (spouses and parents, siblings and children and their spouses) of Sponsors, their respective subsidiaries and affiliates, officers, directors, shareholders, employees, agents, attorneys, advertising, promotion and fulfillment agencies and other representatives and their immediate families, licensed alcohol beverage retailers and wholesalers, or any other alcohol beverage licensee, and any other company involved with the design, production, execution or distribution of this promotion are not eligible. Grand Prize winner's travel companions are required to be 21 years of age or older as of winner notification. Entries not meeting all of the requirements stated herein will be disqualified and ineligible. All applicable federal, state and local laws and regulations apply.

3. How to Enter. To enter, complete the official entry form or hand print your name, address, age, and phone number along with the words "Host Your Reading Group at Sutter Home Winery's Victorian Inn" Sweepstakes on a 3" x 5" card and mail to:, "Host Your Reading Group at Sutter Home Winery's Victorian Inn" Sweepstakes, c/o Harper Paperbacks, Attn: Marketing Department, 10 East 53rd Street, New York, NY 10022. Entries must be received no later than June 30, 2006. Enter as often as you wish, but each entry must be mailed separately. One entry per envelope. Partially completed, illegible, or mechanically reproduced entries will not be accepted. Sponsor is not responsible for lost, late, mutilated, illegible, stolen, postage due, incomplete, or misdirected entries. All entries become the property of the Sponsors and will not be returned.

4. Grand Prize. One Grand Prize Winner will win a three (3) day, two (2) night-stay (double occupancy) at Sutter Home Winery's Victorian Inn in Napa Valley for self and up to 5 members of their reading group, including round-trip coach airfare from major airport nearest winner's home and transportation to and from the San Francisco airport and Sutter Home Winery's Victorian Inn (all travel must be as a group), a dinner hosted by a Sutter Home chef, and 10 copies of Elizabeth Noble's bestselling book The Reading Group and 10 copies of her latest book The Friendship Test. Approximate retail value of prize totals $4,800. All other expenses, including meals, are the sole responsibility of winner and his or her guests. Trip must be taken by June 30, 2007. Certain travel restrictions will apply and may be subject to availability. If trip cannot be taken by that date, prize will be forfeited.

5. Prize Limitations. Prizes are non-transferable and cannot be sold or redeemed for cash. No cash substitute is available. Any federal, state, or local taxes are the responsibility of the winner. Sponsors may substitute prize of equal or greater value, if necessary, due to availability.

6. Odds of Winning. Odds of winning depend on the total number of entries received. Approximately 1,150,000 sweepstakes announcements published. All prizes will be awarded.

7. Notification & Releases. Winner will be randomly drawn on or about July 15, 2006, by HarperCollins, whose decision is final. Potential winner will be notified by mail and will be required to sign and return an affidavit of eligibility and release of liability within 14 days of notification or an alternate winner may be chosen. All travel companions will be required to sign an Affidavit of Eligibility and Liability/Publicity Release and return it prior to confirming travel arrangements. By acceptance of prize, winner and travel companions consent to the use of their names, voices, photographs, likenesses, and biographical information by HarperCollins and Sutter Home, for publicity purposes without further compensation except where prohibited.

8. Additional terms: By participating, entrants agree (a) to the official rules and decisions of the judges, which will be final in all respects; and to waive any claim to ambiguity of the official rules and (b) to release, discharge, and hold harmless the Sponsors and their respective parent companies, affiliates, subsidiaries, employees and representatives and advertising, promotion and fulfillment agencies from and against any and all liability or damages associated with acceptance, use, or misuse of any prize received or participation in any Sweepstakes-related activity or participation in this Sweepstakes.

9. Dispute Resolution. Any dispute arising from this Sweepstakes will be determined according to the laws of the State of New York, without reference to its conflict of law principles, and the entrants consent to the personal jurisdiction of the State and Federal courts located in New York County and agree that such courts have exclusive jurisdiction over all such disputes.

10. Winner Information. To obtain the name of the winner, please send your request and a self-addressed stamped envelope (residents of Vermont may omit return postage) to "Host Your Reading Group at Sutter Home Winery's Victorian Inn" Sweepstakes c/o Harper Paperbacks 10 East 53rd Street, New York, NY 10022 after September 1, 2006, but no later than December 1, 2006.

11. Sweepstakes Sponsors: HarperCollins Publishers and Sutter Home Winery, Inc. d/b/a Trinchero Family Estates, St. Helena, CA.